Book 3 of The Halcyon Cycle

The
DRAGONS
of Sheol

I0641484

PETER KAZMAIER

THE DRAGONS OF SHEOL
Copyright © 2019 by Peter Kazmaier

For more information or to order additional copies, please contact:
Wolfsburg Imprints
2421 Council Ring Road
Mississauga, Ontario, Canada
L5L 1E5
http://www.wolfsburgimprints.com/
For online maps: http://www.wolfsburgimprints.com/halcyon/maps/

Print ISBN: 978-1-4866-1820-0

Word Alive Press
119 De Baets Street, Winnipeg, MB R2J 3R9
www.wordalivepress.ca

WORD ALIVE
—P R E S S—

Cataloguing in Publication may be obtained through Library and Archives Canada

Dedication

To my grandchildren: Adia, Nolen, Abigail, and Walter; may you follow the Master and discover (as I have) that He is worthy of all of your devotion and trust.

Contents

Books by Peter Kazmaier
The Halcyon Cycle

The Halcyon Dislocation
The Battle for Halcyon
The Dragons of Sheol

An apologetic prequel to *The Halcyon Dislocation:*
Questioning Your Way to Faith. Learning to Disagree
without Being Disagreeable

Chapter 1

Dirty Tricks

Dave glowered at the diminutive figure darting and swaying before him like a jack-in-the-box. Wiping the sweat from his swollen left eye, Dave mumbled to himself, "Come here Brandor, you half pint. All I need is one touch with my quarterstaff and you're finished." Not for the first time in this match, Dave wished he had picked a lighter weapon. Maybe then he could land a blow.

His fellow students at Gur Academy stood in a circle around the two combatants, cheering them on.

"Come on Rokodor," called one using Dave's Gurundarian name, "All you have to do is fall on the little squirt to win."

"Brandor, stop with the bouncing around. You make my eyes tired," chimed in another.

Dave fixed his eyes on Brandor's, whose slender form was seventy pounds lighter than Dave's solid, well-muscled body. He could smell Brandor's self-confidence. Then he saw his opponent turn and smile at one of the young women watching them. Dave seized the moment and rushed in, raising the end of his staff for a quick blow.

Brandor evaded the swing easily, crouched and swung a low, sweeping blow at Dave. Dave felt a sharp crack on the side of his leg. It sent him sprawling to the ground, gasping in pain. He moved to get onto his feet.

"Stop!" came the order from the Academy commandant. Brandor was poised to drive his quarterstaff into Dave's head, as Dave crouched, vulnerable, on the ground. Dave dug his fingers into the sand of the practice ground. He could smell Brandor's indecision. He could sense his hatred.

"You're lucky, *skork*. You don't belong here with us. Go back to your own kind," said Brandor through gritted teeth. Sullenly, he pulled his weapon back from the killing blow, then stood at attention, facing the commandant.

Skork was the pejorative used to describe all bent and broken peoples from the zombie-like Apemen, to the Halfmen, and even to Dave's own people who were inferior to the Ancients in longevity, speed, and several other attributes.

Brandor was a young nephew of Arachodor, a member of the ruling Council of Thirteen. Arachodor had objected strenuously to Dave's acceptance into Gurundarian society, after Sirona the healer had called him back from death. In saving him using a healing plant tuned only to Ancients, Sirona had changed Dave's body from that of a *Lesser Man* (what Ancients called ordinary people from earth) to that of an Ancient.

I wonder if Brandor would have killed me if the commandant hadn't stopped the match? No one's been killed during Academy combat training in more than a hundred years, Dave thought.

He stood up gingerly and limped toward the circle of onlookers. The Academy stood high on the western slopes of the Barrier Mountains and he could see the vast expanse of Lake Tolbar shimmering in the distance. His wife, Arlana, came toward him. Clutching his right arm to support him, she walked with him away from the crowd.

Dave was glad she didn't talk about the fight. She had neither his strength nor toughness, but she was as fast as thought. She had deftly handled Brandor in a sparring match the previous week. She still had a bruise where Brandor had flailed out and "accidently" hit her when she had started to walk away after their match. Dave had planned to teach Brandor a lesson today—and hadn't been able to touch him. The humiliation was almost unbearable.

"Well, husband," said Arlana, "are you ready for our expedition test the day after tomorrow?"

"I think I'm ready, Princess. Any idea where we're going?"

"I hear we're heading to the eastern slopes of the Barrier Mountains to replant the guardian trees that were burned by the Halfmen."

"Sounds easy enough," said Dave.

"Things are never easy when we're close to the Skull Mountains," said Arlana.

"I wish we could get some leave and head home," said Dave.

"You're thinking what I'm thinking—how are Al, Pam and Little Thomas?"

"I am. Since we've been at the Academy, we haven't been able to visit our 'mailbox' to see if they've sent us a message from home. They're probably wondering why we haven't answered."

"Shhhh, Dave. Keep your voice down," whispered Arlana.

Dave glanced over his shoulder, relieved that there was no one in sight.

"Anyway," continued Arlana, still whispering, "Since Al and Pam know we're away at the Academy, I don't think they'll be too worried about our lack of communication."

When they finally reached their quarters, Dave went out back to wash in the creek-fed shower. When he returned, he saw Arlana and Ferris, her cousin, in serious conversation. They looked up as he limped in.

"What's going on?" asked Dave. "You look like there's been a death in the family."

"We have trouble, Dave," said Ferris. "Your old enemy, Arachodor, used his influence with some of the teachers. He's made the motion that you shouldn't be allowed to join the cadets on their expedition. They claim your lack of competence makes the trip too dangerous for you."

"Arachodor's concern for my welfare is—well—touching. Can they really do that?"

"They can, and they are trying to do exactly that. I'm about to head over there now, to intercede on your behalf. You deserve to take this first test. Arlana and I have been training since we were very young. You may not have had all the instruction we've had, but you've seen more real combat than half the Rangers in our force. That should count for something. Perhaps they'll listen to a seasoned Ranger who knows you."

Dave sat down and poured himself a cup of *siph*. "What I don't get is why Arachodor's argument for my exclusion is even being considered. After all, we're only going camping alone on the other side of the Barrier Mountains; there will be seasoned Rangers and Guardians on patrol—so where's the danger?"

"Husband, as I said before, anytime we are on the other side of the Barrier Mountains we are in the wild and there is danger. The guardian trees have been destroyed in large measure, so there is no protection from that quarter."

"But I thought," interrupted Dave, "that the Bent Ones had all fled to Abaddon, and the Halfmen would be cowering in the Skull Mountains, nursing their wounds."

"We have no proof," said Ferris, "that the Bent One controlling the Halfmen has left. He may have left. He may still be there. Or maybe a black swamp oak has been established in the Skull Mountains, so that he can travel back and forth to Abaddon. We just don't know, and so we assume the worst. That is why we train so long before venturing beyond the Barrier Mountains. From the cadet leader's point of view, you have had much less training than the other recruits."

After Ferris left, Arlana looked at Dave as if she were deciding whether to tell him something.

"What is it, Arlana?"

"What Ferris said, about us learning to fight from our earliest years is true, you know."

"Are you telling me you know why I'm losing to a pipsqueak like Brandor? I know I'm losing because I'm just too slow."

"You're not too slow. You're actually much faster now than you were before you became one of us. You're losing because he knows exactly what you're going to do a fraction of a second before you do it. Let me show you."

She picked up her light quarterstaff and took up a defensive position with her left foot forward. Look at the muscles in my arm and my calf; do you see how they're tensed? It means I'm getting ready to evade." She shifted slightly. "Now I'm ready to launch an attack. Do you see the difference?"

"So that's why you beat the little twerp. He was so busy watching your beautiful muscles flexing and unflexing that he completely forgot to defend himself."

Arlana jabbed Dave in the shoulder with her quarterstaff. "*Kree ah na koo!*[1] Stop joking. This is serious. In two days you could be out on the mountain slope without me to take care of you. How would it look if you got yourself killed? All the women would wonder if you went out looking for death to get away from me. Think of what that would do to my reputation." They both burst out laughing.

---

1 An expression in the Ancient Tongue meaning "May the Creator help me!"

She knows how to handle me. She's not just good to me—she's good for me, Dave thought.

"One more thing, husband. You probably don't yet realize how much more acute your sense of smell is now that you're an Ancient. By paying attention to your nose, you can tell a lot about your opponent. Is he fearful? Is he confident? Is his anger growing? All these emotions will tell you what he will do next."

They sparred for a couple of hours with only the occasional breather. Dave began to see what Arlana meant and started to anticipate her moves. Then Arlana showed him how to disguise his next move by deliberately attacking from a disguised defensive posture.

The door opened and Ferris entered again. He was scowling.

Dave's spirits flagged. "I take it they won't let me go."

"Actually," said Ferris, "they were surprisingly easy to convince. Your father-in-law, Kelldor, and your adopted father Celyddon, had anticipated this last-minute difficulty and were both there to speak on your behalf. The board of the school logged Arachodor's protests, and then capitulated, agreeing to let you go."

"So why the long face?" asked Arlana.

"It was too easy," said Ferris. "I think all of us have been duped. They're digging a pit for you through the test, and they wanted to register their disapproval in advance. If you have an 'accident,' they'll shake their heads and say, 'We did all we could to avert this tragedy.' Be on your guard and watch your back."

It was getting late and Ferris left. Dave and Arlana began to organize their equipment for the trip. Dave tried on his living cloak, hung a small satchel containing a light gourd around his neck and strapped on his long belt knife, which he had named Skene Dhu. Dave had found his knife, along with his sword, Gram, in a blade tree near the Ancient fortress of Kellburg.

Dave realized he needed a tie to fasten his sleeping blanket to his pack. He had some stout leather, which he had taken from the hide of a Rokash. He took out Skene Dhu and examined the blade lovingly. It had a lustrous blue sheen unlike any other metal blade. The bio-engineered alloy of molybdenum-tungsten steel, protein spacer, and diamond fiber, cut through thick Rokash leather as if it were the thinnest of papers.

He put the knife back in the metal-lined sheath and walked over to Arlana.

"Princess, I want you to take this." He held out Skene Dhu.

"Dave, I couldn't. The blade tree knife came to you. I have a good knife …"

"Arlana, please take it. I need to keep you safe. If you don't have this knife, I'll worry."

She peered into his eyes, as if wanting to wrest his thoughts from him. Suddenly she relaxed, raised herself on her toes, and kissed him lightly on the cheek.

"We'll trade knives. Viper will look after you." She handed him her knife and scabbard and then they both turned to organize their packing.

"No, no ye fool," Grimbor, the Blade Meister growled as he jabbed Dave in the lower chest. "Rokodor, ye canna shift from an evade form directly to a cut or thrust form. Yer feet are not set. It makes ye too slow. How many times do I have to tell ye that ye must use a transition form first?"

Dave was exhausted. Grimbor had summoned him, to offer some extra help on using his sword after yesterday's fiasco with his quarterstaff. Now after three hours, Dave was laboring and Grimbor didn't even seem to be tired.

Dave began to circle once more. Grimbor was shaped like a fire hydrant, with no waist. He was much shorter than Dave, but his shoulders were just as broad. Yet he was fast as well as strong. With his eyes fixed on Dave's, Grimbor's feet and sword moved in perfect coordination, with a grace and fluidity Dave wished he could match.

After another flurry of exchanges during which Dave was barely able to evade and block the lightning attacks, Grimbor sighed and said, "Enough fer today." Sitting down, he gestured to a space on the bench beside him and offered Dave a drink of water.

Dave took a long pull from the water skin and handed it back to Grimbor.

"I know I'm bein' hard on ye lad, but I'm tryin' to get ye ready for the test tomorrow."

"Even if I see a Halfman tomorrow, I don't think he will press me nearly as hard as you do, Blade Meister."

Grimbor's eyes became hard. "It's not Halfmen I be thinkin' of. Fer a youngin, ye have many enemies, and to my way of thinkin', Halfmen are not the most dangerous of 'em. Watch yer back and practice yer forms every night when it's safe to do so. Hmm." Grimbor lapsed into thought.

After a while he spoke again. "Rokodor, ye be fast, and ye have good instincts," he said. "But ye spend too much time thinkin' what to do next, and when ye be thinkin' ye not be watchin' the enemy. I be wantin' ye to use only one form in each of the five categories. Practice those until ye can change from one form to the other without thinkin'. When ye have those perfect we be addin' some more."

With that, Grimbor rose and clapped Dave on the back. "One more thing, Rokodor, find a safe campsite. The safest be a campsite yer enemies canna find. The second safest be one where ye hear 'em coming. Be smart! Be safe! Come back to me alive."

Chapter 2

Survival Test

The next morning the cadets assembled on the parade ground. The cadet leader gave a short speech, organized the students into four squads and then handed out orders by squad leaders to each individual cadet. The trainees, about one hundred in number, dispersed by squad to the exit point through or over the Barrier Mountains. Arlana's squad had to make the trip back to the tunnel they had used when she had first brought Dave to Gurundar, but Dave's pass was the closest exit point, only a day's march from the Academy.

The Middle Pass was a high, winding, rocky notch with cliffs rising hundreds of paces on either side. As Dave's squad walked through in single file, he could see fortifications all along the route. Dave could smell the guardian trees already, a pleasant smell like pine woods. After passing a particularly narrow bend in the path, he saw one of the large rubble traps—a huge collection of boulders held back by a stout timber wall—designed to plug up the defile in case of attack.

The squad leader halted the trainees. Dave sat down for lunch, and looked at the rubble trap. He imagined Halfmen fighting their way through the narrow pass with Rangers desperately holding them off. In his mind he saw one of the Rangers set fire to the pitch-laden timbers holding back the rubble. Suddenly, with a crack, the timbers gave way and an avalanche of boulders, louder than a thunderclap, roared into the narrow defile burying everything. He shuddered as the vision faded. *I hope it never comes to that*, he thought.

"Let's get moving," said the squad leader.

Dave shouldered his pack and followed the others in single file. At intervals they crossed wooden bridges that spanned deep pits. Finally, Dave emerged from the pass with the east side of the Barrier Mountains falling away before him. Below him, smoke still hung in the air from the burned sections of the woods closest to the Skull Desert, the aftermath of the assault on Gurundar by the Halfmen, part of the Battle for Halcyon.

Their squad leader stopped on a promontory and turned to face them. "Cadets you can see why we're here. The Halfmen burned large sections of the lower reaches of the Guardian Forest when they attempted to overrun us last year. With the loss of those trees, our defenses are weakened. We're here to begin to repair the damage by planting guardian saplings. This is no holiday. For you …" he looked directly at Dave. "For most of you, this will be your first time outside the protective ring of the Guardian Forest. You will now be on your own in the wild. Although the Halfmen have retreated back to the Skull Mountains, don't be complacent. Be on your guard. We have given you only a knife and a quarterstaff as weapons. Your job is to stay alive, not to defeat any wild beasts or Halfmen that come along. We deliberately leave you alone because this is a test of self-reliance. You can return here to safety at any time, but if you come back before the recall is sounded, you have failed the test, and will not graduate. Any questions?"

Everyone remained silent.

"In that case open the instruction package you received, and be on your way to your designated tree-planting area."

Dave's area was almost at the bottom of the mountain where the old Guardian Forest had ended and the regular forest began. It was already late afternoon when he reached his work area. Clumps of small saplings, two paces high for planting, had already been delivered and were sitting in the shade of a large rock.

Dave looked around for a campsite. He remembered what Grimbor had said and rejected several comfortable but obvious locations. The meadow, bordered by a small rivulet descending from the heights, offered the most comfortable and convenient campsite, but he had had too many adventures already to chance camping out in the open. He found a spur of the mountain a short distance from the meadow and climbed up to a broad ledge with an overhang at the back. He would leave his supplies down below, and cover his tracks to this hidden camp. He felt certain this location would satisfy both of Grimbor's requirements: invisibility and defensibility.

The next order of business was to gather enough wood for a supper fire and perhaps even for the night. He wished he had been able to bring Gram, his sword. That weapon, hardened and modified in a blade tree, was so sharp and strong it cut through wood as if it were straw. With Gram, he could have cut down some of the standing deadwood. He began a search for manageable pieces he could carry or break. It took a bit of work to carry wood up to the ledge, but after three trips he had enough for a cook fire.

Dave sat at the edge of his campsite and surveyed the meadow below. The wind was blowing out of the south. The air was dry with a hint of the fragrance of cactus from the Skull Desert. Charred stumps dotted the meadow. At intervals he saw piles of charred brush, the remains of felled trees which had been used by the Halfmen to start the fire. Beyond the guardian trees there had been a woodland fringe that gradually gave way to desert a mile or so distant. This had been cut down and new growth was only beginning as waist-high saplings. If Halfmen came from the desert, he should be able to hear them as they trudged through the dense brush.

It was time for supper. He returned to the middle of the ledge and placed some stones around a shallow depression. Using Viper to whittle some soft boxwood, he shaved off thin slices, then piled the tinder carefully in the midst of some dry sticks, and added a bit of dry moss he had carried in his pack. When he struck the brittle steel of his fire starter with flint, a shower of sparks cascaded onto the moss and wood slivers as the fine iron particles spontaneously ignited. He blew gently to get the sparks to light the tinder. Soon he had a vigorous blaze going.

The evening was chilly. After a quick, hot supper, he decided he would let the fire die down rather than extinguish it. Wrapping himself in his bedroll, he laid down beside the fire and went to sleep.

It was about three in the morning when something startled him awake. He heard a sound below. The fire still had the faint glow of embers covered in ash. Crawling to the edge of the ledge, he peered into the gloom, his eyes penetrating all but the deepest shadows. He saw nothing. He heard a twig snap, and knew whatever caused the sound, it was not from the direction of the desert, but well into the trees off to the left beyond his sight.

The next morning after breakfast, Dave was just climbing down from the ledge when he heard a whinny. Turning, he saw a horseman on a rise some two hundred paces away and off to his left. It was

Teledon, Arachodor's son. Teledon gazed at him for a while, and then turned his horse, and trotted off the rise, back toward the remaining guardian trees.

Dave's thoughts churned. *Am I supposed to believe that's a coincidence? Of all the Rangers and Guardians that could have been watching me, I just happened to draw Arachodor's son, by chance?*

Dave walked to the meadow. Unwrapping the cloth from the bundled tree roots, and finding the steel shovel among the saplings, he began to dig a hole.

It was hot and sweat was soon running down his face. When the hole was finished, he used his water bag to pour water into it, placed the sapling into the hole, and tamped the earth down around its roots. As he planted another, and then another, he realized he was enjoying his work, and increased his pace.

That afternoon, a wagon came by with more saplings, just as he was planting his second-to-last tree.

"You're making good progress, cadet," said the driver. "Most of the other cadets haven't nearly planted all their trees yet. I guess they're chasing butterflies. I always appreciate finding one who knows how to work."

Dave felt so good about the praise that he forgot his hunger, and worked until the shadows grew long.

After his work was finished, he ate a quick supper. The night was overcast and dark. The overhang, facing east was even darker. He still had an uneasy feeling about having seen Teledon. So, Dave found his bedroll, repacked his rucksack and placed it under his blanket beside the fire. Satisfied that the lump under the blanket would look like a sleeper, he wrapped himself in his living cloak and settled back in the dark, under the deep shadow of the cliff in a little notch three paces from the bedroll.

His thoughts turned back to Teledon. *Maybe I'm being paranoid, but I can't believe Teledon is here to look after my best interests.*

He concentrated on breathing slowly and regularly. After the day's labours, he quickly fell asleep.

It was early morning when Dave was awakened by the clatter of a rock falling down the cliff. He heard it *plunk* as it buried itself in the soft forest floor. It sounded as if someone or something was climbing up to the ledge. The moon was in the east. Dave stared across the ledge and saw a dark shadow—silhouetted against the moon. The shadow straightened up.

Removing what looked like a quarterstaff from a sling around its back, the figure, the size of a small man, approached the blankets skirting the fire until he was directly between Dave and the bedroll. The cloaked figure raised his staff like a spear, and struck the bedroll.

Gripping his own staff, Dave moved quietly, coming up in a crouch from behind the figure and jabbed it in the back, making it stumble over the bedroll. The intruder yelped from pain and narrowly missed falling into the fire.

I recognize that voice. What's Brandor doing here?

Brandor quickly jumped to his feet, searching the shadows for Dave. His eyes had not yet adjusted to the darkness of the cliff shadow.

He can't see me because he spent too much time looking into the fire, thought Dave as he gave Brandor another jab on the leg. Brandor backed out into the open. Dave followed warily.

Brandor lunged, and Dave gave back a step.

"I'm going to kill you!" snarled Brandor. "There won't be any commandant to save you this time."

An image of his own battered, lifeless body came briefly into Dave's mind. He forced the thought away and concentrated on the fight. They circled. He could see Brandor's muscles tense despite the gloom. Dave could detect a subtle change in Brandor's smell. He knew the blow was coming and stepped back causing Brandor's attack to miss. Dave did not counterattack, knowing Brandor was setting him up. Brandor exuded confidence. Dave cautiously evaded a few more attempts until he felt sure he knew Brandor's tells. When the next attack came, Dave was ready and transitioned from a defensive posture with the form *reverse of the boar*. When Brandor swung around, Dave saw the blow coming and poked him solidly in the shoulder, turning him. A second blow caught Brandor's ankle, and flipped him to the ground.

With his staff end a hand's width from Brandor's face, Dave growled "Drop your staff." Brandor dropped his quarterstaff. Dave kicked it away from Brandor's side. Moving back, Dave kept his eye on his opponent as he reached down, grabbed Brandor's staff, threw it spinning over the lip of the ledge and heard it crash into the bushes beyond the meadow.

Brandor rolled to a crouch, snarling, but did not try to stand.

"Why are you doing this Brandor?"

"I hate you *skork*!"

"But why? What did I ever do to you?"

"You killed my brother."

"Killed your brother? I didn't even know you had a brother."

"Defending the Barrier Mountains, he was killed by the Half-men. You brought the Halfmen to us. It's your fault he's dead."

"If I were smart, I would do to you what you had planned to do to me—but I won't. Now get outta my sight."

Dave made Brandor climb down and watched him disappear into the guardian trees off to the left.

I guess I'm going to have to be careful where I sleep.

From then on, Dave never slept directly in the camp, but found a small hollow or ledge somewhere on the cliff.

Five days of hard work passed. Dave managed to plant a wagon-load of trees after each daily delivery.

Just one more day until it will be time to head home, he reflected. He was just about to take a break when he heard a bellow and scream from the north. The bellow brought back dark memories of his pursuit by Halfmen. He felt the sweat grow cold on his skin.

Grabbing his quarterstaff, Dave plunged through the woods toward the sound, slowing when he heard someone thrashing up ahead. The thrashing stopped. Moving stealthily forward, he saw two Half-men bent over a body in an area denuded of guardian trees. A slender teenage boy was lying face down on the ground, unmoving. From the blood on his head, it looked like he had been beaten unconscious. The two Halfmen were binding him with cords.

Revulsion welled up inside of Dave, and he sprang forward, delivering a solid blow to the back of the first Halfman's head, knocking him to the ground. The second Halfman turned, drawing his blade in one motion. Seeing Dave, he snarled hideously, and raised his sword to strike. Dave cracked the Halfman's wrist with his quarterstaff and then struck him on his side.

Clutching his wrist and dropping his sword, the Halfman plunged into the eastern woods, shouting for reinforcements. Dave moved to the still figure on the ground, and turning him over, saw that it was Brandor. Attempting unsuccessfully to revive him, Dave hoisted Brandor onto his shoulders and carried him back up the mountain, heading for the shelter of the guardian trees. Coming across the wagon trail, he went north.

A few minutes later, he heard the sounds of horses and harness. A wagon came into view around the bend. Dave waved with his arm. The wagon stopped.

"What happened?" asked the driver jumping down.

"Halfmen," gasped Dave. "… attacked this cadet. Need to warn the Rangers."

"Let me help," said the driver. He climbed down and helped Dave hoist Brandor into the back of the wagon.

"Do you want a lift back to the meadow?

Dave hesitated. "I'd better not. I haven't been given permission to leave my post."

"Suit yourself," said the driver, chewing on his pipe stem vigorously.

Waving the driver goodbye, Dave made his way back to camp, then moved his campsite further up the mountain into the shelter of the guardian trees. All night he stayed awake listening for Halfmen, but heard nothing unusual. The next morning, he made his way back to the crag and meadow where his squad had first dispersed.

He was not the first to arrive, but the other cadets did not welcome him with the friendly banter he had expected. But when he glimpsed the Commandant together with Teledon waiting on horseback in the woods at the edge of the meadow beyond the rocky outcropping, he understood. They had a third horse with them. Dave went over to a cadet and said, "Why's the Commandant here?"

"I overheard them saying that you almost killed Brandor."

"I didn't nearly kill Brandor. I rescued him from the Halfmen."

"Oh," said the cadet. "You should be alright then." But Dave heard no conviction in his voice.

Just then, the Commandant and Teledon walked their horses into the open area with Teledon leading the additional horse. "Cadet Rokodor ap Celyddon, please mount the horse," said Teledon. "You're coming with us."

Dave mounted without a word. Teledon did not relinquish the reins but led Dave's horse up the track. Dave thought it best to keep silent for the time being. The true story would, no doubt, unfold. But he sensed that something was terribly wrong and that Teledon was at the heart of it.

When they had returned to the Academy, the Commandant asked Dave to follow him. Teledon went to look after the horses.

The Commandant led Dave to a large room that looked like a study. Two walls were covered in bookshelves, the other walls were covered with maps. A large desk, the size of a wagon bed, was at one end of the room.

"Take a seat Rokodor ap Celyddon," said the Commandant gesturing at an empty chair by his desk. "Tell me exactly what happened on the far side of the Barrier Mountains.

"Dave gave a detailed description of his time there, his selection of his camp, the precautions he had taken for his security, and his tree planting. After he had described the attack by Brandor, the Commandant interrupted him.

"So Rokodor, you claim that Brandor was not unconscious after that beating?"

"Yes, sir."

"Why would he attack you?"

"Well sir, during the fight Brandor said something about his brother being killed by the Halfmen. He seemed to blame me for their attack since it followed shortly after my coming to Gurundar."

"I see," said the Commandant, making a steeple with his fingers. "Go on with your story."

Dave continued until he finished his account with his return to the meadow where he had met Teledon and the Commandant. "So that's it sir. May I ask what I am accused of?"

"Ranger Teledon testifed that he saw you attacking the much younger and smaller Brandor, and he broke up the fight. Brandor confirmed Teledon's statement and claimed that later, you attacked him again and knocked him unconscious because he'd embarrassed you in the sparring contest at the Academy. Brandor also predicted that you would make up some story to cover up the assault."

"But I carried Brandor to the wagon. How do you explain that?" protested Dave.

"That is definitely in your favor. However, Ranger Teledon thinks when you ambushed Brandor a second time, you were afraid you had killed him. So, you panicked and sought help."

Dave shivered involuntarily. He had no friends to defend him. Arlana was in a different squad and could not speak for him. "What happens next?" he asked.

"I'm afraid, Rokodor, the charges of attempted murder are very serious. They require your suspension until all the facts become clear, and an Academy Tribunal can be convened and a judgement rendered. Until that time, you may not return to the Academy."

"In all likelihood, you will miss graduation because of the timing. But my hope is that you will be vindicated. I will only be one of the judges on your tribunal. May the Creator be with you. You will receive the formal charges in a day or two. Dismissed!"

Chapter 3

The Letter

The first view of Abaddon from the encircling mountains is breathtaking. The Abaddon plain is two leagues below sea level. The mountains add another one-half league to the stupendous drop. Yet the plain is the size of a small continent, stretching some three hundred leagues in every direction. In the center of the plain, it is rumored that there is another deep chasm, falling more than a league to an inland sea. Why the enormous pressure of the sea does not percolate through the surrounding rock and fill up this void is a mystery.

A scout standing on the mountains would see the plain climb slowly to the level of the mountain base in the west, in the huge peninsulas that we call the North and South Mandibles, enclosing Fang Bay. Perhaps that is how the armies of Abaddon keep coming to Feiramar to trouble us.

Alas, most of the history of Abaddon is actually a history of Abaddonian attacks on our land culminating in the greatest calamity of all—the treachery of Meglir and the Great Plague he unleashed in the last desperate days of the siege of his great stronghold. Apart from what we learned from several bold climbs to the surrounding mountains, we know little of Abaddon itself. Discounting the implausible tales told by the fantasy writer, Jandor Longwalker, the little we do know has been gleaned from documents captured in the long war against the Bent Ones. No firsthand reports are known of Abaddon itself.

THE HISTORY OF ABADDON
KENDOR AP KARNELLIAN

Dave pushed back from the table in his kitchen and looked out the large window down the long western slope of the Barrier Mountains to Lake Tolbar. After a brief look, he took another mouthful of *siph*, the *Hansa* drink he relished so much. It tasted like coffee and chocolate mixed together. He had just finished telling Ferris the story of his survival test, and of Teledon's charges against him, from beginning to end.

Turning to look at Ferris, Dave waited, expectantly, for his comments.

Ferris was a slender, clean-shaven young man who looked to be in his mid-twenties (although as an Ancient, Dave knew he could be much older). Although Ferris appeared tall because of his slim build, he was a couple of inches shorter than Dave. He had dark curly hair, in contrast to his cousin Arlana's blonde hair, yet Dave could see a resemblance around the eyes. Ferris' skin color today had what Dave would have called a "Middle Eastern cast," not white, but also not the dark brown Ferris would likely choose in intense sunlight, or when he was in stealth mode at night.

I wish I had that kind of control over my skin pigmentation, thought Dave. *I'm still a child and have times when my skin pigments change unconsciously and everyone can tell I'm still just an Ancient infant.*

Ferris cradled his own cup of *siph* and looked thoughtful. "It goes without saying that I believe you Dave. You have always been an honest man who has invariably told me the truth. I think if it were only your word against Brandor's, the tribunal would rule in your favor because of Brandor's behavior in the training combat, and the fact that you carried him back to the wagon for rescue. However, Teledon's testimony as a Ranger will carry great weight, and ultimately, may tip the balance against you."

"So, what's the probable penalty?"

"I think attempted murder is unjustified. You could easily have left Brandor where you found him. Teledon can only testify to the first combat. If he had seen the second, more serious combat, then why did he not intervene and bring Brandor back himself?

"To fully answer your question, in case of a guilty verdict at your court martial, I think the tribunal will expel you from the Academy for 'conduct unbecoming.' With that charge on your record, the Academy would never let you in again. Still Brandor's claim—that you killed his brother indirectly—will give us something to work on."

Ferris allowed his last statement to hang in the air until the silence became awkward. Then he picked up the book Dave had been reading. "Oh, you're reading *Abaddon Journey* by Jandor Longwalker. How Arlana and I loved that book! Longwalker's adventures are so wild and frankly unbelievable that the implausibility may put you off. I think that's why children like it so much; when you're a child you believe almost anything an adult—or a book—will tell you."

"What do you know about Abaddon, Ferris?"

"You have already read *The History of Abaddon*, which I loaned you, so you know what I know, and what the rest of us know, for that matter. Abaddon is the source of all of our troubles. We know well the troubles the Bent Ones have caused us. We know almost nothing about the place itself. A long time ago, our people sent several expeditions to climb the mountains surrounding Abaddon. They reached a pass, saw the sheer drop, and saw the huge Abaddon plain far below them. They observed for a while, and then returned. They did this from many locations."

"Isn't there a map of what these observers saw?" asked Dave.

"Yes, there is a map compiled by Kandor ap Karnelian from a synthesis of maps that various observers drew of the Abaddon plain and the edge of the drop-off to Sheol. But it is obviously woefully incomplete. There are no rivers, mountains, or cities on Karnelian's map."

"How far is the plain below sea level?"

"They took some geometric measurements using the shadow of the rim. In your measurements," Ferris thought for a moment, "in your measurements the plain is about ten kilometers below sea level. Sheol, the huge deep chasm in the center of the plain, is much deeper still."

"But there has to be some way to get from the plain to the coast. How else could they build ships and launch attacks on us? They must have settlements, or at least ship building sites somewhere on the coast. Haven't the Gurundarians looked for them?"

Ferris raised his finger indicating that Dave should hold his questions, then left the room. He returned a few minutes later with a large paper roll, which he flattened on the table. It was a map. "This is the map that Kandor ap Karnelian compiled," he said. "We also believe the Bent Ones must have settlements, or work camps, somewhere on the coast. But we have never found any. In the days before the plague, and the sundering of our people from our brethren to the west, we had a sizeable navy. Our fleet would periodically sail here into Maw Bay and try to surprise their ships to stave off future attacks. We always caught some, but never their whole fleet. There are huge caverns at the end of Maw Bay. The admirals of the time thought the Black Fleet was hidden there. A few adventurous captains tried to take longboats in to reconnoitre, but none ever returned. Eventually the loss of manpower grew too great, and the benefit proved nonexistent. The admirals gave up sending in expeditions. Still, we believe that somewhere in Maw Bay, the ships are built that plague us so."

Dave shrugged. "There has to be a way in and out from the Abaddon plain to Maw Bay."

"Undoubtedly. Maybe one of Jandor's crazy notions hits near the truth. Perhaps there is a subterranean passage that connects the caverns on Maw Bay to the Abaddon plain."

Just then there was a knock at the front door. Dave was just getting up to answer it, when Hanomer came in carrying his pack, sword, and bow.

Hanomer was mammalian, about three feet tall. He had a long prehensile tail with a tuft on the end that opened up into a third hand. His glistening fur was dark. He wore a primitive body armor made of tough, yet pliable leather. On his belt he carried a long knife. He had a quiver with arrows slung over his back and a short bow. The overall impression he gave was of a badger, walking upright.

Hanomer and his mate, Endowyn, and their close relatives had moved to Gurundar as *Hansa* ambassadors at the request of the Council of Thirteen. Their *Hansa* clan had, of course, moved with them since it would have been unthinkable for Hanomer and Endowyn to move without their community. The Council of Thirteen had shown extraordinary trust in letting Hanomer set up a link to The City of the Trees using a pair of black swamp oak acorns. The Gurundarian end of that connection was planted in a well-watered meadow in the midst of the new *Hansa* village so that the black swamp oaks could be guarded day and night.

"Hanomer," said Dave, "it looks like you're going on a long journey. What's up?"

"Friend Dave, I believe I *am* going on a long journey, but I thought that you could tell me what the long journey was about."

"You thought I could tell you? I don't understand. Did someone send you a message on my behalf? As a prank?"

"No message came from you friend Dave. The message came from elsewhere. Endowyn and I were sitting on our new veranda singing to the Creator as we like to do in our morning time of contemplation, when we were interrupted. It was as if someone were speaking to me mind-to-mind as you and I sometimes do when I touch your arm. Only no one was touching me. It came as a poem. Here he began to recite in the Common Tongue.

A path united divided
A day of sundering
A week of trials

Prepare for the journey
Prepare your friend
Prepare to descend

A lamp will light your feet
A goal will loom out of the gloom
Look for new birth out of dying
Look for hope in the hopeless
Look for heaven in hell

"And because of that poem you came here to go on a long journey? What does it even mean?" asked Dave, bewildered.

"Friend Dave, Endowyn and I independently heard exactly the same poetical prophecy mind-to-mind. Although we do not know what it means, we know enough that we were to be parted for a time, perhaps a very long time, and that it would be a trial for Endowyn, me, and our three children. Still if the Creator sends us a message, even if we don't know what it means, we ought to follow it, as far as our poor understanding allows. Perhaps I am wrong. Perhaps I have been a fool to come here with my 'goodbyes' said and my pack loaded for a long journey, but Endowyn and I want to be found ready and faithful to obey the instructions. The Creator is never wrong."

"Well," said Dave, "put your equipment down and join us for some *siph* and a bite to eat on the veranda. It's too nice a day to sit indoors. I'm glad you're here." Dave made Hanomer a sandwich.

Ferris had left, and Hanomer was into his third sandwich when Arlana came into the room holding a letter in her hand. "I found this letter waiting for us in our black swamp oak water meadow." Dave recognized Pam's elegant handwriting, and saw a short note from Al at the bottom in spidery script.

Dave's eyes widened as he read. "She's pregnant!"

Arlana laughed with deep joy. "Isn't it wonderful news?"

"I can't help but think that this will heal some of their hurts," she continued. "We've been away so long at the Academy; this letter could be old news. I'm going to write a quick reply to congratulate them and tell them of your predicament with the Academy." She kissed him tenderly, then said, as if in an afterthought, "With the black swamp oak growing so quickly in our water meadow, I may be able to visit Pam when the baby comes."

Dave felt himself begin to tense up. "You know how I worry about my government back home and what they'll do with you and to you if they find you there. Anyway, do you really relish being scrunched up in the fetal position overnight until the transfer to my world is complete?"

"I wouldn't mind the scrunching. As for the other, I know your worries, sweetheart. I would be careful. Pam and Al live in a secluded place in your world, don't they? I would stay away from trouble. Besides, I would come back immediately if there were any question of government interference or danger."

Yeah, thought Dave, *"immediately" to her means hiding out in a tree overnight until the transfer is complete. She has no idea of police, FBI, police dogs, or snoopy neighbors.*

Dave watched her leave to write her reply, then settled back into his chair on the veranda. Once again, he looked westward down the mountain side. Lake Tolbar glistened like a mirror in the sun. At the horizon he could see the Callabar Islands. Far off, beyond sight, were the forbidden western lands. To the north, storm clouds were forming, large and black.

"Hanomer, I hope you will stay a while before you head back to Endowyn." Hanomer gave Dave a look that said "Didn't you hear anything I said?" but went off to store his gear in the room that he used whenever he visited.

Alone now, Dave settled deeper into his chair on the veranda. Arlana's home was far down the mountainside, nestled near the water's edge, where the healing plant grew that had made him into an Ancient. It was good to be close to her home, but not too close. They needed the space to start their lives together.

He thought of the book he had read, *A History of Abaddon*, in the Ancient Tongue. *What a dreadful place Abaddon seems to be. A continent so far below sea level that the atmospheric pressure is high. Life forms, which need the high air pressure to survive, live there. People full of violence, weird experiments on people and living things—if this book is to be believed. Now I know why people shudder when that name is even spoken.*

After that tome, he had needed some lighter reading. Arlana had suggested a childhood favorite of hers, the fantasy called *An Abaddon Journey* by Jandor Longwalker. It told of the author's imaginary adventure in Abaddon. But Dave was looking for real information, not fantasy. Still, since he had started reading Longwalker's book, he couldn't put it down. Now that he was out of the Academy and supposed to stay home, he would have plenty of time to read. When Ferris came he had been reading about Jandor drifting in a small sailboat after a storm had dismasted his craft. He was being blown into Maw Bay on the west side of Abaddon and his situation looked desperate. Of course, no one could walk around that continent and come back to tell about it.

Dave opened the book and read for a while. Jandor was shipwrecked on the west coast of Abaddon, captured and taken to an underground tunnel that led to the Abaddon plain. But eventually, despite the excitement of the book, Dave felt tired from the tension of the last few days. He closed the book and dozed off. He was soon dreaming a vivid dream of giant reptiles, winged creatures so large they could never fly in our light atmosphere—all warped by the malevolent hands of sorcerers, human experimenters, and Bent Ones. Some were even Ancients that had been so warped and changed that they were unrecognizable, but still, they had that spark of consciousness that made human beings and *Hansa* so different from beasts.

He woke with a start as he heard footsteps on the veranda. It was Arlana. She was pale, her cheeks glistening with tears, and clutching a letter. "I found another letter from Al when I went to send off my reply. Something terrible has happened."

Chapter 4

Trouble in Georgia

There is no such thing as a smart computer, only smart programmers. Certainly, with enough work, ingenuity, and a reasonable amount of computational power, a team of smart programmers can get a machine to pass the Turing Test, but if you look at the machine code, you'll find subroutines, specifically designed after many failures, to eliminate machine 'tells' and fool a person into thinking he's interacting with another human being. It's the programmers who have done all the real thinking.

COLLEGE PANEL DISCUSSION
ON ARTIFICIAL INTELLIGENCE
ALBERT GLEESON

Before going off to teach his classes, Al looked in on Pam.

Pam and Little Thomas were sitting at breakfast. The kitchen smelled of freshly baked buns, making Al hungry. He went to the pan and picked up a golden bun and bit into it. So good! It didn't even need butter.

He looked at Pam. She looked so beautiful in the morning sunlight. She wasn't showing yet, but she had been having bouts of morning sickness. She was reading to her son. Al loved to stand and watch her, especially with Little Thomas. She seemed to glow with the quiet joy of motherhood.

Well, it's getting late. I have to get ready to teach my college class.

He walked over to the breakfast nook quietly, leaned over and surprised her with a kiss. She looked up with a welcoming smile.

"You're off to school, honey?"

"Soon. I'm going in a bit later today because I'll be home late tonight, sweetheart. This afternoon I've been asked to help with a panel discussion on Artificial Intelligence with the Computer Science Department. We're filming it for the students. The school may even upload the clip to the internet. I guess I'm included because I'm the resident sceptic. Then I'll be helping with the basketball team after school again."

Pam looked concerned. "What are you going to say about Artificial Intelligence?"

"I'm going to say that there is no such thing as a smart computer, only smart programmers."

Pam frowned slightly.

"Are you still worried that I'm going to say too much?"

Pam's frown turned to a look of concentration as if she were wrestling with a difficult problem. "Al, I know you have to speak your mind, and that when you do you're gracious and respectful. You're a man of integrity. But we do need this job with the baby coming. I just worry that our world has changed. Society pays lip service to honesty and free speech, but we don't really practice it. If you challenge one of the pet theories of the Computer Science department head—I worry about what that could mean for us."

Al pulled up a chair and sat down. "I hear you Pam. I know I'm often on the opposite side of issues from the *status quo* at the school. But I have to walk a fine line between speaking rashly and being silenced. There's an oppressive climate in education these days that cares more about how statements mold student behavior than what's true or false. Education has become a process of manipulation and behavior modification rather than a search for truth. Hardly anyone seems to believe in following the truth to wherever it may lead. Most don't seem to believe in the idea of truth at all. If I'm to do any good at all for my students, I have to help them become truth-seekers. That's the only way to maintain integrity, and to be connected to reality."

Pam sighed. "I know you're right. But with the baby coming, I'm feeling vulnerable right now. Sometimes my fear undermines my ability to trust in you and in God."

"Hopefully your trust is in God over me. You of all people should see clearly that at best I'm a broken vessel."

Pam smiled weakly but said nothing. Al took a deep breath. "I know Pam. It's tough for both of us getting used to being a part of a college. Academia by its nature engenders a herd mentality. To survive, the academic has to be a part of an approving group. If he ever finds himself alone, with no one to support him, then no matter how right his position or how strong the evidence, his academic career will end and his voice will be extinguished because he's lost his peer-group credibility. His peers will destroy his career with faint praise. I feel a strong pull, against my honest judgment, to say things and take positions that will gain the approval of my colleagues. That's how to maintain my academic credibility. To me that's the great trap—cutting corners and sacrificing integrity to maintain credibility with my peers."

"But shouldn't credibility be automatic if you have evidence and speak the truth?"

"Pam, I think that's how it used to be, when a commitment to the truth over-rode everything else. But now, if you listen to the talk in the faculty lounge, there are so many issues where the focus is not on what's true or false, but rather on getting the public to think or act a certain way or getting politicians to fund a particular project. When the end justifies the means, then often, a useful lie that moves public perception in a desired direction is exalted over an uncomfortable truth. This social pragmatism will be the death of science. When we go down this path, all we will have left is propaganda."

Little Thomas was beginning to squirm.

"Well I think I'd better go," said Al.

"I think Little Thomas wants a kiss before you go."

"No kisses!" said Little Thomas emphatically. "And no hugs."

"He does that with me too," laughed Pam.

"He takes after his dad—err—his step-dad and kisses women only."

"In that case you ought to set him a good example." She lifted her chin invitingly and Al obliged.

"I'll keep dinner warm for you," she said with a smile.

As he closed the front door Al felt a chill come over his heart. It was as if someone were watching him. The feeling only deepened as he drove down the long, tree-fringed lane to the main road.

But Al forgot about his foreboding until he returned home that night. *The discussion on Artificial Intelligence went better than I hoped,* he thought as he steered his car home, *and the basketball players are starting to play like a team.*

The overcast sky made the night dark. He thought again how isolated their property was. He turned into his lane. The wind picked up, whipping the trees. Leaves swirled as if a giant were waving a huge duster. The house was dark. His apprehension deepened as a palpable dread washed over him, paralyzing him for a moment. Murmuring a quick prayer that everything would be alright, he pulled the car near the front of the house. In the glare of the headlights, he could see that the door had been ripped off its hinges. He knew he should call 911, but he had to know if Pam and Little Thomas were safe. Turning off the headlights, he took a flashlight from the glove compartment, went to the shed, and picked up an axe handle. Quietly, he approached the mangled door.

I know this house better than any intruder would. I should have an advantage in the dark.

The inside was even darker than the outside. He heard a shutter bang in the wind. Behind him, the wind chimes tinkled and rattled as the wind gusted. The floor was covered with debris. His feet crunched on what sounded like broken vases from the window sill—in the faint light from the window he could tell the place had been trashed. Al searched the first floor, but found nothing and heard no sound but his own steps and the wind. He went upstairs—no one was there.

He went back to the main floor and turned on the lights. On the mantle, over the fire place was a folded piece of paper, fastened onto the wall with a steak knife. On it GLEESON was written in capital letters. He opened it, and terror filled his heart. as he read,

Gleeson, you stupid—he skipped over the profanity. It's payback time. They're mine. You must have known I'd come for them. I'm taking them where you'll never find them. Maybe later I'll come for you too. Sleep tight.
Bigelow

Al sat down stunned. *Think! You've got to think!*

Bigelow disappeared during the Battle for Halcyon. He wasn't with the survivors and his body was never found. He must have escaped to that continent to the east with the Bent Ones. What was it called? Abaddon—that was its name. How did he get here from the parallel world?

An idea occurred to Al; the radio frequency identification tag. Pam had been so paranoid about Bigelow coming back and snatching Little Thomas, that she had convinced Al, against his better judgment, to implant an RFID tag into Little Thomas. He had found an expensive one listed on the internet that was powered by bioelectricity, using the body's own biochemical energy to emit a digital radio signal over the cell network. It was designed for pets, not for humans, but Pam could be very persuasive.

Al ran to his office and launched the tracking program. He could see the signal. It was a long way off. The map said Little Thomas was heading into Okefenokee Swamp. Al left the RFID-tracking program on and called 911. As he waited for the police, he kept watching the signal. He began to data-log the location coordinates and the signal's intensity. Bigelow's group stopped, as if they were making camp for the night. He wrote down the coordinates.

The police arrived. Al showed them the note.

"We'll talk about this in a few minutes," said one of the officers, "but first we'd like to search the house. Please stay here."

"Sir you really ought to look at the tracking data I have on my stepson."

"Tracking data—what do you mean?"

"My stepson has an RFID chip on him—my wife was worried that he'd be taken. The point is that I can pinpoint his location within a few meters. We need to act on this now." Al's voice had become shrill.

The two officers looked at each other. "Okay Mr. Gleeson, let's have a look at your data." Al took them to his office and showed them the data. The RFID log indicated that Little Thomas was not moving. He was several miles into Okefenokee Swamp.

The older officer called headquarters for a helicopter and dispatched it to the coordinates on a child abduction alert. The two officers began searching the house. In the living room, where he had been asked to wait, Al fidgeted.

Finally, the two policemen returned. The older officer, with "Monroe" stenciled on his uniform, sat down and looked at Al impassively for a few seconds. "Officer Connelly and I have a few questions, Mr. Gleeson. This note you found is rather personal. How do you know this Bigelow?"

"I knew Stan Bigelow from the University of Halcyon." Al recounted the details of the University of Halcyon's dislocation, told them that Bigelow was Little Thomas's father, talked about many of the conflicts he had had with Bigelow at Halcyon, and finally told about their return home more than a year ago.

"Do you know where Bigelow moved after he returned?" asked Monroe.

"But that's just it," said Al, "As far as I know, Bigelow wasn't among those who returned with us. I thought he was either dead or had stayed behind."

The officers looked at Al sceptically. Suddenly the radio blared. Monroe answered it. He said "okay" a few times and then ended the call.

"Mr. Gleeson that call was from the helicopter pilot. There was no one at the coordinates you gave us, nor in the immediate vicinity—not so much as a light, a fire, or a campsite. You've been leading us on a wild goose chase. You'd better come with us down to the station."

Al started to protest, but Monroe put up his hand. "Mr. Gleeson, we can either do this the easy way or the hard way. You wouldn't like the hard way."

They took Al down to the police station and into an interrogation room. Another officer began the questioning all over again. She probed Al's relationship with Pam, how he felt about Little Thomas, curiously enough, even about Al's religious beliefs. It took hours.

It wasn't until morning that they released him. During Al's interrogation, the police had obtained phone records, confirmed that Pam had made a telephone call from the house while Al was teaching, and received independent confirmation that Al had been at the college until late in the evening.

Grim-faced, Monroe and Connelly drove Al home. They didn't even try to make small talk. Before they let him out of the car, Monroe turned to him. "You know, in some quarters, putting a tracking chip into a child would be considered child abuse. We won't charge you, since our state has no specific laws that cover this particular case, but you're definitely in a grey area. If you keep talking about this tracking chip, someone in the District Attorney's Office may decide they have a case against you."

The police left. Al went back to his office and looked at the tracking log. The RFID signal had not moved. But at 3:13:51 a.m. it had abruptly disappeared.

He knew that black swamp oaks acted like huge capacitors. When one stayed in them long enough, the trees built up whatever energy they needed to accomplish the transfer to the sister oak. It happened in an instant. He realized that Bigelow had taken Pam and Little Thomas right out of their world to the other place. Perhaps they were in the continent of Feiramar, but more likely in dreadful Abaddon.

Al couldn't hold the tears back. He dropped to his knees. "God, how could You let this happen? Even if I find them, what will Bigelow have done to Pam? What will happen to our unborn child? What about Little Thomas?"

The thought came into his head: *the most common command in the Bible is "fear not." So why am I letting fear paralyze me?*

He pulled out his Bible and turned to Psalm 91. He began reading out loud. He stopped after verse 10 and re-read verses 9 and 10.

> **Because you have made the LORD your dwelling place—the Most High who is my refuge—no evil shall be allowed to befall you, no plague come near your tent.**

But evil has befallen me. A plague has struck my tent. Does this promise really have any meaning? Haven't others read this and clung to it, only to be disappointed?

Still he knew what he had to do. He had to do his part, and trust that God would do His. Al turned to the only friends he could really trust with this problem. He sat down at his desk and pulled out a fresh sheet of paper and began to write. Fifteen minutes later he walked to the swampy meadow at the back of his property and approached a curious tree with oak leaves. The branches folded in, so that the overall effect was that of a two-meter pear sitting on a ten-centimeter tree trunk. He parted the leaves and placed a small wooden box carrying his letter into the open space in the center of the tree. By some time tomorrow the box would appear in the sister tree in Feiramar.

Returning home, Al emailed his closest friends: Floyd Linder, Tom Chartrand, Dwight Larsen, and his brother Thomas. Next, he wrote a confidential letter to his lawyer with instructions. His lawyer would have to notify the college that a family emergency required Al to take a leave of absence. He put one signed copy in an envelope and left a second signed copy for his friends. Then he called his friend Makalo who lived close by. Al told him he was coming by; he needed his help.

Assembling his camping gear, sword, knife, and crossbow, he wrote detailed notes for his friends, and then left, wondering if he would ever return home again.

Chapter 5

The Burning House

Floyd Linder sat at a table, surrounded by faculty from the University of Halcyon. To his right sat Professor Frederick Aberhardt, his sociology professor. Aberhardt had his hands folded across his chest, eyes closed, with an earnest look of forced contemplation on his face.

Linder choked at the smoke that was filling the room. The heat was stifling. The house was on fire. He was deeply afraid, yet somehow, neither startled nor surprised.

"I'm going to see if I can get out," said Linder.

Aberhardt opened his eyes. "Don't you trust us, Floyd, my boy? We've told you all the doors are locked and windows barred. You're engaging in wishful thinking. You want a way out. Your propensity for imagining fulfilment of your desires makes you think there *must* be a way out. There is none. Face reality. Compose yourself and enjoy the last few moments until the flames reach us and oblivion comes."

Linder slumped back into his chair. *Maybe he's right,* thought Linder. *I'm sure everyone has tried all the doors and windows already. I'd look a fool to try them all again.*

Suddenly Linder looked up and saw a ghostly apparition of his friend, Al Gleeson, standing before him. Linder knew it was an apparition because he could see the smoke-filled hallway right through Al.

"Why are you just sitting there, Linder? Why aren't you trying every window and door to escape?"

"They've all been tried," said Linder. "Everyone says so."

"But wouldn't it be better to be trying to find a way out rather than just sitting there waiting for the flames to reach you?"

"Remember Al, just after my grandmother died, we had that long debate about God, Jesus, and the afterlife. You used the same argument then. "Try it out," you said. "What have you got to lose?""

"Did you try it out?" asked Al.

"No," said Linder. "I knew I would be disappointed and it would turn out to be a sham in the end. Then I'd look like a fool for being taken in. I'd rather keep my pride. I guess I'm afraid of getting my hopes up, beginning to believe there's a way out, only to have my hopes dashed."

"So, you're going to just sit there?"

Linder said nothing.

"You can't really know until you try," continued Al. "Isn't it worth the risk to have a chance to get out of this deathtrap? Won't you try now?" asked Al. "What have you really got to lose? Why wait for the flames to come? What kind of a life is that, waiting for death?" As he said those words, Al began to fade, such that the last words came as if from a great distance.

Isn't that what we all do—just passing time while we're waiting for death? Isn't that reality? Linder thought.

Linder awoke. But he couldn't shake the dream still vivid in his mind. So, he deliberately chose to put it aside, knowing the details would fade quickly as he moved into his day. He didn't have to go to work, since the contract job he had taken three months earlier had ended the day before. He planned to go on an extended trip before looking for something more permanent, and to find another place to stay. He looked at his smartphone and saw an email from Al. "Speak of the devil," said Linder.

But as he read about Pam and Little Thomas, he caught his breath. Getting up, he rushed to get his things together. Life was about to get very interesting.

Chapter 6

Swamp Oak Voyage

Every muscle in Dave's body ached as he woke from a troubled sleep. Having slept in the fetal position in the black swamp oak, he had his backpack in his lap, and was holding his sword, Gram, in the crook of his arm. His bow was digging into his side and his quiver was lashed to the scabbard of his sword.

This had better work. If I spent the whole night in this blasted tree only to find myself back in Feiramar—I'll scream. The stuff I do for Gleeson.

But in the next moment he felt a pang of guilt as he remembered Al's anguished letter.

Dave realized that the smells of the swamp had perceptibly changed from the familiar scent of the wetland near his Barrier Mountain home. He parted the branches and peered out. The swamp looked unfamiliar.

Dave pushed his way through the branches. Standing up, he found himself in the middle of a bog about a hectare in size with cypress hummocks protruding from the water—green peas with toothpicks sticking out—floating in brackish broth. Sunlight dappled the placid surface of the water. Dave looked up. It was going to be a day of mixed sun and clouds.

He turned his attention to finding his way off the hummock that held the black swamp oak. There was no immediate evidence of a path. He didn't expect one. Al would have disguised his approach to the strange tree, just as he and Arlana had for their black swamp oak, the twin to this one. He looked for evidence of the morning sun through the tree canopy and chose the approximate direction to Al's house. Jumping from hummock to hummock and balancing on cypress roots, he finally saw evidence of a path. In five minutes, he was out of the trees and headed toward a modest bungalow, which he recognized from pictures as Al's house. He smelled hay and cut grass. A sport utility vehicle was parked out in front. The porch creaked as he approached the front door.

Suddenly, the door swung open. "Son of a gun, if it isn't Dave Schuster!" said a familiar voice. Floyd Linder wrapped Dave in a bear hug and lifted his two-hundred-forty pounds off the porch easily.

"Whoa, Linder, I'm breakable. It's good to see you. How's Al? Any news about Pam and Little Thomas?"

Linder put Dave down, and ran his hand over his shaven scalp. "Chartrand, Larsen, and I drove up as soon as we received his email, but he wasn't here when we arrived this morning. There was just a note that he was checking out some black swamp oaks south of here. He gave us the coordinates. He also left us a bunch of other stuff. Al's lawyer is a close friend, and he's put all of his assets in trust with his lawyer. Makalo's been designated to provide guidance to the lawyer on Al's behalf. We were just talking about what to do next. Come on in. We helped ourselves to Al's coffee. It's fresh."

Dave followed Linder in to the smell of freshly brewed coffee. Dwight Larsen and Tom Chartrand were already up and greeted Dave warmly. Dave pulled up a chair and joined the others at the table, taking a sip from the cup of coffee Chartrand had thrust into his hands.

Dave felt elated. He only realized, now that they were together, how much he had missed his friends.

"So Arlana let you go?" asked Chartrand.

"The swamp oak is barely big enough to carry one person. I insisted on going first, but Arlana will be here tomorrow morning with Hanomer."

"Oh," said Larsen. "Hanomer is coming? We'll have to be careful to keep him hidden."

Dave sensed Larsen was troubled. "I know. I was worried, too, about Hanomer coming. How do we keep him hidden when one view of him will raise all kinds of questions we can't answer? Still, when Hanomer makes up his mind, he's hard to dissuade, especially when Arlana backs him up, and when he's had some kind of vision that he was supposed to come."

"What's this hocus pocus about a vision?" asked Linder.

"I'll let Hanomer tell you about it when he gets here. It gets worse. Hanomer is convinced he's going to Abaddon to find Pam and Little Thomas. So, he argued he would only be here, in this world, for a brief time, so there would be little danger of his discovery."

"What if we decide going to Abaddon is not the right course?" asked Linder. "Would he go by himself?"

"I wouldn't be surprised if he did go by himself," said Dave. "The *Hansa* have a very highly-developed sense of honor. If he believed it were his duty, he would go even if it meant going by himself to certain death."

Linder shook his head. "Well back to the matters at hand. We were just trying to figure out what happened to Al, and what we should do next."

"Well, if I were Al," said Dave, "and I found the black swamp oaks that Bigelow had used, I would follow Pam straight away. Every moment counts. I would follow no matter the odds."

"He's right," said Larsen. "Al would do a fool thing like that."

Chartrand, biting his lip, added, "No matter what Al does, Bigelow has at least a twelve-hour head start on him. It means we now have two groups to search for. If Al had been smart, he would have waited. He's just made our problem worse by rushing off."

Linder rocked back on his chair. "That train has left the station. I say we head down to Bigelow's bog and locate those swamp oaks. We have to find them if we want to help Al."

There were nods around the table, except from Dave.

"I suppose," said Linder, "you have to be here when Arlana arrives tomorrow morning."

"Yeah," said Dave, "It will be her first time in our world and she doesn't know the first thing about this place."

"You know Dave," said Linder, "Arlana is not the only one we have to worry about. You're an Ancient now. You've got that freaky ability to change your skin color in the matter of a few seconds. Remember how Bigelow's men in Halcyon dubbed you and Arlana both squids when you were in captivity and they saw your skin color change? If that happens now, all kinds of alarm bells will ring. So, I'm asking: are you better at controlling your pigmentation?"

"Yes, I am."

"Still, I think, Dave, you ought to let us take the lead while you stay in the background just so you don't lose it and have a color change when you get excited."

"Okay, I agree."

"If we find enough swamp oaks," continued Linder, "the three of us will travel right away to Abaddon in the hope of meeting Al before he wanders too far. You can drive the car back and pick up Arlana. You'll be back here in plenty of time. In any case, we'll wait for you by the trees in Abaddon."

"You guys can do that? What about your jobs? What about family? Can you just disappear like that?"

"It's all taken care of," said Larsen. "Chartrand and I are still looking for work and Linder's just finished a contract job. Our friend, Makalo, is going to look after our stuff. We're following Al's cue. We've given up our apartments and left notarized letters with our lawyers in case anyone questions Makalo about our disappearance."

"Surely, you didn't write down where we're going?" said Dave.

"No, of course not. We only said we were going on a trip, and that we would be off the grid for some time. We also asked Makalo to pay the taxes on Al's place if that should be necessary."

"Alright," said Dave, "Let's get started."

Chapter 7

Into the Okefenoke

It was late afternoon. The day was overcast. The air was muggy. The four friends had rented a small boat and traveled about three kilometers into the swamp. Linder glanced up from his global positioning device. "Okay, we're close. The black swamp oaks have to be around here somewhere. Keep your eyes peeled."

Chartrand maneuvered the boat to an island about fifty meters in diameter, dense with vegetation. The edge was fringed with pond cypress trees interspersed with bald cypress. Linder attached the painter to a cypress root and pushed through thornless green briar, grimacing at the putrid smell of the plant. "There's green briar all over this little island. Seems to me with that smell to keep the tourists away, this would be an ideal place for a black swamp oak that needs to remain hidden."

"You mean," said Dave, "we're going to have to put up with this stink all night while we transfer to Abaddon? The things we do for Al!"

Linder didn't answer but pushed toward the center of the small island. "Dave, you're the only one of us who's seen a black swamp oak. Why don't you lead and see if you can find one?"

"Well we know this is the right island," said Dave pointing to a pile of brush. Under the dense brush, they could see a camouflage-painted boat.

On the second pass of the island Dave found a cluster of three pear-shaped trees with ten-centimeter diameter stems. Next to the middle tree, he saw a note wedged into a cypress root fork. It contained Al's scrawl.

I took the middle swamp oak. I'll try to follow Pam's trail and leave markers.
    Go with God!
Al

Dave passed the note around. "Now what do we do?" asked Larsen.

"I'm going to stick with the original plan and follow Al right now, said Linder. "Anyone coming with me?"

"I'm in," said Chartrand. Chartrand and Linder looked at Larsen.

"Yeah, I'm coming. I just wish Al had waited for us."

"I'm heading back to pick up Arlana and Hanomer," said Dave. "Tomorrow when you've transferred, Arlana, Hanomer and I will climb into the swamp oaks and join you. But what am I supposed to do with your car, Linder?"

"Remember, Makalo? He lives not far from here near Astoria. I called him last night and told him the situation. He'll store my SUV and drive you and Arlana back here. He'll likely even take the rental boat back for you."

"You know there's a chance that the twins of three black swamp oaks are located in different places in Abaddon," said Dave. "Linder, since you're taking Al's tree, you'll go to wherever he went. So, Larsen and Chartrand, what are you going to do if you end up some place else and don't find Linder on the other side?"

Chartrand looked at Larsen. "I guess after a thorough search of our arrival area, if we can't find you, Linder, we'll come back and line up to take Al's tree."

"Dave, I think you're worrying needlessly," said Linder. "Bigelow had to transport Pam and Little Thomas back as prisoners. Each tree can take one adult and one child or *Hansa*, I suppose. At the most. There's no way this plan would work if Bigelow used black swamp oaks in different locations."

"I hope you're right," said Dave.

Dave watched the men climb into the foliage of the swamp oaks and try to make themselves comfortable for the long night, with their packs nestled on their laps. After a few minutes, satisfied that they could last the night, Dave headed back to the rental facility with the boat.

Chapter 8

Into Abaddon

Before dawn the next morning, Dave waited in the bog near Al's black swamp oak. Finally, when the newly risen sun was casting long shadows on the bog, Hanomer followed by Arlana poked their heads through the foliage. As Arlana climbed out of the oak in which she had travelled, she reached back into it for her pack and weapons. Dave stepped up and pulled her into an embrace before she had completely disentangled herself from the tree. Next, Dave gave Hanomer a hug as well.

Arlana crossed her arms, attempting a scowl in mock severity. "Well husband, that's quite a reception. You'd think I'd been away for a month. What have you learned about Pam and Little Thomas?"

"Come to the house. It's a bit of a story. I'll fill you in on the details while you have something to eat."

When Arlana had finished the omelet Dave had prepared, and Hanomer was on his third helping of home fries, Dave finished his story.

"So, husband, we're going to follow them, I take it?"

"Yes, I think we have to. How much time do you need before you can endure another cramped trip in a black swamp oak?"

"I'm ready to go right now. I didn't find the trip here too difficult. I'm sure it's much harder for you than for me."

"Let me just clean up these dishes, lock up the house, and we'll be off to see Makalo."

Just then he heard a car pull into the lane. Looking out the window, Dave saw a taxi. A man climbed out carrying a backpack and what looked like a rifle case. The stranger paid the driver and headed for the front door. Dave and Arlana opened the door and stepped onto the porch. Startled, the stranger stopped at the bottom of the porch stairs. "This is the Gleeson residence, isn't it? I'm looking for my brother Al."

Dave and Arlana looked at each other. Then Dave descended the steps and held out his hand. "My name is Dave Schuster and this is my wife Arlana. We're friends of Al and Pam. This is their house but they're not here right now. Nice to meet you. I didn't catch your name."

"My name is Thomas Gleeson. Nice to meet you too, Dave." Thomas smiled at Arlana shyly, put down his rifle case, and shook Dave's hand tentatively.

Dave knew about Al's estranged brother but couldn't remember if he was older or younger. He looked older, perhaps because he had a full beard. His eyes were dark brown, almost black. He was taller and more athletic looking than Al, but Dave could see the resemblance when he frowned in concentration as he was doing now.

Dave's silence was growing awkward. "As I said, I'm afraid Al's not here," said Dave blocking Thomas' path to the house.

"Oh," said Thomas. "He's already gone after Pam has he? You're probably here to help. Whatever you're going to do, I want to be part of it."

Feeling sceptical, Dave said nothing. He didn't invite Thomas into the house.

"Listen," continued Thomas, "as I'm sure you know, Al and I had grown apart while at Halcyon. I had left the university before the Dislocation. Ever since Al came back, he's been trying to patch things up with me. We finally met at his marriage recommitment here. He wouldn't have emailed me if he didn't want me to at least have the option to come along. He's my brother—I have a duty to help. If I don't go, I'll have regrets for the rest of my life."

"Thomas, I mean no disrespect," said Dave slowly, "but you can't know what you're getting into. From what I know about where we're going, you *will likely regret this trip* for the rest of your life. We may never get back."

Thomas took a deep breath. "I'm a University of Halcyon alumnus. I read everything about the Dislocation that I could when it happened and I've kept reading after you came back. I know you're going to a strange new world—a dangerous world. Please let me come along. I'm a good woodsman and an excellent shot. You won't regret it."

Dave ran his hands through his hair. He didn't like this situation one bit, but he didn't know what to say.

Arlana came down the steps and put her hand on Dave's arm. "I think we should bring him along, husband. None of us know what we shall meet. But the call of honor on blood-kin is strong, and he has an obligation to help his brother and his relatives. It would be wrong for us to take that choice away from him."

Dave was going to object but changed his mind. He didn't like it, but he'd have to live with it. "Okay, we leave as soon as we can get our things together."

As the implications of Thomas joining the party hit him, Dave came to another decision. "Okay, Thomas," he said, "if you're going to join us, I want you to meet someone. Hanomer, please come out here."

Hanomer came out of the door. Dave heard Thomas gasp in surprise. "Hanomer, meet Al's brother, Thomas."

Hanomer walked up to Thomas boldly and extended his right hand. "Welcome friend Thomas, kin of my friend Al Gleeson."

Thomas reached down to shake the small hand. "This must be one of the *Hansa* I've read about."

"Yes, he is," said Dave, "and now I'm going to tell you what I know about our situation. And you're not going to believe me. In fact, you're going to think I'm pulling your leg when I tell you how we're going to follow Al. Come into the house, put your feet up, have a coffee and something to eat. It's a long story."

Dave told Thomas everything. A few times during the narrative, Thomas' facial expression showed he was startled. During the conversation, Thomas couldn't take his eyes off Hanomer, who sat nearby and listened.

When Dave was finished, Thomas said, "So you're telling me we're going to climb into these small trees called black swamp oaks and overnight they're going to miraculously transport us to a new world?"

"That's what I'm saying."

"But that seems so unbelievable. I don't believe in miracles anymore."

"Why are you so surprised to find the 'unbelievable' in nature? If your brother Al were here, I'm sure he'd say that there are many things in nature that, at first glance, are miraculous and unbelievable. Think of birds navigating for thousands of miles from summer to winter habitats; salmon finding their home tributary, bats, at high speed, using high frequency sonar to locate and eat flying insects at night and butterflies undergoing enormous changes from egg to caterpillar to adult. All these things macroscopically seem astounding and miraculous. Your brother

Al also would say that the chemistry behind these phenomena is even more astonishing. Yet science gives them a name and a mechanistic explanation and then we lose the wonder, the mystery, and the miracle behind all these events. Somehow, they become commonplace because we have named—and perhaps, in our minds at least—explained them.

"Al once said that science was like a basilisk (I think he was quoting someone) and that it takes the life out of whatever falls under its gaze. When science analyzes and explains a mystery, it destroys something profound and essential about the phenomenon by taking away our wonder and our profound sense of the miraculous. We are poorer for it."

"I think you've been around my brother too long. You're beginning to sound like him."

Dave chuckled. "You got that right."

They left in Linder's SUV as soon as all their gear was loaded. About three hours later they were in Clappers Corners, a small hamlet near Astoria, looking for 821 Lee Avenue. The house proved to be a rambling bungalow on a large lot with a barn in the back.

Makalo was out of the house and welcoming them before they had even left their SUV. After Dave introduced Thomas, Makalo said, "Come inside and have some food. You must be hungry. I've put on a fresh pot of coffee. You are hungry, right?"

"Yes, we are!" "No, we're not!" said Dave and Arlana simultaneously.

Makalo laughed as Arlana gave Dave a stern look. "My friend Dave is always hungry," said Hanomer.

Makalo smiled at Hanomer. "I seem to recall hearing from Dave, Hanomer, that the *Hansa* also have a considerable appetite." Makalo had pulled-pork sandwiches and wraps already prepared. The spices he used were delicious, and Dave was ravenous. Between bites, Dave described what he had found in the Okefenokee Swamp, the pond cypress island, and the three black swamp oaks.

"I know," said Makalo. "Al came by and I helped him get to the island. I have his car in the barn now. So, you think Al was right about them travelling over to the other place?"

Then why didn't you stop him? Thought Dave. Out loud he said, "I think so. Hopefully the others have found him safe and sound. For my part I had to pick up Arlana and Hanomer to follow them."

"So, you want me to take you to the island and then bring Linder's SUV back and store it?"

"We'd be grateful if you would, Makalo," said Arlana. "We don't know when we'll be back, but it could be a matter of months."

Or longer, thought Dave.

"I'm ready to go," said Dave, finishing the last of his sandwich.

Dave drove them back to the boat rental facility. They had hidden Hanomer in Dave's large pack. The clerk showed surprise at their repeat rental so soon after the last one but said nothing. Makalo remembered his way through the swamp. He brought them unerringly to the black swamp oak island.

Dave tied up the boat and they went directly to the cluster of three black swamp oaks.

The oaks were empty, and there was no sign of their friends. "Well, they're no longer here, so that answers one question."

Makalo helped them unload their supplies. Dave chose the largest of the three black swamp oaks while Arlana chose the second largest, the same one Al had used.

Dave noticed these oaks were slightly larger than their specimen in Gurundar, attesting to the excellent growing conditions in this swamp. Makalo hugged Arlana and then Dave, and then shook hands with Thomas and Hanomer. Wishing them God's protection, he waited until they were settled in the cocoon-like interior of the bulbous trees. Dave's tree was very similar to the black swamp oak in the water meadow in Feiramar. The thick stem ended abruptly, about two meters from the ground. It then divided into many branches, which bent upwards from the outer stem of the main trunk, leaving a hollow space shaped roughly like an onion.

Dave heard Makalo start the boat motor and the sound gradually diminish. His heart began to pound and his thoughts began to trouble him again. *Everything that I read about Abaddon from the books in Gurundar made it seem like I'm going into hell—a land where the Bent Ones like Meglir rule. A land filled with slaves who are compelled to work for their masters. A land so far below sea level that the air will be like soup. What will I find in eight hours? Will I be able to protect Arlana? What if we die in the first hour? What if my friends are already dead?*

He remembered a scene from the children's book, *The Silver Chair*, where Pole, Eustace, and Puddleglum faced a difficult decision, wondering if they would die if they did what Aslan, the great lion, had commanded. He remembered what Puddleglum said in the book:

"You see, Aslan didn't tell Pole what would happen. He only told her what to do."[2]

Yes, Dave thought, *I have no guarantee of safety. I only know what we must do. So, if we live or die, we will have done our duty.*

He felt an inexplicable lightening of his spirit, and was suddenly overcome with sleep as the tension of the last few days caught up with him.

---

2   C. S. Lewis, The Silver Chair, (New York, HarperCollins, 1953, 1981), 175.

Chapter 9

The Platform Trees

Dave awoke to a feeling that he was breathing thick soup. The smells, although similar to what he had smelled in the Okefenokee, were sufficiently distinctive that he knew he had been transported to the sister black swamp oak in Abaddon. Trembling, he spread the branches and looked around. No dangers appeared to be present. The light was subdued, like twilight at home, but his sight was sufficiently keen that he saw island after island surrounded by peat-stained water.

Stiff because of his cramped sleep, he climbed down. His tree was on the slope of a tiny island. At the crest of the small island was a large tree with horizontal branches starting about twenty paces up the stem. He looked carefully at his black swamp oak. Initials had very recently been carved into the trunk: "FL/TC/DL."

Linder's always thinking. The last thing we need is to wander away and forget which black swamp oaks brought us here. It looks like they all arrived together, thank the Lord.

Dave looked around hoping to see at least one of his friends, but there was no one in sight. He strapped on Gram, tied his bow and quiver to his pack, and then shouldered the load. Still no sign of Arlana or Thomas. Disappointed, he tried his opera-bird whistle, hoping to alert Arlana or one of the others that he was here.

He heard a rustle behind him. On a neighboring islet, Arlana's head appeared. She smiled as she saw him. Hanomer climbed off her lap and down the short tree trunk, scanning the swamp for danger, his bow ready. After looking carefully to the base of the tree for a few seconds, Arlana also climbed down with her pack and weapons. She walked toward Dave as he approached her. Ten paces of water separated them. The water was so brown that Dave could not see more than a few inches into its depth, but he thought he saw the shadow of a large creature glide under the surface. The water rippled at its passage.

"Don't try to cross," he warned.

Arlana nodded and said, "Any sign of the others? Where's Thomas?"

"No sign of Linder, Chartrand, or Larsen, but I found all of their initials at the base of my black swamp oak." Dave called Thomas by name. To his relief, he saw him climb out of a bulbous black swamp oak on a third island.

Arlana climbed part way up the hillock again, and presently called back, "This swamp oak also has all three initials, and a note from Linder."

How are we going to get together, thought Dave, *with these large creatures prowling the depths?*

"Friend Dave," called Hanomer, "look up at the trees that grow up out of the center of each island. They grow their branches together."

Dave looked up. Hanomer was right. It was almost as if they formed a terrace or platform of horizontal branches. Dave climbed to the highest point of his island, where he could see a large tree, about three paces in diameter with smooth grey bark, rising straight up. Moving closer to the tree, he saw that in the bark were curious helical indentations. By putting his toes into one of the indentations as a foothold, Dave found he had enough purchase that he could walk up the helical ramp by holding onto the indentations as the helix circled the tree above his head. In this way he soon reached the platform of branches. The platform stretched off in three compass directions as far as the eye could see in the vaporous gloom, but behind him, about two hundred paces distant, it ended in a rock wall, which marked the southern border of the swamp.

Dave identified the tree that formed the centre of Arlana's hillock and walked towards it. Above the platform, the terrace trees looked normal, with branches bending upward at irregular intervals. A profusion of vines ran from tree to tree. Holding on to these, and proceeding slowly, Dave completed the short traverse to the next hillock where Arlana and Hanomer were waiting for him. From there, Dave led the way to Thomas' tree. The branches that girdled the tree on level with the platform were so dense that they made a floor, so the four sat down to consider Linder's note.

Dave and Arlana:
Al was not here when we arrived. However, he left a
note saying he had found some clues, which had been
dropped by Pam, to show the direction she had been
taken. Apparently, they were taken roughly north by
northeast in a direct line. Al decided to follow, since
he believed time was critical. He's going to leave us
sets of three slash marks as trail blazes to help us follow his footsteps. If he loses Pam and the others, he
told us he would retrace his steps.

The three of us decided to follow him. We're going to try to use these funny trees to get out of the
swamp. Stay out of the water! The water between
the islands is deep and seems to harbor some large
aquatic creatures. I wouldn't trust them. One of
them went for me, when I bent over to wash my face.

We'll follow Al north by northeast. We'll wait
for you at the edge of the swamp if we get back before you arrive.

Floyd, (Tom and Dwight)

"I guess we'd better get moving," said Dave.

They tied a rope to each other with Hanomer leading, followed
by Arlana, Thomas and finally, Dave, acting as the anchor. Hanomer
was in his natural element and walked to the next tree as if he were
strolling on a sidewalk. Arlana also had exceptional balance, and did
not seem to be frightened by the height or the prospect of slipping
into the water.

Thomas was tentative, and took his time crossing to the next tree.
Fortunately, there were many finger-thick vines slung between the two
trees, which provided handholds.

When it came to Dave's turn, sweat began to bead on his face as
he remembered his old fear of heights.

*Funny, when I was anxious to see that Arlana was safe, I didn't think
about the danger at all as I crossed to her island without a rope.*

He called across to Hanomer to wrap the rope around a branch in
case he slipped. Hanomer did so, and Dave crossed gingerly.

Other than the large creatures in the brown, peat-stained water,
there were almost no animals to be seen—either in the trees or on the

islands. When he did see the occasional squirrel or bird, each fled in fear as the group approached.

This swamp is uncanny. I was expecting all kinds of snakes and alligators, and yet it seems so empty of animal life. I wonder if those aquatic creatures kill off anything that comes down to drink?

After crossing the first gap between the trees, Dave's confidence rose. Their rate of progress increased as the traverse from tree to tree settled down to a routine. After several kilometers, the light began to increase. They were leaving the shadow of the southern wall, and the size of the trees was also diminishing.

Dave called a halt and the group rested briefly on a terrace platform near the central stem of a particularly large tree. Arlana was standing, looking ahead. "I think I can see the edge of the swamp a few hundred paces away," she said, "but there's a curtain of white objects hanging from the trees. Almost like fruit or decorations. I can't make out what they are."

Dave jumped to his feet, filled with foreboding. He looked in the direction Arlana was pointing and saw the curious objects, but didn't know what they were either. Opening his pack, he took out a pair of binoculars.

"Oh no," he said.

He handed the binoculars to Arlana. She gasped.

"Let's get moving," he said.

They moved forward with renewed urgency, because of what the binoculars had revealed.

Dave, dreading that something was approaching from behind, looked over his shoulder as they moved, his imagination generating images of horrific monsters swinging through the trees, their jaws dripping with blood,

Finally, they reached the last terrace tree. It was covered with human skulls, hanging like Christmas ornaments. There seemed to be hundreds of them.

But as they looked left and right to the surrounding trees, they saw that there were, in fact, thousands.

Chapter 10

Terror on the Grassland

"Please Dave," said Arlana, "I want to get away from this swamp as quickly as possible."

Dave looked down from the platform. A moat about ten paces wide separated the edge of the swamp from the sparsely treed grassland beyond. The platform trees ended at this moat. There was no way across using the branches.

"How do we get across without getting eaten?" asked Dave.

Hanomer pointed to his right using the hand on his tail. "Friend Dave," said Hanomer, "someone has felled a tree to cross the water."

Dave heard Thomas mutter, "Whaat!" He looked at Thomas who was staring wide-eyed at the hand at the end of Hanomer's tail.

"I am sorry to startle you, friend Thomas," said Hanomer. "I should have remembered you have not seen the *Hansa* before." He opened and closed the hand on the end of his tail. "This extra hand is a great gift from the Creator."

Staying on the platform level, they crossed from islet to islet along the edge of the swamp until they came to the island with the log bridge. A large tree had been felled from the other side of the moat. The four of them climbed up on the one-meter-diameter trunk and traversed the moat. Someone had taken the trouble to remove the branches, making the crossing easier.

On the other side of the moat, there was a band of trees with long thin leaves. Once through this band, grassland opened up before them. The grass came up to Dave's chest. There was no sign of human habitation, but small copses dotted the grassy plain. A few miles distant there was also a series of steep-sided rock buttes that rose several hundred paces from the grassy plain, reminiscent of pictures Dave had seen of Monument Valley. Most interesting of all were rounded humps of deep green, like half-buried soccer balls scattered about the grassland at intervals of a kilometer or so.

Dave scanned the grassland for his friends. "Now what?" he asked. "There's no sign of them. Do we wait or do we continue?"

Still visibly shaken, Thomas shrugged and shook his head as if to say, "I don't know." Dave could see Arlana shudder as she looked back across the moat at the human skulls hanging on the trees. "I don't want to be anywhere near this swamp when night falls," said Arlana. Let's keep a look out for them now while we search for high ground. The buttes would be the best place to look for a safe campsite. We can still watch for the others from there."

Arlana looked back toward the swamp. Dave followed her gaze. Beyond the swamp came a plateau, several kilometers wide covered in deep shadow. Directly behind the plateau rose an impossibly high wall or cliff that rose straight up until it disappeared into a cloud bank. The rock appeared to be black granite with large patches of orange-brown rock reminiscent of rust. Surprisingly, there was little evidence of weathering, with no scree and few boulders or obvious rock slides.

Through the cloud cover Dave could see the sun peeking out. It was very high in the sky, so high that he estimated that the cliff he was seeing must be south of them. He knew from his studies on Abaddon they were ten kilometers below sea level, and that the air pressure was about three atmospheres. *Mount Everest is 8,848 meters above sea level. If I sliced Everest down to sea level with a knife and stood before it, it still wouldn't match the cliff I'm seeing now*, he thought, feeling small and insignificant.

"Looking at the shadows and the position of the sun, I guess we're somewhere on the southern side of Abaddon," said Dave. "I'm willing to bet that those regions very close to the southern Abaddon wall are mostly in shadow."

Arlana came over to Dave, put her arms around him and nestled into his chest. He could feel her shaking. "Dave, I'm afraid. We are out in the open here. Please, can we find shelter?"

Dave looked down at her and kissed her tenderly on her forehead. "Let's head for the nearest butte."

I have the same misgivings, thought Dave. *If we meet trouble out here in the open, this could be the shortest unsuccessful rescue in my brief but brilliant career as a hero.*

"Friend Dave, could I ride on your shoulders for a while?" asked Hanomer. "The grass is too long for me. Maybe on your shoulders I could warn us of danger."

It took only a moment for Hanomer to scramble up. He stood on Dave's shoulders, using his third hand to hold himself in place.

"Do you see anything, Hanomer?"

"Off in the distance to our left I see a herd of massive creatures with huge tusks and a snake-like appendage on their snouts. They have long tails with a bulge at the end. They are not close but they seem to have seen us."

"I see them Hanomer. They do look like what we call elephants, but they must be as big as a house."

"Friend Dave, those huge creatures are facing our way. I don't think they're friendly."

"Are they moving towards us?"

"No."

"Alright Hanomer, you'd best get back down. I figure we should head for that steep butte up ahead to our right, and if we really hoof it, we might get there in about an hour."

"Hoof it?" chorused Hanomer and Arlana together.

"I mean travel at top speed. If we can climb to any height on the butte, we should be able to see our friends if they're anywhere near the northern edge of this swamp looking for us. Arlana, let's put the hoods up on our living cloaks and hope the cloaks blend in enough to hide us."

Hanomer seemed to know the route even though the grass stalks towered above his head, and he set out at a rapid pace. Although the grass was tall, it was not dense enough to really slow them down. Arlana followed him, scanning the horizon, while Dave, with his crossbow out, kept looking back over his shoulders for anyone or anything coming out of the swamp after them. He kept looking back at the herd of super elephants in the distance. They hadn't moved.

The group had covered about half the distance to the butte and were approaching the first of the green hemispheres. "Down!" said Arlana. "Someone's coming."

Arlana, Dave and Thomas all crouched in the high grass. Only Hanomer remained standing.

"Where are they?" asked Dave, after he had crawled forward to join Arlana.

She pointed to the edge of the green dome. "There's only a single person. I think he came from the direction of that butte."

Dave pulled out his binoculars, rose high enough to scan the grasslands all the way to the butte, and then sighed in relief. "It's Linder, coming for us. Why is he waving like a mad man? Let's go meet him."

They rose and, redoubling their efforts, raced towards their friend in the fastest trot they could manage encumbered as they were by the weight of their packs. Linder sped toward them at a fast lope. In five minutes, he had closed the distance. Grabbing Dave's arm he wheezed, "This way. They're coming for you."

"What do you mean?"

"No time," said Linder gulping lungfuls of air as he pulled Dave toward the green mound. They renewed their efforts with Linder leading and Dave right behind Arlana.

The green dome consisted of ten-centimeter-diameter stems armed with fifty-centimeter-long thorns that looked sharp as rapiers. The thorn stems rose to about six meters and then plunged into the ground again, making the arc of a large circle. Many of the arcs rose and descended to make an impenetrable dome structure bristling with spikes. The five reached an area of grass about the size of a football field that had recently been trampled. Dave could hear the ground tremble.

Linder led them to the edge of the spiked structure, pulled out his sword and hacked the nearest thorns off the stems. He squeezed through the stems by pulling them apart.

"Come on, hurry. They're almost here."

First Thomas, then Hanomer squeezed through. A bellowing trumpet sounded as a huge elephant-like creature, over ten-meters tall at the shoulders, charged into the open area. Dave pulled the stems apart with all of his might, urged Arlana to go in, and then followed her.

"Let's move into the center of the hoop thorn grove," said Linder. "Those pachydons are vicious and will try to grab us with their trunks." The thorns all seemed to face outward, so that the inside of the grove consisted of large hemispherical room. What had seemed like a single hemisphere, was actually a series of overlapping hoop thorn chambers. Although the interior stems had no thorns, moving to another room meant squeezing through the stems again.

The five huddled together in the centre of the hoops as the pachydons bellowed and stampeded around the outside. Dave smelled a strong musk-like scent.

"Where did they come from?" asked Dave. "I was keeping an eye on a herd to the west."

"There was another herd directly east of you that was hidden by the hoop thorn," said Linder. "They smelled you and were building up their anger to charge. I could see the danger developing from the butte. That's why I couldn't wait for you."

The noise of the stampede lessened. It seemed the herd was moving away.

"Are you all okay? Did you find Al?" Dave and Arlana's questions intermingled.

Linder put up his hand. "Yes, we're okay. And we found Al, but not Pam and Little Thomas. Where do you think the names 'pachydon' and 'hoop thorn' came from? Didn't you recognize Al's penchant for naming things?"

Dave smiled.

"Anyway," continued Linder, "we need to get off this plain and out of sight as soon as we can. There's a mine at the next butte and there's a lot of activity there. Al, Larsen and Chartrand climbed to the top of the butte to observe the mine, and left me to watch for you. Al says we don't want to be seen by the people manning the mine. We'll have to stay here until dusk when the pachydons form a defensive perimeter for their herd for the night, and then we'll make a run for it.

"I almost didn't see you," said Linder. "Your living cloaks blend in so well with the surroundings. If it hadn't been for the combat fatigues,"—here he pointed at Thomas—"I wouldn't have been able to warn you."

"By the way," said Linder looking at Thomas, "I don't think we've been introduced. My name is Floyd Linder."

"I'm Thomas Gleeson, Al's brother."

"Glad to meet you," said Linder offering his hand, but he looked at Dave as if to say, "What's going on here?"

With that Linder sat down against a stem and told the others everything that had happened in the twenty-four hours since they had travelled to Abaddon.

When the light began to dim, Linder travelled to the edge of the hoop thorns and looked for any sign of the pachydons. Satisfied that they had returned to their herd, he set off at a rapid walk, insisting on carrying Arlana's pack. Arlana let him have it, but took out her bow and nocked an arrow. In twenty minutes, they left the grass and walked up a scree slope. Soon they entered a narrow cleft about three paces wide. Dave could hear the sound of running water but saw nothing. As they entered the cleft, Dave saw the small, clear rivulet in the cleft disappear as it reached the edge of the scree. Further back, the cleft opened up and was blocked by a five-pace rock wall which was wet on one side from the rivulet.

Chartrand appeared on top of the wall and lowered a rope for them to climb. One by one, Dave, Arlana, Thomas, Linder, and finally Hanomer made their way to the top, where they found a lovely, grassy alcove with a few small shrubs, which appeared to be stunted because of the shade. A pool of water rippled at the base of a rivulet that splashed down from the heights.

Chapter 11

Friends Reunited

Al, Chartrand and Larsen were waiting for the five at the top of the wall. Al's jaw dropped open when he saw his brother. "Thomas, when I contacted you I never expected …"

"I know," interrupted Thomas. "I've hurt our relationship by dropping off the grid for so long. I just had to be in on this rescue."

Al gave his brother a hug. There were tears in his eyes. Dave could see that for once, Al did not know how to respond.

"Well," said Al after an awkward silence, wiping his eyes, "come on back into our camp."

The dell was a flat triangle about twenty meters wide on a side. The sides of the triangle were steep except at the back where the butte could be climbed easily.

Once everyone had moved to the back of the little dell, Al dished out some hot soup he had ready on an alcohol burner. Everyone sat in a circle to eat. Al's eyes kept straying to Thomas.

"Al, I know you've already filled in the others on what happened when you arrived here, but you'll have to go over it again," said Dave.

Al took a deep breath. "After I left you the note by the black swamp oak, I climbed into the tree and spent a worried night waiting for the transition to take place. I had my flashlight, so I was reading Psalm 91 and thinking about Pam and Little Thomas. I couldn't help thinking about how hopeless my situation was. Even if I did my best, and was lucky enough to find them, Bigelow would have had them both for so long that he could have done unspeakable things to them just out of spite. I hardly slept at all that night. I'm not exactly sure when the transition to Abaddon occurred, but I do remember feeling the air grow thicker and the night sounds of the Okefenokee diminishing. I waited until daylight; I didn't want to risk leaving the tree in the dark.

"At first light, I climbed out of the tree and found myself in the swamp. I tested the water with a stick and found it was very deep. Something large snatched the stick out of my hand almost pulling me in. It was then that I saw a red kerchief hanging down from the platform trees. I examined the kerchief and saw that it was Pam's. Once I had my starting point, I could see the direction they had gone in. Some of the branches were broken and there were marks on some of the larger limbs where someone had damaged the bark with a rope. For a while there weren't any more signs, but I knew they'd crossed the final stretch of water at the tree trunk, and had headed across the long grass plain.

"Before I left home, I checked Pam's closet to see which shoes she was wearing when she was kidnapped. A pair of boots with one-inch heels was missing. She must have had a terrible time crossing those tree limbs in the swamp with those boots. But they helped me a lot in the grasslands. As you know there were several worn paths where the grass was disturbed, leaving the tree trunk bridge. I hunted around until I found her boot print. Their group didn't head out into the plain like we have, but skirted the edge of the swamp and headed east. I followed them as fast as I could for most of the day until I reached a precipice that dropped about five hundred metres. Below was a flat shelf about three kilometers across. It was covered with trees, meadows, and water courses. Beyond that there was just sky, so the drop could be much bigger and deeper. They skirted the edge of that precipice consistently and headed roughly northwest. Since I had a line on where they were, and I knew you would be here soon, I headed back to meet you guys.

"On the way back, I was thinking about Bigelow's route. He went east and then northwest along the precipice. Why not head straight across the grasslands? I couldn't figure it out.

"It was late afternoon. I didn't retrace my steps but headed a little bit north towards the nearest butte. I needed water and thought the buttes would be the best chance to find some. I saw those huge elephant-like animals. I also wanted to check out those domed structures. But as I approached one dome, I heard this thundering noise. I looked back and saw a group of pachydons lumbering toward me. In my panic, I cut my way into the hoop thorns and stayed inside as they stampeded around the outside. A few times, they tried to reach me with their trunks. They were so persistent that I was afraid I would miss you. But the pachydons left that evening.

"I was very thirsty, so I made my way to the nearest butte and found a stream. I was too far away from the swamp exit, so I kept heading toward the butte that I'd first seen when I crossed the log bridge.

"The pachydons didn't bother me at night. I reached my destination just when it started to get light. I followed the water course up to this dell and made camp. I climbed up higher to watch the log bridge.

"That's when I saw the mine in the next butte. I had a quick bite to eat, while staying as far from the pachydon herds as possible, and kept a hoop thorn close at hand. Then I made my way back to the swamp. And that's how I found Linder, Chartrand, and Larsen."

Linder took up the story. "When Chartrand, Larsen and I finally came out of the swamp, Al was waiting for us. He led us back by a route that always kept us out of sight of the mine and away from the pachydons. Staying here, we could keep an eye on that mine—in case they sent out patrols—and watch for you to arrive.

"We didn't expect you for another day. But just in case, I was commissioned to watch for you. Al was catching up on sleep while Chartrand and Larsen climbed up to the lookout and took turns watching the mine on the next butte over."

At this point Larsen interjected. "There was a steady parade of what looked like Apemen, Halfmen, and a large contingent of slaves moving around the mine. I'm not sure if the slaves were Ancients or regular people."

"Do they have guards at the mine?" asked Dave.

"There were guards in black armor carrying long spears. They seemed to focus more on keeping the slaves working than watching for danger. There's a dirt road heading north that has a lot of wagon traffic. A wagon full of ore leaves every hour with a couple of mounted guards."

Al picked up the conversation. "This makes Bigelow's behavior even more puzzling. He's Meglir's henchman. Why not head straight for the mine, and avail yourself of a ride and an escort? Instead, Bigelow headed east to the edge of the precipice of the canyon and stayed as far from the road as possible. It may be that Bigelow was just avoiding the pachydons, but if we can avoid the pachydons using the hoop thorns, so can he. It's my best guess that Bigelow was running this operation without Meglir's approval. I think we should follow Bigelow's trail. That will give us a chance to avoid detection for a while, if I'm right with my guess."

"How many people did Bigelow have with him?" asked Dave.

"With only three black swamp oaks, Bigelow came back with one other fellow. It looked to me that the party that ransacked our home was bigger. Bigelow may have contacts in our world who planted the black swamp oaks and helped him out with the transportation, the snatch, and then hung around until Pam transferred."

"That makes sense," said Dave, "Pam would have been in a tree by herself. They had to make sure she didn't make a run for it."

"She would never leave Little Thomas." said Arlana. "The sooner we find them the better.

"I have another question, what do you make of all those skulls hanging at the edge of the swamp?"

"No idea, Dave," said Al. "It seems another strong reason to stay out of the swamp and off the plain."

Al waited to see if there were any other questions. "I think we should turn in early and then leave in the middle of the night. The moon is well before the first quarter so there's very little light. With Hanomer, Arlana, and Dave to guide us, we should be able to find our way on the open plains without being seen. Hopefully we'll be well away from the mine by daybreak. If we need to go to ground, the terrain will get very rough once we get close to the lip of the canyon."

"Al," said Arlana, "from your description, your canyon is the lip of what we call Sheol, the Pit. Terrible as Abaddon is, it's nothing like the evil and terror of Sheol. By your measure, the Infernal Sea of Sheol is another six kilometers down from the Abaddon Plain. There are many huge and terrible creatures living at the bottom. Sheol is the black heart of Abaddon. All the evil of this place emanates from there."

"Arlana," said Dave, "you've got to lighten up. You're scaring them. Look Chartrand is shaking in his boots ..."

"I am not," protested Chartrand. "I'm shivering because the night air is cold."

Dave looked at Chartrand sceptically. "Like I said, Arlana, you're scaring the boys. Why should Sheol harbor so many terrible creatures?"

"I don't know why. I do know we should only cross the lip into Sheol in our most extreme need," said Arlana, "and then return to the Abaddon Plain as soon as the danger has passed."

Al was still thinking about Dave's question. "She may well be right, Dave, about huge and bizarre animals living here and in Sheol. Have you ever wondered why the largest land mammal back home is the elephant, and the largest flying bird is the California Condor?"

"No, I haven't, but I have a feeling you're going to tell me."

"It has to do with air pressure. For warm-blooded animals, energy is generated by all of our cells, while heat is lost by heat exchange at the surface of the animal. Since heat generation scales roughly as the cube of the linear dimension and heat loss as the square, there comes a point where a much larger animal will be cooked by its own metabolism. The only way around it is to change the medium to water or increase the air pressure to enable better heat conduction."

"So why do we find such large land creatures in the fossil record?" asked Linder.

"I read a paper once that argued that those creatures could only exist when the air pressure was much higher. Air pressure is much higher here and would be even higher in Sheol. So, we're ten kilometers below sea level here. And Sheol is another six kilometers lower than that. If I assume a constant temperature, I can use the Ideal Gas Law and figure out the pressure on Abaddon Plain and at the bottom of Sheol."

"Whatever," said Larsen, "while Al is using his Ideal Gas Law to figure out the pressure, if I'm not on watch, I'm going to catch forty winks."

They began to disperse. Linder headed up to the lookout, while others decided to catch up on sleep. Dave saw Al and Thomas sit down together for what looked like the beginning of a long, quiet talk. Dave crawled into his sleeping bag. Within minutes, he could hear Arlana breathing regularly and he knew she was asleep. Yet sleep did not come to him. While back in his home in the Barrier Mountains, he had spent a lot of time reading everything the Ancients had written on the continent of Abaddon. What he had read terrified him as much as it did Arlana. Afraid to be alone with his thoughts, he got up. At the back of the triangular shelf, the cliff walls narrowed to a slot carved by the little stream that flowed into the dell. Dave scrambled up an easy climb for more than a hundred meters. The slot opened into a ragged shelf that formed a notch on the side of the steep butte. Linder turned to him as he heard Dave approach.

"I take it you can't sleep," said Linder.

"No," said Dave. "Since I can't, you may as well get some rest. There's no point in both of us staying awake."

"Alright Dave, wake me when you get sleepy." Linder left. After about 45 minutes, Al joined Dave.

"I'm glad you brought Thomas, Dave."

"I didn't want to, but Hanomer and Arlana made me."

"Why didn't you want to bring him? Didn't you know what it would mean to me?"

"I guess I wanted to spare Thomas. This place really bothers me."

"Why?

Dave took a deep breath. "I did a lot of reading on Abaddon when I was back home in Gurundar. Everything I read about it reminded me of what I'd heard about hell."

"Why is that?" asked Al

"Well," said Dave, "we're looking at a continent ruled by a group of Bent Ones like Meglir. Under Meglir are the Apemen, which remind me of zombies, and maybe an army of sycophants—like our turncoats—who are as cruel as they are resourceful. The only role we have in this society is one of slaves." Then Dave began to chuckle.

"What's so funny?" asked Al, surprise tinging his voice.

"I was just thinking that God sure has a sense of humor. You know Al, the concept of hell, more than anything else, kept me from becoming a Christian. And now that I have an uneasy truce with that subject, I find myself brought here to experience hell-on-earth first hand."

Dave could see Al's posture grow more upright in the gloom. "Dave why has the concept of hell been such a problem for you?"

"God is supposed to be a God of love, so why have a place of torment? Why not extinguish people completely if they're bad and unredeemable? In fact, if God is all-powerful, why not make it so that all people could be redeemed?"

"I think you mean 'will be redeemed' rather than 'could be redeemed.' I think I'm correct when I say that most Christians, except the staunchest predestinationalists, would say that all men could be saved. But by free will, they have the right and the power to choose not to be saved."

"But couldn't God make the terrors of hell so real to people that they would avoid it at all costs?" asked Dave.

"I suppose," answered Al, "but wouldn't that be overriding free will another way? Aren't Christians often accused of using hell to frighten people into the faith? Isn't that just another form of coercion? A spiritual shotgun wedding?"

"I suppose," said Dave, "but does that really answer my question? At the end of the day, my question still stands. Can God really love me if he'd let me choose a destiny that involves eternal torment? You love Little Thomas, Al. Wouldn't you choose to override his free will, to keep him safe?"

"I suppose I would while he's a child, but if Little Thomas is to grow into an adult, I have to let him make his own choices, even bad ones. To forever take away his right to choose is a terrible pathology. I want him to choose, and to choose the good.

"Dave in the sciences, when one is trying to answer questions in a new area, one often begins with data that don't seem to fit together, and even that seem contradictory. What I always do is ask myself 'What am I sure of?' I begin formulating my hypotheses starting there. It's like a puzzle where I begin with the corner pieces and edge pieces. I believe all the pieces will eventually fit, but I start assembling the whole puzzle picture using the pieces I'm most sure of.

"For me the same is true of these questions about hell or Gehenna—the Valley of Hinnom—which is the actual term used by Jesus. I begin by believing that Jesus loves all of us enough to die for us. That's what I'm most sure of. In the end, when full understanding comes, then I believe all the things that Jesus said about hell will prove true, but some of my ideas may have been wrong. I believe the word is true, but that doesn't guarantee *my interpretation of it* is correct."

"Al, your letter to us seemed filled with desperation. Arlana and I were worried."

"Yes, it was. I'm dreadfully frightened about what's happening to Pam and Little Thomas. Bringing Thomas and talking to me about things that matter a lot to me have pulled me out of my funk. Thanks, Dave."

"So, talking about hell has cheered you up? Has anyone ever told you that you're really weird, Al?"

"Yes, many times," said Al chuckling.

"I don't know how Pam puts up with you."

"Frankly, I don't either Dave. I'm just grateful she does."

Chapter 12

Necroan Attack

Dave was startled out of a sound sleep by the sudden pressure of a hand clasped over his mouth. Someone was shaking him. When he sat up, Arlana, who was beside him, also began to stir. Linder removed his hand and put a finger to his own lips. In the dim light Dave watched as Linder crawled to the back of the dell, then turned and motioned for them to follow. Arlana led; Dave brought up the rear.

At the back of the dell, the cliff walls narrowed to a slot, which had been carved by the little stream that flowed into the dell. Linder was already well up the slot, groping his way from one foothold to the next. They followed Linder up to the lookout notch on the side of the steep butte. The others were already crouched there, looking south to the swamp and northwest to the mine.

Dave touched Linder's arm.

What's going on?

Linder was visibly startled by the contact telepathy, but he sent a thought back by forming the words in his mind.

We're not sure. We can hear several hundred heavy bodies moving through the grass. All I can see are large blobs. Al is using his night vision goggles to get a better look.

Dave wormed his way to the edge of the shelf and peered over. The moon had already set, yet the starlight was sufficient to make it seem, with his Ancient vision, that he was watching at late twilight. He gasped at what he saw. Several hundred enormous men, perhaps four meters tall, were moving rapidly through the grass toward the mine.

They were covered with hide armor and carried spears with shafts the size of saplings. At their sides swung two-meter scimitars. On their forearms they wore leather sleeves bristling with spikes. Their heads were the most disquieting thing about them. Although their bodies were much taller and broader than ordinary men, their heads were of normal size. These disproportionately small, helmeted heads gave them a grotesque appearance.

What are they going to do?

The formidable troop quickly passed their butte several hundred paces to the west and continued straight on toward the mine. As they passed, the leader began to lope at an even more rapid pace. The others followed his lead. They didn't yell, but the thump of their feet and the swish of the grass as they sped on interrupted the stillness of the night. About three hundred meters from the mine, shouts of alarm sounded.

Dave pulled his binoculars from his pack. A gravel and rock ramp extended from the mine opening to a road that bent north. The invaders reached the base of the ramp. The first of the huge men charged up it with a deep-throated animal roar. A few of the guards who were positioned at the top of the ramp put up a token resistance, looking like children fighting grownups. The enormous men skewered them easily with their long spears. Other guards threw down their weapons and ran for the mine. The giants cut down several of them. Soon the fighting moved into the mine itself. Screams could be heard echoing from the depths. The screams went on for more than an hour, followed by a silence equally terrifying.

Dave looked at his friends. Al kept swallowing. Linder's mouth was set in a line. Arlana had changed her skin to the palest color possible and was averting her eyes.

Then, Dave saw the flickering shadows of several large bonfires in the mine entrance. Harsh singing and coarse laughing began. This went on for another hour. Dave could hear shouts and the occasional scream. After another twenty minutes, chained slaves and soldiers—who were being whipped by the giants—came out of the mine entrance pulling a wagon piled high with corpses. They rolled it down the ramp and pulled it across the grassland towards the swamp. A second wagon followed the first, and a third followed the second. Around these marched the giants, each with several human heads—some as many as a dozen—strung on a rope hanging over his shoulder. Dave watched as the huge warriors threw away the bones they had been chewing on, and drove the captives with the captured wagons back towards the swamp.

The giants approached the edge of the swamp. Through the sparse trees Dave saw the living prisoners push each wagon onto a raft in the moat. There were many more rafts than wagons. Soon the prisoners poled the rafts into the swamp, and drifted out of sight. Several of the smaller giants had collected the ropes with fresh human heads on them. These trophies were added to the skulls already hanging at the edge of the swamp.

Dave felt sick.

Al groaned. "Those poor slaves in the mine."

"While we were escaping from the swamp," said Linder, "we saw huge footprints. They must belong to those giants."

"Now what do we do?" asked Larsen.

"We need to get out of here," said Linder. "Initially I wondered why Bigelow wasn't guarding those black swamp oaks. Now we know. He deliberately planted them where no one in their right mind would search, but it also means he can't leave a guard outpost here to watch them."

"What you say makes sense, Linder," said Al, "especially since Bigelow wouldn't know about the Radio Frequency Identification Tag. He wouldn't expect us to find the black swamp oaks in Georgia."

"Friend Linder," said Hanomer, "I don't think we can just leave. What if there are some survivors left in the mine? I think we have to go there at least to check."

"But what about the patrols and the supply wagons?" asked Linder. "If they spot us, our best advantage will be lost and the hunt will be on."

"We've been watching them for a couple of days," said Al. "The first wagon won't arrive until a couple of hours after sunrise. If, by chance, they do surprise us, we're armed and there are only a couple of guards with the supply wagon. We can defend ourselves or scare them off. I agree with Hanomer, we can't just leave those slaves at the mine. I think we have to take the chance and rescue any that survived. What if they've been chained up and left to starve?"

The debate went on for a few more minutes. Linder gave in when Dave and Arlana sided with Al and Hanomer, but he still insisted they visit the mine, then immediately make their way to the cliff edge.

Together, they descended into the dell and broke camp. When they were ready to move out, Chartrand climbed up to the lookout that faced north to see if anyone was coming down the road. When he reported that the road was still clear, the group hurried across the grassland to the mine.

Linder led them at a rapid walk interspersed with short jogs. Dave kept up without difficulty, despite the twenty-kilogram pack on his back.

My work with the Guardian Cadets is paying off.

Even marching at double-quick time, it took about twenty minutes to get to the base of the mining butte. They reached the road, which bent around the rock from the northeast. The dirt road climbed a steep ramp made of rubble to a flat area. At the back yawned an opening about twenty paces high. The stench of death filled the air. Three bonfires were still smoldering and piles of clothing and armor were stacked beside the entrance of the mine against the cliff face. There were still some bodies around, but everywhere Dave saw bloodstains and gnawed bones.

Taking off their packs, the group readied their weapons.

Al went directly into the mine. Pulling his flashlight from his pack, Dave followed. Arlana and Hanomer were right behind him. After about twenty paces, two galleries split off to the side, one heading left and one right. More bodies. There was not a sound except the faint tinkle of water dripping into a pool. The main shaft then split into three narrow galleries.

Al went into the right gallery, Arlana into the central one. Dave was about to follow her when he heard a faint cry in the Common Tongue. "Help me. If anyone be there, please help me."

Dave went left. This gallery opened up a small chamber with crudely made iron picks, shovels and pry bars scattered about. Four more bodies were lying on the floor with ghastly holes in their chests. The cry was coming from a small crack on the right side of the chamber. It became louder and more insistent as Dave's flashlight beam played off the wall. A trickle of water had cut a channel into the rock and formed a pool at the bottom of a ten-pace deep shaft. A spindly, bedraggled figure was standing beside the pool.

Dave shone his light on him. His face was a mass of hair so that Dave could not tell where his hair stopped and his beard began. His skin was dark, the color of soot. The figure shielded his eyes and then clasped his hands saying, "Praise be, ye be not a Necroan."

Dave shouted, "Over here." In less than a minute Al, Arlana, and Hanomer were standing beside him.

"Who are you?" asked Dave.

"My name be Tandor—you don't be lookin like Meglir's soldiers."

"What do you know of Meglir?" asked Al.

"He be the new lord of this province. I be his slave and have served Meglir and the lord of Seth before him for twenty years. Rescue me and I be to servin' him still."

When Tandor saw Hanomer's face, his eyes went wide. "Ye be not with Lord Meglir, are ye?"

Dave looked at Al and Arlana. They both nodded, so Dave took a rope from his belt and tied a bowline hitch onto his line. Hanomer climbed down into the pit. Dave lowered the loop down to Hanomer. "Sit on the rope, Tandor and I will pull you up."

"Thank 'ee yer lordship." Hanomer helped Tandor drop the loop over his head so he could sit on it and Dave hauled him up. It was easy work; Tandor was light.

This poor guy has been starving for a very long time.

Dave broke out a piece of bread and hard sausage and gave them both to Tandor who ate ravenously saying, "Thank 'ee yer lordship," over and over again between bites. Dave, Hanomer, Arlana, Al and Tandor made their way back to the mine entrance. The others were already waiting there.

"We found nothing," said Linder. He stared at Tandor stuffing bread and sausage into his mouth. "Who's this?"

"This is Tandor," said Al in English. "If we've checked everywhere, we'd better move east before someone comes down the road. Tandor's eyes visibly widened as he heard them speak, but he said nothing and continued eating.

"So Tandor," asked Linder in the Common Tongue, "how did you survive when no other slave did?"

"The pool I be standin' beside in the little pit be deep. When the Necroans be comin' I slide into the pool and hold me breath till they be gone."

Led by Linder, the group hastened down the ramp and followed the road. Dave could see the sun already creeping above the horizon in the east. The road bent northeast, so Linder led them due east. Tandor, in the middle of the group, tried to keep up, but soon fell on his face.

Al knelt beside him and revived him with a drink from his canteen. Linder looked at Tandor and then back at the road.

Dave looked anxiously north. We're so exposed here, he thought. *A wagon could come along any time now.*

Chapter 13

Tandor

"Tandor's too weak to make the long trek to the cliff," said Al. "We need to head back to camp and give him a chance to recover."

"I'll hold Tandor up," said Dave, "he hardly weighs more than a feather."

They retraced their steps back to their butte. Linder was grim-faced but said nothing. With Dave carrying Tandor and the others making a couple of trips, they were able to get their supplies and Tandor up to the dell.

The group sent Hanomer up to the lookout to keep an eye on the mine, while they set up camp. Tandor washed in the stream, then trimmed his hair and beard. Al was roughly the same size as Tandor, and gave him some fresh clothes to wear. They all gathered for a meal. When they had finished, Linder asked Tandor to tell them his story.

Arlana sat beside Thomas, translating for him since he did not know the Common Tongue.

Cleaned and fed, Tandor looked years younger. His eyes seemed more intelligent than they had when they had first found him. He looked each member of the party in the eye. He seemed to make up his mind about something. Straightening up, his face took on more authority than it possessed before. He began this story:

"I spoke slave talk because I thought you were soldiers from Seth. Now I will speak plainly. A few hours walk east of here is the opening of Sheol, the deep pit. The cliff doesn't drop all the way to the bottom. It drops in a series of steps with flat places in between. My people call those flat places 'terraces.' When you stand at the top of the cliff you see the first terrace about seven hundred paces below you. Beyond the first terrace is another cliff, like the first one, and then another terrace.

"As a young lad, I grew up on the second and third terraces as part of a rebel clan. I was well-treated and taught the little knowledge we had. But our rebel clan was in constant danger, and we moved many times. When the Bent Ones from the town of Seth hunted us, we would flee to the lower terraces where the soldiers were afraid to follow. But we could not stay in the lower terraces for long because the dragons would fly up out of the depths of Sheol and attack us. So as soon it was safe to do so, we would ascend back to our home terraces."

"Why didn't the dragons just follow you up to the second terrace, Tandor?" asked Al.

"They are too heavy. They can't fly in the thin air. Only the youngest and lightest, the brown dragons, can even make it up to fourth terrace. The big monsters have to stay further down."

"I am sorry for the interruption. Please go on with your story."

"About twenty years ago, when I was a young battle chief for my clan, the rebel clans came together for a raid, to free our people who had become slaves of the Bent Ones. I was proud. I was reckless. And I led my band into an ambush. I was captured and made a slave in Seth.

"Most slaves, especially those in the lowest tier, don't last long in captivity. However, I was filled with shame and anger. I learned every skill I could and that made me useful. I survived as a slave more than two years and did not give way to despair—the slave's curse and death sentence.

"Finally, my chance came to escape during one of the wars and I joined the Guild in Seth, an outlaw group. I was with the Guild for many years, becoming one of their captains. When we could, we bargained and sold our services to the soldiers and minions of the lord of Seth."

"I don't get it," said Linder, "why would they want your services when they have slaves?"

"Worker slaves give in to despair and stop caring if they live or die. The soldiers and slave taskmasters of the lord of Seth are given tasks to perform and excuses for failure are not accepted. They are desperate not to fail. When it looks like they will fall behind the deadline, they come to us and secretly pay for us to finish it on time. The lord of Seth does not know.

"Still, we were enemies of the Bent Ones and every once in a while, the truce would be broken and the lord of Seth would order the Guild to be hunted. When he hunted us, we would hunt them and become true outlaws until the truce was again secretly established.

"A little over a year ago, I heard rumors in the town that this powerful lord, Meglir, on the continent of Feiramar, had managed to get out of some sort of a trap and wanted to overrun the Guardians, the long-time enemies of the Bent Ones. The Guild was quietly paid to haul supplies by wagon to the seaport outside the Rim Mountains. We pretended to be slaves on behalf of the logistic captains.

"As Guild members, we were against the Bent Ones. We did everything we could to damage the cargo for the fleet. We loaded contaminated food, mis-delivered weapons, and separated arrows from bows. In short, we secretly caused trouble that would become apparent when the Black Fleet fought. We knew we were taking a foolish chance but wanted to strike out.

"When the Black Fleet came back defeated, the Bent Ones went after the Guild with great fury. They were harsh with every one of the Guild members they caught. They gave me hard labor. After the second Necroan attack on the mine, they sent me to the Southern Marches—a place for me to die."

"So, what happened to Meglir?" asked Al.

"Oh Meglir? That's an interesting question. Hundreds of years ago, Meglir was king over Grishfang as well as king in Feiramar. He expected to take the throne here again when he returned. Had he defeated the Guardians, he likely would have been made king in the Council of Thirteen.

"But he was defeated. When he demanded to be made king, the Bent Council said 'No!' Instead they gave him the holding of a minor lord here in the south. The previous lord never made it back from the war. The council is reminding Meglir of his failure. Meglir's not even on the Bent Council now. Instead he sits brooding in his black fortress, plotting his revenge. He's the one who decided to reopen the Necroan mine. He has lots of slaves and the soldiers he assigns to guard duty at the mine are being punished. The soldiers only spend a quarter of the time actually guarding the mine, so they can always hope they're not there when the Necroans attack. The slaves always die."

"Have you ever heard of a lieutenant of Meglir called Bigelow?" asked Linder.

"Aye, I have," said Tandor. "Meglir was given two fortresses. He took the larger one and gave the smaller one to his lieutenant, Bigelow. Bigelow is now lord of Seth. He's an ordinary man like me and a traitor to his kind. I guess Meglir trusts him, as much as he trusts anyone, because without Meglir's protection, Bigelow would end up a slave."

Al looked around the group as if seeking agreement. Then Al turned to Tandor and said, "Tandor, we appreciate the information you have given us. We give you your freedom. Return to your people. We have to head off soon, however we'll leave you here with enough food until you get your strength back. We do ask for your word that you will not tell of us if you are captured."

"That's kind of you to give me leave to go, sir. I've been away from my people on the terraces for more than twenty years. I'm not sure what I'd be coming back to. But before you go, you fine people have asked me many questions. I have a few myself. May I ask them?"

"You may ask," said Al after getting nods from his friends, "but I'm not sure if we can answer them."

"You have equipment I've never seen before." Here Tandor pointed at Thomas' rifle. "From your questions about Grishfang, you don't even know about this place what the youngest child of a slave would know. I don't think you're stupid. You're from someplace else.

"Slaves and Guild members have a prophecy that at some time in the future, rescuers will come and lead us to victory over the Bent Ones. Now, I happen to believe in prophecy. And I hope you're here to fulfill it. So I ask, where are you from and why are you here?"

Al took a deep breath and looked at his friends. "Stop me if I say too much." Then, turning to Tandor he said, "You talked about how the rebels attacked the Bent Ones trying to recapture slaves. Well, we're here on that kind of rescue mission. Bigelow took two people from us, people we love very much, and we're here to get them back.

"You're right, we don't know our way around. We're doing the best we can. Right now, we need to get into Bigelow's fortress and hope we can think of a rescue plan once we get there."

"Are you from Feiramar?"

"Not exactly," said Al. "Dave and Arlana are from Feiramar, but the rest of us are not."

Tandor waited, expecting Al to say more. When Al pursed his lips, Tandor said, "Keeping things to yourself. I don't blame you. As I said, I've been away from my people for a long time. I don't know what I'll find if I go back. I do know, sure as a viper will bite the hand that pets it, that you'll be in irons five minutes after you reach the gates of Seth. I can help you. I can keep you safe. I have friends back in town and I think they'll remember me and help us."

Al looked around the circle. Dave nodded his head. Al turned back to Tandor. "Tandor, you are right, we don't know the first thing about this place we're going to—but how can you help us?"

"Well for one thing, you need know that you're in the country of Grishfang now. Grishfang is full of slaves. These slaves are under the authority of other slaves. There are only a few Bent Ones. The Bent Ones have Apemen, Halfmen, and soldiers to support them."

"Are these slaves Ancients?" asked Arlana. "Do they live for hundreds of years?"

"Oh, no ma'am, we might live for forty or fifty years, but we usually die sooner because of all of the beatings and whipping."

"Oh," said Arlana, half to herself, "You are Lesser Men."

Dave saw Tandor's eyes widen in surprise. "You truly are Ancients then? You really are going to fulfill the prophecy."

"Whoa," said Dave. "Not so fast. First of all, most of us are like you and we're not Ancients. Secondly, we're here to rescue our friends and escape. You need to know that. I won't have you helping us thinking that we're going to stay and help you escape the Bent Ones. We want to rescue our friends and go home."

Tandor smiled. "Funny thing about prophecy. It has a way of coming true whether people believe it or even know about it. I'll help you rescue your friends. Then I'll either be going back to my people or home with you if you'll have me. Either way I'm your man on this quest."

"Okay Tandor," said Al. "so how do you keep us from being captured five minutes after we enter Bigelow's town?"

"First," said Tandor, "we need to go back to the mine and get clothes and weapons from the dead guards and from the slaves. The guards also have badges and passes that we'll need. Next—"

"Whoa," said Linder, "we can't go back to the mine. By now the first wagon will have arrived and we'll be spotted."

"Aye," said Tandor, looking up at the sun, "the first supply wagon will be there. But those soldiers won't stay to look around. They'll be racing back to Seth, whipping their poor horses all the way. No, by now the mine is empty again. Bigelow will need a few weeks to round up enough new slaves to consider reopening the mine.

"That's step one. Next, even with disguises, we can't go up the main road to Seth. Ahead, on the road, we'll be blocked by one of the main gates. A party of soldiers coming from the mine after a wipeout would be highly suspicious.

"There's a better way. The wall that surrounds Seth crosses the plain and then makes a sharp bend northwest and runs right along the edge of the escarpment. That part is less well guarded and only has a few small gates for patrols that go partway down the escarpment to recapture escaped slaves.

"My plan would be to head straight for the cliff and then down to the second terrace to a place I know where we can find water and food until the time is right. When Bigelow sends out raiding parties to recapture slaves, we'll wear our disguises and pretend we're a returning patrol with a couple of escaped slaves."

Al turned white and put his head into his hands. "Oh no! Poor Pam and Little Thomas. What's going to happen to them while we're waiting?"

"It's the only way," said Tandor. "You have to trust me."

"I know it's the only way," said Al. "That's what makes the wait so dreadful."

Just then Hanomer returned from the lookout ledge. "Friends, the soldiers in the black armor have come and gone like Meglir himself was after them."

Chapter 14

To the Escarpment

I was travelling with Mikeloc and his marauders along the southern wall of Abaddon the first time I encountered the Necroans. Mikeloc had led us along the edge of a swamp in broad daylight because he believed we were safe during the day. How wrong he was. Four giants leapt across the narrow water channel at the edge of the swamp and attacked our troop. Two swung long swords with vicious force overwhelming all opponents with their strength and reach. The other two used spears to impale our comrades. Only when they had skewered one of our comrades were they vulnerable and then only for a moment. Our bows saved us. It was hard to pierce the Necroan hide armor. I was able to bring one down with a lucky bow shot into the eye. When the four were finally down, half of our band was dead. Mikeloc was so shaken by the attack, he did not delay our flight to bury our dead, but force-marched us through the night to get to the edge of the Mutandi Highlands.

ABADDON JOURNEY
JANDOR LONGWALKER

It was late morning and the sky was overcast when Hanomer returned to the lookout ledge. Al and the rest, including Tandor, made their way back to the mine. As they were climbing the ramp to the mine entrance, Al saw no sign of the visitors. The guards and wagon had come and then fled back to Seth.

Al and the others approached the mine and searched it thoroughly for any sign of survivors or guards. Linder acted as lookout, using his binoculars to keep an eye on Hanomer for any signal of approaching danger.

After the second search of the mine was complete under Tandor's watchful eye, they began the grisly task of collecting clothes and weapons to outfit their party for their eventual entry into the town of Seth.

When they were done, Tandor convinced them that he was feeling much better and could manage a march to the cliffs so they swung by the butte, picked up their gear, and began the journey across the plain.

As usual, Hanomer scouted ahead. The trip to the escarpment was slow. A light rain began to fall and soon they were thoroughly soaked. As Al had predicted, the first part of the journey was level grassland. The rain seemed to have driven the pachydon herds into shelter since none were visible.

The drizzle dampened both Al's spirits and his clothes. The soggy grass and the muddy track made walking difficult. Linder dropped back to walk with him.

"I don't like it," said Linder. "We don't know the first thing about Tandor, but we're trusting him with our lives."

"I know," said Al, "but what choice do we have? He's right you know. We'll be captured one minute after we show up at the town gate."

"We might find a way to sneak into the town."

"If we do," said Al, "we'll face the same problem all over again. If we ask directions or try to get food we'll give ourselves away."

"I guess we have to take a chance," said Linder, "but I'm sceptical that some random slave we rescue from a mine can be the answer to our problems."

"I guess that's the nub of it," said Al. "I don't really believe in accidents and random events. I've been praying for some help. So Tandor comes along. He feels good, not evil to me. He also seems to have the key for getting into Seth. Even if I'm wrong, even if Tandor sells us out in the end, like Gollum betraying Frodo, I still believe that even the back-stabbing will work out for our good in the end."

"Okay Al, we'll agree to disagree as we often do about these accidental events. However, we both agree we have to take a chance on Tandor for now. But I'll keep both eyes on him."

By late afternoon the drizzle had stopped. Al had hoped to speak to Thomas, but he was with Dave and Arlana who were acting as rear guard. Al felt a sense of panic as a critical voice within him said, *You have offended him now Al. You should have talked to him when he first arrived.* But Al's rational self told him that this wasn't true. *We had to worry about survival of the whole group and that had to come first. Thomas would understand. Anyway, I should be glad he's building a connection with Dave and Arlana. That can't help but make him feel welcome.*

Al could see that they were leaving the grasslands. They were further north than the route he had taken previously so this terrain was unfamiliar. The group climbed a ridge topped with windswept trees. Al identified oaks, maples, and a third tree with three-lobed leaves that he had never seen before. After crossing the narrow band of deciduous trees, they skirted a series of deep gullies and then entered a pleasant dell that widened out into a shallow valley with a small water course at the bottom. The valley sloped gently in an easterly direction toward the cliff edge. Hanomer led them on a game trail, which followed the meandering brook.

Finally, late in the evening, Tandor suggested they halt. "There are patrols that walk a trail that runs along the top of the escarpment. They are looking for Rebels on the first terrace. I suggest we make camp here."

It was only when he stopped walking that Al realized how tired he was. He looked for Thomas and found him sitting on a rock. Thomas looked as tired as Al felt.

Al sat on a fallen tree facing his brother. "Hey," said Al, "I'm so glad you came to help me find Pam and Little Thomas."

Thomas shrugged. "That's what brothers do."

The silence grew awkward. Thomas shifted his position on the rock. "Is it really true that Dalrymple is dead?"

"Yes," said Al, "he died saving some of his flock during an attack by some wolf-like creatures in a place he had founded called New Jerusalem."

"Damn!"

Al was startled. He had never heard Thomas speak like that. "You're upset?"

"It would have been easier—I mean it would have been easier for me to deal with his death if he'd died cowering in a hole, or been pulled down by those wolf-like things while abandoning his people. Now it sounds like he played the hero at the end."

"Why do you say that? Why did you want him to have a coward's death?"

"I hate the guy!" said Thomas. "I want him to be easy to hate. I want the satisfaction of knowing that he's a coward and a cheat."

Al felt an urge to tell his brother the story of how he wouldn't even forgive Dalrymple when he asked for it. He decided not to share. *Bad idea. Telling that story would not help Thomas. It would only make things worse.*

"Dalrymple hurt you a lot, didn't he?"

"He destroyed me!" said Thomas. "I worshipped the guy, hung on his every word. When he told me not to see you because you'd fallen away from the faith and would pull me down, I listened to him. I did what he said. When I finally saw what he was like, I wanted nothing to do with religion or Christianity—I still don't. It's been hell ever since. All my closest friendships are gone. I used to know what I believed and what the future held, but now I don't."

"I saw that happening to you, brother, and it tore me apart. I didn't know how to help. Then you disappeared and my closest friend was gone. Like I said, I'm glad you're back." Al leaned over and punched Thomas in the arm.

"Mind if I set up camp here?"

"I'd like that," said Thomas.

Chapter 15

The Second Terrace

Dave woke up next to Arlana just before dawn. His eyes were gummy, his mouth dry. Arlana looked so peaceful and beautiful lying beside him. Her skin was chocolate brown and her long blond braid trailed down her blanket.

Instead of feeling the pleasure he usually felt when he saw her sleeping, Dave could feel himself grow angry. The warmth, the affection, the love that they had shared since they had been married seemed so far off now that they were on the trail together. It was all danger, hiding, enemies, and huddling together as a group. There was no privacy. There was no time for him and Arlana to be alone. It was a tacitly-accepted group rule that no one must wander off. All had to stay together to remain alive.

I know it's all just part of being a Ranger and being on adventures. But I still don't have to like it.

What particularly irked him—Arlana didn't seem to mind or care that they had no time together. It was as if she expected the distance and the separation and took it in stride. *Did she actually welcome it?*

Dave quietly rose, strapped on his sword and his long knife. Picking up his crossbow and quiver, he headed back to the game trail. No one else was up. Thomas who was on sentry duty, had fallen asleep. They had camped in a rocky bay that cut into the north hill of the gentle valley they were following. Now Dave followed the game trail to the escarpment. The valley bent southeast and ended at a rocky shelf maybe two hundred meters across. The sun was not up yet but soon would be. Dave picked his way across the rocky shelf which was rent with cracks and pits. Beyond was a well-trodden path and then sky.

He looked up and down the path. He was in a shallow dip, so he could only see the trail two hundred meters in both directions where it crested a rise. Dave walked to the edge of the escarpment and caught his breath. The steep-sided cliff descended vertically five hundred meters. To his right the stream they had been following plunged over the edge and disappeared into spray before it cascaded halfway down. Looking straight down, he could see that the bottom of the cliff had a fringe of broken rock shards. Beyond that were large trees and a dense wood with a four-meter-wide watercourse winding through it. The heavily-wooded terrace was three kilometers wide. Beyond that edge, Dave saw nothing but sky. He was so high up, that he could see a second set of clouds in the distance perhaps one to two thousand meters below him.

The bottom of this huge canyon has its own weather system.

Just then, his acute hearing picked up harsh voices and the jingle of armor. Quickly, Dave moved into the deep shadow of a shallow crack, concentrated to make his skin as dark as possible, and waited.

He saw a troop of twenty-five men marching along the path from what he thought was the direction of Seth. Along with them were another twenty-five men in chains. The soldiers were cursing and laughing, the prisoners, sullen. Dave watched as just opposite him, on the path, the lead soldier stepped aside and looked over the edge to the first terrace, then, after everyone else had passed, rejoined the end of the column.

Dave waited until the troop has disappeared over the second rise, and then carefully picked his way back across the broken rock of the shelf to the shallow valley. He raced back to camp.

The others were just waking up when Dave arrived, out of breath. He saw alarm in Linder's face. "Dave what's up?"

Dave held up his hand, and took a few more deep breaths. "Soldiers … on the path … walking southeast … twenty-five … with prisoners."

"Did they see you?" asked Linder.

Dave shook his head.

Tandor had heard every word. "Seth sends regular patrols along the cliff edge to watch for Rebels on the first terrace. We must not be seen."

"What about the prisoners?" asked Linder.

"I don't know," said Tandor. "Patrols normally take captured Rebels back to Seth. From what Dave described, this group is being moved somewhere else. I don't know why."

Linder sent Hanomer and Arlana to scout out the path, while everyone else broke camp. When the rest of the band reached the rocky shelf, Arlana and Hanomer returned. Arlana had found a rise that allowed her to see several kilometers northwest in the direction of Seth. It was deserted.

"Friend Linder, the band Dave saw is still moving away from us along the edge. We are safe for now."

Linder led the group across the rocky ledge to the path and walked out onto a spur of rock, almost like a diving platform. He looked down. "Whew," said Linder, "you weren't kidding, Al. This is huge. It makes the Grand Canyon look like a ditch."

Tandor joined Linder. "This is the edge of Sheol," said Tandor, "my childhood home. It is too dangerous to head down now to the first terrace. We are not in the best place for the descent. We have to follow those soldiers carefully."

Hanomer set off ahead of them, keeping an eye on the soldiers in case their patrol carried them back to Seth by the same route. Tandor led the rest of the group southeast along the cliff edge until he came to a section of the cliff that was riddled with cracks and ledges. Dave recalled Hanomer.

Tandor led the descent, picking a zig zag trail. He stopped frequently, as if trying to remember where he should head next. The climb down to the first terrace was gruelling, often requiring rope work.

The going was hardest for Thomas since he had never had to attempt rock work of this difficulty before. Dave saw Al stay to help him at first, but when Hanomer came back from his lookout post, he took over. Hanomer stuck close to Thomas and lowered a rope for him, coaching him at every step. When Thomas had reached a safe ledge, Hanomer used his third hand to scamper down even the most treacherous rock face, spider-like, to join him. Then the process began all over again.

Al was glad that Thomas and Hanomer had become friends. There was no one better to keep Thomas safe on this climb.

Dave and Arlana were second in line after Tandor when Dave saw a small, winged shape off in the distance well past the edge of the first terrace.

"Tandor," said Dave, "could dragons make it up this high?"

"No, what do you see Dave?"

Dave pointed. Tandor shaded his eyes. "I don't see anything. What does it look like?"

"I see it too," said Arlana. "It's far away."

"It looks to me like a giant bat, with skin stretched over bone. It has a long neck and tail. The tail has something on the end."

"I think," said Tandor, "it's a vul. It's smaller and lighter than even a small dragon, and roosts on the terraces off the Mutandi Highlands where it was first created. They are carnivorous and dangerous and they sometimes roam far looking for prey. Where is it heading?"

"Your description fits. It's dipped below the far edge of the first terrace."

"It hunts for animals trapped on the side of the cliff."

"You mean like us?" asked Dave.

"Yes. We're close to the bottom. If we can reach the trees, we'll be much less vulnerable."

Linder had overheard the conversation. "Okay, let's get moving. Thomas and Hanomer, stay close. I don't want you exposed on the cliff side."

Tandor and Linder started down the last one hundred meters. Reaching a ledge, they waved for the others to follow. Dave and Arlana were halfway there when Arlana glanced up, grabbed Dave's arm and whispered "The vul."

Dave saw the vul climb above the far edge of the first terrace. Its reptile-like body was the size of a horse. It had a long, thick, snake-like neck ending with a blunt head and a mouth filled with teeth. Its thick tail ended in a cluster of spikes.

The vul climbed for height. Dave and Arlana froze. A rock clattered below and the vul changed course.

Dave and Arlana both shouted a warning. The vul turned and dove straight toward them. Dave pushed Arlana into a depression in the cliff, sought a firm purchase for his feet and pulled out Gram.

The vul let out a cry, which was echoed by a second vul rising above the first terrace cliff edge. The first vul banked its six-meter wings along the cliff toward Dave, its clawed feet almost scraping the cliff wall ready for the snatch. Dave hoped his feet would stay firm as he timed his sword stroke. He heard a thunk as Arlana unleashed an arrow into the scaled body of the vul. The vul swerved slightly and then headed straight for Dave.

Dave swung with all his might. Gram cut through both legs, shearing off one claw and most of the other leg. The severed append-age flew off, hitting Dave in the head and chest, and covering him with gore. He heard the spiked tail scape the rock above his head. Then everything went black.

Going limp, Dave dropped Gram and began to teeter over the edge. Arlana lunged and grabbed his belt. She heard Dave's sword carom off the cliff face and bounce on the rocks below. Dave hung limply.

"Dave you have to help me! I can't hold you."

Arlana looked up and saw the second vul coming toward her. Holding on, she steeled herself.

Just then a gunshot rang out. The vul's head jerked and went limp. Its body passed over Arlana and Dave, and crashed into the cliff face. It tumbled twice and plunged into the woods, almost on top of the first vul carcass. Arlana looked further up the cliff and saw Thomas with his rifle.

Al reached her just as Dave regained consciousness.

"What happened?" Dave asked.

"You killed the vul," said Arlana, "and part of it hit you. You could have been killed."

"I killed the vul?" Dave had a smug grin on his face. Suddenly his expression changed. "Where's Gram?"

"It fell down the cliff to the rocks."

They started down. Al wanted to lower Dave by rope, but Dave insisted he was fine.

They made it the rest of the way to the first terrace without incident. Dave found Gram. The hilt was dented, but the blade was unmarred.

Worried that the rifle shot would attract a patrol, Tandor led the party into the deepest part of the forest without delay and crossed to the cliff edge leading to the second terrace. A bow shot from five hundred meters up could travel a long way, but here they were safe. They called a brief halt. Dave washed the blood off his clothes and said he was fine to continue so they spent the rest of the day walking northwest staying under the cover of trees. When they crossed the third meadow, Arlana peered apprehensively at the path at the top of the escarpment. A group of soldiers was watching them. One tried a bow shot, but it fell far short.

"It's too late for them to come down to pursue us," said Tandor. "Still it would be best if we disappeared." They spent that night under cover in a dense thicket.

Arlana passed a restless night, wondering if Dave had any lasting injuries and dreading the sound of soldiers beating the undergrowth for their campsite.

The next morning Tandor searched for a way down to the second terrace to get out from under the watchful eye of the patrols. After a morning of hunting, he found what he was looking for. To Dave, standing on the edge of the second cliff, the second terrace looked very much like the first: a five-hundred-meter cliff and a shelf about three kilometers across, all covered with bountiful vegetation, water courses, and meadows.

"How many terraces are there?" asked Dave.

"The Rebels think there are twelve terraces," said Tandor, "but no one in recent memory has gone down that far and returned."

Pointing to the scarred cliff in front of them, Tandor continued, "This not be the easiest way down, but the patrols always take the easiest way. For us this is the safest way."

The climb down looked worse than it was. Often, they came across a hidden ledge or a crack in the cliff face that made the descent easier. Thomas was climbing more on his own than he had the previous day.

They were almost all of the way down. Below them they could see a lake that came right up to the cliff edge. Dave was following Thomas, when Thomas came to a round opening in the side of the cliff like a three-meter drain pipe with a pile of pebbles like a frozen stream of water cascading from the pipe mouth to the lake.

Thomas stepped onto the pebble-scree to traverse it. Dave shouted, but too late. As soon as Thomas had planted his foot on the stones, the whole tongue of pebbles began to slide. Thomas lurched back and landed on his rear end. With increasing speed, the mass of pebbles raced toward the lake with Thomas on top, his hands digging into the pebbles for balance. With a huge splash, he disappeared below the water along with an avalanche of stones.

The others rushed down to the lake shore. Thomas was already climbing out.

"Are you alright?" asked Al.

Thomas nodded sheepishly. Al helped him take inventory; he had lost his rifle. They dove for it, to no avail. It was either buried under pebbles or had been dragged into very deep water.

Making camp, they built a fire in order to prepare a hot meal and dry their clothes. When they were all fed and dry, Tandor was the first to speak.

"We should get moving again," he said.

"Where are we going next?" asked Linder.

"The Rebels know of many hiding places here on the second terrace. About half an hour from here is a cavern I used to use as a hiding place. I want to leave you there while I scout out Seth."

"You plan on leaving us?"

"Seth lost many slaves in the Necroan attack. I think Bigelow will order a raid here to the terraces to capture Rebels to replace what he lost. We don't want to camp out in the open if the soldiers come. I also want to wait by the gate to see the soldiers leave so that I know how to time our return so as not to arouse suspicion."

At the cavern, Tandor led them to a narrow, hard-to-see entrance on the side of the cliff near the rock fall at the bottom. The inside of the space was covered with bat dung. However, further in, the narrow passage opened up into gallery after gallery of chambers. Tandor seemed to know his way, and led them back and up to a small cave, that opened out onto the sheer wall of the cliff.

"We're a long way into this cavern," said Al. "Are we going to have to retrace our steps to get out?

"Possibly," said Tandor. "You will be staying here for a time, so you have to be safe. Sometimes the Sethian patrols have trackers with them—vicious, smart wogogs that weigh as much as three men, with fangs the length of my little finger. The wogogs hate the bat dung and won't follow you this far into the cavern. My countrymen won't come in this far either. But stay near the lower entrance. If they found you, they might kill you thinking you were a Sethian patrol. In case of trouble, you can escape in single file out of this upper gallery."

Al looked anxious. "Can't we go with you, Tandor? Every hour may be critical to the safety of my wife and son."

"It is easier for one person to hide than a group. I'll wear soldier's garb. If I'm spotted, I may be able to talk my way out of it. Haste will make you walk straight into slavery or death. Dead, you will be of little help to your wife and son. Be patient. I promise you that I will do my best to get you into Seth as quickly and safely as possible."

Tandor seemed to have taken control of things and everyone went along with it, at least for the moment, even if grudgingly. "Can't change horses in mid-river," Al heard Dave mutter to himself. But there was no other choice. Since they had trusted Tandor with getting them into Seth, they had to follow his advice and time table.

Tandor set them to work, setting up camp, organizing a hunting schedule, and cleaning their Sethian armor and the slaves' garb that they had procured from the mine.

"I'm leaving now," said Tandor. "I'll be back as soon as possible. Be ready to leave on a moment's notice. When we go, there will be two guards and a captain in our party. The rest will be dressed as slaves. Understood?"

Everyone assented.

Dave was asleep, but Arlana was awake, troubled. Climbing to the upper exit of the cavern, she sat on the cliff edge with her pack. The sky had cleared and she could see the stars. The moon was in the west, almost at first quarter. She opened her pack and took out a black swamp oak acorn. Invoking the aid of the Creator, she whispered an oath in the Ancient Tongue, "*Kree ah na koo.*"

This is the first secret I have kept from my husband, she thought. *I have broken the laws of my land by planting the twin of this acorn in our water meadow on our side of the Barrier Mountains. I could endanger my people. But what else can I do? I can't just leave us trapped here. I will only plant this one if there is no other way to get home.*

Chapter 16

No Plague Come Near Your Tent

Al sat in a small alcove near the narrow upper opening in the cliff wall reading his Bible. Below, he could see the greenery of the dense wood of the second terrace, and beyond, the edge of the next escarpment. A bank of clouds hung over the third terrace while a white fog sea roiled up against the escarpment edge like waves against the shore. Every once in a while, a wisp of fog would rise up only to dissipate in the gentle wind blowing along the second terrace.

He had been reading Psalm 91 again, as he had every day since Pam and Little Thomas had been kidnapped. Hearing footsteps behind him, he turned and saw Dave approaching. Dave was also carrying his Bible.

"May I join you?" asked Dave.

"Of course. This is about the only place we can sit to get a little bit of daylight. I don't mean to hog the location."

Dave settled down on a stone ledge and stared out into the morning light. Al saw him look at his open Bible. "You must be worried to death about Pam and Little Thomas. It must be hard sitting here and doing nothing."

Al rubbed his eyes. "It shows, does it? I keep reading verses 9 and 10 in Psalm 91:

> **Because you have made the LORD your dwelling place —**
> **The Most High, who is my refuge —**

No evil shall be allowed to befall you,
No plague come near your tent.

"I have always taken the phrase 'no plague come near your tent' as a promise that God would protect my family if I stayed loyal to Him. If I stayed under His protection …

"But now …" Al could hear his voice begin to tremble. "How can I still believe this? Pam and Little Thomas have been with Bigelow for many days now. She's completely in his power. For all I know, he could be treating her abominably every day. Or maybe he's killed her. And Little Thomas, what's he doing to him? I feel so helpless! And I have to sit here, waiting for Tandor to tell me that it's safe to move."

"She's really not completely in his power," said Dave softly. "Humanly speaking, Pam and Little Thomas are in a terrible situation. Still, it seems to me you're assuming that God will do nothing. Isn't that what faith is all about? Believing that God will do something? Maybe not in your timing, and maybe not exactly what you expect or even hope for. But shouldn't you believe He will do something good?"

Al found himself looking at Dave in surprise. This conversation seemed somehow familiar. Al felt himself smile. "Dave, Dave, you keep doing this to me. Remember back in New Jerusalem when I was ranting at Dalrymple and what he had done to my brother through the Dalyites?"

"Yeah, I remember I had a lot of chutzpah chiding you about your lack of forgiveness for Dalrymple."

"Well your chutzpah has helped me again. I feel chastised, as I should. You're right—I'm supposed to exercise the faith that God is doing something—if not what I expected. Just because He's not doing exactly what I wanted doesn't mean He's doing nothing, and certainly doesn't mean He doesn't care."

Dave smiled. "I can't help but dish out a smug 'I told you so.' Isn't Thomas here with you now? Hasn't God worked that out in an unexpected way?"

Just then, they heard footsteps. It was Linder. "Tandor's back," he told them. "We have to move now."

Chapter 17

Into Seth

Tandor adjusted his captain's armor and then helped and Dave and Arlana properly put on soldier's garb and weapons. Dave spoke the Common Tongue well and had the physique of a fighter. Arlana had tears in her eyes when she cut her beautiful hair to a close-cropped brush cut. She completed the disguise by wearing ill-fitting armor to disguise her figure. With a lot of dirt on her face, she thought that she would not be recognized as a woman. Tandor hoped to pass her off as a very young, green, bashful, boy recruit. All the rest wore slave's rags. They would be chained together later.

Dave had his sword and scabbard wrapped up in a filthy rag so that the quality of the blade would not give them away. Additional weapons were strapped to the outside of his pack, which had also been disguised with rags.

Tandor led them up a narrow rock chimney, near the upper exit of the caves, chains clinking in their backpacks. After several hundred meters they emerged onto a narrow ledge. Tandor continued the climb and after another fifty meters, they emerged onto the first terrace.

Tandor urged them to huddle together in the shelter of an evergreen thicket. The shrubs, which Dave did not recognize, had thorns on the outside, but not on the inside, and grew on the fringe of a shallow bowl that sheltered the whole party with gnarled thorny branches forming a leafed canopy.

"I returned to the caverns," said Tandor quietly, "because several raiding parties had just been sent out to recapture slaves all along the wall. The soldiers will go all the way down to the third terrace. The guards at the gate will have changed by now, and I am betting that the new guards don't know all of the soldiers. They are expecting small parties of captured slaves to return to the gates while the main raiding party continues the hunt. We'll wait here for a while to travel by night and to time our return to the town gate just as day dawns. We'll just come back a bit sooner than they're expecting.

"I need to keep you chained from here on, in case anybody sees us. Rest now. As soon as the sun sets, we'll head out."

They ate quietly and drank from the canteens. No one talked. Finally, Tandor gave the signal that it was time to move. With Tandor on point and Dave and Arlana at the back, they walked northwest along the first terrace throughout the night. The moon was in the first quarter, and low in the west, but provided some light. When it finally set—at about 3 a.m.—they continued in the dark. The land was flat and heavily treed. With Hanomer, Dave, and Arlana leading three small groups, they made no missteps. They crossed the occasional small stream, but Dave saw no animal life.

Dave thought, *with the clinking of chains, we're so noisy we may as well shout to announce ourselves to the enemy.*

Despite the noise, they reached the base of the next escarpment without meeting anyone. Ahead was a well-worn trail that zig-zagged back and forth across the face of the cliff.

"Everybody down. Relax and stay out of sight," said Tandor quietly. He headed up the switchback. Dave saw him disappear round a bend. It was well before dawn and the air had become muggy and thick. It felt like rain. No one spoke, but Dave listened for the dread sound of a troop returning to the gate.

What do I say if I'm challenged without Tandor here?

The silence was unbroken.

In a few minutes, Dave saw Tandor loping around the bend of the switchback.

Breathing heavily and out of breath, Tandor knelt down to whisper. "All clear. Smartly now, follow me … We will be … in extreme danger while on this switchback … since all patrols will follow this easy route."

In a few minutes, Tandor's pace up the switchback had Dave—with his heavy pack—puffing. A little bit of regular food and the few days of rest had helped Tandor's stamina enormously. Dave could see that Arlana, ahead of him, was also struggling with the armor and weapons she had to carry.

Dave turned to look back over the first terrace. He couldn't see anything because of the many trees, but he felt exposed on the side of the cliff. He resumed his climb. The path was well used and two paces wide. At each turn there was a ledge that allowed parties to pass each other on the narrow way. In places, the rock had been chiseled out and there were small arched bridges that filled in gaps. Occasionally, a spring came out of the cliff wall and plunged to the terrace below. Muddy boot prints showed where soldiers had stopped to have a drink.

Just before the switchback reached the crest, Tandor called Dave and Arlana together and whispered, "When the gates open and I talk to the guard, keep the prisoners moving. Don't stop, but march them right into the city. Look bored."

Finally, just before dawn, they reached the lip of the escarpment. Tandor marched them to the gate about one hundred meters from the edge of the escarpment. He made a show of cursing the prisoners and jabbing them with the butt end of his spear. The gate opened and a guard came out with a sneer on his face. "You boys be back quick. Usually dem rebs be makin' a better show of hidin'."

"Yeah," sneered Tandor, "the hounds found this bunch cowering in a cave in no time. I'm sorry to be givin' up the hunt so quick. I be lookin' for a bit more fun. The sooner I can unload these rats, the sooner I be gettin' back."

"Suit yourself." The guard waved them in. Arlana led the way, plodding listlessly forward with the chained prisoners following meekly.

"By the way," said the guard as Tandor turned, "who be your commander?"

"Bonecruncher," said Tandor over his shoulder as he kept walking.

Dave, who was at the end of the processions, eyed the guard out of the corner of his eye as he passed. The guard had put his hands on his hips as if he were going to say something, then seemed to change his mind and went back to close the gate. Tandor wisely had the band through the gate so quickly that the guard hesitated to make a scene and call him back.

The town was built of close, ramshackle, multi-storey buildings with adjoining walls. Immediately inside the gate, there was a crossroads, with a road running along the base of the wall. Ahead of them, the main thoroughfare plunged straight in through the close-packed structures. The streets were filthy, with refuse everywhere. The stench of rotting garbage assailed Dave's nostrils. Tandor followed the road into the center of town. He was quiet except for occasional cursing directed at his charges, whenever a pedestrian approached. Fortunately, this early in the morning, there were few pedestrians and no patrols.

After about a kilometer, Tandor turned down a side street on his left and headed southwest. This area was even more dilapidated with the occasional building crumbling alarmingly.

This side street began to zig-zag back and forth as it wended its way between the overhanging houses that had been built in a misaligned, haphazard manner. Finally, they emerged from the narrow street to an open area that would have been a square, except that it was piled high with rubble. The rubble heap was extensive, maybe a four square kilometers.

Tandor directed them to sit down at the foot of a rubble pile under a tilted wall. Gesturing at the extensive heap, he said quietly, "This is what the Guild calls 'the Warren.' I'm going to leave you here while I find someone who knows me, and negotiate your entry into the Guild. Be quiet. Stay in the shadows. Above all, don't move until I get back." He opened up his pack, changed into slave's garb and left them.

After about fifteen minutes, Tandor returned. "Alright," he said, "I have negotiated to have you read-in as probationary servants of the Guild. I'm what's called a 'level seven servant' and I have charge of you who are level one. Dave, Arlana, put on slave's garb. I don't want an agitated Warren-dweller to put an arrow into you because he thought Bigelow was raiding their hideout."

Arlana looked disquieted.

"I know," said Dave, "it's tough to be here with a party full of men. Here, I'll hold a blanket so you can change."

Tandor gave them each a wooden pendant on the chain. "These pendants show who you are. I will teach you the basic passwords. When you enter the Warren or are talking to a member of the Guild, they will be checking three things: your pendant, which could be stolen; your knowledge of the passwords; and who you know that could vouch for you—that would be me right now.

"Follow me. We're going to the district Bossman who will be assigning us lodging."

Tandor led them out of the rubble heap and down the street to a building that had a shingle with a leather pouch hanging over the doorway. Approaching the leather-making shop, they saw that it was closed, but the door opened to Tandor's knocking nonetheless, as if they had been expected. The shopkeeper was unpacking his things, getting ready to open up. Without speaking, but flashing a gold pendant,

Tandor led them around the counter to the back of the shop. Lifting a trapdoor in the floor, he led them down a steep staircase to a tunnel about one hundred paces in length. The sense of direction that Dave had gained as an Ancient told him they were heading back under the street to the rubble heap.

The tunnel ended in a small, square, brick-walled room with three additional tunnels at right angles. The room walls glowed with a pale green light from the lumi-lichen that had grown over the brick work.

They continued down the middle passage. If they encountered anyone, Tandor flashed his gold medallion, while they showed their wooden ones. Nothing was ever said. The underground passage was a maze. Dave was sure he could never find his way out. After about twenty minutes, they came to a large, steel-bound wooden door with a large apple crudely painted in bold strokes on it. The door looked menacing in the green light, as if they were entering a jail. Tandor knocked on the door. A small window at the top slid open and an eye peered out. Tandor held up his pendant. They heard the sound of heavy bolts being drawn. The door opened to a huge man with enormously broad shoulders.

The man seemed to recognize Tandor, who showed his pendant again, allowing the other to examine it minutely. The huge man nodded and stepped aside, allowing them to enter.

Inside the room, they saw a smaller man sitting at a desk. He wore an eye patch. On the desk were a stack of papers and a bucket filled with what appeared to be metal disks. He looked up. "What do you want?"

"I'm Tandor, a seventh level servant escaped from the mines. I am here requesting lodging and membership in your battalion with some probes I brought with me." He showed the man his medallion.

"Yeah," said the Bossman. "I remember you. You were taken a couple of years ago in the great purge when Meglir returned. Good to see you still alive. You're lucky to be alive after a stint in the mines. How did you escape, anyway?"

"I was lucky. The Necroans killed everybody else, but missed me," said Tandor.

"I hope your luck holds. You know the rules, I give you lodging, first month free, but triple rent due at the end of month two. You know what it means to be in arrears. It would be a pity to sell you and your probes back into slavery because you can't pay your debts. Here's a list of passwords. Use Entrance 21. You can take over Apple-641—it's been empty for six months." He looked at each of the others and then picked up two small bronze disks and gave them to Tandor. He pointed to a second heavy door at the back of the room.

Tandor led them through the door to the neighborhood called 'Apple.' Inside the Apple Quarter, there was a great deal of activity. Just inside the second door was a small square with booths and shops. A small fountain in the centre of the square bubbled fresh water into a shallow pool before draining away. Beyond this were hallways with more shops set up along the central corridor in little alcoves. Tandor approached a shopkeeper and asked for directions, then led the group down a hallway directly across the square. At the end of this corridor they turned right and came to a door with a crude apple and 641 carved into the wood. The hinges were rusty, but they managed to get the door open, revealing their lodgings. The interior space consisted of a central room and four additional chambers. Tandor took the largest room as befitted his station. Dave and Arlana took another, while the six "slaves" were crammed into the last two rooms.

Dave unpacked their supplies. He pulled Arlana into an embrace and kissed her. "I guess this is our new home. It's not much, but I always feel better when I have a place to hang my hat."

"Hang your hat? But husband you don't wear a hat."

Dave smiled. *This is definitely beginning to feel like home.*

Chapter 18

Vixa and Alandro

The realization that the system of slavery does not work surprised me. Slaves in Abaddon, especially those at the bottom tier, are without hope. Eventually despair seizes them. In black despair the lash, imprisonment, and even the threat of death no longer has any effect. They want to die. The Grishfang leadership, called the Cloaks, can issue all the orders they want, but if the slaves are so listless and despairing that the work doesn't get done, then the wrath falls on the soldiers, stewards, and merchants who are supposed to be carrying out the Cloak's orders.

That's where the Guild comes in. They pretend to be slaves, and for a price, make up the shortfall. The Guild lives on a knife edge — supported by the middle class but hated by the Cloaks. Every once in a while, a purge is ordered and then the Guild resorts to thievery and retaliation. Still, it looks to me as if the Guild is the only thing that keeps the Grishfang society from total collapse.

ABADDON JOURNEY
JANDOR LONGWALKER

Dave heard Tandor calling them together. He sighed and released Arlana after a second, long kiss and picked up his sword.

When Dave reached the main chamber, Tandor was passing around a vellum sheet. "Learn these passwords. When we leave here, we'll be dressed as house slaves and have slaves' headbands. We get those from the Disguiser."

Tandor passed out the bronze disks, each with a small apple crudely engraved on it. "Attach these to your wooden pendant."

When everyone had done as he instructed, Tandor squatted down. "This whole country of Grishfang is run by a ruling class called Cloaks. Most Cloaks are different from us—they are Bent Ones. They live much longer than we do and they have power to compel men and command beasts." Here he looked searchingly at Dave and Arlana.

"But many are also humans who have been so long in the arts of the Bent Ones that they have made themselves exceedingly evil. The highest rank of the Cloaks are the Redcloaks. Meglir, members of the Council of Thirteen, and particularly high officials and beings of power will all have red cloaks as a signature of office.

"Blackcloaks are just below them and are perhaps even more dangerous. They want to prove themselves. Bigelow is a Blackcloak. If he were Bent, he would be a Redcloak, and that must torment and anger him. There are many Blackcloaks and Greycloaks of much less exalted position. I'm telling you this because all Cloaks are dangerous. They can kill a soldier, a merchant, and certainly any slave with no questions asked. Avoid them at all costs. They are deadly.

"I've just learned that, luckily for us, Bigelow has few Blackcloaks and Greycloaks in his service, because he is not a Bent One. But he does have many soldiers, merchants, and stewards. Everyone else is supposed to be slaves, and slaves are expected to do all of the work. Except, the system of slavery fails. There are shortages everywhere.

"However, failure to complete the tasks assigned by the Cloaks means slavery or death to the underlings. That gives the soldiers, stewards, and merchants a very strong motivation to work with us on the sly—as long as they don't get caught by the higher-ups.

"So, I will get us slaves' headbands and get you some work. When you earn some silver, keep half and give the rest to our general fund to pay the Guild for food, for these holes in the Warren, and for protection. Do you understand?"

"I have a question," said Dave. "What keeps the soldiers and stewards from just chaining us up when we've completed our work, and keeping the money?"

"Dave, that's always a risk, especially if the steward is in trouble or about to be enslaved himself. The Guild looks after its own. That steward would never get any help from us again. He might even find that his slaves were running away a lot. It may turn out his collaboration with the Guild might become known to the higher-ups. In extreme cases, the steward might even be killed during a robbery."

"Still, we're in a dangerous business. Eventually we go to the mines. It works because we need coin and food. The stewards and soldiers need our help to meet quota."

"So how do I find Pam and Little Thomas?" asked Al.

Dave felt a pang of regret. *How quickly I think of myself and forget the real reason we're here.*

"I haven't forgotten our purpose, Al," he said. "We need to find where they are and how to get them out. I'll look at every job we can get at the fortress. I know the grounds' steward, Blackthorn. Once we're working there, we'll find out where they are, and when we can get them out. I promise you."

There was a knock at the door. Everyone went silent. Dave made sure his sword, Gram, was well wrapped. Tandor walked to the entrance, gave everyone a final look, and opened a small shutter at the top of the door to look out. He opened the door.

A slender, dark haired young man with a goatee and an insolent smirk leaned against the door frame with his arms crossed.

"Ah," he said, "the rumors are true that this ... ahem ... apartment is occupied once again. We are your neighbors and wanted to pay our respects."

"We?" asked Tandor.

Straightening up, the man uncrossed his arms and bowed. "Let me introduce ourselves. I am Alandro, a fifth level servant of the Guild, and this is my sister Vixa."

Alandro pointed around the corner. A young woman with long black hair and a dress that accentuated her exquisite figure sauntered into the room.

Dave was drawn to look at her. He didn't. But the effort *to not look* made him aware of her every movement.

"I'm pleased to meet you," said Vixa. She drew out the word "pleased" as if it were a caress. She looked everyone in the eye in turn.

This is a really dangerous woman, thought Dave.

He glanced over at Arlana. She still had her boyish clothes on and had not cleaned the dirt off her face. Her short hair still made her look like a young boy. Dave could tell by the set of her mouth and her rigid posture that Arlana was bristling.

Vixa's eyes swept the room again as she made a small circle in the center of the company. When she came to Dave, she put her hand on his arm. "Are you in charge?"

Dave could feel himself blushing. He wanted to darken his skin to cover his blush but remembered, just in time, that he mustn't give himself away. Instead, he stammered awkwardly, "Nooo, I'm … I'm not in charge."

"I think you should be," Vixa said.

Tandor interrupted. "Alandro and Vixa, it was kind of you to grace us with your visit."

Alandro looked sharply at Tandor as if offended at the interruption, but Tandor continued to speak with a tone of such courtesy that Alandro relaxed.

"But," continued Tandor, "we have only just arrived and we are embarrassed to meet a fifth level servant neighbor when we have not had time to freshen up nor buy supplies for a proper welcome cup. Could we send you an invitation when we are more able to receive you?"

"Of course; come Vixa."

Vixa flashed Dave a big smile and, giving his arm a squeeze, she turned and walked out the door.

Chapter 19

The Servants' Guild

I first learned of the Guild shortly after being ship-wrecked and captured in Maw Bay. The soldiers of the Bent Ones marched me through the Black Caverns for ten days, to the capital city of Ra on the Abaddon plain, and attached me to the slave company of the chief steward of the city. We were building an arched bridge over a small canal. Of the one hundred slaves in my company, about half were filled with despair or had been driven to madness such that they were all but useless for the work. The despairing slaves were whipped until their backs were raw and bleeding, yet still did their work poorly and lethargically. They did not care if they lived or died. The mad ones cackled and laughed at the whippings. They would sometimes drop stones into the canal instead of bringing them to the scaffold. Then the overseer would kill them. I worked with a will. I met one other "slave" who worked as well as I did. He actually organized the bridge building. That's when I found out he wasn't a slave at all, but secretly hired himself out to the overseer from the Guild.

ABADDON JOURNEY
JANDOR LONGWALKER

The next morning, Tandor took Dave to the Disguiser in a booth in the central square and had him dressed in slave's garb along with a headband that indicated his ownership. Tandor then escorted Dave to a side passage that led to Entrance 21.

"Rokodor," said Tandor, "although Apple has four entrances, you must always use Entrance 21. The guards will get to know you and will verify your identity. To enter somewhere else could cost you your life."

Passing through Entrance 21, Tandor and Dave climbed a set of stairs, opened a door and came out into the back of a butcher shop. They were given packages to carry to the front of the shop, allowing them to move about the store unobtrusively and leave by a side entrance when there were no patrons.

Tandor led Dave south—even at this distance, the southern wall was so high Dave could see it.

Eventually, they arrived at the South Gate. Tandor asked for an overseer by name. The overseer attached Dave to a group of slaves that was repairing a portion of the wall that was crumbling. The group wore the same headband that Dave did. Dave watched them, followed what they did, and worked with a will.

Dave out-carried and out-worked the slaves so that he was bringing two stones from the wagon to their one. At the end of the day, when the slaves were being chained up, Dave wondered what was going to happen to him.

The overseer took him aside, checked that no one was watching, and gave Dave two silver pieces. "Come back tomorrow. You worked well. I'll need you to supervise the stone work tomorrow."

With that, Dave quietly disappeared and walked back to the Warren. He took one wrong turn, but eventually found the butcher shop. It was empty of customers. Walking to the back of the store, he opened the trapdoor, and descended the stairs to the tunnel. At Entrance 21, one of the guards who had been there that morning was there again, but he still questioned Dave at length and examined the disk on his pendant closely. Finally, the guards opened the inner door.

Dave had no sooner stepped through the entrance than he saw Vixa lounging against the tunnel wall. Seeing him, she straightened up with cat-like grace, blocking his way in the narrow passage. She was wearing a tight dress that revealed too much. She smiled. "What a surprise to meet my neighbor here."

"What are you doing here Vixa?"

"I was waiting for my brother." She reached out and stroked Dave's arm, causing him to flinch. "I'm glad I saw you though."

Dave found himself blushing furiously, wishing again that he had set his skin color to a darker shade. *What is she doing? Why is she doing this?*

He could see her smile broaden.

Dave became angry. *She's enjoying my embarrassment.*

"Don't you work? How do you have time to be lounging around Entrance 21?"

"I work at night." She smiled seductively. Dave didn't know where to look. "I'm a cat-burglar. I work when the moon has set," she added.

"I … I … I really need to go," he stammered, taking a step to the right. She mirrored his movement, effectively blocking his way in the narrow tunnel. "Are you blocking me?" he asked.

"Blocking you?" Her eyes widened in mock surprise. "Rokodor! You shock me! And you a married man. How could you think that? There is nothing between us. There can be nothing between us!"

Dave felt alarmed. *What's happening?* In desperation and without thinking it through, he put his hands on her waist, picked her up—she seemed light as a feather—and set her to his left side. Continuing through the tunnel at a faster pace, his thoughts raced.

He knew he had to tell Arlana what had happened, yet every time he practiced the conversation in his mind, it came out badly, and he could imagine Arlana misunderstanding. Saying the words without the body language lost so much of the message.

He was still agitated when he came home. Only Arlana was there. She seemed happy and excited to see him and kissed him in welcome. "How was your day?"

"Fine," said Dave. A polite fiction. He was still engrossed in trying to figure out what to say and how to say it.

"What's wrong?"

"Nothing." Dave wasn't even paying attention to the conversation.

"I know something's wrong. What is it?"

Dave realized, in his distraction, that the conversation he had been dreading had already started badly. He took a deep breath. "I'm sorry honey. I've been distracted."

"So, I've noticed. What happened?"

Dave took another deep breath. "The day went fine. I completed my work as a pseudo-slave and earned two silver pieces." He gave the two silver pieces to Arlana.

"When I came home through Entrance 21, Vixa was waiting for me."

Dave could see concern playing over Arlana's face.

"Vixa, our neighbor? Why would she be waiting for you?"

"I don't know. Maybe she wasn't waiting for me. She said she was waiting for her brother."

"So, what happened?"

Dave recounted the conversation word for word. "And then I picked her up and set her aside and rushed home."

"You picked her up?"

"She was blocking my way."

Arlana's expression was—well Dave couldn't really define it except to say she looked dangerous. Dave wondered if she was getting angry at him.

Finally, she said, "She's a beautiful woman, isn't she?"

Of course, she's a beautiful woman! On top of that she wears that skimpy dress that she pops out of so that I have no place to look except her eyes. And she knows how to use her eyes! She lethal. She's pure poison.

All he said was: "I suppose so."

"You suppose so?"

Dave didn't know what to say.

"Why was she waiting for you?"

"That's what I can't figure out. I mean we only met yesterday."

The silence grew uncomfortable. Arlana had her face set in concentration. She was thinking about what to say. "Dave, you and I both know that Vixa is a beautiful and alluring woman. She's also unabashedly flirting with you. In all honesty, she makes me feel inadequate ..."

"Inadequate. Why?"

"Well, I'm just not like her. I don't think I could flirt like that with you even in private. It's just not me. I would feel foolish and manipulative. Still, I know you well enough that there is probably something in the flirtation that you like—and I know I can't give that to you right now.

"I trust you Dave. I trust you to guard our relationship. But as a woman I may know more about the weapons she can bring to bear on you than you do. You're going to stay away from her, aren't you?"

How can I stay away from her when I have to come in Entrance 21 and she could be waiting for me anytime I come back from work?

"I'll stay away from her."

Arlana smiled and kissed Dave on the cheek. "I love you and trust you." She went back to her work managing the records and funds for their group.

Chapter 20

Rokodor's Dilemma

It was before sunrise when Dave rose and prepared for another day of hard work at the city's southern gate. He had slept very little. Vixa's behavior troubled him. He was determined to stay away from her, but, if her actions thus far were any indication, she seemed equally determined to insert herself into his life.

Maybe I'm overreacting. Perhaps everyone in this strange country acts the way Vixa does towards me. Maybe it means nothing. He didn't really believe it.

Arlana made him a breakfast of fried eggs, onions, and potatoes.

"You'll need a good breakfast if you are to have the strength to work hard today."

Dave sat down at the place she had prepared for him and pulled her onto his lap and kissed her.

"Husband, the others are getting up."

"I don't care." He kissed her again. "When I finish work today, why don't you come to meet me in the square?"

"I would love to husband, but Tandor has been working on a special project for me. He may need me today to close the agreement."

"I thought we could spend some time together. You could take the time to do some shopping."

"Shopping? Are you feeling ill, my husband? You would rather be treed by raging Rokash than go shopping in the market with me."

"I just thought," said Dave, "it might be a way for us to spend some time together apart from the group."

"If I finish early with Tandor, I promise to wait for you in Apple Square."

Dave gently lifted her off his lap, rose, kissed her again, and then gathered his things. Looking at the breakfast table he had just had an idea. "May I take a loaf of bread?" he asked.

"Sure, we have many. They are only a few coppers a piece."

Dave made his way from Entrance 21 to South Gate. The overseer put him in charge of the slaves and left with a warning that he expected to see a good deal of progress when he came back. Dave's heart broke for the wretched slaves. Except for the fact that he was part of the Guild, he could be one of them. In fact, if he made one false move as a Guild member, or the overseer took exception to him, he *would* be one of them.

Dave sighed and started work. He looked the dispirited crew over carefully and gave directions to all of them. Some worked, others pretended to work, and some simply stared off into space, not caring. Dave began the repairs with half a dozen slaves who still had a will to work and ignored the others.

After two hours, he called a break and gave a bit of bread to those who had worked. He gave more to those who had worked hardest. Some of the slackers came over and he gave them a bit of bread as well—just a lot less than the others. Finally, he gave some bread to those who had lost all hope.

He had just put the bread back into his satchel when he sensed danger. Twisting around, he saw one of the slackers rush him, brandishing a piece of lumber.

Dave reacted without thinking. Grabbing his assailant's club hand, he threw him onto the ground. With a growl the man rose to his feet and rushed again. But the big slave was clumsy and slow. Dave decided not to land a blow. He didn't want to kill the poor, miserable fellow.

The second rush ended like the first. The slave lay winded on the ground. "Back to work," said Dave.

Now with a bit of food in their bellies, the slaves worked even better in the afternoon than they had in the morning.

The overseer arrived and looked over their progress. "Any problems?"

"No problems," said Dave. "The men worked well." Dave saw relief on the faces of the slaves, especially the big man who had tried to club him.

"You accomplished more than I expected," said the overseer, paying out the agreed-upon amount.

I did more than expected? thought Dave. *He really doesn't even see these men as people.*

Dave headed back to Entrance 21, determined to spend a little more on bread tomorrow. As he approached the safe house that hid the tunnel entrance, he felt a cold chill envelope him. *What if Vixa is waiting for me again?* He looked around to make sure no one was watching, and then walked across the street to the deserted rubble heap that covered the Warren. He sat down and waited.

If I delay my entrance, then even if Vixa is waiting to pounce, she can't hang around the entrance forever. I'll stand a better chance that Arlana has finished her business with Tandor. Dave felt like a coward, taking steps to avoid a one-hundred-twenty-pound girl. Still, he sensed that she had the ability to ruin his life.

After half an hour he entered the house that hid the tunnel to the Apple quarter and breathed a sigh of relief when the inside hallway was clear. Entering Apple Square, he saw Vixa leaning on a pillar. But he also saw Arlana get up from a table on a patio in front of a small tavern nearby. He entered the patio as she came over to him. Arlana kissed Dave thoroughly, so that he could feel himself blushing up to the tips of his ears.

"Come husband, I have something to show you." She sat him at her table, then went to the back of the tavern and came back with two steaming cups of *siph*. The aroma was heavenly. The taste was superb.

"Arlana, this is the best *siph* I have ever tasted!"

She leaned close and whispered. "It had better be, Hanomer is putting all of his skill into making it."

"Hanomer," Dave hissed. "Is that wise?"

"He was getting tired of hiding out at home. He and Thomas work here, in the back. Thomas doesn't have to talk to anyone, and Hanomer is in a sealed off section so it looks as if Mute Thomas makes all the food and drink.

"Tandor thought it was a wonderful idea. He needs everyone to contribute to make ends meet, and neither Hanomer nor Thomas can work as a hired slave. Tandor insists it's too dangerous out there for me or any woman"—Arlana grimaced— "so I run this *siph* tavern to keep up appearances, make a little money for us, and keep our account records in my spare time."

"How did you find this place in such a short time?"

"The previous owner was killed while out on a job. This pub had everything we needed and the higher-ups were glad to rent the whole thing to Tandor in the hopes of recouping some of the money owed by the deceased owner."

Tandor and the rest of the crew strolled up to them. Chartrand said in his best Common Tongue, "I hear this is a great place to eat and drink."

"So it is," said Dave. Arlana was beaming.

A few others came into the patio, and Arlana rose to serve them. One of the newcomers tried to grab her, and Dave started to rise from his seat, his anger kindled. Tandor's arm shot out, restraining him. But Arlana was quick and the fellow never touched her.

The troublemaker's companion nudged his friend and tilted his head in Dave's direction. The troublemaker looked over and then grew paler as he saw Dave scowling. When Arlana came back with their order, the two barely looked at her.

The supper hour was busy so the friends lingered over an extra cup of *siph* until the small tavern cleared. Finally, after putting a chain across the patio entrance to show they were closed, Arlana and Thomas came to join them carrying their own plates heaped high with food.

"What do you think, Dave?" asked Arlana.

"I think you'll do a smashing business, but the place needs a name."

The Copper Kettle was proposed, followed by The Doubtful Dragon. Many more names were suggested, but they kept coming back to The Doubtful Dragon.

"The Doubtful Dragon," mused Tandor. "I don't know how that name will be received so close to Sheol. Even though they can't fly in this thin air, dragons are still a fear that's on everyone's mind."

Still, they decided to try it. First by word of mouth, and then they would have a sign made. Thomas was already sketching a few designs on a piece of parchment.

Arlana and Thomas went out back to close the tavern. In a few minutes, Thomas came out carrying a knapsack, followed by Arlana. Walking back to their lodging, they let Hanomer out of the haversack. A formal invitation to Vixa and Alandro's home was lying on the floor.

"It's for tonight," said Tandor. "We had better go."

Dave wanted to plead off, but Tandor insisted that he go. Everyone except Hanomer and Thomas went next door. The party was in full swing and several other neighbors were already there. There was food aplenty on huge platters. Beer and wine flowed freely and everyone was laughing. Vixa came directly over and took Dave's arm almost out of Arlana's grasp. "Come, I must introduce you to my friends."

Dave looked at Arlana as Vixa dragged him away. Her mouth was a line and there was fire in her eyes.

Vixa dragged Dave from friend to friend, Arlana trailing behind. After making the introductions, when Arlana was busy greeting the others, Vixa would "accidently" rub up against Dave. He was furious, but didn't know what to do. *How do I not make a scene and embarrass both Arlana and myself?*

Finally, the introductions were finished. Dave reached with his free arm and pulled Arlana to himself and kissed her. Vixa released his arm and drifted away.

"Husband, have you had too much to drink already? And here I thought you had hardly touched a drop?"

"Can we go? I want to get out of here?"

"It's Vixa, isn't it?"

"Yes, she gives me the creeps," whispered Dave.

"The creeps—what does that mean?"

"It means she makes me feel very uncomfortable. If she were a man, I'd punch her in the mouth. I can't very well punch her, can I?"

"No, you mustn't, but I might …" said Arlana, her eyes again flashing, "… but I don't think beating our neighbor to within an inch of her life would endear me to Tandor. It's probably better for all if we head home."

Chapter 21

The Fortress

At the end of the week, Dave returned from his final day working at the South Gate. Arriving at Apple Square, he was surprised to see their whole crew eating at The Doubtful Dragon. A newly painted sign with a perplexed-looking dragon holding its chin in a clawed paw hung over the entrance.

"What's up?" asked Dave as he sat down.

Looking around, Tandor whispered, "My quiet inquiries into building projects in Bigelow's fortress have finally paid off. Assistant Steward Blackthorn is reworking some crumbling drainage channels inside the fortress. You're to report there tomorrow morning."

"Bigelow knows what I look like. What if he sees me?"

"I should be the one to go," said Al.

Dave regretted his objection immediately. "No," he said. "Tandor's right. I've already had experience with stone work, so I know what to expect. I spoke too quickly. I'm the right person to go. How do I find out where Bigelow is holding Pam and Little Thomas?"

"You don't need to do that. Just find a way to get Vixa and Alandro into the fortress. Use your work on the drainage system to do that. Don't do it right away—Blackthorn is pretty thorough for a Steward—he may check up on you early to make sure you're only there to work."

Kree ah na koo, thought Dave. *First Vixa and now Blackthorn checking up on me. The things I do for Al!* But he felt a pang of guilt at his thoughts.

"Why are Vixa and Alandro even involved?" asked Dave.

"They're professional roof rats," said Tandor. "Once inside the fortress at night, they'll be able to move all over, find out who's there, and overhear conversations that will tell us where Pam and Little Thomas are."

"And they're doing this out of friendship?" asked Dave.

"No, I'm paying them handsomely. I have a bit of money in the Guild bank from before I was sent to the mines. Now, no more questions. Have something to eat, get cleaned up, and then I'll tell you all I know about the fortress. Early tomorrow morning you need to go see Blackthorn, Dave. You can't afford to be late."

Shortly after dawn, Dave presented the parchment from Blackthorn, that was to be his entrance ticket, to the guard watching a small side gate at the fortress. With a grunt, the guard waved Dave through, and resumed his sentry position.

Inside, Dave looked around to get his bearings. The outer wall was about five meters thick and about twenty meters high. He could see the citadel that Tandor had told him about to the north, rising above the buildings. Even higher than the citadel wall, was the somber black keep, where Bigelow reportedly stayed.

Like all fortifications designed to withstand a long siege, the problem was finding a supply of water inside. According to Tandor, just inside the citadel wall was a spring that gave rise to a small creek. After flowing out under the citadel wall via an underground channel to a pool, it drained and flowed through the fortress to the town and then to the escarpment and on into the depths of Sheol. Rain water from the fortress drained into this creek. All Dave had to do to find Blackthorn and the building crew would be to follow the street drains to the underground creek.

He found the first drainage outlet ahead and began walking toward the citadel. No street followed the arrow-straight water channel directly, so Dave had to veer east or west and then double back to locate the next drain. A patrol stopped him once, but when Dave showed his parchment from Blackthorn, he was given a shove and sent on his way with a kick.

Around the next bend he saw the work party. He approached the foreman, who read his paper, and then sneered. "Lucky you. You get to climb into the hole and work with the crew underground. I'm sure the lazy sacks of refuse are doin' nothin' down there right now. I'd better see some action before the day is done."

Dave touched his forelock in the slave's salute and eased himself down the hole in the cobblestone street. He climbed down a broken channel for about five meters and joined a group of slaves standing around at the edge of the creek. One slave banged two stones together to keep it from being too quiet.

"Do you want us all to get whipped?" asked Dave.

No one answered, but he could see their blank stares in the dim light.

Dave began clearing the rubble from the drainage channel in preparation to lay some new stone work. He worked with alacrity for half an hour by himself, making reasonable progress. Finally, another fellow joined in. Mixing the mortar and selecting the stones to get a good fit, the end of the runoff channel began to take shape.

The work up top seemed to stop. Dave washed his hands briefly in the creek and opened his pack. Taking out a loaf of bread, he broke off a generous hunk for the fellow who had worked with him. "There's some here for the rest of you, but you have to help." Soon half the crew was working.

The drainage channel had really begun to take shape when Dave finally heard the call from up top for everyone to come out. Emerging, the slaves were chained together and led off to their quarters by a soldier. Blackthorn, a dark-haired man with a hook nose and a permanent scowl on his face, was there to inspect their progress. Unlike the foreman, he actually climbed into the hole.

After he emerged again, he looked Dave up and down and said, "You have made reasonable progress." Turning to the foreman, he said, "Close it up."

The foreman asked Dave to help him seal the opening. They rolled a large, heavy wooden disk over the opening and piled it high with brick and stones, leaving a small opening for water to drain out.

Now I know how to let Vixa and Alandro in, thought Dave. *But not today.*

Blackthorn sent the foreman away, and then paid Dave.

As Dave retraced his steps to the small gate, he was sure he heard footsteps behind him. But he didn't look back. The guard at the gate didn't even ask to see his parchment. Dave rounded a corner and then waited, looking back from the shadows. A man in servant's livery appeared at the gate and spoke briefly with the guard. The guard pointed in the direction he had taken in to town.

So, I am being followed.

Dave walked slowly back to the Warren. When the streets became quiet, he could still hear the servant following him at a distance. Instead of going directly into the Entrance 21 safe house, he ambled into the broken piles of rubble that covered the Warren and waited. The servant did not follow. When he was certain it was safe to do so, Dave emerged from the rubble and entered the safe house.

Chapter 22

News

A week later, Dave was working with a new crew of slaves building a shed by the stables for Blackthorn. These slaves, like the others Dave had met, were dispirited creatures with no ambition. They seemed to have lost the will to live. Their foreman used the whip viciously and enthusiastically, but the beatings seemed to have almost no effect on the group, who obviously thought life little better than the prospect of death. Dave found it hard to work and to mind his own business in the midst of such suffering.

Al had been insisting that he join Dave at the work site, so Dave had obtained clearance from Blackthorn. Al was instructed to play the part of a hardworking mute. The foreman left Al alone, and Al worked very hard, accomplishing more than what four whipped slaves could accomplish.

When Dave had first taken on this job, he had hoped to get some information about Pam and Little Thomas. The initial plan had been for Vixa and Alandro to find out what they could about Pam and Little Thomas, yet despite Dave getting them into the locked citadel for several nights through a drainage hole, which he had deliberately left a little too large, Vixa and Alando had not reported any information about the two.

Dave decided he had to do something himself. He knew it was a risk. He was too well-fed to pass close scrutiny as a slave; however, the foreman and the steward took no notice of him, and treated him like the other slaves except, that as a Guild member he was never beaten.

Still, he knew that if he were to become too inquisitive, all that disinterest might change.

So far, all of his jobs were away from Bigelow's sprawling citadel on the hill in the high point at the north end of the fortress. He never entered the citadel itself. He continued to bring food with him and surreptitiously shared it with the slaves when the foreman left the work site. The last while he had been working alone with a slave called Grigor, a grizzled, emaciated old-timer who somehow had found the purpose and will to survive.

On this day, Dave and Grigor were repairing a collapsed stable roof on the south side of the fortress. The foreman had just left, pleased with their progress, so Dave shared some of his food with Grigor.

"Grigor," said Dave, "have you been up at the big boss's citadel?"

"Yep." Grigor continued eating as quickly as possible. "I've even been in the keep."

Dave handed him another slice of stale bread. "Ever been to the dungeons?"

"Yep, I used to muck 'em out."

"Does Bigelow have a lot of prisoners?"

"Nope, he sent most of them to the mines when he first arrived. He still has a couple of foreigners, but he doesn't keep them in the dungeon."

"Foreigners?" asked Dave.

"Yep, a woman and child in strange dress. They're not from around here. Must be from those people they attacked across the sea."

"Where does Bigelow keep them if not in the dungeons?"

"They be up somewhere on the third floor. Bigelow didn't take them along on his trip."

"Trip?"

"Yep. I hear Bigelow left three weeks ago with his personal body guard. One of the slaves overheard his body guards talking about goin' to the Mutandi Highlands to meet a wizard named Zambor, or some such name. The citadel has been mostly empty ever since. Our lives have been a bit easier since he be leavin'."

Chapter 23

Storming the Keep

Dave could barely contain his excitement as he made his way back to the Warren. He even found himself whistling at one point, something that slaves never do. After that glaring mistake, which had drawn surprised looks from a couple of passing slaves, Dave kept his head down and tried walking with that listless, shuffling gait common to those in bondage.

He was later than usual, and The Doubtful Dragon had already closed for the night. When Dave returned to their lodgings, he was disappointed to find that he was the only one home.

He paced back and forth for a while, and then laid down. He fell asleep quickly—his hard work of the day having overruled his excitement at hearing news of Pam and Little Thomas. Arlana shook him awake, telling him he had not heard her call for supper. Everyone was already eating and talking by the time he arrived at the table.

But Dave couldn't eat until he had shared his news. Having done so, everyone wanted to ask questions.

"You say Bigelow is away right now?" asked Al.

"That's what Grigor said. I have to admit the citadel seemed pretty quiet. In retrospect, I realize more should have been going on if Bigelow were home."

"Then we need to move right away," said Linder. "When should we try a rescue?"

"If we're going to try it, we should do so tomorrow night. I'll be working there tomorrow as usual. The main gate will be locked and guarded at night. Instead of leaving at the end of the day, I'll hide inside. I can let you in, and we can search."

"Okay," said Al, "you'd better draw us a map to the gate. During the day, I'll make sure I can find the right gate in the dark. We'll make a run for it as soon as we have them, so we'll leave town shortly after the town gates open. What do you think Tandor?"

Tandor did not seem pleased. After thinking a moment, he said, "I think it'll work. Those guards don't pay much attention to people leaving, especially at the main gate. Getting out is possible. But then what?"

Al answered. "I know this is not what you wanted to hear, but I will take my wife and son back to our home as quickly as I can. We may not be the answer to the prophecy. But I also believe in genuine prophecy, and I do think your prophecy will still come true."

Tandor shrugged. "I gave my word. You'll have my help. I will get a safe house ready in case we cannot leave the city, and the guard decides to watch the Warren closely after the escape."

Dave worked hard all the next day. When the time had come, he made his way to the main fortress gate. Once out of sight of the stables, he doubled back and hid at the back of the construction site. There was a pile of fresh straw in the back corner behind a pile of lumber. He planned to hide in it if a patrol should come through as part of a late-night inspection. But no such patrol came. With a New Moon, and a very dark night, Dave was confident that he could see much better in the dark than the guards. At about 1:00 a.m., Dave crept from his hiding place. The streets inside the citadel were deserted. He skirted the front gate, expecting to see sentries on duty with lanterns burning in the gate house. But there were none to be seen. In the quiet, he heard the distant sound of singing and the occasional faint shout.

What's going on? Is it a riot or a party?

Arriving at the postern gate, Dave sat down for a few minutes to watch, in case of a sentry. But there was no noise and no movement. He crept closer and unlatched the gate from the inside. Pulling it open, he looked out. "Are you there?" he whispered.

Several figures separated from the shadow of the buildings across the street and moving stealthily, entered at the gate. Dave locked it.

Al whispered. "We brought everyone. We figured the more we had, the faster we could search the building."

Without further discussion, Dave led them through the grounds to the citadel itself. He knew the gate was open during the day but hoped they didn't lock it at night. The citadel was surrounded by a dry moat and crossed by a stone bridge. The gate beyond was open.

Dave crept forward, thankful that he had worn his darkest clothing that day. He entered the yawning mouth of the gate. The noise of the singing and shouting had grown louder as he approached the entrance to the keep and now it was almost deafening. Ahead, light streamed from under a closed door.

There must be some party going on. Let's hope that keeps them busy.

Inside the citadel wall a series of buildings abutted the wall. Beyond the buildings was a square. At the center of the square was a huge circular keep that rose in a series of three concentric towers, each segment bordered with battlements. The whole effect reminded Dave of a three-layered stone wedding cake.

The main gate of the keep was directly across from the citadel main gate and the singing and shouting seemed to come from inside the keep. Just inside the keep main gate, off to the left was a small spiral stairway. Straight ahead was a grand staircase. Dave decided to try the spiral staircase as the safer choice. He headed up one floor and stopped. This floor also seemed deserted.

Linder gave instructions, assigning the party in groups of two or three to search each of the corridors. "Do a quick search to see if anything looks promising but meet back here in five minutes. There will probably be a guard at Pam's door. Don't try to take him unless he sees you. Come back here." They soon returned after a fruitless search and then moved up to the third floor.

Dave and Arlana took the left corridor. There were many doors, but none looked suspicious and none were guarded. Finally, at the end of the hallway, they saw one door that looked different. The door was heavier, and was fastened with a sliding bolt. Inset into the door, near the floor was a small, latched sliding door with an empty tray beside it. There were two chairs outside of it. Dave touched Arlana's arm to speak by contact telepathy.

I think this is it honey. We had better go back and tell the others.

They retraced their steps. In a few minutes the others all returned and Dave told them about their discovery. No one else had found anything worth investigating. Al could not be held back. He rushed down the hall to the door and quietly pulled the latch back. A small light gourd cast its light on the room. Two figures were asleep on the straw mattress, a woman and a child.

Dave watched as Al hesitated for a moment and then crept forward. He knelt down beside the woman and gently touched her shoulder, his other hand ready to stifle any scream. She looked up. But it was not Pam.

A little girl sat up on the other side of the bed sat up. "Mommy what's going on?" she asked in English.

"Who are you?" asked the mother.

"We've come to rescue you," said Al, disappointment tinging his voice. Who are you?"

"My name's Kyra and this is my daughter, Sophie. We were captured by Bigelow in Halcyon and brought here when he fled. Are you working for him?"

"No," said Al, "get your things and come with us." In the dim light, Dave saw despair in Al's face.

The woman hesitated, but only briefly, then rose to gather her things. Al ushered everyone out. Leaving the room, Linder latched the door. Al gave the woman and the girl the dark cloaks he had brought for Pam and Little Thomas.

As they crept out of the fortress, Dave couldn't help wondering about what would happen next.

Now what? I was so sure we had found them. Now we know no more than we did when we first arrived in Abaddon. A deep sense of gloom and hopelessness enveloped him.

They returned to the postern gate. When they were outside, Al spoke again, but his voice sounded hollow and flat. "We had better go to the safe house," he said, "to question them and decide what to do."

Chapter 24

Contract Bridge

Al had not been able to sleep. He rose while it was still very early in the morning. The safe house had an upper window, which was shaded by a smooth-barked tree with long narrow leaves. As Al sat in an armchair by the window, not even the beauty of the night and the magnificence of the stars shining through the gaps in the tree's canopy could fill him with joy. His dashed hope about Pam and Little Thomas had brought him as close to complete and utter despair as he had ever been in the last few years.

Lord, get me out of my Slough of Despond![3] Al felt tears trickling down his cheek. A creak on the stairs made him turn around. Floyd Linder appeared carrying a light gourd.

Linder came into the room. As the light fell on his face, Al could see Linder begin to speak, then bite back his words. Linder sat down on the sofa and looked at Al thoughtfully. He seemed to come to a decision and said, "Al, I have a question. I know we talked about this when we had our long discussion about God and death after my grandmother died.[4] But the discussion still seems incomplete to me."

Al felt annoyed at the interruption, but long practice made him give Linder his full attention. "How can I help?"

3   Bunyan, John, Pilgrim's Progress, (Chicago, IL, Moody Publishers, 2007).

4   Kazmaier, Peter, Questioning Your Way to Faith, (Winnipeg, MB, Word Alive Press, Wolfsburg Imprints, 2013). [https://www.amazon.ca/Questioning-Your-Way-Faith-Disagreeable-ebook/dp/B00CSX6VDW/]

"Well," said Linder, "Do you think God is sometimes forced to choose the lesser of two evils?"

"As I understand it," said Al, inexplicably warming to the discussion, "God would never commit a moral evil such as lying or being malicious, but he might be forced to choose the lesser of two calamities in order to preserve his gift of free will to us."

"But isn't God omnipotent? To me, that means He can do whatever He wants. So why does He have to choose something He doesn't desire?"

"If I'm an author," said Al, "when I'm looking at a blank page I'm as omnipotent as a human being can be. But as soon as I write the first line, 'The murder happened just before midnight on the moor,' then I'm no longer omnipotent because I'm limited by the specifics of my own creation. God has to follow His own rules and be faithful to His own gifts and pronouncements. If He gives us free will, He has to live with that choice."

Linder shifted on the sofa. Al looked out the window marshalling his thoughts. "Yeah," said Linder, "I don't really get what you're saying."

"Do you play bridge Linder?"

"Yes, I like to think what I do with the cards could be called 'playing bridge'."

"Let's do a thought experiment. Let's pretend you and God are bridge partners playing a couple of world class players. How would the game proceed? For example, would God, sustaining the universe at every point, simply manage to deal Himself thirteen-trick hands all the time?"

"Speaking hypothetically, since I don't believe in God, I would say 'no.' That would be too much like God playing the card sharp. He may have the power to give himself all aces, kings, queens and a jack, but the rules of the game are predicated on every player receiving a statistical distribution of cards. Furthermore, it would destroy the game by making it completely unfair and, frankly, boring."

"Would God let Himself know what's in your hand or the hands of your two opponents?"

"No, again. Playing with that information would be equivalent to peeking at the other player's cards, and again, would be against the spirit of the game and would ultimately destroy what is most fun about it."

"So, my point then Linder, is that God, by limiting Himself to the rules and spirit of the game, may lose hands playing bridge. He may lose hands because, by adhering to the statistical nature of the game, he will periodically receive hands so bad that it will be impossible to win any trick no matter how well He plays. On other occasions, you, his fallible partner, may make an error that causes a loss, which God has to accept because He has partnered with you.

"To choose otherwise would not only be unfair to the other players, but would also destroy the game."

"So how will God being my partner make a difference?" asked Linder leaning back on the sofa.

"The rules of the game allow God to play every hand as well as He is able. Given the constraints of the game, He will still play every hand better than anyone else could play His hand. There will likely be imaginative choices and playing styles not yet discovered. At every point, God will play according to the rules and spirit of the game."

Al leaned forward in the arm chair. "It's clear He will not allow Himself to see other player's hands, but He would likely go beyond that. You might think since He will know each individual so well that he can predict what their involuntary facial expressions indicate about their hands, that He would use this data to improve His play. But I think even in this grey area, He would act in a way that is within the spirit of the game—only making use of this information when it is proper to do so."

Al could feel himself smiling. He had, for a short time, forgotten his despair. He saw Linder stifling a grin and a suspicion began to dawn on Al. "You didn't open up this line of questioning because this question had kept you awake tonight, did you? You were trying to cheer me up and get me out of my gloom, weren't you?"

Linder smiled broadly. "Did it work?"

Chapter 25

Back to the Swamp

"Now what do we do?" asked Linder.

The whole group was huddled around a light gourd in the safe house a few blocks from the city walls. Dawn was only a couple of hours away. Kyra and her daughter Sophie were asleep in the next room. Kyra had not seen or heard of another set of captives from Halcyon. She did know that Bigelow had been angry about some development. He had apparently gone to a place called the Mutandi Highlands to meet a wizard called Zambor who was going to do something to give Bigelow some kind of weapon or advantage. Captivity had made Kyra lose track of time.

No one responded to his question, so Linder tried again. "We have to decide what to do about Kyra and Sophie. It seems we only have three options: one, find a safe place for them in Abaddon; two, take them with us as we search for Pam and Little Thomas; or three, send them back home through the black swamp oaks.

"I think we have no choice but to send them back home," said Al. "They are Bigelow's victims. We have it in our power to rescue them, so that's our duty."

"Whoa," said Linder. "Think about what sending them back would mean. It will have been noted back home that they didn't return with the Halcyonites. They've probably been listed as dead. Their reappearance will attract the interest of the authorities. They'll be interrogated. Soon everyone back home will figure out the business of the black swamp oaks. Don't you see what that will mean? We'll have incursions by the powers-that-be from back home. Once we open that Pandora's Box, we won't be able to close it again."

"I know," said Al, "and that worries me too. But we don't have the right to condemn Kyra and Sophie to a life here when we have the power to send them home. The end never justifies the means."

"Yeah, but do the means justify the end, even if the end means having this place overrun by opportunists and exploiters of Darwin Blackmore's ilk from back home? I thought that was one of the reasons we fought against him at Halcyon."

"You're right in what you say Linder, but you're asking us to strand Kyra and Sophie in this inhospitable country where they will be slaves, when we have the power to send them home. They are people of infinite worth. Every person is. We need to do the right thing by them, and trust that whatever happens, it will somehow work out for the best."

"Friend Al is right," said Hanomer. "it is our duty to make sure they are returned home safely.

"Let's look at Linder's three options," said Dave. With regards to option one, we don't know of any safe place for them. They can't go to the Guild since Bigelow and his cronies will be looking for them. If we tried to take them to the Rebels why would they help them? The Rebels have enough problems, and have no history or blood ties with Kyra and Sophie. Kyra doesn't even know the language.

"Option two is also out. We have to move fast and under cover. We can't do that and take them along. That leaves only option three. I agree with Linder that this will open the floodgates to the people who share Blackmore's mindset, but this place could use some shaking up. At any rate, even if the government wanted to invade Abaddon, they can't really launch an invasion with three black swamp oaks as the only means of transport. I say, let's take them back. Don't go directly out of the swamp. Confuse the way. Whoever takes them back can take them directly back to their family and then disappear. Maybe with the confusion and stress, Kyra won't be able to lead them back to the swamp oaks. Maybe their untimely emergence will be attributed to a bookkeeping mistake followed by post-traumatic stress syndrome.

"Maybe," said Linder, skeptically.

"Tandor, am I right in what I said about the Guild and the Rebels?"

"Yes, you are right."

The discussion continued for a few more minutes, but Linder, who wanted to continue the search for Pam, and hide Kyra and Sophie, had to concede in the end.

"Alright," said Linder, "I see the way the wind is blowing. How do we take them back? We can't just load them into the swamp oaks and leave them in the middle of the swamp back home. Someone has to go with them. I'm willing to go, but how do I find you when I get back?"

"I don't think you should go alone," said Al. "We have three oaks, so we can send back three parties. I think we should blindfold Kyra and Sophie as you take them out of the trees on the other side, so that they can't guide the authorities back to the oaks. When you get back to our space-time, contact Makalo and have him pick you up. Try to keep Sophie and Kyra from seeing Makalo, otherwise he'll be in even more trouble than he already is.

"And there's something else. We need a way to try to find Pam and Little Thomas. I've been thinking we need a way to track Little Thomas's chip here. We can't track it because there are no cell towers here, but back home they do make military grade mini-towers that are used by oil companies and others who are working out in the bush. They're small enough to carry, and they work on solar. Why not bring one back? We'll have to be within a few miles of Little Thomas, but that's a whole lot better than what we have now."

"All good ideas," said Linder. "So, who's going with me, and how do we find the rest of you when we get back?"

"I'll go with you," said Thomas.

Al pulled a small package out of his pack, the size of a large chocolate bar. "These bread crumbs are how you'll find us. I'm always looking for new hiking gadgets and I thought this might come in handy here." He opened the package. "There are thirty solar rechargeable battery-powered transmitters here. We'll leave them every few kilometers behind us. When you come through, you'll use this direction finder to locate the nearest transmitter—just like picking up bread crumbs."

They woke Kyra and Sophie and told them about the plan, including the blindfolding once they returned to America. Kyra was very nervous, but the thought of going home made her willing to attempt the return journey.

Shortly after dawn, the whole group left the town along with a throng of workers going to the fields. When they were well away from the gate, they left the main road and again retraced their steps back to the Necroan swamp. They crossed to their camp on the Butte and saw that the mine was still silent. Without Bigelow back to restart it, it looked like no one was willing to man the dig.

The trip back to the black swamp oaks was uneventful, although Kyra and Sophie had to be helped to cross from island to island on the tree limbs. After Linder, Thomas, Kyra and Sophie settled into their black swamp oaks, the rest of the company spent a sleepless night waiting for them to depart. They huddled on one of the natural platforms made of interlaced branches, dreading the possibility that they might hear sounds of the Necroans crashing through the underbrush and leaping from island to island. But they heard only animal noises. Early in the morning grunts mixed with the occasional bellow had them on edge. When the noise died down, they all fell into a troubled sleep.

The next morning, Tandor, Al, Dave, Arlana, Chartrand, Larsen, and Hanomer climbed down from the platform, verified that the three black swamp oaks were empty, and left the Necroan swamp as quickly as possible. The search for the Mutandi Highlands, and for Zambor, Bigelow, Pam, and Little Thomas began once more.

Chapter 26

Horatio

Even though the grass was generally above Hanomer's head, his hearing, sense of smell, and intuition still made him the best scout. With Hanomer up ahead, and Dave and Arlana covering their advance on the right and left respectively, Chartrand, Larsen, Tandor, and Al made their way across the grassland in a southeasterly direction. Reaching the edge of the escarpment without incident, they hid a bread-crumb transmitter in a large bush with a note indicating their direction, then began following the rough trail, which bordered the cliff edge in a southeasterly direction.

Dave knew they were in even more danger on the edge of the escarpment than on the grasslands. The low hills and short grass, interspersed with bushes, meant Hanomer's keen eyes provided not nearly as much protection as before. Without sufficient warning, the group was in danger of being surprised by Bigelow and his company's return. To counteract this danger, Dave and Arlana took turns joining Hanomer in scouting well ahead of the party. Hanomer's woodcraft was such that he could hide almost anywhere, while Dave and Arlana's living cloaks made them almost impossible to see, even in open terrain.

The scouts saw the occasional herd of pachydons in the distance, but only once did the party take cover over the precipice edge as the bulls charged. Eventually, the trail began to turn due east and the escarpment changed. The first terrace stopped, and the escarpment cliff descended into the depths as one unbroken wall, sinking straight past a bank of clouds that they could see a thousand meters below the edge.

Off to the east a series of higher hills appeared on the horizon, hazy in the distance, with even higher hills behind them. The short grass and scrub brush gradually gave way to a mixture of meadows and trees with the copses growing larger the further they progressed. The meadows they encountered were crossed by small creeks that disappeared over the edge of the precipice, dissolving into mist as the water plunged hundreds of meters into the cloud-shrouded depths of Sheol.

The trail began to climb the first forest-covered hill. Rock—jutting out like giant raisins in a pastry—broke the contour of the hill. Cliffs twenty or more paces high redirected the trail into an irregular switch back. The path entered an upward-sloping narrow crack between two large cliff faces and emerged at the top of the first hill. The crest was composed of bare rock with small depressions that were filled with soil and small yellow flowers. By unspoken consent, they stopped to catch their breath and to have a meal in the sunshine. Looking ahead, Dave saw the trail plunge back into the trees and emerge on the next hill, which was both higher than the one they were on, and bare of trees. The hill ahead reminded Dave of the back of a monk's crown-shaven head.

Linder pointed into the sky far to the east. "What's that?"

Dave and Arlana both shielded their eyes. "They look like bats," said Dave.

"Very large bats, given the distance," added Arlana. "Their wing span must be twenty to thirty paces."

"What are they?" Dave asked, looking at Tandor.

"I can't say for sure. We know the wizards make many weird and terrible monsters with their experiments. That's why we don't come here."

"They could be really large given the high air pressure here," said Al. "Tandor didn't you say that dragons were not able to fly to the higher terraces because they were too large?"

"I don't think they can be dragons," said Tandor. "There are, however, flying creatures that are smaller and lighter than dragons called vuls, which, although mainly carrion eaters, can kill large animals. It's my guess you are probably seeing those."

"But they are still very large," said Arlana shading her eyes.

"Back home," said Al, "the largest flying creature is the California Condor. It has a wing span of up to three meters. But here, with perhaps three times the air pressure, much larger creatures could fly because the accessible wing loading would be higher. Those things could be big enough to carry off a man, so we had better be careful."

Chartrand gave Al one of his indulgent looks that said, "Too much information, Professor."

"Yeah," said Dave, "we need a break. But let's not stop here where we're exposed and easily seen. Why not move under the shelter of the trees? We should be safe there. I don't like the look of those bats or birds, regardless of the—err fascinating speculation about their wing loading."

They repacked their knapsacks and moved into the trees. The shade was more ominous and less pleasant than the sunlit open crest. A gloomy mood seemed to seize everyone. They ate hurriedly, and then followed the trail into the valley. At the bottom, a small river blocked their path. The trail appeared to cross the river at a ford, but the waters were swollen from recent rains and no one wanted to attempt the crossing there. Dave headed upstream with Arlana while Al headed downstream with the others looking for a better place to cross.

Suddenly a terrible smell assaulted Dave; a smell of carrion and death, and he heard a squeal of terror off to their right. Looking in the direction of the noise, he saw nothing; the trees were sixty to ninety centimeters diameter with an undergrowth of bushes, which limited visibility. Glancing back at Arlana, he signaled for her to wait. She shook her head vigorously. Sighing, Dave crept through the trees cautiously. The stench grew stronger, and the squealing was replaced by loud, anxious barking. An armoured monstrosity, the size of a small cow with a spiked tail, came into view. With its back claws on the half-eaten carcass of a pony-sized animal, the monster was digging vigorously into the bank. The barking, filled with terror and growing more frantic, came from under the bank.

Dave stepped onto a twig with a loud snap. The monster backed out of the shallow depression it was digging, and turned to face him. It was grey, with a thick, rhinoceros-like hide, its head resembling that of a crocodile. It squinted at Dave, narrowing its small red eyes, then moved cautiously toward him, each step snapping twigs in the undergrowth. Its stolid, unhurried approach unnerved him. As it cleared the hillside, its spiked tail swung back and forth in a wide arc, scything through branches as if warding off an attack from the rear. Dave and Arlana shot. The arrow and bolt stuck in the neck and shoulder of the creature, but did not penetrate deeply. The creature's eyes seemed to blaze at the wounds, and it increased its speed to a lope, crushing even moderate-sized branches in its charge. It still gave no cry. Dave whipped out Gram while he and Arlana split up, forcing the monster to face one of them. The creature turned toward Arlana. Its forelegs were long, powerful, and clawed. Dave waited for the tail to flash by, then rushed in and hacked at it. The sword cut deeply, severing the appendage. The monster bellowed in rage as black blood spurted out of the stump, as the monster turned towards Dave.

Dave backed up. The creature's long, clawed paw struck out, gashing Dave's living cloak. Dave stumbled backwards in surprise at the creature's reach, but stopped his fall by steadying himself against a tree. Another claw lashed out. But Dave was ready, and sliced the forearm off with a clean stroke.

The monster hissed. It was visibly weakening from the loss of blood. Arlana rushed in and hacked furiously at the monster's flank, making only a few shallow cuts in its armoured hide. But at last, the monster stopped moving. Teetering for a moment, it toppled over. The blood flowing from its wounds stopped.

Dave cautiously stepped around the carcass and walked to the den. A grey pup was whimpering inside. Dave spoke calmly, but the pup would not come out of its hiding place. Dave took some food from his pack and held it out. The pup slowly emerged, nosing at the dried meat. Dave rubbed the pup around the neck, as it munched on the food, then he looked back at Arlana. She was examining the carcass in front of the den. "You know what that is don't you? It's a lup. When it grows up it will be a killer. You're not thinking what I think you're thinking are you?"

"Look at him Arlana. I can feel his thoughts when I stroke him. He's hungry and scared. He'll starve if we leave him."

"Husband, I will say this in the most loving way I can. Taking a lup as a pet is one of the most stupid—perhaps *the* most stupid thing you have ever done. He's going to grow up to be a killer. How do you know you'll be able to control him? He and his kind are products of the Bent Ones, or their forbearers anyway. In the state of mind you're in, you'll only realize you've made a mistake when your 'pet' kills someone. How will you feel then? How can you even take that chance? Our histories tell us the ancient Bent Ones warped and blended wolves and humans to make creatures like him. When they did so, they unleashed a great evil on the world. Creation of the lupi was a big mistake."

Dave felt stubbornness well up inside him. *I know she's probably right. But I just can't let the little fella starve.*

"You may be right, Arlana, but how do we know that this mistaken creation can't be redeemed? After all, I'm also a bent creation, in a way. If I can be redeemed, maybe this little fella can be too. We can't know if that's possible unless we try. We can always destroy him if we have to. Shouldn't we at least give him a chance? Shouldn't we try to mend before we destroy?"

"You don't even know if the other lup parent is dead. What if he comes to waylay us? Lupi are smart and deadly. He could track us for miles."

Dave didn't answer, but picked up and caressed the little lup.

Arlana threw up her hands in exasperation, then pursed her lips. Dave carried the lup in his arms as they retraced their steps back through the woods, found the river, and continued their search upstream. Just ahead, the river rushed through a narrow cut in the rock. A massive tree had fallen across the river. Dave gave the pup to Arlana and climbed out on the fallen tree. He began lopping off branches with Gram. When he reached the other side, he came back and said, "I think this will do. Let's tell the others."

When Arlana and Dave rejoined the group, the others were pleased to hear about the fallen tree, but were as displeased by the prospect of a lup whelp in their company as Arlana had been. Still Dave would not relent, so they gave up arguing. Dave announced he would name the lup "Horatio."

Dave placed the pup into the top of his pack so that it could peep out, and they resumed their journey.

The group crossed the fast-flowing river using the huge fallen tree. Rejoining the trail, they climbed the next hill. Avoiding the open glades, they kept to the woods, looking up frequently for the winged creatures they had seen.

After twenty minutes, as they were approaching another open glade, Dave, who was leading, heard a hiss like a steam engine. He put up his fist and everyone stopped. Creeping forward to the edge of the glade, Dave saw a large form with folded, bat-like wings crouching over a mound in the middle of the glade. The mound looked like a partly eaten antelope. The harsh cries of other flyers rang from above as the winged monstrosity tore at the flesh of the antelope, looking into the air after each bite to see if anything would challenge its kill. The vul's body was the size of a cow, but long and thin. It ended in a snake-like neck, terminated with a head the size of an elongated basketball with a rounded mouth filled with razor-like teeth. Its wings served as a second set of legs, with claws at the wing joint. Its hind legs were long, and ended in huge claws, which were embedded in the flesh of its prey and had been used to kill the animal, judging by the deep talon rips in the antelope's hide.

When the vul saw the group, it gave out a shriek and a hiss, unfolded its wings and carried its prey into the upper reaches of a tall tree where it resumed its meal.

"Wow," said Al, "I don't much like the look of that." It could certainly kill us and carry us away if we were caught in the open." Al decided to leave a breadcrumb transmitter at the site. He tied the device to a tree on the crest, along with a note about the vuls.

The band returned to the trail and followed it down a gentle slope. Soon the trail bent to the right around a rock outcropping. Al crept out onto the ledge to have a clear view ahead, outside the cover of the trees.

When he returned he said, "It looks like we have another valley ahead and then the trail switches back and forth to climb a large cliff. The cliff is an effective barrier and stretches many kilometers to either side. Once we reach the cliffs it looks as if we won't have any trees for cover until we get to the top."

When they reached the valley, they startled a deer, which ran away from them in panic down a game trail. As the deer passed under an arch that was formed by two trees whose branches met over the trail, they heard a series of twangs, as if several bow strings had been released. They watched as the deer lifted high into the air.

"What was that?" asked Larsen, fear tinging his voice.

"I think that tree just killed the deer," said Chartrand.

Al picked up a small branch and approached the still carcass of the deer hanging about two meters above the trail. Its body was pierced by five or six barbed thorns, each at least sixty centimeters long. Working from a distance, Al used the branch to lift the broad green leaves from the left stem of the arch tree, uncovering an arsenal of thorns. Each of the tree's branches was secured by a vine-like fiber attached to the tree's trunk. Al touched the thorns, but nothing happened.

"Al," said Dave, "look at those vines that stretch from trunk to trunk just above the trail."

Al used his branch to touch one of the vines. The vine snapped immediately, shooting two thorns into the path before retracting upwards.

What have we gotten ourselves into? thought Dave. *Even the plants are killers. We haven't been nearly careful enough.*

"More work of the Mutandi wizards," said Tandor. "They will always find ways to kill people through their infernal creations. Luckily, there usually be only few of each kind, or so our knowledge teaches. It wouldn't do to meet a thicket of these arch trees."

Chapter 27

Vuls

The next morning, the group moved at a slower pace. Their experience with the arch tree fresh in their minds, they kept a careful watch not only for dangerous animals, or the approach of armed men, but on every tree. Horatio seemed content in Dave's pack, and did not bark or make any other sound.

It must have been about 10 o'clock in the morning when they finally reached the edge of the forest and the trail entered the broken rocks that formed the beginnings of the cliff they had seen earlier. Stopping for lunch, Dave let Horatio out of his pack. The little lup ran around their camp and up to everyone for a scratch or pet like an ordinary puppy. Dave and Al searched the cliff face to see the trail and to look for danger.

Dave pointed about halfway up the cliff face. "Doesn't that look like a nest there? It's huge, but we would expect it to be huge for those vuls."

Al scanned the cliff face with his binoculars. "Yes," said Al. "Now that I know what I'm looking for, I think I see three or four more. I think those vuls are going to cause us a real problem if we're in the open and near their nesting area."

"On the other hand,' said Dave, "we know this trail has been used recently by Bigelow, and so it must be possible to climb to the ridge. I suppose we could wait until nightfall."

"How do we know those vuls need to see us? Maybe they can find us by smell. At least during the day we can see them coming. At night only you, Arlana, and Hanomer will see well enough to have a chance."

Ahead of them, the trail crossed a rock-strewn stretch, and then snaked between large boulders. Checking that the way was clear and that there were no vuls in the air, they made a dash as a group to the shadow of the first boulder. Al gave Dave a nudge. Looking up the cliff, Dave could see that several vuls had left their eyries and were now gliding parallel to the cliff.

Led by Al, the group made a second dash to the base of the cliff. Dave glanced up nervously. By now at least a dozen vuls were circling overhead, their deep-throated cries echoing off the cliff face.

"Let's keep moving," said Al.

Dave waited for the others to pass so he could cover Arlana's back. *If one of those monstrosities comes down, it's not going to get her!*

The cliff was dusky brown sandstone with flecks of quartz. The path began to climb from ledge to ledge in a series of steps with a scramble up a steep section in between. They cowered under an overhang as the dark shadow of a vul swept past them silently.

Ahead was another vertical scramble up to the next ledge.

"Everybody wait here and cover me. I'll head up and then cover you when you come after me," said Al.

Al waited until the sky was free of vuls, and then started climbing to the next ledge. The path went up at an angle of approximately sixty degrees. Al had to pick his way from step to step.

"Watch out!" shouted Dave. A vul with talons outstretched banked in an attempt to snatch Al off the scramble. Al flattened himself just in time, and the claws scraped on the rocks. Dave dashed out with Gram and swung at the vul as it tried to bank away from the cliff. The sword sheared off a claw and the vul shrieked in fury, leaving a trail of black, foul-smelling blood.

When Al had made it to the top of the cliff, Arlana went next. Dave marveled at her lithe form as she ran up the scramble without seeming to have to look for the next step. She had adjusted her skin color so that it was almost the same dusky brown as the rock.

Nice trick, thought Dave. *I wish I had that kind of control over my skin color. All I can manage is really light and really dark.*

The wounding of the vul seemed to provide a break, so Larsen, Chartrand, and Tandor went next, while Dave covered them with Gram drawn. When they had also made it to the top, Dave followed. Another vul swooped. Peeking out of the haversack, Horatio let out a low growl. Dave was only halfway up the scramble, but braced himself, and swung his body around to face the incoming vul. His pack prevented him from getting onto his back, but he braced his legs, held Gram at the ready, and waited for the vul. The vul veered away, so Dave continued his dogged scramble to the next ledge with one hand, holding Gram with the other.

Crouching under an overhang with the others, Dave looked around. The others looked frightened. Arlana had more fear in her eyes that he ever remembered seeing before, even during the worst of the Battle for Halcyon.

We can't stay here, he thought. The path did not head up to another ledge, but disappeared into a long narrow crack in the cliff.

"I know that the trail has been pretty obvious since the last bread crumb," said Al, "but I want to put a transmitter here. I wish I could have left them a note to go back. I don't know how they'll manage this climb, harassed by vuls, as a party of two."

"You know Linder," said Al. "He wouldn't turn back no matter what you wrote in your note. He'll manage. He'll stick with us and he'll also find a way while looking after Thomas. Al tied a bread crumb with a note to a small bush eking out a meager existence on the side of the cliff.

"Alright, is everyone ready?" asked Dave. There were nods all around. Dave went first this time. The crack was narrow but the trail continued on with no immediate danger in sight. The sheer walls rose several hundred feet and he could see hazy blue sky above. Dave waved for the others to join him. With Hanomer leading, they travelled single file along the rugged path. Rock shards littered the ground, and from time to time, a vul flew over them. After about two hundred meters the crack opened up into a circular space about seventy meters across. It looked as if they were at the bottom of a well. The walls were relatively smooth and unbroken. Vuls sat on the rim of this rock well, looking down at them, their screeches filling the air. Across from them was the circular mouth of a tunnel, and the path ran straight across the circular space and disappeared into the blackness. Off to their right, a thin trickle of water from the wall formed a small pool.

"If we have to go into that tunnel, let's take a break by that pool," said Dave. "The vuls can't get us here easily if we stay close to the wall. If they try to land and attack us, we'll make them pay."

"Surely you're not thinking of camping here for the night?" asked Al.

"No, I still want to try the tunnel in daylight, otherwise we won't see the exits if it's dark outside."

Keeping a sharp eye on the vuls on the bowl rim, they refreshed their water bottles from the pool and had a quick meal back in the crack. Stroking their light gourds to illuminate them, they crept around the perimeter of the bowl and headed into the tunnel.

The tunnel mouth was about ten meters in diameter, but quickly narrowed to a square passage about three meters on a side. The tunnel ran straight. It looked as if some sections had been deliberately widened a long time ago. After about one hundred meters, the passage opened into a large chamber. A beam of light from a fissure in the roof played on a large section of rock that had fallen from above ages ago.

They lost the trail. There seemed to be several passages out of this cavern.

"Now what do we do?" asked Chartrand.

"I think," said Al, "we ought to split into three groups and follow each of the passages for a few hundred meters and then return here to decide which way to go."

Dave and Arlana took the left passage, which narrowed so much that they had to wriggle forward. It opened up again into a series of chambers. The fourth chamber, which was considerably larger than the other two, had a slope of broken rock at one end. A beam of light illuminated the top of this ramp.

Dave eagerly scrambled toward the shaft of light. He squeezed through the narrow opening and stepped out into twilight in front of a pier of rock thrusting out of the ground in a forest glade. The air was filled with the acrid smell of sulfur dioxide. Arlana joined him, and made a face at the fumes. They began to explore the glade to get their bearings, while scanning the sky for vuls. Arlana moved to the east and a few minutes later called to Dave to join her. He found her standing on a ledge looking east. Across a narrow valley and behind a shallow ridge they saw an area devoid of plant life. This shallow bowl behind the ridge was rent by fissures. Out of several of these fissures, plumes of smoke rose, blowing directly toward them. The shallow bowl had areas of hardened slag, some of which had spilled over the rim of the bowl and scorched the surrounding vegetation. In the midst of this desolation, high on a rocky crag rising out of the slag bowl, stood a fortress. Below them, in the valley, they could see the trail leaving the trees at the fringe of the devastated land and winding its way to the fortress main gate. The road looked recently repaired, where the vomit from the fissures had temporarily blocked it. The evening light was fading fast.

"I think we ought to head back, husband, to find the others."

"Yeah, you're right. I wonder what Bigelow wants from this forbidding place?"

Retracing their steps, they crawled back into the cavern through the narrow passage. This proved much more difficult than they anticipated since it meant crawling down a steeply sloping part of the passage, head first. When the passage opened up and they were able to turn around, the going became easier. In twenty minutes, they were back in the cavern with all the side passages and waited. Another thirty minutes passed and Dave began to be alarmed. Finally, Larsen and Chartrand came running back.

"Tandor and Al been captured," gasped Chartrand as he bent over to catch his breath.

"They were captured by … by lizard men," added Larsen.

"Lizard men?" asked Dave.

"Trogs!" said Arlana, growing pale.

"What are Trogs?" asked Dave.

"They are another of the bent races made from the first men. They live underground and have scales instead of skin. They eat human flesh."

"We need to go after them right away," said Dave.

"We did go after them," said Chartrand, "and we followed them until they left the underground passage and headed toward this fortress on a high rock. We won't catch them before they're inside. Hanomer's still following them."

"If we have no chance of immediate rescue, maybe you'd better start from the beginning, Chartrand," said Arlana.

"Yeah, I think you're right. Hanomer, Larsen, and I took the passage on the right. We came to a fork and kept to the right. After about one hundred meters, that passage came to a dead end. We retraced our steps and took the left fork, which joined another passage at a tee intersection. We thought we might have joined Al and Tandor's passage, so we turned right, thinking that going left would take us back to our starting point.

"We heard Al shout. Then there was the sound of a scuffle with roars and curses in the Common Tongue. The curses had a strange timbre, unlike any sound made by a human—almost like hissing. We ran as fast as we could, but the distance was further than we thought.

Hanomer found Al's pack thrown into a shadowed corner, and scuff marks on the ground.

"With Hanomer leading, we continued down the passage as fast as we could go, hearing talk in the Common Tongue ahead of us. The accent was strong, but it sounded as if the leaders of the band were debating what to do. One wanted to take the captives back to their village cavern while the other insisted they had to take the prisoners to the wizard, Zambor. The first speaker said they couldn't go out into the sun. The second said it was only a short trip and that it was already twilight.

"We followed them to the exit. The sun was nearly down, but there was enough light to see the band head up the road to the fortress. They were too far ahead for us to catch up. There were about twelve of these Trogs. We would be seen. That's when Larsen and I decided we should come back to report and figure out what to do next.

"Show us where the attack happened," said Dave.

With Chartrand leading, they retraced their steps to the widening of the passage. Chartrand indicated where they had found Al's backpack. Their weapons and Tandor's pack had disappeared. Dave showed the others a section of what appeared to be rock, which was in reality a cleverly disguised wooden door with a rock-like coating. Pulling one of the protuberances, Dave pulled open the noiseless door to reveal another passage. They could see where the attackers had positioned themselves for their assault.

"I think this is an outpost set by Zambor to intercept visitors," said Dave. "I expect those Trogs will be coming back here soon to resume their post. We'd better leave."

"Arlana and I found another way out. Let's head back."

They emerged from the narrow passage to the cavern and sat under the trees where they could keep an eye on the fortress and the road. Having darkened their skin color, Dave and Arlana were almost invisible to the others in the darkness. Dave had no trouble seeing in this level of light.

Arlana touched Dave's arm. *Look husband, there's a group leaving the front gate and heading down the trail. They're Trogs—ugly brutes. I see twelve of them. That looks like the lot.*

"They must be heading back to their ambush post," whispered Arlana. "That must mean that Al and Tandor have been left in the fortress."

"Pam and Little Thomas are in there as well."

Larsen said, "Hanomer will be coming back to our meeting place. I'll go back and wait for him."

Dave studied the fortress carefully. The walls were at least twenty meters high with towers every fifty meters. In the centre was a massive keep that dwarfed the walls and rose perhaps two hundred meters above the top of the rock. A crenelated platform at the top was on level with their perch.

Clouds moved in and a gentle rain began. The four retreated back into the tunnel and continued the discussion.

"We should go right now," said Dave. "We haven't seen anyone on the walls. With this rain there will be even fewer guards."

"But even if we're successful in getting over the wall undetected, what do we do then?" asked Chartrand. "We don't know the layout. We have no plan to hide ourselves and we don't know where the prisoners are held. How can we proceed without a plan?"

"I don't know," said Dave. "I think we need to reconnoitre the fortress to see if there's a way in. Maybe find a way to make a grappling hook to scale those walls—I know it's a long shot."

They waited in silence until Larsen and Hanomer rejoined them.

Dave had been looking in the direction of the fortress for a long time. "If Al were here, I'm sure he'd tell us we should pray for something …"

Larsen chuckled, "You mean pray for one of those events, as Al would say, that atheists ascribe to improbable coincidence and Christians ascribe to providence? Yep, that sounds like a plan—sort of."

"One more thing, while we're thinking about what to do, we have to make sure that Linder and Thomas don't walk into the same trap that we walked into. Two of us should wait by the trail to warn them."

"Why don't you and Arlana stay here," suggested Larsen. "Your eyesight at night is so much better than ours, and with your skin color change, you can blend into these rocks much better than we can.

"Chartrand and I can take turns watching the trail during the day. We'll also leave a bread crumb with a note outside the tunnel, telling Linder and Thomas what happened, and to wait for us."

"Friend Chartrand, I will watch with Arlana and Dave," said Hanomer. "I think they have the harder task. Watch should be kept up for twenty-four hours a day, in case something happens that affects our friends."

Chapter 28

What Happened to Al and Tandor

Some time earlier, Al, looking back, watched Dave and Arlana disappear into the tunnel on his right then observed the others as they headed to the tunnel entrance on the left of the cavern.

Tandor said. "I'm ready." Hanging his light gourd from a shoulder strap, he picked up his spear in both hands, and started down the centre tunnel.

Al followed him into the tunnel mouth. The green-yellow glow of lumi-lichen illuminated the walls and Al could see that the tunnel was round, as if it had been eaten out of the rock by a rock-borer, the giant armoured beasts he had encountered before. From time to time, he saw chisel marks. The tunnel had been widened and squared off. He could hear the slow drip of water.

After about one hundred meters, the two reached a tee intersection. Tandor nodded, questioningly, at the side tunnel heading off to their right. Al shook his head, so Tandor continued straight ahead. Al felt a sense of apprehension. Tandor moved even more slowly, cautiously, and as silently as possible, picking his steps forward. After some time, the tunnel widened. Tandor raised his fist, signalling Al to wait, while he advanced cautiously. Suddenly from out of the darkness, a floppy object flew at Tandor, and wrapped its many snake-like arms around him pinning his arms to his side.

Dropping his pack, Al rushed forward, sword drawn, and sliced off the grape-fruit-sized head of the octopus-like creature. Its tentacles relaxed, and the creature fell away from Tandor. In the same moment something hit Al in the back, and he felt his own arms pinioned by tentacles, even as he saw a third creature attack Tandor. Al rolled onto his side trying to crush the boneless beast on his back. But its tentacles were very strong. He couldn't break free.

As Al struggled, a hideous man-shaped figure approached him. It was shorter than he was, but broad-shouldered. It seized Al, lifted him to his feet, and held him twenty centimeters from its face. The creature's jaws protruded forward and were filled with teeth. The pupils of its eyes were cat-like slits; its face was covered with fine, snake-like scales. Yet the creature spoke in the Common Tongue, "Hisst. Get up meat. You walk if you know what's good for ya. Hisst." A forked tongue showed between its teeth. It spat at Al's feet.

"Trogs," exclaimed Tandor, spitting in disgust. The Trog at Tandor's side hit him so hard he fell down. But the Trog forced Tandor to his feet again. "Hisst," it said. "Walk, vermin."

Al looked around as he staggered down the tunnel in the direction they had been going. He counted twelve Trogs, many carried the eight-armed creatures on their shoulders so that they looked as if they had two heads. The creatures, carried by the Trogs, had straps around their bodies with an attached loop, which aided the Trogs in throwing them.

The tunnel ran on for several hundred meters, wider than before. It curved slightly to the right, and then to the left. When Al stumbled, he received a kick in the ribs before being roughly dragged back to his feet. As he was getting up, he noticed that the Trogs did not wear shoes, but had wickedly clawed feet.

The acrid stench of sulfur dioxide in the tunnel made several of the Trogs cough. Eventually, the tunnel grew brighter, and they rounded a bend emerging into twilight. Some of the Trogs moaned at the light and covered their eyes with crude cloth veils.

The trail was made of hard-packed sand and ash. All around them Al could see fissures and craters, some of which emitted a red light from their depths. The heat was sweltering. Sections of the road had been newly repaired, as if the earth's convulsions regularly destroyed it.

Al looked up. A massive shape—a huge rock or small mountain with a fortress on top—rose out of the fissured land. About a kilometer ahead, he could see the road zig zag across the face of the rock as it climbed up to the fortification.

His ribs were aching painfully by the time they reached the mountain. The climb up the switchback exhausted nearly all of his strength. Just as he thought he would fall down for the last time, the road entered a tunnel in the rock wall, emerged to cross a stone bridge, and entered an open gate.

Inside, the Trogs stopped before armed guards who were clothed in black and red livery. "Hisst. We are here to see Zambor for our reward. We captured these spies in the long tunnel. My people are hungry and have not eaten man-flesh in a long time. Hisst."

An officer approached in pure red livery and a gold torq around his neck. "You will get your agreed upon reward in due time. Right now Zambor is up in the black tower embarked upon a great work. It may take many days. When he finishes, he will decide which of his slaves and prisoners he will send to you for your feast."

Two of the Trogs walked up to Al and Tandor and stroked the eight-legged octos—causing the creatures to release their grip on the prisoners—then hoisted them back onto their shoulders. Other Trogs handed Tandor's backpack and their captives' weapons to the soldiers. Without another word, the Trogs hurried out the gate.

Two guards escorted the prisoners down a long, spiral staircase. They passed several landings and side exits but kept descending. The stairs were so long that Al thought they must be at the level of the bottom of the small mountain, and nearly at the level of the lava. He noticed the temperature had become much hotter. When they finally reached the bottom of the staircase, they met a jailor, and a second small man who cowered whenever the jailor looked at him.

"Bring them!" said the jailor to the soldiers. "Show them the way, Trog meat," he added, looking at the smaller man.

With keys dangling at his side, the small man took them to the end of a long horizontal dungeon passage where he unlocked a door with a key as long as his hand. With the help of one of the soldiers, he wrestled open another rusty door, its hinges squeaking, and the door scraping across the floor. They thrust Al and Tandor inside, then forced the door shut. Al heard the key turn and the bolt slide into place. The light under the door gradually disappeared as the small man and the guards returned to their duties.

Al touched the wall by the door and made a slow circuit of the cell. The walls were rough. At intervals, he felt wetness. The back wall was even rougher than the side wall, and Al felt a trickle of water cascade down to a small drain hole on the floor. He continued his circuit. There was moldy straw in one corner and a foul-smelling bucket. Reaching the door, Al completed the circuit. He estimated the cell was a crude square, roughly four meters on each side.

Al could hear crackling as Tandor settled onto the straw. Slowly sinking to the floor, Al put his face into his hands.

Now what do I do Lord? Who's going to rescue Pam and Little Thomas? My arrogant decisions haven't helped them, and now I've led my friends into disaster.

Rocking back and forth with his hands clasped around his knees, a thought came to him, a scene in a favorite book called *The Silver Chair*. The characters, Eustace, Jill, and Puddleglum had been captured in their pursuit of Prince Caspian.

Puddleglum had said that Aslan's signs never go wrong. Following the signs doesn't mean that you will always be rescued, but you are doing your duty. Like the servant in King Lear *when Gloucester's eyes are being put out, and the third servant tries to intervene and is stabbed in the back.*

All I can do is my duty. And do it to the end. Even if I have to pay for it with my life.

Al bowed his head, prayed for Pam, Little Thomas, the coming baby, and his friends. He pleaded for rescue for all of them, but in the end, he resolved to do his duty no matter what happened, even if these were his last days. Even if he was sent to the Trogs for their feast.

His despair did not leave him, but his mood lifted a little. In the silence, Al heard the drip of the water along the back wall. Then he heard the sound of footsteps approaching. Light played through the crack under the door. There was a scraping sound and a rectangle of light showed in the door a foot above the floor.

The face of the small assistant with the keys appeared in the rectangle. He was holding a lantern to shine through the little door. "My name be Weasel, and I be the assistant jailor. I see one of you be a Rebel, or at least from the Guild by the looks of him." He looked furtively over his shoulder to be sure no one was listening. "I be wanting to bargain with ye."

"Why would you want to help us?" asked Al.

"Many years ago, I be captured while serving in the Guild. I was sent to run a message to soldiers on patrol. I was captured and sold to Zambor as a slave. I find being a slave go against my grain and I been plotting to escape. So ever since Zambor be furious with me and send me to watch dungeons under the head jailor. No light and little food. Now that Zambor owes a meat debt to Trogs, I be sure I be on the menu. Only thing saving me be Zambor is busy. Will ye help me or no?"

"How can we help? Why do you need us? If there's a way out why not just go on your own?"

"A lone man will never escape. I'm hoping ye have friends waiting for ye."

Tandor got up and approached the door. Lowering himself onto all fours, he peered at the face. Lapsing into slave talk, Tandor said, "Ye do be vaguely familiar. Who you are ye?" After several exchanges, Tandor seemed satisfied and said he recognized Weasel's name and knew some of his history. "I say we trust him."

"I agree, what have we got to lose?"

"Weasel, trust goes two ways. Open the door and come talk to us and tell us what you want," said Al.

Weasel pulled his key, unlocked the door, and came in with his lantern. He was shaking.

"We're men of our word Weasel. We won't hurt you, or treat you treacherously. What do you want for our help?"

"I be wanting to go with ye. As I said, alone, I have no chance if Zambor looses the Trogs and hounds. Just take me away from here before Zambor finishes his work in the tower with his guest."

Al decided to trust Weasel further. "This guest, I take it he came from Seth?"

"Aye."

"This guest brought a pregnant woman and a boy with him?" Al probed. "Where are they?"

"Sir, there be no pregnant woman and boy with the guest from Seth. I would know if there were. The slaves talk."

Having sensed a glimmer of hope that through Weasel he might find Pam and Little Thomas, at Weasel's words utter darkness and despair crowded into Al.

Tandor took over the conversation. "Weasel we will help you escape. Bring us a bit of light and our packs. That would be a good beginning."

"I only have your pack sir. Your weapons be stored upstairs for Zambor's inspection when he be waking from the plant."

Al roused himself. "What is this plant we keep hearing about?"

"High up in the main tower, Zambor has this huge grey plant, which be looking like a giant cabbage. Most of the Mutandi wizards have one. When he be experimenting and creating a new animal, he puts the animal to be operated on, on one side and he lies down on the other side and the plant closes up. He uses the plant to make changes in the animal. After many days he comes out, and some new monstrosity be born.

"This time the guest came with many guards and wanted Zambor to work on him. The guest be saying he wants to be like the old ones, living long, and being very powerful."

What was Bigelow up to?

"How long do we have until the process is done?"

"Don't know. Zambor and the guest went into the plant last night with this fellow you call Bigelow. The time be depending on how big the change be. The jailor has gone home for the night, leaving me in charge. We should be leaving as soon as possible. Zambor could wake at any moment."

"I have to check for the woman and the boy—they have to be here."

Weasel became very agitated. "No, kind sir, don't you be trying that. They catch you for sure. Please don't sir. Poor Weasel be killed right away and then you'll be right back in your cell. I be getting us out so no one sees."

"He is right, Al." said Tandor. "Your wife and child are not here. We know why Bigelow came. They don't have a role here. If Bigelow had them, he would have left them back in Seth. Something has happened to them, but they're not here."

Al knew Tandor was right. This wasn't just about him and his family, but he had to think about getting his friends out of this pointless danger. Even so, he couldn't just abandon the search for Pam and Little Thomas. He had no idea where to look next. *Oh God, forgive me if I blow this!* Al took a deep breath. "Alright, we'll go as soon as possible. How do you plan to get us out of here, Weasel?"

"This fortress be hollowed out underneath with many chambers and passages. The dungeon be the lowest level so far. In me time here, I go exploring and looking for a way out. There be earthquakes in the lava field that be opening up new channels from time to time. I be following a new crack that opened up, and I already followed it a long way. I just be needin' to find a way to the surface. There be many side passages to explore. One of them be leadin' to the surface."

Chapter 29

Cracks in the Broken Plain

Weasel returned Tandor's pack. And every night, after the jailor had retired for the evening, he came in to eat with the two prisoners.

Al doubted Weasel would have the strength to escape, since his food allowance was so meager. When Al asked him if he'd found a way out, Weasel's answer was always the same: "I still be searchin'." Al was growing impatient.

Finally, on the fourth day, Weasel opened the door to their cell. Standing in the doorway holding their weapons, he announced, "We go now."

He led them down a side passage to a crudely cut staircase that descended to a storage area filled with jars, crates, and sacks. Behind some mouldering boxes, the passage opened to a long, narrow pool of water. Weasel skirted the water and disappeared into the shadows on the far side. When Al followed him, he found a natural passage with undressed stone and pockets of cooled lava flow. Holding his lantern high, Weasel walked down the passage. Chalk marks appeared on the stone at intervals, particularly where side passages opened. "Every trip I made had a different mark. Bein' careful to follow the last marks."

They descended even lower and the temperature increased. Finally, Al felt the faint hint of a draft. Ahead of them, at the edge of the lantern light, the passage sloped upwards. But there was no sign of daylight.

"This be the way," said Weasel, and climbed up the narrow passage.

The opening was too narrow for Tandor to carry his pack on his back. He took out a length of rope and tied one end around his waist. Holding the other end, Al waited with the pack. Twice the rope caught, and Tandor had to delay his ascent to loosen it. Finally, the rope stopped paying out, and Tandor's voice came down the tunnel. "I'm ready to haul up the pack."

Al tied the rope to the pack, stuffed the excess line inside, gave a tug, and watched as the pack was dragged up the channel. On hands and knees, he followed it. In a few minutes Al emerged into the night air. He got a whiff of sulfur dioxide. Behind him, he saw the eerie lights on the wall of the fortress and in the lower windows of the central tower. Suddenly, a bright yellow light appeared in the upper most windows of the tall keep. A long mournful horn sounded.

"We hurry now," said Weasel, fear edging his voice. "Zambor be finished. He be sending for prisoners soon. The hounds be after us. We best be far away if we be wanting to live."

Chapter 30

Flight to the Edge of Sheol

It was the day after Al and Tandor had been captured. Very early in the morning, Dave and Hanomer had searched the lava field and found another route to the walls. Hanomer had crept all the way around the base of the fortress without seeing anyone up on the walls and, then had climbed up the rough stone, but could see nothing except the occasional guard lounging about. Horatio had tagged along and had also become friendly with Hanomer. While Dave was waiting for Hanomer to return, Horatio's sniffing around one of the fissures had Dave wondering if an underground passage might lead inside. Tonight, he would try a search around the walls himself to see if he had missed anything and maybe even search in the fissures to see if an underground passage would answer. Hanomer would try a more thorough exploration of the inside of the fortress. However, he had reported to Dave that the guards had hounds on patrol. Hanomer could hide from the guards, but the hounds would find him, no matter how cleverly he hid himself inside the fortress.

Several days passed. Each night, Hanomer climbed the walls and crept around the battlements. He reported overhearing guards gossiping that two prisoners were being held deep in the dungeons. Everyone seemed to be waiting for someone called Zambor to finish a task that occupied his time.

"So let me get this straight," said Dave to the group as he counted on his fingers, "One, Hanomer can't explore the inside of the fortress because the hounds can smell him; two, we know Al and Tandor are in there, but we have no idea where they're being held; three, we have to gamble that, improbable as it seems, one of these cracks in the lava field somehow penetrates the fortress and four, we can pull off a rescue. Failing that, then five, we launch a frontal assault on a fortress containing hundreds of vicious soldiers and hounds." He glared around for confirmation. Everyone looked away, including Arlana, who had tears in her eyes.

Dave grumbled, "Yep the odds are about what I would expect travelling with this crowd."

Arlana looked up. "Husband, stop complaining—you're frightening the men."

"Arlana, I'm used to these long odds. Look at the odds we faced rescuing Al from captivity in Halcyon—why is it always Al that needs rescuing, by the way? I'm just saying this seems to be 'business as usual' for us. That doesn't mean I have to like it. All I want is an unfair advantage once in a while."

Since their only hope, short of storming the fortress, was finding an underground passage, they focused on searching the pathways. The fissures opened up to a labyrinth of passages. One led to a river of lava deep underground, others led to dead ends. Horatio proved very useful; three times Dave found himself lost, but each time Horatio brought him back.

The three were at the lookout they had discovered on their first day, discussing their next exploration moves, when Dave heard a sound in the passage. Signalling to Arlana and Hanomer, they crouched together and pointed their crossbows at the passage opening. Tom Chartrand's head poked through. Dave breathed a sigh of relief. Dave helped Chartrand up, who was followed closely by Dwight Larsen. Floyd Linder's shaved head appeared next, followed by Thomas, Al's brother. Finally, the clean-shaven, brown face of Edward Makalo came into view. "Surprise!" he said, smiling. "You didn't expect to see me here."

The friends hugged, clapping each other on the back. Linder described how the three had followed the electronic bread crumbs to find Arlana, Dave and Hanomer. The vuls, apparently, had caused them much less trouble.

Dave told the newcomers about his own group's explorations around the fortress and in the fissures underground. Finally, he turned to Makalo. "You're right," he said, "I didn't expect you here."

"Well," said Makalo, "I knew as soon as you left that it would be a long trip. I sold my place and put everything into trust with my cousin, who's an investment broker. I told him I was going on a long trip and he wouldn't be able to reach me. We set up the trust through a lawyer with power of attorney, so that no one would accuse my cousin of foul play. I also had my cousin pay the taxes and utilities on Al and Pam's place, and he found a caretaker to look after the house and re-place the damaged door.

"I also bought more equipment. We each brought back two high powered rifles and as much ammo as we could carry. We have night vision goggles and a portable cell broadcaster so we can keep in touch. Given that you didn't come back right away, I figured it could be months or even years until we get home."

"So, what happened with Kyra and Sophie?" asked Arlana.

"We used the boat to make our way back out of the swamp at night," said Linder. "We phoned Makalo using the portable cellphone we had stashed with our cache before we set out, so he was waiting for us at the landing. Then we drove Kyra and Sophie to their families. We warned them to keep their captivity quiet if they want to be left alone by the media and the government."

"Do you think they'll listen?" asked Dave.

"No, not a chance," said Linder. "You can't keep a big secret like this quiet for long. It will get out, and I wouldn't be surprised if the Feds start combing the swamp for our departure point.

"I hate to say 'I told you so' but that's why I didn't want them going back," he added. "Things here are bad enough without opening a window for the Feds to send black ops teams here to explore this new world."

"I don't see that we had any choice," said Dave. "We couldn't very well have kept Kyra and Sophie here against their will."

"No, not against their will," said Linder. "Well, enough said. That train has left the station. We'd better deal with what we have before us right now. Shouldn't we be talking about how to get Al and Tandor out?"

Linder unpacked a black box about the size of a shoe box and set it up on a tripod. "This is the mini cellphone tower, Al asked me to bring back."

Linder took out his own smartphone and typed into it. "I'm searching for Little Thomas' radio frequency identification tag fre-quency using the mini tower."

He waited for a few minutes and looked disappointed. "Nothing, he's not within range. The range is about ten kilometers."

The discussion continued, but no good options surfaced. Some wanted to keep searching the underground passages, but the majority of the group wanted to act directly. They finally settled on sending Hanomer up onto the wall with a rope, and then climbing after him. Hanomer could search in the depths of the fortress while the rest watched his back and prepared to fight their way out. No one believed this reckless plan had much chance of success, particularly since the dogs would smell them, but their situation was desperate.

The others were trying to get some sleep before the attack, while Dave kept watch. Suddenly, he saw lights come on in the uppermost chamber of the central tower of the fortress, and then a long horn blast sounded. When he started to see activity on the walls, he groaned. "Our chances have just gone from 'low' to 'no chance at all,'" he said aloud.

He woke the others and they joined him in his watch. Presently Dave saw three figures emerge in the lava field, wending their way around the smoking fissures. Dave pulled out his binoculars to make sure—"It's Al, Tandor and a third guy!" he exclaimed. "They seem to be making a run for it! We have to move. They don't know where we are."

Dave, Arlana, and Hanomer raced down to the lava field and chose a path to intercept Al's group. Loping around a pillar of hardened lava, Dave saw the third man ahead of him. Weasel stopped and tried to go back. Al stepped around him. "Dave," Al said, as he ran up to give Dave a bear hug. "I am so glad to see you. This is Weasel. He helped us escape and we promised to take him with us."

"We've got to move," said Dave. "Not that way. Follow me."

They retraced their steps until they rejoined the rest of the group. Just then, the main gate opened and a troop of soldiers marched out along with several hounds of prodigious size.

Weasel said. "They're going to find us. Our only chance be to make for the escarpment and go down the terraces out of their reach. This way."

Dave looked back. What he saw made him shudder. A figure about three meters tall was striding among the solders. He had a head like the Necroans, disproportionately small for his body. At this distance Dave couldn't see clearly, but the bearded face seemed familiar.

Weasel led them in a northerly direction over broken country. The baying of the hounds was rapidly getting closer. The dogs had their scent. Horatio growled, but Dave put his hand on the shaggy pup, who then followed Weasel quietly.

Abruptly, the group came to a deep chasm, a rent in the rock that descended down at least forty meters. The path they had been following crossed a stone bridge. But the bridge was broken and impassible. Dave stopped short. He heard the faint sound of water gurgling below them. He looked up and down the mouth of the chasm. There was enough light that he could see a fair distance with his enhanced night vision. "We go left," he said heading off at a lope.

After travelling about five hundred meters, they crossed a rock arch that spanned the chasm. They were in the midst of crossing when the first of the hounds—trained *lupi*—appeared. Their baying had stopped, but Dave heard the quiet brush of their paws on the rocks. These *lupi* were black as night with yellow eyes, and bodies the size of ponies. The *lupi* bolted straight for the rock bridge.

Makalo, Thomas, and Linder fired their rifles and Dave saw *lupi* shudder and stumble as the bullets went home. With Horatio behind him, Dave ran back across the rock bridge, drawing Gram as he ran. He finished off the wounded *lupi* as one by one they staggered forward to continue the attack.

On the other side of this first chasm there was a second. Dave led the group to the nearest end of the chasm mouth, where they rejoined the path they had been following before their way was blocked. As they neared the trail, they saw their pursuers appear on a rise about seventy meters behind them, separated by the chasm.

"Down!" said Linder.

As one, they dropped to the ground. Dave looked back to see who was coming. The huge figure, well-muscled, wearing clothes that were far too small for him, strode to the edge of the precipice and shouted.

"Gleeson, I know you're there," he said in a deep voice. "You're looking for Pam. You'll never get her. She's dead. I killed her myself and threw her body to the jackals in Sheol. You won't find my son, Little Thomas, either. I sent him far away to be brought up properly.

"I want you to think about what I've just said as I hunt you down, flay every piece of your skin off of you, and use all my arts to give you the slowest, most painful death possible."

What's going on? thought Dave. *What's happened to Bigelow? Is this what he came here for—to be made into a monster?*

Just then Dave heard a rifle shot. Bigelow, the monster, spun, and dropped out of sight. Instantly, his troops started surging along the chasm toward the stone arch. Others fired crossbow bolts across the narrow chasm. Dave heard three more rifle reports and three crossbowmen collapsed. The rest took cover.

"Let's move," said Linder.

The group followed Weasel north at a quick trot until he stopped and waited for them to catch up. Ahead of them yawned the edge of Sheol. A bank of clouds hovered thousands of feet below them.

"How do we get down?" asked Linder, alarm in his voice.

"I don't know," squealed Weasel. "I only be getting us here. We find a way down. I thought we be having time."

"Let's head northeast along the edge," said Linder. "That way we can't be cut off and surrounded if some of those soldiers find another way to the edge."

With Hanomer, Dave, and Arlana leading, they hurried along the edge of Sheol looking for anything that could be a pathway down. More *lupi* were coming up and the baying grew closer.

Finally, Hanomer disappeared over the edge followed by Arlana. Dave waited at the top and guided the others down. Weasel started descending just before Dave. As he followed, Dave thought he saw movement a few hundred meters back, from out of the corner of his eye.

Dave dropped over the edge of Sheol and came upon a series of ledges that formed crude steps—giant steps since the ledges were several meters apart. Far below he saw Hanomer climb down to the next ledge, with the others following in single file. Dave was last. *Hurry, hurry, hurry. Bigelow's men are coming up fast*, he thought in near panic as he watched Arlana ahead of him.

At last, Arlana climbed down to the next ledge and Dave followed her. Once there, he ran along the rock shelf for thirty meters and then climbed down to the next giant step. Fortunately, there was an overhang, so they were only visible to the soldiers at the top when they crossed the lip of the next step.

They must just about be here by now. Dave could almost feel an arrow enter his torso. Still nothing happened. When Dave finally reached the fourth ledge, the first arrows began to fall, but they were wildly inaccurate.

The ledges ended and Dave could see Hanomer leading the group down a long chimney. The descent was time consuming and arduous, but Dave kept going. Arlana, lithe as ever, moved tirelessly. Dave was almost down, when he heard shouts and then gunshots. He increased his rate of descent to a reckless pace. When he was about ten feet from the bottom of the cliff, above a narrow fissure, he saw several large bipedal reptilian creatures emerging from under his position. Linder, Makalo, and Thomas fired again as the Trogs charged. Dave leapt down with Gram unsheathed. A rifle shot ricocheted off the rock, narrowly missing Dave's shoulder. A Trog threw an octo at him, but Dave sliced it in half with Gram. No more Trogs emerged from the tunnel. Dave charged silently after the now-retreating Trogs, cutting down any that turned to fight. Linder and Al followed. The fighting ended.

"Is everyone okay?" asked Dave. Gradually those still under cover came out of hiding and joined the group.

"Where's Weasel?" asked Al. Dave called his name, but there was no answer. Tandor said, "He is here." Weasel lay dead, skewered by a Trog spear, his body partially hidden by a dead Trog that had fallen on top of him.

"He wanted to get away from Zambor to escape the Trogs," said Al, sadness tinging his voice. "But a Trog killed him anyway," he added. "He was a good man, despite his name."

"Without him, we would have had an impossible task in prying you out of that fortress," said Dave quietly. "We owe him a great debt."

The group made a litter of Trog spears and carried Weasel's body away from the site of the battle, further into the terrace woods. Using the spears, they dug a shallow grave on a small hill that rose out of the trees, and buried Weasel, covering his barrow with stones. Al fashioned a small cross and said quietly, "Friend Weasel, you trusted and helped us. I wish I could have brought you out of captivity to your people. May our loving God have mercy on your soul and grant you grace."

The company planted the Trog spears in a circle around the barrow and stood with heads bowed. Hanomer, who was on watch, came to the hill and said, "Friends we have to move. Our enemies are not giving up, but have found the way down. They will be on us in a few minutes."

"That Bigelow never gives up. Lead on Hanomer," said Al. "Take us down to the next terrace as quickly as possible."

Chapter 31

Desperate Measures

Bone tired, Dave rested his hand on a boulder to steady himself. He felt the cool texture of the limestone. Horatio wiggled in his backpack. Dave felt the lup whelp's breath on his neck. He needed to see how far Bigelow was behind him, but Dave was so tired that his eyes didn't focus. He concentrated on a large oak tree, hoping his vision would clear.

The group had descended to the fourth terrace, much to Tandor's vehement objections because of the dragon danger. But Bigelow did not relent. His band of about one hundred men kept pursuing them, long after Zambor's men had turned back.

After Dave's eyes focused, he looked back on the terrace wall. Bigelow's men were using a doubled-up rope to lower themselves down the steep precipice. Dave had seen at least one soldier fall as Bigelow drove them at a pace bordering on lunacy.

Dave took a deep breath. The air had been thick in Abaddon, but now it was definitely thicker. He felt as if he were inhaling liquid. Still, that's how he had felt when he first came to Abaddon. His body had acclimatized and he had forgotten all about the change as it became "normal."

"This can't go on," Dave muttered to himself. No one had slept in more than forty-eight hours because of the pursuit. If they had to attempt the next descent in their present physical state, there would be trouble. He had already seen the others stumbling as they fell asleep on their feet. He, Arlana, and Hanomer, although tired, were much more alert than the others. It was another one of the remarkable things he had learned about his new "Ancient" body. He could go without sleep for much longer than before. He would be able to make it down one more level to the fifth terrace, but the others could not, and there would be casualties. A lot of casualties.

Dave walked over to Al and Larsen who had both fallen asleep as soon as they had sat down. Arlana touched his arm. "Husband, they can't go on."

"I know, sweetheart, I know."

Makalo, Thomas, and Chartrand were supposed to be on sentry duty, watching the progress of Bigelow's company, but they had also fallen asleep.

I hope their guns have their safeties on. Dave thought.

"Husband, do you want Hanomer and me to scout ahead to find a place where we can make a stand so they can get some sleep?"

Dave looked at her, thinking furiously through his thick mental fog. "But there's a hundred of them. We'll never hold them off. And even if we did, once we're pinned down, they can rest as well as we can, and simply bide their time until they have us."

"Except for the monster that used to be Bigelow, they are as tired as we are," said Arlana. "We three can hold them off, while the rest of our party get some sleep. We have rifles and much ammunition. That should discourage them. If not, we'll just have to trust for a chance to get away." She looked up into the overcast sky and sniffed. "I think it will rain soon. That may help our eventual escape."

Hanomer approached. "Friend Dave, the next precipice descent—to the fifth terrace—will kill us if we continue blacking out on our feet, as our friends are doing now. Let friend Arlana and I scout ahead. I think I see a promontory northwest of us, right on the edge of the escarpment. It looks promising. With a defensible position right on the edge of the precipice so that we can't be surrounded and starved out, we can hold them off with our rifles. Perhaps we can even find some water. The farther we descend, the more rivulets and streams seep out of the cliff wall."

Dave nodded his agreement. Arlana and Hanomer set off at a fast pace.

Dave checked the rifles of his companions, verified that his own had a bullet in the chamber and sat on a rock to watch Bigelow's progress down the rock face to their terrace. The soldiers were two kilometers away, but Dave could see them clearly. Suddenly a scream echoed off the far precipice wall as another of Bigelow's men fell to his death. The other soldiers in Bigelow's company stopped. He could see some argue with Bigelow while others seemed to be asleep, slumped against the cliff wall. Suddenly Bigelow lifted one soldier high into the air, threw him off the cliff, and then went to the nearest soldiers and kicked them awake. The band started down again, but they went slowly whenever Bigelow was off haranguing someone else.

Arlana is right. They are spent. Thought Dave. *They won't come on very fast.*

Dave alternately watched Bigelow's progress from his lookout post, and then descended the shallow slope to the cliff edge to help keep himself awake. After about forty-five minutes of this routine, Arlana and Hanomer returned.

"Do we move?" asked Dave.

"We covered about two kilometers along the edge of the precipice to the rock projection Hanomer saw. That pier of rock is like a finger of hard stone that has not eroded away. We will have to descend a shallow ravine and climb the thirty-pace tower of natural rock rising out of the cliff. The back is very steep. A section fell into the abyss long ago," explained Arlana.

"We could make a stand there, friend Dave," said Hanomer, "but the climb up the stone finger is very difficult."

"What do you think, Arlana?"

"It's strong, but there is no cover. We would be attacked on three sides and the top is bare. The climb looks more difficult than it is. I think we wouldn't stand a chance. Fighting against so many under a hail of arrows would force us to take cover. The first wave would overwhelm us. There would also be no water at the top. Bigelow could simply wait us out if he wanted."

"The song of our last stand would be remembered for generations if there were any bards to compose and sing it," added Hanomer wistfully.

I don't really want to us to be thinking about last stands. There has to be a way out, thought Dave.

During his walks to the cliff edge, Dave had thoroughly examined the cliff face leading to the fifth terrace. "What about down there?" he asked. The first part of the drop was not vertical but sloped away at a seventy-degree angle. About one hundred meters down, a buttress of rock that looked like a thirty-meter tower of pancakes rose vertically. Beyond this sentinel, the precipice resumed its descent at a much steeper angle.

"We would be under constant arrow bombardment from up here," said Arlana.

"True," said Dave, "but with that pancake structure, it looks like there are lots of ledges and overhangs to protect us. Furthermore, Bigelow has a difficult choice. If he sends his men straight at us, we'll be firing at them for the whole descent, since the sloping cliff is smooth with little cover. If he stays far away from us for the descent, say over there to the left or off to the right, he still has to send them across the face of the steep slope to reach us."

"I don't think we could get the others down that slope safely," mused Arlana.

"Arlana, use our ropes with bowline hitches and string them all the way to the bottom of the pancake tower. Everybody ties to the rope with a loop knot that tightens if they fall. I'll go last and bring the ropes with me."

The three of them fastened the ropes they needed, with Hanomer fastening the one furthest down. Twenty minutes later, Dave and Arlana began to wake the others. Arlana led the first one to the ropes while Dave went to the others and convinced them to give one last push. He finally roused Al and walked with him to the precipice edge. He made a loop and attached it to Al's climbing harness with a carabiner.

"We had to move," mumbled Al. "I've been praying that you found something."

"I think we have," said Dave, "but we have to make an easy descent to our mini-stronghold. One more push and then you can sleep."

Al groaned, but said nothing more. The others were already part way down. A couple had slipped, but the loop and the angle of the slope helped to stop them before they crashed into the others. When they did fall, Arlana or Hanomer were there to help them find a foothold and get moving again.

Dave climbed back to his lookout position with one of the rifles and crouched down. For the last hundred meters beyond the lookout, the trees thinned and low bushes dotted the landscape. He stayed out of sight, but had a good field of view.

There was no sign of Bigelow's men yet. *They're as tired as we are*, thought Dave. He hoped his friends were making rapid progress, walking down the steep slope of the cliff with the aid of the ropes. The prospect of rest and sleep had seemed to spur them to one last superhuman effort.

Just then Dave saw some movement in the distance. A few figures with bows and swords staggered out of the trees and stumbled toward him. It was a long shot, Dave didn't have the heart to fire at them.

Linder would have done what's necessary, thought Dave. *I'm being sentimentally stupid.*

Dave saw two soldiers on the left of the line stumble and lie still. Then Bigelow's towering figure appeared and, in a rage, he kicked the two soldiers to get them up. One responded and came stumbling forward. The other one collapsed again. Cursing, Bigelow drew his sword and swung at the fallen soldier. Dave's eyes clouded over with anger, and he raised his rifle and took a shot at Bigelow. He shot wide. Bigelow dove back into the woods before Dave could fire a second. He could see the enemy not only advance directly on them, but also move left and right just inside the woods.

They're outflanking me. Time to go.

Dave, ran back to the precipice edge, untied the rope and threw it over the cliff. Doubling his own rope over a knob of rock, he moved down the steep incline as fast as he could. Coming to the end of the first rope, he untied the end, and stuffed it into his pack. He repeated the procedure with the second rope.

He was just about to untie the third and final rope when he saw, far above him, heads peering over the edge in the gloom. He started to untie the knot when he looked up and saw Bigelow towering over his men. "There he is! Shoot him," Bigelow screamed.

Dave pulled out his knife and cut the last rope, then looping his own rope over the projection he started to run down the seventy-degree slope as fast as he could using the rope to keep his feet on the smooth rock. Arrows began to clatter on the rocks around him. He recklessly increased his speed and then leapt the last five meters to the base of the of the pancake tower. *That jump would probably have done serious damage to my knee in my old body. Thank goodness for that healing plant!*

He didn't bother to untie the third rope, but pulling his own rope free, got to his feet and began to ascend the first pancake of the tower, moving toward the back to get out of the sight of the archers. He moved quickly. Sheltered by the stone tower, he began to climb up to his friends. A rope snaked down from above. He looked up and saw Al at the other end. Al gave him a thumbs up, and Dave ascended rapidly.

At the top, he found his friends under an overhang peering up the cliff.

"What's Bigelow doing?" asked Dave.

"I think he's going to send them straight down to follow you. We'll make them pay," said Chartrand. Dave gave his rifle to Larsen who was the better shot. The shooters picked their targets and kept up a slow but steady fire.

"Well, it didn't take long to discourage them," said Chartrand. "Now they're moving to plan B. They'll likely come down in two bands, one on the left and one on the right. I'm expecting them to rush us from both sides at once."

Nothing happened for about twenty minutes. Then Linder shouted, "Here they come." The gunfire continued sporadically, but the shooters had trouble seeing their enemies in the dim light. When Bigelow's men had crept closer, they began to fire crossbow bolts. It became very dangerous for Larsen and the others to return fire. Five minutes later, twenty, maybe thirty of Bigelow's soldiers were crouched under the lowest pancake overhang at the base of the tower. Two more parties had taken cover and were firing their crossbows to keep the defenders pinned down.

"Here they come again," said Linder. Simultaneously, the soldiers started the ascent while arrows rattled off the stone overhang. Dave gave up trying to lean over to shoot and began to drop rocks over the edge to dislodge the attackers. He heard a shriek as a rock found its mark.

This is what I was afraid of. It's only a matter of time, Dave thought.

Chapter 32

Brown Dragons

There was a curious whoosh in the air that had a high-pitched whistle as an overtone. Tandor shouted. "Everybody hide; I see dragons!"

Dave instinctively flattened himself on the rock floor. Overhead, he heard a loud flapping like the crack of a whip. A smell similar to a sickening mixture of kerosene and burned flesh assailed his nostrils. The shrieks of the men on the mountain side sounded terrifying.

"We need to stay still," hissed Tandor. "If those dragons see us, we're dead."

A wave of heat passed. The screaming stopped, and an eerie silence followed, broken by an occasional crunching sound.

Where's Arlana? thought Dave. *Lord, let her be all right.*

After a few minutes more, Dave couldn't wait any longer. He peeked out over the edge of the ledge. About forty meters away, a dragon was eating something. It's long brown worm-like body was the size of a horse. Suddenly, it looked up from its meal and two pale yellow streams of liquid shot out of its mouth. After about two meters, the streams converged and caught fire clinging to whatever surface they touched as if they were inflammable jelly. A bush caught fire. The dragon launched itself into the air, labored to fly back and forth parallel to the cliff. It passed within a few meters of Dave and his friends as it banked away, then glided into the depths, disappearing into the cloud far below.

"Whew," said Dave, feeling shaken, "that was close."

"If I had not seen it with my own eyes," said Al, "I would not have believed that a living creature could spew fire without burning itself up."

"I think that dragon we saw was a small brown dragon," said Tandor. "Our dragon lore says the larger red dragons, and especially the big mean black ones never fly this high."

Linder and Larsen appeared from around the other side of the rock. "So now what do we do?" asked Linder. "I watched that dragon for a while. It had to work very hard to fly at this air pressure, and rested several times on the cliff face. But if we descend, those dragons will be able to fly more easily and linger longer. Descending, we're facing certain death.

"But if we climb up, how do we know that Bigelow won't be waiting for us at the top?" asked

"Is Bigelow even alive?" asked Larsen.

"I didn't see him among his men," said Chartrand. "He's so big we couldn't have missed him if he was there."

Dave felt relieved at the sight of Arlana and Hanomer who had just descended from higher in the pancake rock formation.

"Friends," said Hanomer. "I will scout up to the previous terrace to see if it's clear, and determine whether Bigelow has given up. When I come back, we can decide what to do."

Hanomer left their stronghold and climbed up the cliff. Even with their excellent night vision, Dave and Arlana could barely follow the *Hansa* up the cliff face. Soon he was lost to view.

Dave climbed down the pancake tower to retrieve the rope he had left behind in his mad dash to safety. It had been burned up by the dragon's fire. At some places, the flammable jelly was still burning as it clung to the rock face. There was no sign of the enemy soldiers.

Dave climbed back up to the tower ledge. Even though he and Arlana were worried about Hanomer, they finally succumbed to sleep.

Dave felt Linder shake him awake. "Hanomer is back," said Linder.

Dave and Arlana joined the others.

"Friends," said Hanomer, "the news is not good." I was able to climb up to the next terrace without being seen. I even crept into Bigelow's camp—yes Bigelow is very much alive and furious. They are afraid to come back down here because of the dragons, but they will keep us from coming up. They are cutting down trees, soaking them with pitch and building a fire wheel to roll down on us.

"What's a fire wheel?" asked Dave.

"Friend Dave, a fire wheel is a thick tree trunk with spokes to make a long cylinder. Smaller tree trunks join the outer edge of these spokes. The inside of the cylinder is stuffed with branches. I see pitch being heated on fires. These fire wheels are mounted on a platform at the edge of the cliff. When all is finished, Bigelow will soak them with pitch, light them, and roll them down the steep slope at us.

"I heard Bigelow discuss his plans with his lieutenant. Bigelow believes the fire wheel will bring up the dragons again if he can't burn us out. Even worse, I heard Bigelow discussing with his lieutenants that Zambor is expected to return at any moment with more men from outlying settlements. Bigelow will meet Zambor on the third terrace after he burns us out and attracts the dragons. There will be so many men up there watching for us to emerge that it will be very difficult to evade them. Some of the more courageous will even sneak down to the fourth terrace to hide and watch to see if we try to out-flank the watchers and re-emerge. I think we must go down to the fifth terrace to be safe."

"Fire wheels!" said Dave. "If they crash and stick to the pancake tower, we are so dead."

"We'd better go down to the fifth terrace," said Linder. "No one will follow us that far down. Then we can retrace our steps all the way to the great cliff where the terraces end and climb back up."

"I have a bad feeling about this," muttered Dave.

Chapter 33

Fire Wheels

"We've all had a bit of sleep while Hanomer was away. We have to move now," said Linder. "From the sounds of it, they could begin to roll their fire wheels down at any moment. If the wheels don't kill us, those brown dragons will come back when they see the conflagration and finish the job for Bigelow."

"Leaving is one thing, but where do we go?" asked Larsen.

"We head down one terrace level, turn left, and follow the terrace all the way to where it stops. Then, we climb back up hoping like hell—pardon my French (here Linder glanced out of the corner of his eye at Al)—that Bigelow isn't waiting for us when we climb up."

I have a bad feeling about this, thought Dave. *Why am I so sure that Bigelow will be waiting for us when we try to climb up? That guy seems to hate us beyond all reason.*

Everyone seemed to catch Linder's urgency and they began to pack up their equipment. Below their stacked-pancake tower of rock, the cliff again became vertical as it descended to the next terrace about a five hundred meters below. They doubled up a rope, and Hanomer descended to a ledge that would serve as a suitable resting point. Linder went next, and then was followed by the others.

After the others had all started down, Arlana began her descent. Dave looked up the cliff to Bigelow's position nervously. He saw a flare of light and heard a loud rumbling noise like a freight train rolling down a nearby track. "Incoming," bellowed Dave. "Everybody duck and get a safe hold."

Dave leapt over the edge and slid down the rope, feeling a sharp pain as his leg scraped on the rock. Reaching Arlana, he pressed her into a shallow indentation and covered her with his body. An enormous crash shook the cliff side directly above him. Dave looked up. The stacked-pancake rock formation seemed to shudder at the impact. Huge, flaming, tree trunks fell into the depths to either side, broken in two by the pancake tower. The heat from above was intense, but luckily the indentation in the cliff and the bulk of the tower shielded them from the cascade of embers. Dave's surprisingly cool living cloak spared them from the worst of the heat. Their climbing rope fell away, burning, into the depths.

It was too hot to move. More fire wheels rolled down from above and some of them wedged into the base of the pancake tower, making it an inferno. Embers and fiery slivers of wood kept falling into the depths. Smoke swirled around them. Dave saw Arlana take her living cloak and pull a corner over her mouth. Dave tried the same and was amazed that the cloak filtered out the choking smoke particles, and he could breathe more freely again.

Then Dave heard a beating of wings. *Here they come*, he thought. He glanced down and could see a brown dragon laboring to ascend at a forty-five-degree angle along the cliff face. Dave kept perfectly still and quiet. He looked and saw three more brown dragons ascending, obscured from time to time by the smoke from burning logs that had fallen to the next terrace. Smoke from burning fragments lodged on the cliff wall, rolled in black billows along the cliff face. The first dragon was now above him. Time seemed to slow. Finally, he heard voices—strange deep voices in a strong accent but speaking the Common Tongue with many words from the Ancient Tongue mixed in.

"Much fire," said a deep rasping voice.

"But no meat," said another.

"I can hardly breathe," said a third. "Much smokier than dragon fire. Must go down soon."

"Fly along edge, one more time. Then we go and report," said the first.

Dave heard the flapping of huge wings as the dragons took off. After five minutes he saw them gliding into the depths and sighed in relief. The thick, black smoke from the pitch had diminished and visibility had improved. The brown dragons seemed to have gone.

Dave pulled a rope from his pack, doubled it over a rock, and let Arlana make the first descent. He followed and soon reached the ledge where the others were waiting. A small stream of water seeped out of a shallow cave and everyone was quenching their thirst. Dave was relieved when he counted heads and realized that everyone was there safe and sound.

"We were so relieved and thankful when we saw Arlana begin to climb down. I thought you were goners so close to the fire, with dragons hunting you," said Al.

"Goners?" asked Arlana.

"He means that he thought we'd been killed," said Dave.

"Ah," said Arlana. "We also thought we were 'goners' at first. I am grateful to Linder and Hanomer for urging us out of there in time. The pancake tower is an oven. We would not have survived."

"Funny thing," said Dave, "those brown dragons can talk. It's pretty much the Common Tongue with a smattering of the Ancient Tongue. And they're understandable."

"Are you serious?" asked Larsen.

"Aye, he is right," said Tandor. "The Spectres—the evil ancient sorcerers—descended into the depths so that they could change themselves through their arts into monstrous, powerful beings that were so large they could only live in Sheol. Still, at their core, under the monstrously changed flesh, they are still men."

"You mean like Bigelow, only worse?" asked Dave.

"Aye, only worse. They pursue and hunt others, especially men, whom they hate."

"And that's where we're going," muttered Chartrand.

It was twilight when they finally reached the fifth terrace. The plant life changed again. In the darkness, almost every plant exhibited phosphorescence. There were brilliant blues, greens, and reds. One particularly striking tree, a cone-shaped conifer about ten meters tall, had large globular fruit that glowed white as if the fruit were decorations on a Christmas tree. The ground vegetation was broken up by enormous trees with trunks about six meters in diameter.

Linder led them on a route that skirted the bottom of the cliff as they headed along the terrace in a northwesterly direction. Their path was littered with broken rock, which made hiking slow and difficult, so Linder picked a route just inside the edge of the forest.

Dave saw several rodent-like creatures the size of jackrabbits scurrying through the bushes. Presently, they came to the edge of a large, elongated lake. The waters were dark when compared to the phosphorescent flora.

"We need to rest, Linder," said Al. "I'm so tired I can hardly stand up."

Dave, Arlana, and Hanomer had no trouble at all seeing in the phosphorescent evening light. From the jumble of rocks, a fast-flowing creek tumbled over the broken rock into the lake. Following the creek back, Dave saw it emerge as a torrent from the cliff face. There were several other tunnel mouths nearby—the stream must have changed its course several times in the distant past.

The group fell exhausted onto the pebbly floor inside one of the cave entrances while Dave took up a guard position just outside. Arlana came and put her arm around him. "Husband, I'm going to get some sleep. I will wake up to relieve you so you can get some rest." She kissed him gently and then walked back into the cave, swaying and stumbling from lack of sleep.

Dave tried to stay awake but had to get up and scramble around the cave entrance when he caught himself starting to nod off. Finally, Hanomer arrived with his small bow to watch in his stead. Dave fell asleep as soon as he wrapped himself in his cloak, and put his head on his pack.

Chapter 34

The Debate

When Dave awoke, it was daylight. The others were already busy repairing their torn packs, washing, or hunting for food. Dave took some time to wash in the creek in the cave mouth. The water was surprisingly warm. When he had rearranged his pack and properly stowed the ropes that he had put away hastily the previous night, Hanomer returned with a brace of trout from the lake.

"The fish were biting, friend Dave," said Hanomer cheerily. Hanomer finished cleaning and fileting the fish and soon, the delicious smell of fresh, pan-fried trout wafted over their little encampment. Dave realized how hungry he was.

They sat in a circle, eating together, naturally taking up positions that let them watch for danger from all directions. *We have unconsciously become a veteran fighting force,* thought Dave. *I can't think of a better set of friends with whom to take on a dangerous quest like this.*

With the sun in the southwest and the cliff wall just behind them, this terrace would be in shadow for most of the year except possibly in high summer. It was definitely a land of shadows. Dave's attention was attracted by Linder's voice suddenly rising in vehemence.

"Al, the only reason you're unwilling to admit that all the unusual flora in these isolated ecosystems is another striking example of evolution at work, is because you're so damn committed to your Christian worldview you can't even accept this obvious evidence to the contrary."

Those two! thought Dave. *Here we are fighting to stay alive and they still have time to get into one of their interminable evolution debates!*

"So, Floyd, are you claiming that evolution is a defeater for a belief in Christianity?"

"Not only do I say it, but Christians say it tacitly by fighting against it so much when the evidence for evolution is so overwhelming."

"I think you're dead wrong, Floyd. Let me show you why with a thought experiment. Let's say that you had an application on your cell phone that let you scan back in time and actually see what happened in the past rather than speculating about it from circumstantial evidence."

"Ah this is new. Where are you going with this?"

"Bear with me. There is a point to this thought experiment. Let's say your phone was able to verify every one of the claims made by Darwinism and our current theory of the origin of our solar system and planet: the earth is about five billion years old. The moon was formed by a massive collision with the proto-Earth, and then water from comets formed Earth's oceans.

"From this hostile environment then, the incredibly complex, stereospecific molecules of life formed, and self-assembled to give rise to life on earth. In other words, my hypothetical app supported Darwinism on every point."

"I'm listening," said Linder.

"Now let me use our little time machine for one more point. Let's say we went to Palestine about two thousand years ago and followed the life of a carpenter's son who claimed he was Yahweh, the God of the Israelites come in the flesh. And our cell phone application showed that this carpenter had indeed died by crucifixion and then rose from the dead followed by his inexplicable disappearance. Then, using our app, we confirmed, as we read in the book of Acts, this risen carpenter was not dead, but continued to interact with his followers. What do you think, given those two verifications by our app, has Christianity been defeated?"

"You tell me," said Linder.

"I think that if Christ had not risen from the dead as the Apostles and all the first-generation Christians testified, then that is definitely a defeater for Christianity and our confidence in the truth of our beliefs is null and void. But being wrong about Darwinism is not a defeater."

"But doesn't that mean the Bible is wrong and misleading when it talks about creation in seven days and an earth without a sun or moon?"

"Not necessarily. The Bible can always be right, but our interpretation of it can be wrong. Look, from my understanding, God is always reaching down to communicate with us. That means He steps into time and talks to us using *our words* and our *world view*. When he spoke to the Hebrews, he constrained Himself to their language and their understanding of the world in order to communicate. After all, if God is using the Hebrew language to communicate, then He can't very well speak in quantum mechanical terms or relativistic terms since the Hebrews at that time knew nothing about such things and had no words capable of communicating those concepts."

"So, if that's true, why do you guys fight against evolution so much?"

"Because many of us simply don't believe that the evidence supports it. I don't believe that one can grow these complex living organisms by chance, no matter how long one waits—and we don't have to believe it because we don't need evolution to explain the world. If one believes in God, one doesn't need a timeline that is so long that the patently impossible apparently becomes possible. We recognize that no practical experiment can be carried out that verifies this evolutionary assertion. You see Floyd, *loss of Darwinism is a defeater for your world view of Materialism*, but real substantiation of Darwinism is *not* a defeater of my theistic world view. That's why you and others in the atheistic camp have to go to such enormous lengths to defend Darwinism. That's why many people in your persuasion spend so much time taking anyone to court who even criticizes Darwinism in the school system. You can't just say 'since we all agree to search for the truth, let's put all the data on the table and talk about it.' You cannot even have a reasonable conversation about evolution with us. It's your camp that has to shut down the opposition. You have things exactly backwards."

"Al, you're saying this two-thousand-year-old carpenter is still alive and presumably is still talking to you? Do you realize how crackers that sounds? If you weren't my friend and I didn't know you as I do, I'd figure you were an escapee from a mental institution."

Dave could hear Al chuckle. "Yeah, I know Floyd, I get that a lot. Yes, my relationship with Jesus is very real to me, but I can see how it looks to someone with different beliefs."

Dave couldn't help smiling. Arlana came over to him, sat down, and nestled up to him. "Why are you smiling? I haven't seen you smile for days, my love."

"Why? I guess just listening to Linder and Al go at it with their verbal jousting made me realize that some things never change no matter the circumstances. Their passionate arguing brings back a little bit of home. It tells me things are not as hopeless as I'd imagined. I know it doesn't make a lot of sense, but these little throwbacks to our earlier history seem really important to me now."

Arlana hugged his arm. "You have told me, husband, that there is nothing we can do and nowhere we can go where we are separated from the Creator and His love. You sometimes talk as if you don't believe that."

"I do believe it, but belief happens at two levels. On one hand, I believe it with my mind, but I don't always believe it with my gut. It's like swimming across a lake. My mind may rationally tell me I can easily make it, but when I step into the water, my gut still tells me I can't. I guess hearing Linder and Al arguing has made my gut trust that we will get through this."

Dave saw Larsen stir. It was the signal he had been waiting for. Everyone had had a chance to sleep and now was they must not dally. "Honey, it's time to get moving. We want to get off this terrace as soon as possible before the dragons return and find us."

Dave and Arlana rose and shouldered their packs. Horatio also jumped up on a rock and nuzzled Dave. Dave could have sworn that the lup had already grown larger in the short time he had had him.

Linder and Al also busied themselves closing their packs, having set their discussion aside for another day. Dave led the group along the fringe of the lake. It was more than a kilometer wide but must have been about twenty-five kilometers in length. The trees were sparse on their side of the lake and undergrowth was minimal. Walking on the green sward was a delight after all of the rock work.

Dave saw a globe conifer ahead. It smelled faintly of cinnamon. The air was calm so Dave could hear birds chirping in the trees, and the rustle of one of the jack-rabbit-sized rodents in the long grass. The turf was springy and made walking easy.

They crossed two more streams that descended from the escarpment and emptied into the lake. After about three hours, Dave, leading the group, rounded the end of a small bay and saw the end of the lake about two hundred meters ahead. They rested there for the night.

The next day brought them to a point where the cliff wall formed a large bay like the letter U. The terraces followed the indentation. Looking across the arms of the U, at a distance of about eight kilometers, Dave could see the many layers of terraces bending back to follow the contours of the rock bay or canyon. Over this section, the edge of the next terrace did not block a view of the terraces below.

Linder stopped beside him and cursed quietly. "Because of this bend, we can see all the terraces across this gap down to the cloud cover. That means if Bigelow has scouts anywhere above us, they'll see us as we round this bend and tell him exactly where we are."

"The forest is pretty dense," said Dave. "If we stay in the trees and push it, maybe we'll get by."

"That's what we'll do," said Linder. "I won't chance walking at night. We'll rest again and leave at dawn, and move as fast as we can until we round that rock promontory on the far side of this canyon. With luck, there will be some fog or rain to give us a bit of cover."

The next morning, the cloud cover was well below them. Linder took to the forest and pushed them hard all day. Finally, by mid-afternoon, they left the rock bay and were out of sight of prying eyes from the higher terraces. Linder called a halt.

After a short rest, they resumed their journey. Linder led them at the fringe of the forest next to a rock fall from the escarpment on their left. The trees had huge leaves and were criss-crossed by vines resembling lianas. Dave could hear bird calls as the treetops teemed with life. They had travelled for about a kilometer when Dave was startled by a loud roar, which was quickly followed by a second roar.

Everyone stopped and looked at one another in fear. Linder whispered, "No talking, let's move at double quick time along the fringe of the forest. I don't like the sound of that at all." Hanomer ran up and joined Linder, paralleling his course inside the forest.

After another kilometer, Dave heard a sound high in the trees and saw a large brown ape peering at them. A moment later, it raced through the trees, deftly using the lianas to jump from tree to tree. It was heading into the forest.

I wonder if that thing was responsible for the roar, wondered Dave.

After twenty minutes, Linder stopped. The trees ahead of them were filled with dozens of apes. The largest roared a challenge.

Linder led them up into the broken rock to their left to put some distance between them and the apes. However, the apes kept pace, racing from tree to tree. Finally, the big ape roared again, and the apes climbed down and charged.

Chapter 35

Green Dragons

The loose rock slowed the ape's charge. Linder fired a warning shot and the apes halted. The leader roared again and the apes came on. In desperation, everyone now shot at the charging apes with guns or crossbows.

The apes retreated back to the trees and Linder led his companions on. The group was traversing the broken rock just under the cliff when the apes attacked a second time. Linder and the others took up defensive positions and shot at the first group of apes that raced toward them, but others kept coming. Finally, Linder led his friends to a shelf of rock right up against the cliff face. Dave realized it was only a matter of time before he and the others were over-run. Some apes were climbing the cliff wall; others continued to press the frontal attack.

Dave heard a whooshing sound and a fountain of flame erupted on the cliff face, swallowing up several of the apes. Dave saw in amazement that a long green shape glided along the cliff face, periodically spitting out a jet fluid that burst into flame as it shot towards the apes. Dragons!

The flames scoured the apes from the cliff face. The apes in the rocks raced for the trees. There must have been a dozen dragons. They ignored Dave and the others but settled on the charred carcasses of the apes and fed greedily. Dave and the others huddled together, not moving, surrounded on all sides by dragons.

Finally, one of the dragons approached the group. Chartrand raised his rifle, but Linder put his hand on Chartrand's rifle to lower it. The dragon had a long narrow body but was about the size of a horse. Its wings were folded in. It stopped about five meters away. It spoke in a raspy voice. "Who are you, and why are you here?" The words were Common Tongue, mixed with words from the Ancient Tongue, but the pronunciation was hard to understand.

Arlana stepped forward and spoke. "We are fleeing enemies from above. We were driven here and wish only to go to the end of the terrace and ascend to the Abaddon plain."

"None who come here make it out. Do you not know that?"

"When death follows closely, a dangerous path must sometimes be chosen. Are you our enemies?"

The dragon seemed to consider this question and turned to face the other green dragons. Turning back, the green dragon said, "Green dragons have many enemies. Perhaps you number among them. We are outcasts, hunted by the brown, red, and black dragons. And so, we hide up here, where the brown rarely come, and the red and black are much too large to fly.

"We are hunted by the brown dragons too," said Arlana. "If we have a common enemy, perhaps we can be friends?"

"We have no friends. If we were to be friends, I can see how we could help you, but I cannot see how you would help us."

"Who can say what would happen if we fought by your side. Why are brown dragons your enemy? Are they not your kindred?"

"Because our color has turned from brown to green, we are marked for death by all the other dragons. We have given up our enmity with all things, and seek to return to the Creator. We are cursed by our designers, the ancient sorcerers, with this color change to green, which tells all other dragons that we must be killed because we are abandoning the great rebellion to return home. With dragons, all inward thoughts are manifested in outward appearance. Alas, not all evil can be undone. We can go no higher, and to descend lower is certain death. We are living on the front porch of death. Yet we are not sad that we have changed our thinking."

"You said just now that you were designed. What do you mean?" asked Dave.

"Long ago the great sorcerers descended into Sheol to shape terrible creatures that could not live in the lighter air. They first turned men into dragons through their arts. Dragons are first hatched as brown dragons. As they grow and their wicked deeds increase they become red. Finally, they become huge and black, the most terrible dragons of all.

"The sorcerers knew that some might turn back and not follow through with this rebellion. They made us so that if any chose to go back, our color would turn green and so all other dragons hunt, kill, and eat green dragons as traitors, as escapees to the Great Enemy. I led my friends up here hoping to survive for a while. We are enemies of the great apes who steal our eggs and kill the very young hatchlings. That is why we destroyed them."

"And in doing so, you have earned our gratitude and favor. Let us see if we can repay you in some small way?" answered Linder.

"Begging your pardon, sir," said Tandor. "I have been living in the upper terraces most my life, and I have never heard of green dragons."

"That may well be true little sir. We are a blemish to be destroyed, and so are rarely seen. Yet can you deny you see a green dragon before you—a green dragon which has not burned you to a cinder on the spot? Would any brown, red, or black dragon act the same?"

"Aye you are right, sir. No dragon I ever heard about ever talked before scorching us."

"We are grateful," said Arlana, "that you came to our aid unasked. Is there anything we can do for you?"

"What could weak, little things do for us? Could you save us from the black dragons? Could you give us safe homes?"

"We are weak and small," said Dave, "but what we can do, we will do for you." Here Dave gave a sweeping bow, which seemed to amuse the dragon. Changed as the dragon was, there was still a hint of humanity about him.

"I can't help but sense a kinship with you. Is it our old human blood calling to us? Perhaps, someday you will help us in unexpected ways, but right now you need our help. These woods stretch for days' walk for slow creatures like you. As soon as we leave, the apes will fall on you again. Walk now as fast as you can, and we will circle overhead. When night falls, climb well up the cliff. Tomorrow we will come again and lead you to our caves."

For the rest of the day, the band skirted the edge of the forest. Dave saw the occasional ape watching them from high up in the trees, but none ventured down. When twilight began to fall, Linder led them on a climb to a ledge, about forty meters up the cliff. It turned out to be a shallow ledge so the band had to disperse to several small ledges in the vicinity. Dave, Arlana, and Hanomer took turns keeping watch. In the first watch, Dave saw the apes searching the rocks at the foot of the cliff, but none ventured up.

The next morning as the band climbed back down, the dragons returned. Within two hours the forest ended, and they crossed another stream that emptied into a lake. Ahead they saw rough terrain of hill-sized rocks with crevices in between. The green dragon, who had given his name as Hiszt on the second day, crouched on a rock waiting for them.

"Since the apes stole our eggs, we watch this approach to our caves constantly. You will be safe from the apes now," rumbled Hiszt. "Keep walking down this cleft between the rocks and it will take you through." Hiszt rose, unfolded his wings, labored to get into the air, and sped away northwest.

Two more hours brought them to a flat, rocky, open space. Up ahead the terrace narrowed to a point, ending at a sheer cliff, unbroken by terraces. The cliff was dizzying in its height. They crossed a stream and walked all the way to the end of the terrace. Looking down, Dave could see clouds far below them. Ahead of them, stretching kilometers into the distance, was a sheer cliff that would be an impossibly arduous technical climb. *I guess this means we have to go back up. What happens if Bigelow is waiting for us?* thought Dave.

Turning to look at the cliff just above the dwindling terrace, Dave saw a series of caves. Hiszt waddled out of one of them, came over to a pool and took a deep drink. After his drink, he waddled down to them and said, "You may use the cave on the far left. We have no need of it."

The dragon sniffed the air and looked up. "I think it will rain tonight."

Arlana bowed again and thanked him for the use of the cave. Everyone felt safer once they were in the cave. They built a small fire and prepared supper. There were numerous birds on the cliff above them and Hanomer brought them enough eggs to make a delicious meal.

They held a council among themselves and everyone agreed they needed to climb up to the Abaddon Plain as soon as possible before Bigelow cut them off. Since the trail ran very close to the edge here, they ought to be able to find it and head back to Seth.

The next morning, they bid farewell to Hiszt and started the arduous climb. This was much harder than the descent. Arlana and Hanomer took turns climbing up solo to fasten a rope to a rock. The others followed, using the rope as support. More than once, a loose rock came hurtling down, forcing everyone below to flatten against the cliff wall.

After two gruelling days of climbing in the rain they reached the first terrace and made camp. Dave had an uneasy feeling. His sense of foreboding had been growing since the climb started.

Hanomer approached him. "Friend Dave, my sense of danger has been growing. I feel an inner prompting that tells me that I must climb up tonight to see if we are walking into an ambush. If I am not back by morning, friend Arlana can help you climb up.

Hanomer started climbing the wall. For a while Dave watched him go until Hanomer disappeared over a ledge. The slope of the cliff kept him out of view. Dave told Arlana what Hanomer was doing, and then both told Al. They checked their gear and turned in with Linder taking the first watch.

Dave felt himself being shaken awake. Hanomer's badger-like face hovered over him. Hanomer's hand on his tail held a light gourd that cast a light about the cave. "Friend Dave, we must leave now. Bigelow is here. By morning light, he will send scouts down to the first terrace. He has out-thought us, guessed our every move, and is setting an ambush."

Now Dave was wide awake. He and Hanomer soon roused everyone else. Hanomer had to explain everything twice, including exact details of what he had seen to convince everyone that they had to leave. Reluctantly, at Al's insistence, they packed up and moved to the cliff edge leading to the second terrace.

"Bigelow may be a snake, but he's smart. His scouts will find evidence of our campsite, you know," said Linder. "They'll follow us as far as Bigelow can drive them. We'll have to go all the way down again."

"I know," said Al, concern edging his voice. "I don't know where we go next."

Chapter 36

Dragon Riders

Bigelow had again been chasing them for several days. Dogged and determined, yet with despair hovering around the edge of his thoughts, Dave climbed down as rapidly as he could to the fifth terrace. He still felt a twinge of vertigo because of his fear of heights, but he seemed to have spent so much time climbing in Feiramar, and now in Abaddon, that his fear only gave him occasional pause.

Hanomer had chosen not to lead them down the same route by which they had ascended; they were a few hundred meters east, where they could make the descent more rapidly. Suddenly Arlana who was next to Dave hissed, "Down!" Dave flattened himself onto the cliff face as a brown dragon banked away from the cliff wall below them and dove for the fifth terrace.

That was close, thought Dave. Luckily, the monster's attention had been directed below.

Dave squeezed Arlana's shoulder in thanks. The gliding brown dragon disappeared behind a buttress of rock. Then the air was riven by a roar, followed by a loud hiss—as of sizzling bacon on a monstrous scale—such that the sounds seemed to shake the cliff face.

"I think the green dragons are under attack by the browns," said Arlana.

Arlana and Dave were about one hundred meters above the terrace. They climbed down to a narrow ledge and waited for the others.

"Did you see that brown dragon that buzzed us?" asked Linder. Dave nodded.

"The green dragons are under attack. You can hear the fighting. What do we do?" asked Arlana.

"Friends," said Hanomer, "there is only one honorable thing to do. The green dragons rescued us, so we must come to their aid."

There was silence. Al looked from face to face. "He's right. I'm going to go with Hanomer. Is anyone coming with us?"

"Which way do we go?" asked Dave.

"Follow me," said Hanomer as he began to race along the ledge. The ledge ran unbroken for about seventy meters, when a gap of about seven meters stopped them short. Hanomer had already fastened a rope across the gap and had disappeared around a rock buttress up ahead. Arlana and Dave crossed first, followed by the others. They left the rope behind.

When Dave rounded the buttress, which took some climbing, he saw Hanomer up ahead on hands and knees peering cautiously over the rim of the ledge. About two dozen brown dragons were circling overhead. The outnumbered green dragons could just be seen crouching at the entrance of their caves, sending forth bursts of flame whenever a brown dragon strayed too close. Dragon carcasses littered the rocks in front of the cave. It looked like the bodies of two greens and one brown. Several brown dragons landed and approached the cave entrance nearest to them, blasting a continuous wall of flame.

The three gun-bearers arrived. "Can you take a shot?" asked Dave.

"Makalo is the best shot, let him shoot. We're running short on ammo," said Linder.

Makalo took aim at the dragons on the ground who were attacking the cave.

"Friend Makalo," said Hanomer putting his hand on Makalo's arm, "do not shoot from here. The brown dragons will see us after your first shot. We have no chance to survive here. Follow me. I know a better place nearby." Hanomer carefully climbed down another seven meters and moved horizontally along the cliff face. Then he disappeared.

Dave and the others followed, warily keeping an eye on the battle raging ahead. He saw what Hanomer had been making for—a small opening in the cliff. Makalo took up his position at the mouth while the others went down the narrow passage. Makalo fired off his first shot. Then another, then a third.

"How did you know about this place, Hanomer?" Dave asked.

"When we were staying in the cave that Hiszt assigned to us, I went exploring while you were asleep. I found many passages and openings. This was one of them."

Just then Makalo raced back from the opening and bolted down the passage. "Head down the passage," he shouted, "They're coming!" Everyone jumped up and raced down the winding passage. Dave heard a whoosh behind him, felt intense heat, and sniffed a sweet smell that reminded him of a chemistry experiment he had once done. The companions flattened themselves against a wall.

"Are they following us in?" Dave whispered.

"I don't think so," said Makalo, "the outer passage is filled with flame. I'm not sure those dragons could squeeze through the narrow parts of this passage."

Dave could feel a draft blowing from the lower parts of the cave, feeding the raging fire with oxygen. *It's like standing in a chimney*, he thought.

They started moving again, further down the passage with Hanomer in the lead. Luminescent lichen covered the walls of the passage and gave it a dull green-yellow light. After a few minutes, the cave began to feel familiar to Dave. He saw daylight up ahead.

Makalo edged forward along with Linder and Thomas. All three began shooting. Dave had to see what was happening. He crouched at the cave mouth, deafened by the shots. Green and brown dragons were flying in tight circles like an aerial dogfight with columns of flame filling the air. He watched one brown dragon first dodge, then fly straight into another's flame, light up like a burning torch, and plunge over the edge of the terrace into the depths beyond.

Then the battle was over. The rocky terrace in front of the caves was littered with carcasses of dragons, most brown but some green. The greens dragged the brown carcasses into a heap and then burned them. They dragged the greens into the far cave.

Dave and the rest of the band sat at the cave mouth and pulled out their trail rations to eat as they watched for a second attack. After some time Hiszt came out and approached the band. "Little ones, you have saved my mate and my tribe. How did you kill those browns from a distance?" Hiszt was looking at Makalo.

Dave answered for Makalo who was still learning the Common Tongue. "We have a weapon, Hiszt, that can kill at a distance. It shoots a small piece of metal at great speed that causes enormous damage when it hits its target."

"A formidable weapon. Arrows are deadly but can be avoided. Your weapon's teeth I cannot even see. Come we must talk. You mustn't think we are safe. The browns that escaped know where we are and will bring more browns. Many more. We will not survive the next attack. By the way, what brought you back? I thought you were returning to the uplands?"

"We were walking into a trap, Hiszt," said Arlana. "Our enemy was waiting for us up top, and even now, is climbing down to pursue us. We don't know where to go next."

"Wait here," said Hiszt, "perhaps we can help each other." Hiszt waddled back into the burial cave.

After about twenty minutes the dragons emerged and stood in a semi-circle before the companions. "We have a proposal to make," said Hiszt. "An alliance between our peoples. We have to find a new home. We have to leave. What if we took you across the gulf to your home? We can't fly that high, but we might find a home near you. What do you say?"

Dave and Al looked at each other, "How would you take us across the gulf?"

"You would ride. It means we have to glide to lower elevations to support the extra weight of a rider on our backs, but we can fly long distances and make it to the other side."

After a few minutes of discussion, the dragons and the group of friends agreed upon an alliance. As Dave looked at the proposal, he realized they had no choice but to accept it. Attempting to traverse the sheer, six-kilometer-deep rock wall that separated them from the terraces below Seth or climbing down to Sheol and then edging along the shore of the infernal sea to climb back up to Seth, both seemed sure tickets to extinction.

The next step was to pair the riders with the dragons. Hanomer was too small to ride alone, so he was paired with Arlana. Dave and Hiszt talked about how to keep the riders on the dragons should they fall asleep during the long flight and discussed the idea of improvising saddles.

"I am sorry now that we burned all the brown dragon carcasses," said Hiszt, "dragon skin, especially from the belly, would make an excellent 'saddle' as you call it."

Al and Hanomer searched the cliff leading to the sixth terrace for any dragons that might have crashed there. Sure enough, the bodies of two brown dragons had become wedged into the cliff as they fell. Al and Hanomer skinned the belly hide off the carcasses, and using ropes, worked the hides back up to the Hiszt's terrace. They also collected dragon intestines for the sewing required.

The process of scraping the hides clean, washing them in the creek, and drying them took days. When they were dry, Dave used his tree-grown knife, Skene Dhu to cut the tough dragon hides into saddles and strips. With Dave handling all the cutting, the others spent time completing the sewing.

While the companions were finishing the saddles, they had some disquieting news. Hiszt had sent several of his scouts to search the lower levels. One had spotted a growing band of brown dragons that was gathering four terraces below them. They were preparing for an assault. It appeared that time was running out.

With renewed urgency, Dave and the others worked in shifts to sew the straps and loops that served as stirrups onto the saddles using the dragon intestines.

The work progressed so slowly, Dave expected the brown dragons to appear and begin another battle.

The weather turned ugly. Black roiling clouds churned far below them. *Maybe the browns can't fly in this weather*, thought Dave, redoubling his effort to finish his work.

Three days later, the saddles were finished. The friends strapped the saddles onto the dragons, and allowed them to take a few test flights without riders. When the dragons were comfortable, Dave mounted Hiszt who was poised at the edge of the cliff, while Arlana and Hanomer clung to Hiszt's mate, Hirsa. Dave had sewn loops into the front and back of each saddle, to which the riders could attach their climbing harnesses, so that even if they were unconscious, they would not fall out of the saddle. The others were also assigned to dragons.

The clouds below them were still thick, and the scent of thunder was in the air. The storm had not abated, but had turned more violent.

Hiszt turned his fanged head to Dave. It struck Dave as eerie to see the long snake-like neck allow the dragon's head to turn completely around and look at him.

"Are you ready little one?" asked Hiszt. "We will all have to glide a long way before the air is thick enough for us to fly with your additional weight. We will try to stay close to the bottomless cliff where few dragons fly."

Dave swallowed hard as he looked over the cliff into the black clouds flecked with lightning bolts. The clouds seemed to be rising. "I'm ready."

Hiszt launched himself off the cliff with wings extended wide. The other dragons also launched themselves into the air and plummeted until the air was thick enough that they could bear their burdens. They quickly picked up speed even though their angle of descent was only about ten degrees. The dragons banked left and glided along the long, sheer, unbroken cliff, which Hiszt had called the Bottomless Cliff.

There's no place to land. Either we make it or crash, thought Dave.

They plunged into the thick clouds where visibility was zero. Dave hoped the others were nearby. Hiszt began to emit some high frequency chirps, that struck Dave as being completely incongruous considering the dragon's size. Lightning blinded Dave's eyes, and the sound of the thunder was deafening. How could he keep from getting disoriented? *If we fly into that cliff wall …*

Hiszt banked right, still emitting his cry. The wind picked up until Hiszt was buffeted back and forth. Still chirping amid the cacophony of thunder, Hiszt continued to glide.

We're totally lost, thought Dave. *We'll never find the other side.*

Chapter 37

The Black Dragon

Dave could barely see Hiszt's head, but he could hear the dragon laboring, sucking in air in prodigious gasps. *This can't go on much longer,* he thought. But his ears popped, so he knew they were still descending.

In the midst of the gloom, there was a part of Dave's mind that encouraged him. Somehow his confidence grew that they were going to make it. The winds were so strong that he knew no other dragons would be flying in this weather. *Perhaps the weather is a blessing rather than a curse?*

The clouds began to thin and were replaced by a torrential rain that beat down, soaking him. Far below, Dave saw little white flecks. *Waves,* he thought. *It can't be! We can't be this low.* Ahead he saw a small island, perhaps about ten kilometers in diameter with a squat volcanic cone rising about five hundred meters. Hiszt banked and made for the island, his high-pitched chirping changing tone. Dave looked behind him. He could see the other dragons following them. Hiszt stopped chirping and landed on a flat, rocky, crevice-filled plain near the volcanic cone. Dave leapt off and began to remove the saddle.

"No, no," gasped Hiszt. "Leave it on. We're in great danger here. Too tired to go on. We need rest, but have to leave quickly. We're on the Infernal Ocean in Sheol. Middle of dragon country. Never meant to come here."

The rest of the dragons had also landed and discharged their riders. Dave could smell the fear in them as they cowered in whatever cover, crevice, or boulder, that they could find. Hiszt was breathing in great gasps and had lain down like a giant dog, resting.

Dave began to explore their surroundings. Two of the smaller, riderless dragons were not as tired as the others and had begun to waddle away in the storm looking for food. They wandered toward the volcanic cone, and Dave saw a flash of fire coming from the direction of the cone. Curious, he climbed a small rise and saw the green dragons had surprised some goats and were devouring the goat carcasses greedily. Then another movement caught his eye. From the rocky knees of the volcanic cone, a black head, the size of a pickup truck emerged from the mouth of a huge dark cave. The head reared back and a jet shot from its mouth like water from a powerful fire hose. The stream, which was many times the size of what he had seen from any other dragon, caught fire, the flames engulfing the feeding green dragons. Dave's shout of warning was lost in the storm and the whoosh of the conflagration. The two greens were charred instantly. The huge head of the black dragon was followed by a long neck the diameter of a sewer pipe, and forelimbs like tree trunks.

Dave watched the black dragon lumber from its lair, stop at the smoldering carcasses of the two green dragons and begin to feed, then Dave raced back to the others.

"Black dragon," he cried between gasps, "it's coming." But no one moved. Several of the green dragons were so exhausted they lay sprawled on the rocks. But Al and Linder understood the urgency of their situation and implored the green dragons to get onto their feet. The creatures were too weak to fly but took shelter among some large rocks on a peninsula at the end of the small island.

Dave heard a rock roll on the other side of a ridge. *The Black Dragon!* He pulled Gram and flattened himself into a crevice less than a meter wide just in front of him. As he lay there he felt a wave of despair. Then a powerful compulsion assailed him, commanding him to show himself. It took his full will power to keep from standing up. He knew if he succumbed to the summons, his life would end in a fiery inferno.

He looked over his in horror as two of the smaller green dragons came waddling over a low rise, moving as if against their will.

I have to do something, thought Dave. *I can't just let the black dragon fry them.*

He looked back at the black dragon as it came over the low ridge from. Its forelimbs were thick, keeping its body about two meters off the ground. Its gigantic wings were folded in. The huge dragon's eyes were focussed on its prey. It never looked down. Its legs shook the ground as it lumbered toward his hiding place.

Sinking as far into the crevice as he could, Dave looked straight up. *Dave, you're an idiot. Only an idiot would do what you're about to attempt.* Adrenaline made him almost giddy. *It's barbeque time! And I'm on the menu.*

The scaly underside of the black dragon's head came into his field of vision, then passed by. Now he saw its colossal neck, almost two meters in diameter. He could see the muscles rhythmically contracting and expanding as it prepared to vomit more destruction on its prey.

Dave sat up and climbed out of the crevice. The ground shook with each of the monster's footsteps. Dave ran towards it, expecting this foolhardy attack to be his last.

Lifting Gram, Dave threw his full weight behind an upward thrust, into the beast's throat. He expected resistance. To his utter astonishment, the blade sliced through the ten-centimeter-thick scales as if they were soft butter and slid, effortlessly, into the dragon's neck, right up to Gram's hilt. Black blood oozed out around the blade. The monster roared, twisting and lifting its neck upward. Dave, still holding desperately onto the hilt with both hands, was lifted upwards. Gram sliced through the dragon's neck bone and muscles like soft tallow. More black blood spewed out of the gaping neck wound.

The monster reared onto its hind legs, freeing Gram. In its death throes, the dragon began to topple.

I'm lost, Dave thought. *I'm going to be crushed by tons of dragon.*

Al was just putting his saddle away when he heard a shout. In the distance he saw Dave stumbling toward him down the side of a ridge. Black dragon? *What is Dave shouting about? Doesn't he know we are trying to maintain a low profile?* Then the words began to make sense, and a wave of fear stirred him out of his torpor. Al went over to his green dragon and worked hard to rouse it out of its sleep. The dragon rose slowly and began to move away from Dave's shouting. Al ran alongside it, urging it to move faster until it moved out of sight behind a pile of rocks.

Al turned back to help Dave, who was still waving his arms frantically, while occasionally looking back to the top of the ridge. Al saw Dave look at his feet, and then disappear into the ground, just as a monstrous black head appeared in a cleft of the ridge. It fixed its stare on two smaller greens, which were off to Al's right, and only now were moving to follow the other greens to safety.

Al could feel despair engulf him. Amid his powerful sense of hopelessness, he also felt a strong urge to walk toward the black dragon. *No! Lord, help me!* A voice inside him was urging him to take cover. He saw the two greens change direction and amble back toward the black. The black's forelimbs came through the ridge cleft, and it lowered itself close to the ground, its concentration fully fixed on the two greens stumbling reluctantly toward it to their doom.

Al dove for cover just as he heard a loud whoosh and felt intense heat. He looked up, unable to move. He knew he was going to die, but he couldn't take his eyes away from the black dragon. *I'm sorry Pam. I didn't do enough. I should have seen Bigelow coming.*

A figure rose out of the ground as if out of the grave underneath the dragon. He thrust a bright sword thrust up to the hilt into the neck of the black dragon. The black roared, twisted and lifted its neck high, dragging the sword bearer into the air. But not for long. As he was lifted from his feet clinging to Gram with both hands, the sword cut a long gash across the dragon's neck and the figure fell back to the ground. The dragon rose on its hind legs, its partially-severed neck flopping, as black blood rushed from the wound spraying everywhere. The monster fell forward, its bulk covering the ground where Dave had fallen.

Arlana rushed by Al with a cry, followed by the others. Coming to his senses, Al raced after her. Arlana skirted the pool of dragon blood, and tried to push on the monstrous carcass to get to Dave, but to no avail.

A moment later, Arlana cried with delight, as Dave crawled out from under the beast, dripping with its blood. He had managed to dive into his crevice just as the dragon had fallen.

Between sobs, Arlana kissed Dave's face repeatedly, saying "You fool, you fool ..."

"Honey, I'm a mess and I don't even know if this stuff is dangerous. Look what I've done to my living cloak. It's soaked."

Holding him at arm's length she looked at Dave critically. "Your cloak will be fine. By tomorrow it will have cleaned itself and the dragon blood will provide some much-needed nutrients to keep your cloak healthy. But your buckskin is ruined. You will have to bathe and change into your other clothes."

Hiszt ambled up to them. "I have never heard of a black dragon being killed by anything other than another black dragon. Your sword, little one, has a mighty bite. Still we must leave soon. The other black dragons will know that one of theirs has died, and they will come."

Hissa approached them. "We can't fly in this weather and neither can they. Should we not rest while we can, and then leave with the small ones as soon as the weather breaks?"

As if to underline her words, the rain began to fall again in torrents. They did not want to stay near the black's carcass but moved back to the peninsula where the green dragons curled up like huge cats and fell asleep.

Al was just about to fall asleep when he saw Dave walk into the surf and wash the dragon blood off of himself as best he could.

Al was hot, even with the rain. He stripped down to his shorts, and rolled into his blanket, wondering if he would wake up before the other black dragons arrived.

Chapter 38

The Eighth Terrace

Dave woke up as he felt Arlana move. He was wearing nothing but his shorts, which had also served as a bathing suit, but he was still hot and sweaty. "Now I know why they call this place Sheol," he muttered to himself. "It has only two thermostat settings: hot and muggy, or really hot and muggy."

Arlana sat up. How beautiful she looked in her brief top and shorts. She looked at him and seemed to read his mind. "Don't even think about it husband. The weather is clearing."

"What do you mean?" he asked, feeling himself reddening. "How did you know what I was thinking?"

"You seem to forget, husband, that you're not the only one with an acute sense of smell. Among Ancients, we derive much more information about what others are thinking by our sense of smell than Lesser Men do. So, yes, I can usually tell what you're thinking and feeling. A more mature Ancient, with training, would be able to disguise the signs. However, you aren't able to disguise them very well yet."

"So, you've always known," he gulped, "—what I've been thinking and feeling?"

"Pretty much, although early on I did not know how reliable my sense of smell was when it came to Lesser Men. But when you became one of us Ancients, I knew I was reading you correctly. But enough talk, husband, we have to prepare ourselves and the dragons for flight as quickly as possible." She smiled as Dave felt his embarrassment growing.

The wind was abating and the rain had diminished to a drizzle by the time the dragons were ready. When Hiszt indicated that the weather was barely acceptable for flying, one after another the dragons lumbered into the wind and flew off in a westerly direction. The Infernal Sea had monstrous waves but the dragons gained enough height to miss the tops of the worst of them. They occasionally saw an island far below. Some of the small islands had ruins on them, but no one wanted to stop. Then the flight settled down to one long monotonous endurance trial. Dave fell asleep.

When he woke, the wind had died down and Hiszt had climbed high enough that the huge waves looked like small whitecaps. They were just below the cloud layer. Hiszt flew into the clouds and began emitting his periodic chirps. Dave could hear the nearby dragons chirping as well.

Soon they were through the clouds and could see the terraces rising as steps before them. Hiszt seemed to be at the end of his strength. He headed toward the terrace ahead, found a meadow, and landed. He was breathing hard.

"I cannot go higher, little one," he said. "I think we are at the eighth terrace from the top. The trees should protect you from the other dragons, but beware, red dragons can reach this height. Without you on our backs we will fly as high as we can and find a place to rest. We'll come back and protect you as well as we can on your climb, after we have rested and have our strength back."

"Do you want me to take your saddle off, Hiszt?"

"No, little one. It's not very heavy. We may need them again, and you can't carry them up in your climb. We will leave them on, trusting that you will join us on the fifth terrace to take them off."

After those words, Hiszt and the other dragons took flight, resuming their climb to the higher terraces. Linder led the band into the woods. The gloom increased since the trees were tall and hardly any light reached the forest floor. Dave let Horatio out of his pack. He had only travelled a short distance, Horatio sniffing at his side, when he noticed high up on a tree, a two-meter-diameter web, coated with water drops and glistening in a beam of sunlight like diamonds. Even at this distance the strands were the thickness of string, not at all the gossamer threads of spider webs that Dave was used to seeing.

The webs appeared with greater frequency but remained high in the trees. Finally, the band came to an area dense with webs. They could see the occasional arachnid, with a body about thirty centimeters in diameter waiting by the webs, some of which were three meters across. Ahead Dave saw an enormous cocoon or hive about thirty meters high. A steady stream of arachnids was going in and out of holes in the globular structure.

"I don't like the look of this," said Linder. "Let's try to go around by heading left. It looks like the webs are strung a little less densely there."

With Dave leading, they headed a substantial distance to the left. The frequency of the webs did decrease, but after a while they increased again, and off in the distance Dave saw another one of the large cocoons.

"These arachnid colonies seem to go on for ever," said Dave. "Maybe we should just cut our way through the webs at the edge of the colony. We must be less than two miles from the next escarpment."

There was general assent, so Dave took out Gram and sliced through the web impeding their way. A spider with a dinner-plate-sized body rushed along the strands toward them.

"Let's move people," said Linder. "Dave, you lead and clear the way. Chartrand you're with me."

Dave was running through the trees, cutting any webs that impeded their progress. Behind them he could hear a buzz and a click like chitin scraping against chitin. The frequency of the webs decreased remarkably and they were now confined to the tops of the trees.

Dave slowed to a brisk walk to let everyone catch their breath and to let Linder and Chartrand catch up. The spiders came running through the trees. "There's something big coming. Let's go at our best pace." Without waiting for an answer, Linder sped past them. The others followed. Dave waited, looking back. He could see nothing, but Horatio growled and then darted after the others.

Dave took up the rear-guard position following the others. After about fifteen minutes the trees thinned out and the escarpment to the next terrace loomed before them. Linder was already picking his way across the broken rocks that littered the base of the cliff.

Following, Dave could still hear the buzz and click, although a little more faintly. When he reached the escarpment, the others were already climbing up the cliff. Dave lifted Horatio into his pack and began to climb also. As he looked back he saw a torrent of arachnids pour out of the woods and begin to crawl over the rock field. Dave shouted to the others and began to climb as fast as he could.

The arachnids had no trouble with the cliff and were able to walk up without apparent difficulty, like spiders climbing a house wall.

Dave reached a ledge. "I think we need to make a stand here," said Linder. "I don't want them attacking us while we're climbing."

Picking up what loose rocks they could, they threw them at the arachnids as they methodically climbed toward them. When a rock hit one of the monstrosities, there was a satisfying plunk and the writhing spider plunged onto the rocks below.

"Look!" shouted Dave, pointing down to the rock field. In the middle of the rock field, a sedan-sized arachnid with a swollen abdomen over one-half its length climbed onto a large rock and watched the attack with its multifaceted eyes.

"Makalo, Chartrand. Get your rifles and take that queen out. Maybe that will stop the attacks."

They needed no further urging, and within seconds they were targeting the grotesque head. The arthropod reeled when bullet after bullet ripped into its head and thorax. It slipped off the rock leaving a smear of green blood.

The attacks stopped. All of the arachnids that had been approaching them stopped. Then slowly, one-by-one they turned around and headed back down the cliff.

Everyone sat down from their exertions to catch a quick rest. Dave anxiously watched the edge of the forest to see if the arachnids would return.

Finally, Linder said, "We may as well get going. None of us want to stay this close to those things in case they come back.

Chapter 39

A Parting of Ways

After two days of hard climbing they reached the fifth terrace. Hiszt and the dragons had returned shortly after Dave and the others had met the arachnids. A platoon of dragons glided back and forth along the cliff, keeping an eye on their climb. From the cloud pattern below, it looked like another storm was in full swing in the depths of Sheol.

The fifth terrace on the west side of the Sheol rift was a pleasant place with green meadows, huge trees, and abundant game. The dragons liked it; it was at the limit of their flying ability and so would rarely attract brown dragons from below. They only lacked caves for sleeping and nesting.

After the group caught up on their sleep, Linder called a planning meeting. "Al, we're wondering where we're heading next."

Al looked uncomfortable. "I don't know Floyd. I know I can't go home, because I know in my heart that Pam and Little Thomas are still alive. But I'm out of ideas." His voice quavered. "Everywhere we have looked has turned up evidence that they are probably dead."

"For my part," said Linder, "I've set up the mini cell tower and scanned for Little Thomas' signal. I've seen nothing. I know it's hard Al, but perhaps circumstances are telling you it's time to head home."

"I just can't do that." Al couldn't keep the pain from showing on his face. "Listen, my friends, you have done more than I have any right to expect. You've gone far beyond the call of duty. I think you should head home. I cannot in good conscience keep you here when I don't even know where to go next myself."

The discussion continued. Thomas, Dave, Arlana, and Hanomer were adamant about staying with Al. Linder, Makalo, Chartrand, and Larsen reluctantly decided to head home. Tandor had remained silent but said after everyone had decided, "I will go with them in case they meet some of the rebel clan, but I will return once they are safe on Abaddon Plain.

Al gave Makalo a hand-written power of attorney on paper taken from his notebook, along with a short video recorded on Makalo's cell phone in which he signed the document, instructing Makalo to look after his assets and continue to pay the taxes on his property. He also gave each of his returning friends a letter reaffirming that he was on a long trip and could not be reached. The next day, the home-bound friends packed up their gear for the long climb up to the Abaddon plain. Linder had left the mini station for Al. Dave was reorganizing his pack when he overheard Al and Thomas talking.

"Thomas, shouldn't you go home too? You have done more than any brother should."

"I don't want to leave you in the lurch again, Al."

"And you won't. Dave, Arlana, and Hanomer all have a reason for staying, since this is their world even if it isn't their continent. They will look after me, and they will help me keep looking. It would be a comfort to me to know you are safe at home."

Thomas reluctantly agreed to return with the others.

The group that remained worked to make their camp more permanent. They built lean-tos, fished, and smoked the fish they caught, repaired torn clothes, and patched their shoes.

Four days after Thomas and the other five had left, Dave returned to the dragon camp from another early morning fishing expedition. Although Al loved to fish, he had not gone with him, but had gone off by himself. Since he had not yet returned, Dave worried about his friend and went in search of him.

He found Al sitting at the edge of the cliff with his Bible open and head bowed as he looked into the depths of Sheol.

I guess he needs some time to pray about what to do next, thought Dave.

He quietly went back to camp and found Hiszt waiting for him. "Little one," said Hiszt, "we found a cave a one-minute flight away, but it may be a rock-borer hole. Will you come explore it with me?"

"Sure Hiszt." Hanomer and Arlana wanted to come along. The three walked northwest in the direction Hiszt had indicated. An hour later they saw Hiszt standing at the entrance of a round hole about three meters in diameter. A slope of pebbles the size and shape of marbles at the entrance of the hole looked like the discharge from a pipe.

"Sure looks like a rock-borer hole to me," said Dave. "Can you burn rock-borers with that fire of yours?"

"I think fire would cause them some discomfort, but not kill them. The great black dragons have such power in their thoughts that they can control rock-borers and bend them to their will. I am too weak to do that alone, but I thought, little one, since I have felt the power of your thoughts during our flight, perhaps together, we would be strong enough to control one."

"I'm listening."

"Put your hand on my flank to link telepathically."

Dave did so and found he no longer had to speak.

Reach out with your thoughts little one. The rock-borer will feel cold and unfriendly.

Dave did so, but could feel nothing.

Let us go in, little one. Keep your hand on my flank and keep reaching for contact with your mind.

They walked forward down the tunnel. Dave tried hard to concentrate, but also had to mind his feet to avoid stepping into narrow chasms that frequently crossed the tunnel floor.

Do you feel the mental touch yet, little one?

Dave tried hard and could almost imagine a mental presence—cold and alien. The mental touch grew stronger.

Yes, I think I feel it Hiszt.

They walked further. So far, they had not reached any side corridors. The mental touch grew stronger.

The rock-borer is coming toward us, Dave. Now bend all your strength with mine to turn it.

They stopped walking and Dave reached out to that touch and commanded it to turn. It kept getting stronger. It kept coming nearer.

It's coming for us. We have to get out of here, thought Dave to himself.

Steady Dave, steady. Keep thinking. Keep commanding.

Dave shoved his fears aside and redoubled his effort to control the rock-borer. He sensed the creature stop. There was a change in the coldness he was feeling. Implacable enmity became reluctant compliance.

Now we make our dragon dens, little one. Thank you. We are not strong enough alone to bend a rock-borer to our will, but now that we control it, one of us will be sufficient to guide it. We will have to take turns until the job is done. I think once we release the beast it will flee to keep us from snaring it again.

Hiszt took the first shift. Dave and Arlana went back to camp and packed up their supplies. It was mid-afternoon and Al had still not returned, so they left him a long note describing what they were doing and where they were, should he need them, and inviting him to join them when he was ready. They picked up their supplies and made camp outside the rock-borer hole.

Dave tried to catch a couple of hours of sleep. Arlana and Hanomer looked after hunting and meal preparation to enable Dave to take his shift in controlling the rock-borer. When Dave awoke, he ate a quick meal and went to look for Hiszt. He found the dragon further into the cave than he had left him, and saw the rock-borer working his way back to their main camp, cutting an opening every hundred meters.

As long as the rock-borer was under control, one of them was enough to control it. To assume his shift, Dave joined Hiszt in the link. While linked, Hiszt described his plan of four entrances. He had already caused the rock-borer to cut a passage into a small cavern, which would serve the females as a nursery.

Dave took over. Hiszt stayed with him a few minutes to make sure Dave didn't lose control of the rock-borer, then said "goodbye," and waddled out of the tunnel.

It was a grim six hours as Dave concentrated on directing the rock-borer, but doing so proved to be easier than he had anticipated. The rock-borer made a thumping sound as it advanced. It seemed to know exactly where it was in the rock, so over time, Dave was able to capture a mental picture of where they were with respect to the cliff face. If the rock-borer found a crevice or a pit, it could discharge the gravel there, otherwise it had to make the trip back to the nearest tunnel mouth to spew out the debris.

Dave drove the borer on relentlessly. His control of the creature was getting so good that he could stop the rock-borer when less than six inches of rock separated the beast from open air. In this way, he constructed a set of secret entrances, which would only be opened in an emergency.

This is fun!

Chapter 40

Hope Renewed

Al had spent a number of hours at the edge of the cliff reading his Bible and praying for guidance. Should he give up his search and follow his friends home? But he couldn't do that. He couldn't give up. But where should he look? He had no direction and no plan. While he had something to do and a plan to follow, he had hope that shielded him from despair. An intolerable weight seemed to settle on his mind. For some reason two Bible verses popped into his mind. The verses, from the book of Exodus tell of the Israelites at the moment when they were trapped against the sea by the pursuing Egyptians. The people were in despair facing the prospect of a return to slavery or death.

> *"The Lord will fight for you, and you only have to be silent."*
> *The Lord said to Moses, "Why do you cry to me? Tell the people of Israel to go forward."*[5]

Wow, thought Al. *Given my circumstances, those verses smack me in the head. I didn't think I'd ever read a verse that told me to stop praying and get busy. I need to get up. Enough praying and thinking. I need to do something. I need to find a next step to take.*

He got up and walked back to camp. The birds here were beautiful but much larger than higher up in the lighter air. Even the

---

5   Exodus 14:14-15

butterflies and dragon flies were huge, although they didn't bother him. He walked through the woods and jumped a rivulet that made its way to the cliff edge and then left the woods for a stretch of meadow that fringed the cliff face leading to the fourth terrace. Al heard a rock clatter down from the cliff face. Looking up, he saw two tiny figures climbing down. He pulled out his binoculars—it was Larsen and Chartrand.

What's happened? Where are the others?

Al rushed back to camp looking for the others but found no one there.

At his own tent, he found Arlana's note, which described Dave's tunnel-cutting activity with Hiszt. At any other time, he would have been amazed, but now he felt he needed to find out what had brought his friends back to him in such a rush.

Donning his climbing gear, he took his best rope and ran to the cliff edge. Chartrand and Larsen had made rapid progress. They had just dropped a long rope down to the broken rock at the bottom of the cliff and Larsen was rappelling down. Al steadied the rope.

"Where are the others?" asked Al. "Are they alright?"

Larsen was out of breath from his exertions. He shook the rope to signal for Chartrand to descend.

"All okay—couldn't reach you by phone—news," he gasped. He bent over and breathed air in great gulps. "Need water and food."

While Larsen recovered, Al steadied the rope for Chartrand. After Chartrand was down, Al led them both to camp and gave them water and some cold fowl from the previous night's dinner.

When they had slaked their thirst and taken the edge off their hunger, Al asked, "Now what's going on?"

Larsen began the story. "We made the climb as fast as we could to the fourth terrace. We realized we were quite a way northwest of where we wanted to be, and decided to travel some distance along the fourth terrace. Tandor knew of a rebel encampment nearby, so we climbed up to the third terrace and entered the village of a rebel tribe called the Hawks. The chief had heard of Tandor and treated us kindly when he heard our story. That's when the bombshell dropped."

Here Chartrand jumped in. "The Hawk chieftain had heard of other-worlders (that's what he called us) being rescued from a Seth raiding party some time ago by the next rebel tribe over—the Eagles. The rescued were a woman and a child. Linder decided there was no time to waste. Who knows what Bigelow is planning next. Linder,

Thomas, Makalo, and Tandor headed immediately to contact the tribe and make sure Pam and Little Thomas are safe."

"Whoa," said Chartrand, "we don't know for sure that it's Pam and Little Thomas. Don't set Al up for another needless disappointment."

"We need to leave right away," said Al. "How soon can you start?"

Larsen looked at the cliff shadows. "We're ready to go as soon as we finish eating." If we hurry, we can make it up one terrace before it gets dark."

Al rushed off to Dave and Arlana's tent and wrote them a detailed note explaining where he was going, and urging them to follow. Then he packed up his gear and rejoined Larsen and Chartrand just as they were finishing their meal. Chartrand looked at the note and drew a small map to the Hawk's camp on the third terrace.

"Let's go," said Al eagerly. "I'm sure Dave, Arlana, and Hanomer will follow us as soon as they get back."

Al rushed ahead to begin the climb. He found himself impatiently waiting for Larsen and Chartrand. At one-point Chartrand foolishly stepped on a loose rock and slid about three meters onto a narrow ledge, hanging alarmingly over the edge of a deadly drop.

I'm being stupid, thought Al. *They are exhausted and if I don't slow down and take it easy I'm going to get them killed.*

Al climbed down to see if Chartrand was okay.

Chartrand looked up at him sheepishly. "I'm okay. I was just being stupid and rushing my climb."

"I am sorry fellows," said Al, "I am the one who is being stupid and blind. You pushed yourselves hard to bring me the hopeful news. In my eagerness to find Pam and Little Thomas, I'm pushing too hard. Let's take a break. Have another meal, and then we'll take our time climbing up to the fourth terrace. We'll still make it before dark."

The climb went much better after that. It was dusk when they finally reached the fourth terrace. They hastily set up camp and Larsen and Chartrand were fast asleep shortly thereafter.

Al stayed alert keeping watch. As the night wore on, he refused to wake either Larsen or Chartrand.

The next morning, Al woke to a bright morning. The sun was in the east, which he was used to seeing in these terraces. The smell of roasting meat reminded him of how hungry he was.

"Wake up sleepy head," said Chartrand jovially. "You know, as sentry, you should be shot for falling asleep while on duty."

Al grinned. "The person who should be shot is the one who didn't get up to relieve me so that I could get some sleep. But seriously, sometimes we just have to trust that the Lord will protect us—we all needed the sleep after that climb."

After breakfast, they walked in the direction of Seth. Al wanted to search for the Eagle camp without the interruption of stopping at the Hawk camp. When Chartrand and Larsen judged they had just passed the Hawk camp, they started another climb to the third terrace. It took about two hours of strenuous rock work to complete the ascent of about five hundred meters. They were too exhausted to continue, but rather set up their tents on the cliff edge, had a quick meal, and then fell asleep.

The next morning, they were much refreshed. Chartrand and Larsen took turns leading the way to the Eagle camp, walking roughly in the middle of the terrace, so they would have the best chance of seeing the encampment.

They had traveled perhaps six kilometers along the terrace in a south-easterly direction, when they saw a band of travellers, mostly women, hurrying toward them carrying bundles on their heads. The few men with the band had huge packs on their backs. They all looked exhausted.

Al, Larsen, and Chartrand took cover. When the lead traveller was almost on top of them, Al stepped out holding his hands up in the universal peace sign. The men leading the group were so startled that one of them stumbled.

"We are friends and come in peace. We seek the Eagles," said Al in the Common Tongue.

"You come from the Hawk camp?" asked one of the men.

"Yes, we have been there and we seek the chieftain of the Eagles."

"We are from the Eagles. Alas the Eagles are no more. We have been overrun by Halfmen and soldiers of the overlords. Our fighting men have been captured. Our clan is destroyed. We are part of a remnant that has escaped. We run to join our clansmen, the Hawks, but doubt that we will be safe even there for long."

Chapter 41

Ambush

Filled with dread, Al was anxious to push on, but he knew better than to barge ahead with enemy skirmishers about, so they crept forward. Soon they heard the tramp of feet, curses, whips cracking, and the snapping of branches. Al stole ahead to have a look and peered out from under an evergreen bush.

He saw a band of twenty chained prisoners guarded by six Halfmen. The Halfmen were marching the prisoners diagonally across the terrace to the cliff wall. He was filled with anger at Bigelow and the Halfmen.

Saying a quick prayer to help him think more clearly, Al watched the Halfmen whipping their prisoners. They were clearly taking delight in the pain they inflicted. *They're completely taken up with guarding the prisoners. They're not expecting to be attacked.*

Al signaled his friends to fade back into the woods, then led them at a trot to the base of the escarpment. When he reached it, he saw a narrow trail wending its way up the cliff face and knew that the chained men would be able to climb up this path. *The Halfmen have to be coming this way. If they start ascending the narrow trail, any attack will cause the Halfmen to pitch their prisoners over the edge to their death. We have to intercept them before they reach the cliff!*

Al led his friends back along the path looking for a good ambush site. He found what he was looking for in a small glade with a creek that meandered through it, surrounded by dense brush. He could hear the crack of a whip and the guttural shouts of the Halfmen as they goaded their captives along.

"When I let fly with my crossbow, only then do you shoot." Al instructed, as they hid themselves in the brush.

They didn't have long to wait. The first captives, staggering under the blows of their captors and bound by a long chain, appeared at the edge of the clearing. When they reached the creek, the captives rushed down to the water and threw themselves down for drink. The mad rush toppled the stragglers at the end of the line and chaos ensured. The Halfmen, cursing and whipping every prisoner in sight, were not watching the forest.

Al took careful aim at a Halfman who was raising his whip to beat the last fallen prisoner cowering on the ground. The bolt took the Halfman in the side. He dropped his whip. His cry was lost in the ensuing shouting. Al reloaded his crossbow as quickly as he could.

When he looked up, he saw one guard racing down the path. Al shot at him but missed. Everywhere else the guards were down, having been shot by Larsen and Chartrand. Al raced after the Halfman who had escaped, but could not catch him. Satisfied that the guard wasn't going to double back, Al returned to the glade and saw that the prisoners had already been released. Larsen had found a key on one of the corpses and unchained the prisoners.

"I don't know how much time we have," said Al, "but we should leave as quickly as possible."

"Al," said Chartrand, "these prisoners are near death. They need to drink and then have something to eat otherwise the trip will kill them."

"Alright, let them have a quick drink. Then we'll head back into the woods and find a defensible place until they've had a chance to eat something. We'll question them about Pam and Little Thomas while they're eating."

Al led them into the woods, following the creek, which was soon joined by a second creek from the cliff, becoming a small river. Al chose a place to rest by a deep pool. He could see trout dimpling the surface as they fed on insects. At another time this would be a wonderful place for some fly fishing. He was filled with longing for that time when Pam and Little Thomas weren't in danger.

Chartrand broke out the rations and gave each rescued prisoner a chunk dried fish about the size of a child's fist. They devoured the food eagerly.

Al approached the one who seemed to be in command. Speaking in the Common Tongue, Al introduced himself.

The leader of the band nodded his head to Al and responded to the introduction. "My name is Camgar, second in command of the Eagles after Loktor my chief. I give you thanks, stranger, for your rescue, yet I see you are not of the Hawk clan but look like the strangers who have come into our midst."

Al's spirits lifted. "Strangers? Was there a woman and a young boy among them?"

"Yes," said Camgar, "The lady, Pam, and her son. We rescued her many weeks ago from a raiding party coming up from the land of the Necroans as they walked along the edge of the terrace cliffs on their way to the town of Seth."

Al felt an elation he had not felt since before that dreadful night when he had come home from the college, found his home empty, and his family gone. "Where are they now? Are they safe?"

Camgar's face clouded. "Safe, no! They have fallen into Bigelow's accursed hands, that sorcerer's spawn of an overlord. Through treachery, he knew exactly where we were and attacked without warning at dusk. All were killed or captured. Only two bands, mine and Loktor-the-chief's band escaped by joining forces and cutting our way out past our encircling enemies. We watched for a while from a high point on the cliff wall and saw all of our people taken by the encircling ring of enemies. None that were not with us, escaped. Then, with our enemies in pursuit, we split up into smaller groups in hope of warning the Hawks. In our long history, no one has pursued us so far down the terraces. We must reach the Hawks and warn them that they likely have a traitor in their midst (as we did) before Bigelow surprises them as well."

"Are you sure they—Pam and her son—are captured?"

"I am sure. We were completely surprised and surrounded. No others escaped. Only we were strong enough to cut our way out, and it was a near thing. I am sorry for your loss my friend. I am sorry to start our friendship by bringing such terrible news.

"We have little time. Come with us now."

In a daze, Al followed Camgar's band. The pace Camgar set was gruelling, but Al found himself plodding along so numbly that he wasn't aware of his surroundings. Still, they covered the ground quickly since Camgar's men seemed familiar with the route.

They reached the Hawk camp late that evening, and Al was so sleepy he and the others simply lay down on some grass and fell fast asleep.

He was awakened after a few hours by Camgar. "The Hawks are breaking camp and moving to a new location immediately. Don't be left behind!"

Another brutal day of travel started. All along the way, Al could see the Hawk scouts and lookouts keeping watch over their trail to warn of Bigelow's expected advance.

Later in the day, the Hawks began to climb down a well-hidden trail to the fourth terrace. That evening the Hawks made camp on a small butte raised about ten meters above the floor of the terrace, right against an overhanging rock wall leading to the third terrace.

Al was just returning from an exploration excursion of the camp, when he saw Camgar approach. Larsen and Chartrand jumped up from their lounging to greet him.

Camgar bowed. "Friends of Lady Pam, I have come back to wish you 'goodbye.'" I am about to head back with some of the Hawk scouts to look for my chieftain, Loktor. He does not know the Hawks have moved their camp, so he will need guidance."

"Friend Camgar," said Al, "we are deeply grateful for your help. As Pam's husband, I am very worried about her and my son, Little Thomas. I ask you again and mean no disrespect by the asking, is it certain that they were captured by the enemy Bigelow?"

"I did not see Lady Pam captured since I was fighting for my freedom and the freedom of my chief," said Camgar gravely. "What I did see was the whole camp surrounded when the attack began. As I said before, in my estimation, there was no escape for anyone without a fight that would break through the cordon. We only escaped because we were the only force strong enough to fight through the ring. Even so, we barely had the strength of arms to escape. If I were you, I would deal with the grief of Lady Pam's capture. Most assuredly she is now in Seth, with the other captives."

"Thank you, friend Camgar. I will not shame myself or you by asking that question again. I wish you the Creator's blessing on your journey."

"I thank you, friend Al. It has been a long time since I believed that the Creator could bless this accursed land. It is good to hear you wish it. I will take it as a sign for a hopeful tomorrow." With that Camgar rose, tugged on his forelock by way of salute, and left their campsite.

Al, Larsen, and Chartrand watched Camgar leave the camp with four warriors. Finally, Chartrand broke the silence. "Al, what do you mean to do?"

"I can only think of one thing to do. I have to get back into Seth and find Pam and the others."

"But that's madness," said Larsen, "Bigelow is at war and will be guarding the gates like a hawk."

"Will he?" asked Al. "All of Bigelow's best men will be used in the hunt. There is a constant stream of slaves flowing into the town and they will have to be guarded. With the rebels on the run, why guard the walls so carefully? If you were in charge, would you not thin out the guard on the walls and reinforce the prison guards, making sure that you don't have a slave revolt on your hands?"

"When you put it like that, it makes sense," said Chartrand. "Still it's a gamble."

"I overheard Camgar call this place their last refuge," said Larsen. "We're not even supposed to be here. If you ask to leave, I don't think the Hawk chieftain will let you go."

"I have to go," said Al. "I can't leave Pam and Little Thomas in Bigelow's hands. Maybe in the confusion I can get them out."

"But how are you going to pull it off?" asked Larsen. "The cliff here to the third terrace forms an overhang over the whole encampment. That makes it impossible to climb, at least for me."

"For me too," said Al. "I walked around a little bit and I found the entrance of a tunnel that climbs up inside the rock. I think it's a backdoor escape. It emerges above the overhang where the cliff wall is much easier to climb."

Al looked around at his friends and saw worry and doubt on their faces. "I'm not asking you to come. It isn't your fight. You have done more than any friend could ask."

"I'm coming," said Larsen.

"So am I," said Chartrand.

Al felt a broad grin break across his face. *You can't put a price tag on friends that always have your back, even when the potential exists for the cost to be so high.*

Chapter 42

Back to Seth

When night had settled and the camp was asleep, except for the sentries at the edge of the butte who were watching for trouble, Al and his friends quietly packed up their belongings and crept up the broken rock below the overhanging cliff. Al led, testing each rock for stability before putting his weight on it. They had done this so often that stealth was second nature.

When they reached the cliff wall, Al entered the tunnel, turned on his flashlight, and followed the route he had scouted earlier. Emerging above the overhang, they began their ascent, protected by the overhang from curious eyes in the camp below. The moon rose well past midnight, just four days from a new moon. Still even this wan light helped them find their way. It was clear that a path had been prepared here as an escape route, or as a route for messengers to the third terrace. Although the path took advantage of every natural chimney and crevice, Al could see and feel places where rock had been chiseled away to make the ascent a steep hike rather than a climb. They made good time. In two hours, they reached the third terrace.

They marched along the cliff edge towards Seth on the third terrace. When daylight came, they rested. Then Al used his binoculars to see if he could detect an easy way up to the second terrace.

As night fell, they stealthily crossed the terrace and Al unerringly led them to the start of the path he had selected for them to try. The ascent was gruelling and dangerous. But they took their time, and four painstaking hours later, they were on the second terrace.

They pushed on and completed another ascent to the first terrace. In sight of watchers from the Abaddon Plain, they hid all day in the deep brush and began their final push at dusk along the terrace until they were below Seth. Al chose a well-worn path for the ascent, which led to one of the gates of Seth. This was the most dangerous part of their approach, since many returning combatants would use this well-travelled trail to return home. Al took some time, with his binoculars in low light mode, to look for a party on the cliff face.

"It looks like Bigelow is keeping everyone on the terraces to fight," said Al. "I don't see a single party returning home by this route."

"It would have been better if we had caught Pam and Little Thomas on the trail where we could surprise their captors. One more prayer not answered," mumbled Larsen.

Al led the way up, walking as fast as the steep trail would allow. He wanted to reach the top while still dark. It was almost morning when they finally reached the edge of the cliff, about one hundred meters from the town wall. Al stayed just below the top of the cliff and worked his way northwest to find a secluded spot where the group could rest. About five hundred paces along, he found a trickle of water coming out of the rock and a shallow grotto that they could use. The opening was narrow and heavily overgrown with shrubs, mainly species he had named bushy rhubarb because of the large leaves.

They pulled out their sleeping gear and fell fast asleep. Al woke up to the sound of heavy rain outside their grotto. He briefly wondered if the rain would affect the flow of the rivulet, but the volume of water seemed the same.

Al had learned from Tandor that many of these small streams held an edible salamander-like creature that stayed in the water but foraged for insects on the cliff face at night. These creatures massed about a kilogram and made a delicious stew. He crept out and stayed still hoping to catch one as it returned from a nocturnal foraging expedition. He was in luck. After about fifteen minutes, one crept down the rain-slick rock to return to a small pool, and Al was able to hit it with a rock.

When he had skinned and cut the meat into bite-sized chunks, he decided there was so much mist along with the rain that he would risk a small fire near the entrance. He had breakfast going along with Halcyon tea when the smell of hot food woke the others. The stew, with a few added potatoes he had dug up a few days ago, was fragrant and tasty.

When they had finished, everyone relaxed. Al was reading his Bible and then opened up his cell phone to read some of his digital books. He checked the battery. He would have to recharge his phone using fabric solar energy panels on his backpack in the next day or two.

When it was dark, they packed up, put on their rain gear, and headed out. The rocks were slick and the fog thick, so that Al decided they should climb up to the top of the cliff and take their chances. Although they would be within sight of the wall, on a foggy night like tonight, bumping into another party would be the biggest risk.

They moved silently in a northwesterly direction, listening for the dreaded sound of tramping feet. Every few hundred meters, Al would work back to the Seth wall to make sure they hadn't walked past the point where the town wall made a sharp turn west. When he could no longer locate the wall, he realized they had walked too far. With Chartrand and Larsen in tow, he doubled back until he again found the wall. Then, he walked east toward the corner until he found a series of shallow holes and depressions, which made hand and footholds up the wall. The Guild had cut these into the wall at this location precisely because, even at the best of times, this section of wall had limited surveillance by the town watch. It was far from the barracks and was in a section of town where the buildings had collapsed because of neglect.

Al climbed the wall quickly, clambering through the embrasure to the broad stone way. The merlon was crumbling, and he had to be careful not to drop rock fragments onto his friends below.

Al dropped a rope, and first Larsen and then Chartrand climbed up onto the wall. When they reached Al, they looked around, but saw no sentries. With the fog, they could only see about twenty meters in any direction. Al walked over to the inside edge of the wall and saw a mass of crumbling buildings directly below him. There were no lights. A short distance to his right there was an open stone spiral stairway that made its way to street level.

Al went back and touched his companion's arms. They nodded, and followed him to the staircase. The dripping water sounded loud in the fog-shrouded darkness. The rain made the stairs treacherous, so Al kept his right hand on the wall to steady himself as he descended. A loose step halfway down caused him to stumble, and only the wall kept him from careening all the way down.

When he reached the bottom, he paused. *Now what do I do? I have to contact the Guild. I know they were setting up new digs here, but they won't know me. Do I risk it? They may have completely different passwords*, he thought. But he decided he had to take the chance.

He led Larsen and Chartrand into a crumbling building that had enough of a roof left to give them shelter from the strengthening rain. "You fellows wait here," said Al. "I'm pretty sure the Guild is setting up here, but I don't know the passwords. I'm going to try to talk my way in, but if they're afraid, they may silence me with an arrow before I even have a chance to speak. If I don't come back, you're on your own. I suggest you climb back out and make your way back to the Hawks. Our rescue will have failed."

"Hurry back," said Larsen tersely. Al left the shelter and began to pick his way across the rubble. Since this was a fairly new Guild hideout, he expected all of the underground passages from legitimate buildings had not yet been constructed.

He was about one third of the way in, when he was jumped. Three guards threw him onto his back. Two held his arms and the third put a sword to his throat. Each of the three wore a cloak with a hood that covered his face.

"What's the password, bloke?" asked the man with the sword.

"I'm from the Warren. The last password I was given before my trip was 'nighthawk.' The response was 'early supper.'"

The swordsman said nothing, as if deciding whether he should run Al through with his sword.

"I have my medallion," said Al.

"Let's see it," said the swordsman. Al produced it. The swordsman examined the medallion carefully.

"I remember you. You were part of Tandor's gang. Where's Tandor?"

"We were with the rebels. Bigelow launched an attack. He took out the Eagle clan and is now searching for the Hawks. Most of my gang were captured. I'm here to free them."

"Let him up," said the swordsman. "You don't know then, that the Warren has been overrun?"

"No, I didn't know. It seems I should be thankful I came here first because you're so close to the wall."

"Yeah, you're lucky. The Warren was overrun as soon as Bigelow came back from his trip," said one of the men still holding Al's arm. "He surrounded the digs and then moved in. He lost a lot of his soldiers underground. But our losses were also heavy. He killed or captured about half our people. Luckily, he didn't know about all of our bolt holes. People are still drifting back here after lying low. You're not the first one.

"These dust-ups happen from time to time. It means we stop cooperating and finishing projects, and instead raid Bigelow's soldiers for whatever supplies we can get our hands on. While we're doing that, we're cutting new passages and bolt holes here, as well as setting up our next back-up digs."

"Okay, enough jabbering. Let's go see the chief," said one of the other guards.

Al was blindfolded. Guided by the two guards, one on either side, he was soon out of the rain. They led him well and he only stumbled once. They led him into a room where a new voice questioned him further. Then after a substantial pause, the voice said, "I believe him."

Al's blindfold was removed, and he looked into the eyes of a stranger with piercing brown eyes and brilliant red curly hair.

The red-haired man didn't give his name, but he looked Al in the eye, and asked a further set of questions to do with Al's association with the Guild. At length he seemed satisfied.

"Okay, we'll show you to your quarters. You'll get the first two months on loan and then you have to starting paying. We want the loaner months paid off a year from now, or before you leave. Got it?"

"I understand. May I bring in the rest of my team?"

"Yes, if you vouch for them. We're in raiding mode now. We can't farm ourselves out for jobs until this brouhaha with the Cloaks blows over. The quartermaster will tell you how much the raided goods are worth. I don't need to tell you, it's best to build up a supply to get ahead of the curve. The password is 'Apeman' and the answer is 'Black Dragon'."

The red-haired man called a guard, and soon Al was led to their quarters, which consisted of two rooms. In one corner water trickled from a clay pipe into a basin with a drain.

Al inspected the quarters for a few minutes and then returned to the surface where he found Larsen and Chartrand. At the entrance, he gave the new password and showed his medallion. Larsen and Chartrand also showed theirs. The guards recorded their names and noted that they were working for Al.

When the three had settled in to their rooms, they planned what to do next. Al explained that the rules had changed because of Bigelow's crackdown on the Guild.

"So, what do we do?" asked Larsen. "Do we go raiding after supplies to pay our rent?"

"That wouldn't be my first choice," said Al. "Do you remember how Tandor advised us to hide the bulk of the gold and jewelry we received as payment for our services? He buried it in our old lodgings. Maybe it is still there."

"Won't the old ruins still be under guard? This sounds risky to me," said Chartrand.

"There may be some guards there," answered Al, "but we know many more entrances than they do. Besides, with Bigelow's offensive on the terraces, how many guards would he leave in the ruins? We know many prisoners from the Guild were captured in the raid. I think that he would assign the few guards that he has left in the town to guard the prisoners first, and the rest he'd have watching the walls."

"That won't help us if we're caught," grumbled Chartrand.

"There is no risk-free alternative," said Al. "I'll go along with whatever the team decides, but I vote to dig up our treasure."

Chartrand and Larsen didn't like this idea, but it was clear that they liked the prospect of attacking supply trains to earn the needed rent money even less.

Chapter 43

Treasure Hunt

In their previous participation in the Guild's activity, Al and his friends had walked around Seth freely, disguised as slaves belonging to one of the military commanders. Now, with most slaves serving in slave work-battalions or dedicated to re-supplying Bigelow's army, any slave wandering around Seth would arouse suspicion. So, Al, Larson and Chartrand had to sneak around by night—a dead give-away that they were Guild members, and up to no good.

They slept the day away, and then left at sundown along with many others from the New Digs to sneak about the town. Al led them through dark back streets until they came to a hill overlooking the rubble of their old hideout. The streets were empty, and they did not even see a single patrol as they had moved from shadow to shadow. The fear in Seth was palpable. Even the houses seemed to sense it with their windows shuttered. Most houses were dark, and no one appeared to linger in doorways or on balconies.

Al was not surprised. *It is as I thought. Every available soldier is committed to battle. The garrison doesn't have enough men left to patrol the streets at night, so they are safely holed up in the citadel and everyone else is afraid to be out.*

Al pulled out his night vision binoculars and searched the broken rubble of their old Warren for guards. He saw no one. Still, he didn't believe that there were no guards or spies. He led Chartrand and Larsen off the hill to Creek Street, a narrow cobblestone road, which ran along Seth Creek. The creek ran in a stone-walled channel, which formed a chest-high barrier. Al led them to a wrought iron gate with a chain lock. He pulled out his lock-pick set and quickly opened the padlock. Letting them in, he re-fastened the lock.

"What church did you go to Al?" whispered Chartrand. "They taught you lock-picking in your Sunday School class?"

"Shh," said Al and chuckled, "No, I took lock-picking instruction from one of the old-timers when we were in the Warren. I am glad I did. Now quiet!" he shushed his friend. "The creek goes underground a short distance ahead, and our whispers carry."

"I was joking," whispered Chartrand.

Al lit a dark lantern, which was baffled so that light only fell directly at their feet. He had bought it at the New Digs supply depot on credit.

The creek stank from the run-off of the streets. It ran under the bridge of a cross street, then continued for about one hundred paces where it entered a tunnel. Al led the way, stepping from rock to rock to remain as silent as possible. He stopped to listen for voices but heard only the gurgle of the creek as it ran over rocks. They passed a set of stairs climbing the wall. It led up to a solid iron-framed door to a house, which was built over the creek, but Al kept going until he saw what he was looking for, a side tunnel about two meters by two meters square. Al stepped into it and led them down the storm sewer. Now, he had to find the entrance to the old Warren.

He missed it, but when he reached a place where the large tunnel bifurcated into two one hundred and fifty centimeter by one hundred and fifty centimeter channels, he realized he had gone too far. Retracing his steps, he saw the broken remains of a staircase. Climbing up the stairs, he felt around until he found the cleverly disguised trapdoor and pushed. It was open! Lifting it, straw fell down on their heads. Once inside, Al replaced the straw to hide the door, and then led them to their old home. The door to their lodging had been torn off its hinges and lay to the side. Inside, their belongings had been rifled and scattered. Nothing of value remained.

Al took his friends to a storage room. Inside, he moved a storage shelf, which had been tipped over, then began to dig in the dirt at the spot where the shelf had lain. Larsen and Chartrand heard a "thunk" as Al's knife hit wood. Carefully, Al continued his digging until he uncovered a heavy wooden door.

"Larsen, you stay here. Warn us if you hear anything. Chartrand you're with me. Al lifted the door and climbed down into a small space, still holding the lantern. "This was Tandor's idea. Only Dave and I knew about it. Tandor was adamant that we never fall behind on our Guild payments, so he stored the excess loot here without letting anyone know how much we had."

Al and Chartrand filled up their packs with enough loot to pay off their debt, and enough reserve to rent their home at the New Digs for an extra month. Al insisted they take enough that he could start a treasure cache at the new place. Climbing back out of the space, Al reclosed the trapdoor, filled in the dirt, and moved the broken shelf back on top of the door.

Using a bundle of straw, he swept up the footprints they had made in the dust, like a golfer covering tracks in a sand trap, until they came to the trapdoor to the storm sewer. He gave the lantern to Larsen and sent his companions into the sewer first, while he made sure to hide the exit under a pile of straw.

From there, the three made it home without incident.

Al traded some of their loot for food at the New Digs commissary and then prepared a meal of stew, a few potatoes, and some stale bread. He steamed the bread, making it a bit tastier, and they found the stew palatable. The beer was weak and watery, but it would have to do until they contacted their old friends who would sell them provisions, including good beer, on the black market.

After their meal, they rested until evening. Al felt much better now that he could see their way forward. Locating Little Thomas and Pam among the rebel prisoners seemed less daunting now that they were settled back into the Guild.

For the next two weeks, the three reconnoitered Seth until they located the prison camp where Al thought Pam and Little Thomas must be. There was a depression in the western part of the town that was bounded by the town wall on the west and south, and a low fifteen-meter cliff on the other two sides. There were only three places where a road had been cut down to this Low-Town, and so the prison camp could be guarded with a few soldiers on the outer wall and at the hastily-constructed gates that barred the roads.

Tonight, would be the big night. After sundown, Al, Chartrand, and Larsen, wearing guard uniforms they had purchased from the Guild supply store, snuck through the town, once again, by moving from shadow to shadow. As usual, the streets were deserted. In half an hour, they approached Cliff Street. The houses were dark. "This is it," said Al, gesturing to a two-story stone house surrounded by a two-meter stone wall.

"Are you sure it's deserted?" asked Chartrand.

"I've watched it for two nights. There has been activity in some of the other houses on the crest of the cliff, but not this one. Not even so much as a light."

In the center of the wall was a rusty iron gate secured with a padlock. Al unlocked it, and then replaced it with another lock to which he had the keys.

"Here, each of you gets a key. I'll keep the third and we'll hide the fourth across the street."

Al refastened the chain, and then the three crept around the side of the house to the back. There was no sound, light, or other indication of inhabitants.

"Here goes," said Al, and then picked the lock to the side door.

"First, we explore. Then we plan, based on what we find here. After that, you lower me down into the Low Town prison camp."

Entering the house, they split up and searched the main floor. The kitchen had a large fireplace on the side wall. The ashes inside it were cold. There were pots and dishes in the cupboards. Mold-covered dishes on the table spoke of a hasty departure. The kitchen floor was dirty. Clearly, it had not been swept in a very long time.

In the living area, there were five dusty armchairs, stained with spilled wine. Empty wine bottles were cast about the room. A cabinet held no books but was filled with a few full bottles of wine and a clay tankard of something else. There was one bedroom on the main floor, but everything except the straw mattress had been taken.

Al carefully climbed the stairs. Despite his care, the straight staircase creaked at every step. The stairs ended at a hall running the length of the house from front to back with four doors to additional bedrooms. Al approached the window at the end of the hall and looked down on the prison camp. He could see the light from four campfires.

Turning, he walked the length of the hall to another window and looked out onto the deserted street. The upstairs bedrooms were the same as the ones downstairs—no belongings, discarded rags, and straw mattresses on the beds.

The cellar was partly cut out of the living rock, but made use of a natural depression in the ground. At the base of the cellar stairs there was a solid wooden door leading to a large cold storage room that contained potatoes and other root vegetables. The main area of the cellar was littered with stacked piles of old, discarded furniture. Al worked his way to the back wall by squeezing past old cabinets and chairs. Here a stone wall had been built to fill a gap in the rock and two large windows were set in the cellar wall overlooking Low Town. With Larsen as lookout on the main floor, Al and Chartrand moved the furniture in the cellar so as to clear a space before the windows and block easy access to this new secret space. Both windows were stuck, but with a bit of work, Al was able to open one of them. He took a rope from his pack and fastened it onto a wooden post supporting the floor above. He also took out a roll of fishing line.

"Surely you didn't bring fishing gear on this rescue mission, did you?" asked Chartrand.

Turning red, Al whispered, "I brought my smallest telescopic rod, a few lures and some fishing line. Good thing that I did," he added. "The line is going to come in very handy. I'm going to lower this rope and climb down. When I'm down, pull up the rope."

He attached a length of fishing line to the end of the coiled rope, and tied a brick to the other end of the fishing line. Next, he lowered the brick over the cliff, followed by the length of rope.

"If I have to get out in a hurry, I'll use the fishing line to pull down the rope and climb out, even if you're not here."

"What do you want Chartrand and me to do while you're looking for Pam?" asked Larsen. "Shall we hide here until you come back?"

Al hesitated and thought. "I think I would like you to stay until about three in the morning, in case I find them right away. After that I'll leave the decision up to you. You can head back to the New Digs and come back to check on me at night when it's safe, or you might decide you'll take a chance staying here. Just don't try to leave during the day. There are too many eyes, even when we're wearing Bigelow's uniforms."

With that, Al changed from his soldier's uniform into rags, and then rappelled down the cliff face to a deserted road that ran along the base of the cliff. Running across the road, he hid in the shadows to watch as Chartrand pulled up the rope. Al saw the brick shift as the invisible fishing line was drawn taut.

Stepping out of the shadows, Al gave Chartrand a thumbs up and then crept down a narrow alley that ran towards the center of Low Town. The houses were built right onto the alley. A door to the left banged in the wind. The large hemispherical double gate of a court-yard showed evidence of pounding, but the lock had not been forced. He crossed a wider transverse street and continued along an alley that led in the general direction of the fires he had seen from the window.

Up ahead, two men in rags ran from a doorway carrying something small. Seeing him, they scurried away.

One more cross street, and Al came to an alley on which every house showed evidence of having had its door forced. Finally, he entered a large square with a fountain in the middle and four bonfires, spaced equally around it. Al could see the silhouettes of men, women, and children crowded close to the fires.

Leaning against a house wall near the end of the alley, he looked intently for Pam. After about fifteen minutes, a woman and a child came out of an alleyway and walked towards him. Al grew tense. They were about thirty meters away when a figure rushed out of the doorway of a nearby house, pushed the woman to the ground, and tried to wrestle something out of her hands.

Al leapt to his feet and charged toward the conflict. It wasn't Pam. The woman and her assailant were wrestling over a dead rat. "Let her go," Al demanded.

The man looked up. His feral eyes looked desperate, and held a hint of madness.

"It's mine," whined the man. Dressed in rags, his legs and arms were emaciated.

"Let her go," said Al gently. He had no stomach for this fight, but he had to see the woman keep the food, no matter how repulsive it seemed.

"I have to eat," screamed the man. "I haven't eaten in days and I'm going to die."

"You have to let her go."

Frothing at the mouth, the man let go of the rat and leapt to his feet pulling out a sharpened stick. He stumbled toward Al, raising the shank to strike.

Al sidestepped him easily and grabbed his wrist. With the other hand he lifted him off the ground. The man was light and weak. "Easy there. I don't want to hurt you," Al coaxed. "You need to conserve your strength and try to find some food."

The man struggled weakly. Al saw the woman take her little girl to her side and hold onto the dead rat.

Two men carrying clubs separated from the crowd at the fire and came toward Al and the struggling man. "What's going on here?" said the larger of the two men.

"I don't want to hurt this fellow, but there was a disagreement about the ownership of a rat."

"Yours?" asked the big man.

"No, that woman's," said Al pointing with his chin.

"Is that true?"

"Aye," said the woman, "that man saved us after the other fellow attacked."

"Okay, we'll take it from here."

"Could you go easy on him?" asked Al. "He's weak from hunger and is almost out of his mind."

"Don't tell us how to do our job." They took the shank out of the starving man's hand.

Al noticed they treated the poor fellow with some kindness, and released him to the two guards.

Al sat down and leaned against the house wall again. The woman, with her daughter in tow, went to the fire and began roasting the rat on a stick. Al kept looking, hoping to see Pam.

After about half an hour the woman returned with her daughter. "I wanted to say, 'thank ye' and give you this." She held out a small leg with a mouthful of meat on it.

"I thank you," said Al, standing up, "but I would be glad if you gave it to your little girl."

"Thank ye, sir"

"There is something you can do for me." Al saw a shadow of fear cross her face. "I have lost my wife and small son. They were captured by Bigelow, the ruler of Seth. Have you seen a woman and a boy alone?"

The woman seemed relieved. "There are many women here without their husbands. What's her name?"

"Pam. Our son's name is Little Thomas."

"Strange names. If I hear anything, I will let ye know."

Al sat back down and watched her move toward the nearest bonfire. He watched for another half hour, hoping to spot Pam's familiar gait.

Finally, he rose and retraced his steps back to the cliff, where he ran his hand along the rock face until he felt the fishing line on his wrist. A quick pull brought the rope down. He briefly looked up and down the road, and then began his climb.

Chartrand was at the top, waiting to help him through the window. After pulling the rope back up, Al leaned out and looked at the street to see if a spy had spotted him. Satisfied, he joined his friends for a bite to eat and a quiet talk.

"I take it you didn't find them," said Larsen.

"I didn't," said Al. "The camp is in a bad way. Everyone is starving and the stress is leading to anarchy. Thankfully, some members of Loktor's war band have taken up the role of vigilantes and work to keep the peace. There are many women and children. Everyone is desperately trying to survive. There are so many captives that it may take some time to find my family. I need to go back. Don't expect me for a few days."

Chartrand looked at Larsen who nodded. "We've decided to wait here for you," said Chartrand. "As you said, no one has come into this house recently, and we have enough supplies to hold out for a week with rationing. There is also a well in the courtyard and the water is passable."

Al nodded. "Thank you. You fellows have been great friends. You have come through for me once again when I most needed it." His eyes moistened. Rubbing his eyes, he said, "I need to head back."

Al climbed back down to Low Town and retraced his steps to the bonfire. As he reached the square he noticed that he could see much more clearly. Suddenly, across the square he saw people begin to run for the houses. They raced for an alley, only to emerge a few minutes later followed by a group of armed men with whips, nets, and swords. A group of perhaps one hundred captives had been trapped by the armed guards.

Al crept nearer in the dawn light. He had to see and hear what was going on.

"I want two dozen of the vermin men," said a gruff voice. "And mind ye, no half-starved weaklings that we'll have to kill on the way down."

"Sit down all of ye," shouted the voice. The men with whips lashed anyone who was slow to obey. The guards then searched every man they had corralled, selected the strongest-looking ones and herded them to a separate area where a group of soldiers with a long chain and hammers fastened them at the ankles into a chain gang.

"We also need half a dozen women for the fighting boys. No hags and no women with brats—they're too weepy." The soldiers placed ropes around the women's necks and gathered them into a weeping group with one soldier holding each rope, all the while leering at them and peppering them with lewd remarks. Finally, they marched their captives off towards one of the gates.

After they had left, people emerged from hiding, many crying openly.

Al was filled with dread. *What if Pam had already been taken as a soldier's slave? She is so beautiful, she'd be sure to be one of the first to go.*

Al sat down and tried to still his pounding heart by exerting his will, to no avail. His active imagination showed him Pam in the clutches of one of the unwashed, cruel, and vindictive soldiers he had just seen. He imagined him doing unspeakable things to her as she cried out for him, but he was not there to help her. In his imagination, the soldier tired of her, beat her raw, and killed her. Pam seemed to look straight at Al as she died.

Gloom settled on Al, and he folded himself into the fetal position and wept. A voice inside seemed to say, "Stop it, Al. Don't let the enemy control your mind. Even if Pam were to die, it would never be that way."

Al raised his head. *I am at the mercy of my imagination. Faith means knowing God so well that I can imagine good outcomes that may come true because God is supremely good. He will give us a happy ending, if not in this life, then after we pass the long sleep.*

Al chose to deliberately imagine the same nightmare again, but this time, with a different outcome. He saw a defiant Pam who stood up to the abuse like the warrior princess she was. Although chained, she was not cowed. While being beaten, she picked up a pot and struck the soldier on the head, knocking him senseless. She removed the rope around her head and snuck from the tent seeking to escape.

I know I am making this story up; I have no expectation that it is true, but why should I let the enemy make me think the worst? Should I not honor the Lord Christ by believing that strength can be given to Pam in the midst of the worst nightmare? Should I not believe the best of You, God, rather than the worst?

A little bit of light seemed to enter his gloom.

Three days later, Al once again climbed up the rope to their refuge. When he reached the top and saw Chartrand, he was surprised at the look on his friend's face.

"Al you look terrible."

Al sat down. He had expended his last energy returning to the safe house. "I feel terrible."

"What's wrong? Are you sick?" asked Larsen, joining Chartrand at the window.

"I can't find them," said Al. "I've searched the whole camp and asked everyone who would talk to me, and I can't find any trace of Pam and Little Thomas. I think they've been taken by the guards."

Al felt tears coming, and buried his head in his hands. "I don't know what to do. I feel so alone, so hopeless—so forsaken."

Chapter 44

Despair

Staring into the darkness at his feet, Al heard one of his friends pull the rope back up and then move off down the hall. The other one shuffled over and sat down beside Al. There was a period of silence. Finally, he heard Chartrand speak. "Al, where's your Bible?"

Al looked up, turned on his flashlight, and opened his pack, pulling out his well-worn English Standard Version Bible.

Chartrand opened it up to the back page. "Remember that break-up I had a couple years ago that threw me into despair. I was asking: 'Why God, why?' You drew this diagram for me." He pointed to a thick dot with an arrow going to the right. "You told me this dot represented my birth and my short life to the present time. The rest of the arrow represented the rest of my life stretching out to eternity. However bad my life may look at this point in time, even if the despair continues for the rest of my time here on earth, God has more than enough time to make it right. In fact, you told me that after a few thousand years of my eternal life had passed, those memories would be like a trip to the dentist, a lost football game, or a tough exam. Your words didn't make things better right away, or even the next day, but I started to think that God would give me grace, so what seemed like the end of the world to me at the time, was something I would be able to get over."

"My own words," said Al, "seem less believable now that this cloud that is hanging over me. I feel like I'm drowning in quicksand."

"Here's something else you told me Al. 'Think back and remember a promise God has made to you. Hold onto it and start to do something that He has told you to do. Any step of obedience is going to be a step out of your gloom.' You were right Al. It took a few days, but your words helped me a lot. Now you need to listen to your own advice. You don't really know what has happened to Pam and Little Thomas. It's all your imagination. Don't let the enemy fill you with despair. Remember the promises you've received. Take a step that God wants you to take." Chartrand handed the Bible back to Al, and left to help Larsen prepare their meal.

Holding his flashlight against his body, Al opened his Bible and started reading the book of Isaiah, but he couldn't keep his eyes open. So, he laid down on a mattress. As he fell asleep the words came to him from somewhere "Fatigue makes cowards of us all."

The following evening, Al joined Chartrand for supper just as the sun was going down. There was an awkward silence after Larsen had prayed a prayer of thanks for their meal.

"I want to thank you for your words of encouragement," said Al, "and also the space you gave me to work through my emotions. I still feel hollow inside, but I know I'm here to do a job. In my reading, I kept coming back to a passage in Isaiah chapter 42 verse 7 where God says what He's going to do. He says He plans: 'to open the eyes that are blind, to bring out the prisoners from the dungeon.' I'm here—we're here—to set these captives free."

Larsen seemed to gag on his mouthful.

"How are we supposed to do that?" asked Chartrand. "We're only three."

"I don't have it all worked out yet, but here's my plan so far." Al began to talk. He still felt a great pressure as if he were keeping a terrible fear at bay, but he could feel himself getting excited as he talked about possible plans.

After dinner, Al climbed back down the rope and returned to the camp. Since the night that he had come to the rescue of the woman with the rat and her child, he had worked hard to get to know the vigilantes who kept order in the camp.

He sought out Loktor's lieutenant, Ragnor, who headed the vigilante crew that kept lawlessness and predations at bay in the camp. "Last week you asked me if I wanted to join your band to help keep the peace in the camp," Al said. "And I said 'No.' Now I would like to say 'Yes.'"

Ragnor's eyes held suspicion. "What made ye change yer mind?"

"I was desperately looking for my wife and young son. I've looked everywhere, but they're not here. I think the soldiers may have already taken them."

"They don't normally taken women with children," said Ragnor. "Why would ye believe that?"

"She's a beautiful woman. When they saw her, I think they might have made an exception."

"You're not from my tribe, the Eagles. Are ye a Hawk?"

"No, although I have been welcomed by the Hawks, I'm not from around here. I'm a friend of Tandor's. He was helping me search for my wife and son."

"Why would Tandor do that?"

"I rescued him from the mines after a Necroan attack wiped everyone else out."

"Ye survived a Necroan attack?"

"I was lucky. They didn't see me."

"Hmm" said Ragnor. He looked at Al for a long time. It was clear that he did not yet trust him. Finally, he called to a man sitting by the fire, "Raynor, come over here for a minute."

Raynor came over. "This fella wants to join our ranks. What think ye?"

"He handles hisself well enough, though he be a stranger."

"Look after him, Raynor, on a trial basis to see how does, remembering he be a stranger."

So it was that Al found himself attached to Raynor, who seemed more his personal guard than his commander.

After a couple of days, they were on a patrol to the part of the camp that was closest to the house where Larsen and Chartrand were hiding. Al saw a red kerchief hanging out of the window at their hideout.

Al said to Raynor, "I want to check something out." He walked into a house across the road from the cliff, with Raynor right behind him, he found a bundle standing in the corner. He unwrapped it as Raynor looked on with suspicion. The bundle contained two swords, a bow, and a dozen arrows.

"How did ye know that would be here?"

"I have contacted some of the Guild in Seth. Some of my friends are able to buy weapons from them and I mean to arm your war band. Our people are starving. I think we ought to break out."

"Our people? How do I know this isn't just a trap?"

"A trap?" said Al. "We're already captives, and completely under the power of Bigelow and his soldiers. What possible value would he have to send a spy into your midst? There would be nothing for him to gain by giving you any weapons at all."

Raynor shrugged. "How many more weapons can ye get us?"

"If my friends have to buy them on the Guild market, they'll trickle in a few every day. If we want to use the weapons we have and put together a raid by our war band on the armory, we could get a lot more."

They carried the weapons back to Ragnor and explained Al's plan for a raid on the armoury. Ragnor was suspicious, but Al could tell by his haggard look that he was desperate.

"What do we have to lose? How many men do ye need for the raid on the armory?" Ragnor asked. "How do ye get us out of the camp?"

"If my friends can buy some more weapons from the Guild, we would have maybe nine armed men for the raid. I know from them that Bigelow has almost everyone fighting the rebels, so Seth is undermanned. With a little bit of luck, we'll find that nine will be enough. If you think I'm wrong, we could wait a week or so, and maybe have double that number of armed men. What do you think Ragnor—shall we move quickly, or wait a week?"

"To speak plainly," said Ragnor, "My men need food as much as they need weapons. Let's move quickly. We're burying bodies every day because of starvation. If we scout the armory and we don't have enough, we can always wait a week."

Ragnor got up and paced back and forth. After a couple of passes, he came back and squatted down. "Here's what I want ye to do. Leave me a sword. Raynor, ye take a sword and a bow, and scout out the armory with Al. Then report back to me."

Chapter 45

Rebellion

Al and Raynor returned to the base of the cliff as twilight was falling. Al walked across the street, looked up and down, felt for the fishing line, and then pulled down the rope. Raynor picked up the nearly invisible filament, shook his head and began muttering to himself. Al climbed the rope and Raynor followed.

Chartrand sprang up from his mattress in alarm, but visibly relaxed when he recognized Al's reassuring voice. Al introduced Raynor to Chartrand and a very groggy Larsen. They broke out some food and Raynor ate ravenously.

When it was completely dark, Chartrand led the way into the city. They had moved about in Seth at night so often now, they knew the best routes, the routes avoided by the few patrols that were still active. Some of the way was at street level, but much of it was on the rooftops of buildings long abandoned. Finally, they approached Bigelow's stronghold, the barracks, and the armory.

The main gate was closed and guarded, judging by the subdued light in one of the gate towers.

"Now what?" whispered Larsen.

Al smiled. "The Guild is devious. Dave worked on some repairs to the drainage system of the fortress on behalf of the Guild when we first entered Seth. I was part of the work detail. The Guild always has an angle and an eye to the future. Getting into Bigelow's stronghold was one of the things they thought about. Follow me."

Al led them back a couple of streets to a small creek that ran in a bricked-in channel. Steep stone steps ran at intervals down the channel walls to the water. Al opened a rusty iron gate and led his comrades to the water's edge. The water level was low, so it was easy to walk on the fringe of the channel without getting wet. Soon the channel dove under the street. Al used a light gourd; the channel bent to the right. Finally, they came to a grate with some crude markings on the adjacent stone.

"Guild markings," said Al. "I think this is it." A pin held the grate locked, but was easily removed. Al climbed into this side tunnel and led the way to the first vertical drainage channel. It had a heavy grate on top. Al climbed up and looked at it with his flashlight, then came back down. "When the Guild was repairing the drainage grates in the stronghold, they were supposed to bolt them from the top so that they could not be opened from below. But on one of them, they sawed the shank of the bolt off, and then glued the shank in places so it only looks like it's bolted down. The actual lock is on the bottom. This one is bolted shut as it should be, so we keep looking."

Three vertical drainage channels later they came on one that had four levers cemented into the stone, which locked the drainage grate in place from underneath. Once the four levers were disengaged, the heavy grate could be moved aside. There were protruding stones on the side of the shaft that made access easy. When they emerged, they saw this grate had been well chosen. It was in a dark, dead-end alley with no doorways or windows. Al slid the grate back into place and headed for the armory.

The armory was guarded. A sentry stood outside a large, very heavy, open door. Light streamed out. Inside, even at this hour, there was the sound of hammering, the clanging of steel being thrown on the stone floor, and the loud hiss of bellows.

A grimy slave with black streaks on his face and hands, came out of the armory pushing a creaking wooden wheelbarrow. He began to shovel coal from a pile to the right of the open door into the wheel barrow, and then struggled to push the load back into the armory. The bored guard barely gave the slave a glance, and began a slow pace to the corner of the building.

Presently, Al heard the clop of hooves on the cobblestones. A covered wagon came into sight, with a soldier sitting in the wagon seat, leaning forward on the toe board as he snapped the reins and cursed at two horses. The gangly, underfed horses came to a halt just as they passed the door. Putting on the brake, the soldier climbed down, stretched himself, and went over to talk to his comrade.

"Jed, ye flea-bitten excuse for a soldier, what brings ye at this cursed hour to this midden heap?" asked the sentry.

The wagon driver scratched himself just under his helmet at the back of his head. "The higher-ups want a load of weapons delivered for the big push to finish off the mangy rebels. We're to leave as soon as it starts to lighten up. The wagon has to be at the side gate, loaded and ready to go in two hours."

"Why two hours?" asked the guard at the door. "It's a long time 'til sunrise."

"Never ye mind," said the wagon driver. "It only natch-ral that I want a few pints and a sleep before I haf to go down to those accursed terraces."

The sentry cursed soundly, then said, "So it's finally started. I hope it's over soon. We're undermanned here and I have a bad feelin' about this place when so many of the lads are away fighting. It's like a storm is going to break."

"Keep yer traitorous mouth shut, if ye know what's good fer ye," said the wagon driver. "Now git the slaves out here and loading so I can get some bloody sleep before I have to drive this load down that switchback to the supply depot on the first terrace."

The loading began as six slaves were made to carry out swords, spears, bows, and arrows, depositing them into the wagon box.

Having seen and heard enough, Al beckoned his companions to follow, and led them back to the grating. After fastening it from underneath, they left the stronghold. Al led them to a place where they could watch the main gate in the stronghold wall. Presently, the gate opened and the wagon rolled out. After the first couple of turns, Al realized the wagon was heading to a side gate near the main switchback that descended to the first terrace. Heavily loaded, the wagon moved slowly. Al left the others behind and sped through the back alleys at a quiet trot to get to the side gate.

The wagon arrived shortly after he did. The soldier unhitched the two horses and then, after looking around, disappeared into a well-lit tavern filled with laughter and cursing. Al returned to the shadows to wait.

When the others arrived, after stationing Larsen to keep an eye on the inn, Al uncovered the wagon and then began unloading about sixty of the weapons. Together with Raynor and Chartrand, he carried the arms into a nearby empty house and hid them under some debris. Finally, he restacked the weapons in the wagon less efficiently, so that things looked undisturbed once the rawhide cover had been lashed back into place.

Carrying as many weapons as they could, the four companions made it back to their cliff-edge house. Al and Raynor climbed down the rope and then the others lowered the weapons down to them. In two hours, Ragnor had most of his war band armed.

Ragnor and Raynor joined Al, Chartrand, and Larsen in the house as they planned their next steps.

The following night, after retrieving the cached weapons, sixty-four armed men were huddled in the sewer, waiting for Al to open the grate into the stronghold.

I worry that we're moving too fast, thought Al. *We don't know what we're facing. Still, now that I have started this, I have to finish it.* His mind was tormented with images of torture and mutilation as he saw himself and the others being overwhelmed and captured. *They're not going to capture me alive.*

Chapter 46

Besieged

Dave was just finishing his bone-weary stint controlling the rock-borer. He had directed the animal to finish the dwellings for the green dragons, and had just completed a special project, a spiral tunnel up to the fourth terrace. He finally released the exhausted rock-borer and walked down to the green dragon lairs on the fifth terrace.

He and Hiszt had been working so hard to complete the rock-borer diggings that the passage of time had become a blur. When Dave returned to Hiszt's spacious cavern, he found Arlana and Hanomer with their hands on Hiszt's flanks, in contact-telepathic conversation with the dragon.

Dave placed his hand on the green dragon and joined the conversation.

Your mate, friend Dave, just sent to me that she believed it was time to rejoin your friends on the higher terraces.

I agree with her Hiszt. Our friend Al left some time ago to look for his mate and his youngling. It is time to find him and help him, now that we are done here.

I will be sorry to see you three friends go.

Friend Hiszt, sent Hanomer. *I believe we will meet again before long. Our meeting has not been a mere accident but has a purpose.*

It is hard for us to leave, sent Arlana. Her sending was filled with warmth and tenderness. *You have become a life-friend. Life-friends are worth more than gold or jewels.*

We have become life-friends, sent Hiszt, *haven't we? We have begun to redeem the long enmity between dragons and the Ancient Ones. We have accumulated the life-debt—saving each other's lives. It means we are bound to each other.*

They communicated many more things. Dave had a lump in his throat as he thought about this new bond that had been forged, and how much he regretted leaving Hiszt, who didn't seem as ugly or terrifying as when they had first met.

The next morning, after a long sleep, Dave, Arlana, and Hanomer made the twenty-minute walk up the spiral ramp to the fourth terrace. They emerged into dense undergrowth in a bluff only ten meters from the cliff-edge, overlooking the drop to the fifth terrace; Dave and the rock-borer had dug the ramp in a well-shielded tunnel.

From here, Dave reflected, *the dragons can keep a close eye on their camp below, and glide down to fight in a matter of seconds if danger threatens.*

There were several tunnel mouths in this bluff and nesting female dragons had begun to create a lair. Soon all of the females would reside on the fourth terrace while the males guarded the lower entrance.

Hiszt had been amazed at the idea of having a second camp—beyond the reach of all but the smallest brown dragons—and a ready escape from any impending attack on the fifth terrace.

Arlana, Dave, and Hanomer began the climb to the third terrace. After two hours of climbing, they rested briefly. Then, following Al's map, they made the long journey southeast to the most recent Hawk camp. But upon arriving there, they found the site deserted.

They had just put their heads together to decide what to do next, when they were surrounded by a dozen Hawk warriors. Without a word, the Hawks removed the friends' weapons, but the warriors showed surprise and fear when they saw Dave's sword and knife from the blade tree.

Now weaponless, Arlana, Dave and Hanomer were tied together and covered in partial blindfolds, such that they could only see their feet. Two warriors marched on either side of them.

Time passed slowly. They had walked for a considerable time when, to Dave's surprise, they began to descend again.

The Hawks must be in real danger, he thought. *They only risk the small brown dragons on the fourth terrace as a last resort.*

After some hours, Dave could sense from the coolness of the atmosphere and the echo of their footfalls that they had entered a tunnel, which continued the descent. Soon, Dave heard the sounds of a camp: pots banging, swords being sharpened, and muted conversation. He heard a tent flap being opened, and felt the cool air of a shaded tent.

"Sit down!" commanded one of the guards. When the three had done so, their blindfolds were removed.

Two grim-faced men stood before Dave, Arlana, and Hanomer.

"Is this one of the men who visited you just before the betrayal?" asked one of them in the Common Tongue.

"No," said the other, "but he was very much like them. They have the same blanched skin, and eyes that are too straight. We have to be wary of all strangers now. You must keep them locked up or they may tell Bigelow where to find us."

"What do we do with the strange creature that is with them?"

"I have never seen its like before. It clearly belongs to them. It is a stranger too. I think you should also lock it up."

Dave tried to speak, but the guards dismissed him. He, Arlana, and Hanomer were led out of the tent. Dave looked around. The camp was on a mesa surrounded by a palisade. The cliff above them had a pronounced overhang so that they could not be spotted from the third terrace.

The three were marched to a large box constructed of stout logs that had been nailed together and situated close to the overhang. Forced up a ladder to a trapdoor at the top of the box, they were lowered inside while still bound. The box was about five meters on each side with fifteen-centimeter spaces between the wooden beams. They would be observed by guards at all times.

Huddling together, they used contact telepathy to communicate. What would they do next? Escape seemed impossible, yet the sense of doom was palpable. Dave felt the electrical agitation of an impending thunderstorm in the air. When would the clouds burst?

Evening fell. A loud crack of thunder, and the rain began. Wind was blowing in from Sheol, so even the overhang did not keep the captives dry.

Having watched the prisoners for a while, the guards departed when the rain and lightning began. Stealthily, Hanomer used his tail hand to untie first his cords, then Arlana's, and Dave's. Finally, he untied his empty tool vest and belt. He and Dave quietly moved to a part of the cage where two adjacent vertical logs were bent away from each other. By expelling his breathe, with Dave using his strength to spread the ten-centimeter logs, Hanomer was able to squeeze through the narrow opening.

Dave and Arlana waited anxiously as the rain continued. They were cold. The lightning had moved out of sight onto the Abaddon plain from over the Sheol abyss, but flashes still reflected off the clouds every few minutes. About half an hour passed. Dave grew anxious, and began to fidget.

I wish I could get up and pace, but then everyone would know I'm untied.

Dave tried to calm himself. He sat with his arms behind him, holding onto the ropes as if still tied. He looked over at the bundle of clothes that was supposed to mimic Hanomer sleeping.

As long as it doesn't grow light, that pile should do the trick of fooling the guards.

But no guards returned to check on them. Finally, Dave and Arlana heard a faint rustle, and Hanomer returned carrying Gram and Dave's blade-tree dagger.

After Dave had helped Hanomer climb back through the log barrier, Hanomer touched Arlana and Dave on the wrist.

Friend Dave and friend Arlana, your weapons were in the warlord's weapons storehouse with guards. I think the warlord was frightened by the weapons. I overheard the guards saying that they had strict orders none were to approach the entrance to the hut or touch the weapons. Apparently, the warlord tried to use Gram, and when he sliced through his tent pole with a gentle swing, he proclaimed it 'a wizard-weapon' and had it put away, along with the dagger in a guarded chest. The chest was not locked and I was able to take the weapons easily. The wizard-weapon warning may give us time before they discover the absence of Gram.

Even if they do discover they are missing, sent Dave, **they may think these weapons have the ability to return to their wizard-owner. We had better bury them in case they look for them here.**

Using the dagger as a shovel, they quickly dug a trench in the hard ground in the corner where they sat. Then Hanomer tied up all three of them again, using a knot that he could undo quickly. Finally, they laid down and tried to get some sleep.

Dave woke as the trapdoor to their box was opened and a rope ladder lowered. A young warrior came down and tested their bonds briefly. He cursed when he realized how loose they were and retied their hands in front, then handed each of them a quarter loaf of bread and one water skin. They had just enough mobility to eat the bread and pass the water skin around.

The warrior kicked at the dirt and straw as if looking for something. He looked like he was about to speak and then changed his mind. Leaving the water skin, he climbed back up the rope ladder, refastened the trapdoor, and left.

The young warrior appeared to leave them alone, but Dave caught a glimpse of him creeping back to spy on them. Dave edged toward the others and then touched hands.

Did you see the young warrior come back?

Yes! Sent two different voices.

I think they discovered the missing sword and dagger. Now they have something to think about.

The three friends remained huddled together, discussing possible plans by contact telepathy. Occasionally, by agreement and to allay suspicion, they spoke loudly about commonplace things. They also deliberately spoke about things they had done that would help to underline their innocence, in the hope that the Hawks' warlord might relent and let them help defend the camp.

Dave woke to the sounds of a commotion in the camp. Everyone seemed to be running somewhere. He looked to see if the secret watcher who had crept close to hear them speak was still in his place, but he, too, had left. Everyone was in a panic.

Soldiers approached, along with the young man who had spied on them the previous day. He let down the ladder and brought them better food than the day before and another water skin.

"Yer boss is here," he said.

"Our boss?" asked Dave, puzzled.

"The Lord Bigelow, from Seth," continued the young man. "The chief is negotiating with him now—your safe return for a long truce and our departure from Bigelow's realm."

"He's not our boss and he won't go for it."

"From what I hear, he's extremely interested in trading for ye. The negotiations apparently are going much better than expected. Bigelow must want ye back rather badly, since he's being accommodating."

Dread tightened into a knot in Dave's gut. *Of course, Bigelow wants to trade for us. He cares more about locking us up or killing us, than he cares about subduing the rebels. Staying here was a big mistake. We should have escaped as soon as we weren't welcome. Now it may be too late.*

Outwardly Dave tried to hide his feelings, but he saw Arlana grow pale as the same realization hit her.

"Thank you for the food," was all that Dave said.

The young man shrugged. "We can't send ye back to your master looking half-starved, even if we have been feeding ye as well as we feed ourselves. Don't worry. Ye won't be here much longer." With that he climbed back up the ladder and relocked the cage door.

The soldiers left and the three friends realized they were unguarded. The warriors' false assumption that they would be happy to be traded to Bigelow was the one bright spot in this dreadful development.

"We have to get out of here now," whispered Dave.

As soon as Hanomer loosened their bonds, Arlana and Hanomer began digging for Gram and the dagger while Dave positioned himself so as to block their activity from view. Now it was Dave's turn to work. He decided on the dagger and went to the back corner of the cage and pushed it into a ten-centimeter-thick log near the ground. The dagger sank into the hardwood as if it were soft butter. Dave repeated this action five times, cutting through the log. In this way, he cut away three logs.

Quickly, Dave helped Arlana through the opening he had made, followed by Hanomer. Finally, he crawled through, taking one last look to make sure no one was watching, then lifted the sagging roof of the cage while Arlana placed the three cut logs back into the gaps.

The camp seemed deserted. Dave led the way back along the cliff wall rising to the third terrace, looking for a way up. Only once did they have to scamper for cover as a group of warriors came by at a trot.

Finally, they reached a rock wall where Dave saw a path among the boulders. Hanomer began climbing the path first. Around a large boulder they came upon a tunnel entrance. Trying something she had just mastered, Arlana caused her hands to glow with bioluminescence and followed Hanomer up the tunnel.

I have to learn how to do that glowing hands thing, thought Dave.

When they reached the top of the tunnel, Hanomer studied the rest of the climb for a moment and then selected a route that gave them maximum cover. Arlana followed Hanomer.

Reaching a shallow ledge, Hanomer called a halt. Dave crawled to the edge and looked over the camp. He could just see the outer wall over the overhang. Around three sides of the camp, everyone was congregated behind a shallow, hastily constructed wall. Dave could see Bigelow's army. It was huge. *He must have emptied Seth. The Hawks have no chance.*

Yet there was no battle. In the distance Dave saw a huge pavilion with guards in Seth livery and others who were clearly from the rebel camp. They were having their parley, and apparently negotiating Dave, Arlana, and Hanomer's trade for safe conduct.

Chapter 47

Fight in the Streets

Al undid the latches holding the storm sewer closed and pushed the heavy grating up enough that he could see the alley inside the fortress. It had begun to rain. The alley was deserted. Al tilted the grating up even further, slid it to one side, and loaded a bolt onto his crossbow.

Silently the other sixty-four men climbed out of the storm sewer and formed up in the alley. Those with swords clustered near the entrance of the alley. When they were all out, and the grating had been replaced, Al led them to the armory.

The armory was guarded by a single sentry who marched up and down in front of the entrance with his spear on his shoulder. When he turned his back, Al, Chartrand, and Larsen jumped him.

Chartrand grabbed him from behind and shoved a wet towel into his mouth, while Al showed him the point of his sword. Some of the unarmed men took over, bound the guard hand and foot, and placed him in a corner. One of the others assumed his cloak, and with his spear, resumed sentry duty.

The main loading door was closed, so Al went to the small side door and opened it a crack and listened. There was no hammering. The forge seemed to be quiet, which wasn't really surprising since it was three o'clock in the morning. Probably everyone was asleep.

Al led them through the dark building. The men picked up additional weapons from the stacks by the forge. The group split up and began to look for the storage area. A large door ahead opened up to a warehouse stacked with weapons of all types. Al split the party into three groups.

Raynor—with one third of the men—was to secure the armory.

Ragnor, Chartrand and Larsen, taking most of the remaining men, snuck to the Barrack Gate, where they waited for Al.

Taking five men with him, Al went to the stables and hitched up three wagons to carry weapons to the captives in the lower city. He could see by their quiet competence that the men Ragnor had given him were all seasoned warriors from the Eagle's war band. They would know how to move silently, and how to fight when the time came.

The men drove the wagons toward the Barrack Gate. When they were still a good two hundred paces from the gate, Chartrand appeared in a shadowed doorway and gave Al— in the lead wagon—a thumbs up.

At the gate, Al climbed down, and hammered on the guardhouse door. A red-eyed soldier opened it.

"Whata ye scum want, wakin' a man from his sleep?"

"We got word weapons are wanted," said Al.

The guard called to two others who began to open the gates. As they did so, two dozen Eagles swarmed into the guardhouse. Immediately, the gate belonged to the rebels.

"Larsen you hold the gate at all costs," commanded Al. "Raynor can hold out in the armory for a while since it is fortified. Ragnor, bring most of the men. We're off to the prison camp. We should have many more warriors if I can arm the captives."

Al opened the gates and led the wagons out.

Everything was going smoothly until they met a patrol. The patrol captain was about to yell at Al's band, when it dawned on him what was going on. Before the captain could react, Al shouted "Attack!" and rushed at the band. If the captain had lost his head and stayed to fight, it would have been all over in a couple of minutes, but he ordered the patrol to scatter and head back to the town gate. Now it was a foot race.

Al chased the captain but didn't have time to give orders to his men. The captain ran up an alley, but Al was quicker. It dawned on Al that his opponent was allowing him to catch up. *He is pacing himself. He wants a fight when I'm alone.*

Suddenly the captain reversed direction and attacked him with an overhand swing, but Al blocked with a high guard. From long practice, Al instinctively defended with the Maiden's Repulse. The captain's sword swung and Al was able to shift from defensive to offensive forms.

Al attacked with a sequence of strokes called the Scythe, forcing the captain to retreat awkwardly. Al wished he had Dave's sword instead of his own sabre, good steel that it was. With Gram he would have been able to slice through the crude steel of the Bent One's weapon easily. His sabre, made of the best steel science could produce was very good, but not that good.

The captain regrouped. He had expected an easy victory, but now became more cautious. With his sword held in the high guard position, he began to edge toward Al's left. Al cut him off, moving his own sabre in a rhythmic motion, which Tandor had called the Butterfly. Suddenly, the captain lunged using the Widowmaker. Al should have been expecting it. The captain's sword point flashed towards Al's chest. Al's moving sword added a fraction of a second to his speed and he deflected the blade using the Charging Bull. He wasn't fast enough, and the deflected blade bit into his side. The pain was intense but, reaction born of long practice, took over. Swinging away from the cut, he came around and caught the captain on the neck with his full strength, severing the captain's head from his shoulders.

Al turned away. He couldn't look. This kind of combat was so personal. You looked into your opponent's eyes as you fought. He had seen the fear in the captain's eyes as he knew he was about to die. He walked back to look for the wagons.

After the initial pain of his own wound, he had forgotten all about it in the heat of the moment and with the relief of still being alive. Now it began to hurt again. He could feel the sticky wetness on his shirt. He sat down at a small water fountain and took a drink of water from his water bottle. Opening his satchel, he took out his med kit. First, he cleaned the blood off his sabre. Then he took his shirt off. The cut had glanced off his ribs. It was fifteen centimeters long and about one centimeter deep. He cleaned his hands with disinfectant and then put some into the wound itself, wincing at the pain. There was a lot of blood. Next, he used the clips he had to close the wound. Finally, he attached a large self-adhesive bandage. He knew he should really wrap a bandage around his torso, but he didn't have one large enough. He cleaned his hands as best he could, and washed his shirt in the fountain. After wringing the shirt out, he put it back on and began looking for the others.

Making his way to the Sheep Gate—one of the entrances to the Low Town—he found his men crouching in cover.

"What's going on?"

"Several of the company we surprised, made it back here and warned the guard in those gate towers. The place is locked up as tight as a laced-up boot. A couple of men were wounded when they tried to rush the tower."

"Well," said Al. "We have to work around this setback. The important thing is to get the weapons we have to the captives in the Low Town. You're in charge here. I will leave half the men with you. Keep the soldiers in the gate towers from escaping. See those walls on either side of the gate? Make sure you have a couple of men in each of those houses that butt up against the wall. The soldiers inside must not be allowed to raise an alarm. Understood?"

The warrior thumped his right fist against his chest in the warrior's salute.

Al selected ten men and took the wagons up the street to their safe house. He set eight men to carrying the weapons into the cellar with the window overlooking the cliff surrounding the Low Town district. Once that was started, he took two men with him to the cellar window and lowered one of them down to the base of the cliff. He and the other man began wrapping the weapons in a sack made from the wagon tarp. Everyone worked with zeal. After fifteen minutes, Al turned to Ragnor. "Could you go and get the warriors from the square to come and pick up the weapons?"

Ragnor looked at him, puzzled. "My people be dying, Lord Al, and ye have done something to save them. Ye don't have to ask me. Ye can command me. So, my answer be 'Yes, sir!'"

What was that all about? thought Al. He wasn't thinking straight. *I've lost too much blood.*

Two of the warriors lowered Ragnor down and he disappeared between the houses at a run. The transfer of weapons continued. After about fifteen minutes the prisoners began to trickle in from the square. After they had picked up a weapon, they came up a second climbing rope that Al had let down.

It was getting close to dawn. Al selected five lieutenants to help him, including Ragnor. He sent three groups to the three small western gates overlooking the escarpment to the terraces. He kept one group at the house. He sent another group to the Iron Gate at the other end of Low Town to see if they could capture it. Finally, Al took most of the men back to the fortress and the citadel within it, since he knew that with dawn coming, there was bound to be trouble there.

The first glimmer of dawn had just begun to show when Al finished giving his orders to capture the citadel and to hold the gates.

With his final instructions, the faces around him became strangely indistinct.

He was aware that Larsen was anxiously trying to get water into him. Al felt so tired he could hardly keep his eyes open. His vision narrowed to a tunnel and that was the last thing he remembered.

Chapter 48

Gleeson's Legion

Al woke to find himself in an enormous bed in a gargantuan room. Light was streaming in a bay window, which took up most of one wall. Chartrand was sitting in a chair beside his bed with a broad smile on his face. "Ah, the sleeper awakes."

"How long have I been out?"

"More than forty-eight hours if you don't count your semi-conscious states when we tried to get some water into you."

"Forty-eight hours!" Al rubbed his temples. *Oh, my head aches!* He sat up, only to fall back as dizziness overwhelmed him.

"Whoa, take it easy Al. Everything is under control. We have control of Seth."

"What?"

"Everything worked out. The barracks were nearly empty and the citadel had only a minimal guard. In fact, Bigelow's slave steward was the only one attentive enough to see what was going on, and he didn't raise the alarm, but let us into the citadel through a postern gate. We have it all: the gates, the citadel, and all the store houses. Even the guards at the Low Town gate towers surrendered."

"Have you freed the slaves?"

"Provisionally, the final decision has to be made by the new Lord of Seth."

"The new Lord of Seth? Who would that be?"

Larsen laughed. "That would be his imperial majesty, Al Gleeson."

"What?"

"Sorry, old chum, you have no choice—that is, unless you want to insult the whole rebel nation. Apparently, they have a long-established custom that if a war-leader rescues captives, they automatically owe allegiance to him for at least a year. If a war leader captures an enemy stronghold, he automatically becomes lord of that stronghold. So, it seems old chum, in your usual bumbling ways, not only are you Lord of Seth, but you have several thousand followers, many of whom are seasoned warriors."

Al's mind was reeling. This was too much to take in. Finally, he said, "Where's Larsen? Is he well?"

"Yes, he's fine. He's negotiating with the Guild. We thought it would be best to reassure them that we're not after them, especially since we know their lair so well. Larsen is offering to re-establish the old arrangement where they work for gold—it turns out Bigelow had a huge stash of gold that he used to trade with other fiefdoms and the Mutandi wizards. We can use that to pay for the services of the Guild to get this town running again. As a gesture of good will, we released all the Guild members from the dungeons, and those that had been enslaved. We offered to let them return, but they seemed to be covered by the same honor pledge as the rebels. Er, I hope we didn't overstep our authority."

"Overstep? No, of course not."

Chartrand looked out the door and rose. "I want to introduce you to someone, Al"

He went to the door and brought in a man with long gray hair, a long face, and intelligent brown eyes. "This is Klengar, Bigelow's slave steward who helped us secure the citadel, and has been of inestimable value since. For example, he negotiated the surrender of the Low Town gate towers."

"Lord Gleeson, my pleasure and honor." Klengar dropped to one knee and offered up his rod of office with both hands. "To you Lord, my rescuer, I offer my fealty, my loyalty, and my life."

He obviously expected an answer. Al tried to think of a reasonable response. He could only think of Denethor's response to Merry from one of his favorite books, and gave it his best approximation. "Klengar, steward of Seth, I accept your pledge of fealty. I will reward loyalty with honor, fealty with love, and treachery with judgment." Klengar seemed satisfied.

Al slowly sat up. "Steward, please give me a brief report of what has been done."

"Lord, we have great stores accumulated for the army. The stores are guarded by your men and my staff, that is, those I deem most trustworthy are rationing out the food and clothing as needed. Bigelow's captured men are held weaponless in Low Town. I have begun assigning houses around Low Town to families as an added guard against escape. The deeds to these donated homes are being duly registered here.

"Most of the warriors have taken up residence in the barracks. Former slaves have been assigned shops, duly registered. We should soon be able to buy and sell goods. We plan to use the Guild gold currency, augmented by your treasury as money. Everything has to be paid for as the vice-lords Larsen and Chartrand have been instructing." Here Klengar bowed again to Chartrand.

"I have kept all of my former staff, who were slaves under cursed Lord Bigelow. For room and board and a nominal wage, they were glad to stay on and run both this household and the day-to-day activities of the town."

Al gave Klengar a long look. *There is no hint of treachery or deception in those eyes.* Al always told the truth and somehow that commitment seemed to make it possible to see when others were lying. "You and your staff have done well, Klengar. You seem to know that I value justice, fairness, compassion, and mercy. Let those be your guiding principles. Thank you."

Klengar bowed and left. Al turned to Chartrand. "Bigelow could be wiping out the Hawks right now, and maybe our friends with them. I need to get up and mobilize the army."

"You're not ready to ride out. You need time to heal."

"If I'm really their lord, I have to be there even if all I can do is sit in my saddle. Chartrand, I need you to work with me on this."

Chartrand shook his head. "I will get your battle chiefs."

An hour later the four battle chiefs met in Bigelow's old bed chamber. Al insisted he sit in a chair for their visit. Ale was passed around as the battle chiefs, Klengar and a red headed man sat around Al in a semicircle.

After some preliminary pleasantries, Al's tone became more earnest. "We have some tough decisions to make. I have asked Klengar, my steward, and Red, the chief of the Guild, to join us. Klengar knows more about Seth than any of us do. Red, on the other hand, is still deciding if he can trust us. I want him to hear our plans. I am hoping he will help us run Seth in such a way that Guild members and free men alike will benefit." Red looked shocked at Al's straightforward analysis of the situation.

Al looked around, the battle chiefs were attentive, but no one asked any questions. "Bigelow has emptied Seth to wipe out the Eagles and the Hawks. As far as I know the Eagles have been scattered and perhaps even destroyed. I don't know if we are in time to save the Hawks, but we will try. I'm looking for suggestions on how to carry the fight to Bigelow."

"If I be Bigelow," said Ragnor, "I would use the switchback road to haul supplies down by wagon to the first terrace. I would set up a supply camp there. The wagons can't continue down to the second terrace because there be trails but no roads. Bigelow likely has long lines of slave porters carrying supplies further down on the few trails between terraces. The fortified camp would be expecting attack from roving rebel bands on the second terrace, but not down the switchback."

Al asked, "Won't they see us coming down the switchback from below? We'll be easy to destroy because our line will be so stretched out."

"Yes, very true. We'll have to sneak down the switchback in the dark of the night and launch our attack at first light. If we be lucky, the camp will be lightly defended because all opposition on the first terrace will already have been destroyed, and they be feeling relatively safe."

"Any comments?" asked Al.

"If we're moving on foot to attack," added Chartrand, "why not use all three routes from the three eastern gates? That way we could attack from three different directions. Even if the force down the switchback is discovered and stymied, we could still mount a credible attack."

"There's another reason to use the three-prong attack," continued Larsen. "We don't know the timing of the shipments to the camp. In the intervening days, before we can launch our attacks, there will have been several missed shipments and the camp ought to be suspicious. It may be that they've already sent a scout up to the gate and he's figured out that his boys are no longer on watch. They may be waiting for us. Or even worse, Bigelow may have abandoned his attack on the Hawks and may even now be marching on Seth. It would be just too bad if we sent our whole army down the switchback only to have Bigelow come up one of the other tracks and recapture Seth behind us. We need a force on all three approaches."

The discussion went on for another hour, but the final plan involved a main force down the switchback and two forces down the other two trails with an attack at dawn if they were not discovered. If they were discovered—well, everyone would have to use their best judgment.

The sky was overcast, and a gentle drizzle began. After an afternoon of frenzied preparation, the larger force of five hundred men under Ragnor and Raynor set out down the switchback as darkness fell. The continuous rain made the switchback treacherous. Al rode a horse down, well back from the vanguard. The horse's hooves were wrapped in soft boots to aid in footing and to keep the horse as quiet as possible. The other two forces of about two hundred men each started down the trails from the other two gates at the same time.

Ragnor had selected his people well. Al heard the occasional clink of metal on stone, but no one talked. They made it to the designated way point.

The bulk of the force on the switchback settled down for a miserable night on a shelf about seventy meters from the terrace. This shelf was broad enough that the bulk of the force would be invisible from the terrace below. Others found crevices and small shelves along the route, or they crowded on the road itself away from the edge to remain out of sight. There was no talking. Scouts crept as close to the first terrace as possible in order to observe the camp, and particularly the sentries.

Although Al was soaked to his skin, he was feeling better. He did not sleep, but had a quiet consultation with scouts that had crept back up from the terrace to report. There was a ditch and a palisade but only Halfmen patrolled the camp. There were no true sentries. At dawn his force would attack. He hoped the other two forces had been able to position themselves such that they would also be able to attack from the flanks.

Finally, it looked to be about half an hour before earliest light. Everything was wet and soggy. The main force crept down the road to the terrace. Al expected the alarm to be given at any moment. He heard a clink of metal on stone, and a dislodged rock bounce down the cliff, followed by a loud thud and grunt as the rock careened into a soldier on the lower switchback.

It was too much to hope that five hundred men could be absolutely quiet as they crept into position.

Al heard what he had dreaded, the eerie howl of a Halfman giving the warning battle cry. Dragging himself to the edge of the ledge, he peered over to see what Ragnor and Raynor would do.

Launch the attack, blast you! Launch the attack now! Do I have to send down an order?

It was a little lighter now. Al could see the men moving in force across the terrace silently. The fighting had begun, but his force was not using any battle cries.

Al felt guilty about misjudging his commanders. Ragnor and Raynor were handling this better than he would have. Fighting in silence was a brilliant idea. Anything to slow the response for a few seconds would get more and more of his men onto the terrace and threaten a larger section of the palisade, stretching the defenders.

Al pulled out his binoculars. Now he could see Chartrand's force from the northwest begin to move on the camp. They were here! There was nothing on the other side. Where was Larsen?

Now the tents and huts in the middle of the camp began to empty of troops, mainly men. They rushed to attack Chartrand's forces, which were closest. Chartrand's men were thrown back, but the main force was rapidly advancing with little opposition.

Finally, he saw Larsen's men coming in almost unopposed from the southeast.

Suddenly, as if on signal, the enemy broke contact with Chartrand and ran for the woods on the far side of the camp, abandoning everything. The Halfmen did the same. The commanders sent about half their force to pursue the enemy, while the rest secured the camp, manning the crude palisade and gates.

An hour later, Al sat wearily in one of the tents, which had been cleared to serve as his command headquarters. They had captured about one third of the men in the camp. The rest were being hunted in the woods by small parties of warriors.

Al rubbed his wound. When the reports were finished, Al said, "We need to locate the Hawk camp and Bigelow's army as soon as possible. If we're too late, our effort will be in vain. They will likely be on either the third or the fourth terrace, but we can't count on that. Have two scout groups walk along the edge of this terrace, one heading right, and the other heading left.

"I want two more scout groups on the edge of the second terrace looking down on the third. Finally, scout groups five and six go up and down to the edge of the third terrace, looking down on the fourth. Bigelow's army can't hide, but we need to find them as quickly as possible, if we don't find anything on the upper levels.

"Any questions? No? The rest of us need to be ready to move as soon as the scouting reports comes back."

Chapter 49

Who's Surrounding Whom?

Al was on the third terrace looking down on the Hawk's camp. Below him was the rise of a natural butte which provided a fortification for the Hawks. An overhang, which projected from the wall of the five-hundred-meter drop to the fourth terrace, obscured much of the Hawk camp. However, Al could see the edge of the butte. The Hawk camp was completely surrounded by a large army. Every outlying fortification had been overwhelmed. It was only a matter of time until Bigelow's forces would overrun the butte.

After his scouts had found the two armies, Al had worked feverishly to get his forces into position. It was dusk now and the attack on the butte had stopped except for the occasional probing foray by Bigelow's soldiers, and the even less frequent courageous sortie by the Hawk warriors.

I should be down there to lead our men. Al looked at Ragnor, his personal bodyguard. Ragnor, sensing his desire to join the army, quietly shook his head.

Ragnor's not my bodyguard—more like a jailer!

Behind Al, well back from the edge of the escarpment, a strange contraption loomed like the masts of a sailing ship. There were three long masts on hinges. When tilted forward, they would lean over the top of the escarpment so that they could be seen by his forces pretty well anywhere on the battle field. The right mast would hold a flag designating an army, a division, a brigade, or a warband. The middle flag would indicate an order or action, while the left mast would indicate a location or direction. In his debate with his commanders to let him join the battle, Al had only agreed to stay up here when they convinced him they needed him to oversee the battle and give directions to reduce casualties. Now he wondered if it was all a ploy. *I am sure when the battle frenzy is on them, they will completely ignore my signals and simply go at the enemy with all vigor, regardless of the danger to themselves.*

Al looked to the right and saw the First Brigade move into position.

He laughed at himself. *Brigade! What hubris. His whole "army" did not have enough warriors to make even one brigade.*

Still, even in the three days it had taken to find Bigelow and get the rebel forces into position, their army's numbers had increased. He would have preferred to wait for even more warriors, but there was no more time. They had to try to save the Hawks by morning.

Al turned his attention back to the preparations at hand. They were well back from Bigelow's sentries. Off to the left, the smaller Second Brigade had reached its position and gone to ground. At dawn, just as Bigelow launched his attack on the butte, his own two attacks would begin and hopefully win the day by surprise—they certainly did not have superior numbers, nor were they likely to be as effective as Bigelow's trained troops. "Lord, help us," he muttered.

It was too dark to see now. Fires at the base of the butte had begun to spring up. Bigelow apparently thought there might be a large sortie under the cover of darkness. Perhaps even a breakout. *Lord, please don't let them try anything as foolish as that. If they wait until tomorrow, we have a chance at least. Tonight it would be a massacre.*

"Supreme Battle Chief," said Ragnor, "I had promised the other commanders that I would make ye sleep."

"Make me sleep? You might force me to lie down, but even you cannot make me sleep."

"Please, don't ye make this harder for me than it already is."

"Ragnor, the commanders did not specify where I had to sleep, did they?"

"Nay, my Lord."

"Well I choose to sleep here, close to the edge, so I can be ready for any attack in the night.

Ragnor ordered that some furs be brought to Al who finally rested, confident he would hear noise if anything happened below him in the night.

He rested his head on the furs expecting not to sleep a wink.

The next thing he remembered was Ragnor shaking him. "My Lord, first light be not far off. I can hear Bigelow's army below, preparing for the final assault."

"Thank you, Ragnor." Al silently berated himself for sleeping so soundly. *I was supposed to stay awake for my men.*

Crawling to the edge of the precipice, Al peeked over the edge. It was overcast and still too dark to see anything, but the clink of armor and the rattle of weapons was unmistakable. Bigelow's men were getting ready to attack.

Ragnor brought him some dried meat, some heated wine, and some heavy, dark bread. Al ate as he strained to see what was going on below. *I wish I had Dave's new, enhanced night vision. I would wager he could see what is going on down there.*

It was gradually getting lighter. Al thought he could see his men moving into position. *Hold your ground. Make them commit. Please Lord, don't let them attack too soon. It only takes one over-anxious fighter to completely destroy our advantage of surprise.*

Al's heart leapt to his throat when he heard a war whoop. It was Bigelow's men rushing the butte from all three sides. He saw the first wave charge up the steep side of the butte, only to be mown down by the fighters waiting for them at the top. Arrows filled the air. Now he saw his army advancing silently. They tore into the rear echelons of Bigelow's reserves before the reserves even knew there was an enemy in their rear.

Al frantically signalled for the flag poles to be tilted over the edge. The poles were lowered into position at a forty-five-degree angle.

He pulled out his binoculars. One of the war bands, who called themselves the Ferrets, was penetrating too far into Bigelow's ranks. If they kept going they would be surrounded and destroyed.

"Signal, the Ferret war band, 'Hold your ground. Blow a signal blast to let them know a signal has gone up," Al instructed.

The loud horn rang out its deep, booming blast, shaking the rocks of the escarpment. Al waited to see if anyone would heed his command. Sure enough, the Ferrets held their ground and took up a defensive posture while the flanking warbands caught up."

"Signal the Ferrets, 'Resume your advance'."

An hour later, Al surveyed the battlefield. The surprise had cost Bigelow dearly. Two thirds of his reserves had been attacked and their numbers thinned. Only the reserves at the edge of the drop to the fifth terrace were intact. Still, Bigelow had such a huge numerical advantage, that it seemed to Al the tide was turning against his side. He could see his men were weary. The Hawks had sortied from the butte when his attack had started, and had succeeded in joining forces with Al's troops northwest and southeast of the butte—right next to the escarpment to the third terrace. However, further in, Bigelow's men had regrouped and were beginning to regain the ground they had lost.

Movement far to the right caught Al's eye. He took out his binoculars, adjusted them for maximum magnification, and clicked on the anti-vibration compensation. *No, it can't be!* Far to the right, hundreds, no thousands of spider-like creatures were boiling up over the lip of the escarpment from the fifth terrace. A sinking feeling took hold of his gut. These were the arachnids they had disturbed when they had climbed out of the abyss. They had not been left behind. Now they were going to kill all of his men, and in fact all of the men of both armies.

"Signal: 'Twelfth Brigade; enemy in rear; southeast.' Sound the signal horn when the flags are up."

He saw the commanders looking in the right direction, but the terrain prevented them from seeing the approaching bugs. It was no good. The arachnid numbers were too great. He had to abandon the southeast flank if he was to save his men.

Al swallowed hard, not sure if he was doing the right thing. This would cost him any chance of a victory. "Prepare another signal: 'South army, retreat onto butte.' When ready blow the signal horn!"

Nothing seemed to happen. They were confused by the order.

"Signal them again, Ragnor. Add the urgent flag!" Finally, the south army began its retreat onto the butte with the Twelfth Brigade acting as rear guard. A cry of victory went up from Bigelow's men as they gobbled up the positions abandoned by the south army.

Just then the arachnids charged out of the woods into the rear of Bigelow's men. The sounds of victory turned into cries of anguish and desperation. There was a rasping and clattering of chitin as Bigelow's men faced the new threat. Twelfth Brigade redoubled their efforts to reach the butte.

Bigelow's men hacked hundreds of bugs to pieces, but more kept coming. Finally, that whole wing of Bigelow's army was overwhelmed by sheer numbers.

The arachnids kept advancing. Now they were at the butte. The men were fighting valiantly on the butte and the arachnids were temporarily stymied. Still they ate further and further into Bigelow's army and began to swing around the outer edge of the butte.

A sinking feeling came over Al. It was only a matter of time before the arachnids overwhelmed everyone: soldier and rebel alike. They were trapped.

I have to give the order to get the north army onto the butte. We're into the endgame now. I could see us losing, but not like this.

Chapter 50

Clan Hawk's Last Stand

Dave looked over the edge of the broad ledge on which he, Arlana and Hanomer were hiding and onto the Hawk camp below, which was surrounded by Bigelow's army. Bigelow and the Hawks were still in negotiation. The parley before the battle.

What could they possibly be talking about? Bigelow wants to destroy the rebels once and for all. I thought they were negotiating our trade. It looked hopeless for the Hawks. Dave's inner voice was one of recrimination. *Why did I not foresee this? Why could I not have been more convincing? If they had believed me, this might have come out differently.* His mind was torn. On the one hand he was angry with himself and the Hawk chieftain for doubting Dave's loyalty. Another, vindictive part of his mind, wanted the Hawk chieftain to realize his mistake.

He needed to think analytically and reasonably. He needed to get out of his mental obsession with his failure. He needed Gandalf telling him, as the *Lord of the Rings* character had told Theoden, to take up his sword. Dave began to pray for wisdom. At first it was hard to even think the words. But then the incessant self-recrimination began to dissipate like acrid smog dispersed by a freshening breeze.

I can't redo the past. What is, is.

He looked again and saw a small party of Hawk warriors leaving the tent in the midst of Bigelow's army heading back to the Hawk camp. The Hawk chieftain and Lokodor, the Eagles' chieftain, were not with them.

Where are they going without their boss?

He watched their progress and then the answer to his question hit him with a jolt. Bigelow had been negotiating with the chieftains for him and Arlana. They were the only bargaining chips the Hawks had. Now Bigelow had struck some kind of deal, and there would be carnage when Bigelow realized that he, Arlana, and Hanomer had escaped.

Dave inched away from the edge. He had planned to wait until nightfall for their next move, but there was no time. Generally, the rebels kept scouts right above the camp on the next terrace up. If the scouts were still there, he, Arlana, and Hanomer were bound to be spotted, especially if they moved away from this ledge.

"We have to move now," whispered Dave. Arlana and Hanomer nodded. Dave led the way along the face of the cliff in a north-westerly direction. He tried to choose a path that kept them out of sight of the camp below.

Suddenly, he heard a shout. The returning warriors, approaching the butte, had received word they had escaped. They searched the cliff face, and saw them. A horn sounded three short bursts.

They must be warning the scouts above to trap us if we try to climb to the next terrace.

Dave sent Hanomer ahead since he was the best climber and had an unerring sense for picking the best route for keeping them out of sight. Dave waved Arlana on. She was about to protest; she was a better climber than he, but one look at his face and she bit back her words.

Warriors came out of the tunnel from the butte; others were running along the bottom edge of the cliff and then climbing, intending to cut them off. Dave thought he saw movement at the top of the cliff as well.

The vice is closing, he thought grimly.

Up ahead, Hanomer began to sniff the air.

Dave kept climbing, and then he smelled it too, the unmistakable scent of water—a lot of water. Ahead was a narrow, deep split in the cliff face, as if the wall had been pulled apart.

The slit here was barely wide enough for Dave to squeeze through, but he followed Hanomer and Arlana. Looking up, he saw patches of blue sky peeking between the boulders.

The split was deep, and as they made their way further into it, the smell of water grew stronger. Beads of moisture coated the rock walls. They proceeded through an irregular tunnel entrance. The path descended in a gentle slope and ended in a narrow cavern with a small river running through it.

Even in the subdued light Dave could see well enough to know there were no obvious exits in the cavern on the other side of the river. Hanomer was already walking along the river's edge. The river moved gently and exited by a tunnel at the northwest end of the long, narrow cavern. It was flowing roughly parallel to the cliff face.

The river, about twenty meters across, moved languidly. Hanomer stepped into the water and walked into the tunnel hugging the tunnel wall. The lumi-lichen provided enough yellow-green light to see by.

The tunnel and the river turned sharply to the left and the current began to pick up. Dave thought he heard the clatter of a rock behind him.

Hanomer must have heard it too since he quickened his pace. The rocks became more slippery. Now the tunnel became lower so that he could no longer stand upright.

Dave tried to go deeper into the river, but the bottom dropped off quickly. His foot slipped. Desperately he tried to dig his fingers into the pebbly river bottom, but the current carried him away. He found himself swept past Arlana, and then Hanomer.

Righting himself so that he was swept downstream feet first, his speed picked up. Thankful that his sword and dagger were strapped securely to his body, he used his unstrung bow to fend off the walls. Suddenly, his speed increased even more. The river foamed down a steep tunnel. Dave held his breath and plunged under the surface of the water, using his bow and his free hand to fend off the smooth tunnel walls as the water's turbulence swung him from side to side. His speed increased even more. He was in free fall.

Am I heading back to Sheol? Am I going to hit a rock?

His falling abated and he floated again in a fast-moving current. Dave had lost all sense of direction. What seemed like minutes passed. It was completely dark. Dave could hold his breath for forty-five minutes thanks to the extra hemoglobin in his Ancient body.

He continued to be carried along by the water's current, flung toward the outer edge of the channel. He thought there was a change of direction but couldn't be sure. Suddenly he realized there was daylight above him and he was racing toward it. Although he was completely disoriented now, the current finally slowed. Dave swam toward the light and bobbed to the surface of a lake.

He looked around frantically. First Arlana, and then Hanomer also bobbed to the surface. Arlana smiled until she saw Hanomer floating lifeless in the water. Two powerful strokes brought Dave to Hanomer. He held Hanomer's still body over his back on top of his pack while Arlana, treading water, compressed Hanomer's chest to help clear his lungs. After she gave the Hansa several whacks on the chest, Hanomer began to sputter and breathe.

Dave's slow breaststroke brought them to shore where they climbed out onto a rock in the sun. Hanomer spit up some more water and took several deep breaths. Baring his teeth in a smile, Hanomer stood up and bowed. "Thank you, friend Dave and friend Arlana. I cannot hold my breath like you two, so I was nearly undone by that underwater journey."

"You frightened us half to death, Hanomer. After all your sputtering, your smile was never more welcome."

"If I had perished, friend Dave, perhaps you could have written a glorious poem about my underwater journey, and how I entered the halls of the Great King our Father from the watery channel."

"I don't think I could have done justice to your tragic demise, Hanomer. I much prefer you alive." Dave rose to his feet. After emptying his wet boots, he put them on again and then emptied his pack to dry its contents in the sun.

"I'm going to look around," he announced. "We're obviously on a terrace, but which one?"

He headed into the woods behind the small lake. The bright sunlight gave way to a dappled shade. The squish, squish of his soggy boots was annoying. Birds were singing and he heard the rustle of a small animal in the dense undergrowth. The trees were of a kind he had not seen before with smooth bark and long, narrow, ribbed leaves.

Dave decided to head northwest along the terrace. He walked through the woods roughly halfway between the vertical wall on the right and the drop off to the next terrace on the left. The land struck him as vaguely familiar, as if he has been here before. Suddenly, from up ahead he heard a noise in the brush that sounded like a larger animal. Dave crouched and held perfectly still. The head of a small lup pushed through the underbrush. The lup had a black bar down his tawny muzzle. *Horatio!* Dave stood up and the lup raced towards him and bowled him over. Rolling on the leaves, Dave hugged the pup and scratched him behind the ears.

Concentrating, Dave was able to connect through contact telepathy with the lup. He saw him making his way back to the fifth terrace where the green dragons made their home. Horatio had stayed with the dragons, and had decided to go on a hunting expedition, when he had scented Dave and gone looking for him.

So, we're on the fifth terrace, big fella, close to the green dragons.

Horatio's reaction to the mental picture of Hiszt told Dave he had read him correctly.

That means I'm heading the right way. The dragons are northwest of us.

With Horatio following, he walked back to the lake.

Arlana and Hanomer were surprised to see Horatio again. They had collected some potatoes, in Dave's absence, and Arlana had brought down a large flightless bird with an arrow. Dave's mouth watered at the sight of the game, and his stomach growled with hunger. While the food preparation continued, he told Arlana and Hanomer how he and Horatio had found each other, and his guess as to their location. When the food was finally ready, they sat down to eat. Horatio went off into the woods to continue his hunting. The new potatoes and greens were delicious and the roast bird reminded him of eating duck.

When they were full, Dave told Arlana and Hanomer to put their feet up and relax while he made tea. He stoked the fire and placed two large logs, which he had cut with his sword, on the periphery of the coals. He crushed some dried Halcyon tea leaves and placed them into his all-purpose pot to make Halcyon tea.

As he sipped his hot tea Dave said, "I think if we head northwest along this terrace, we'll find the caves that we helped dig for Hiszt and his clan. I'm worried about the Hawks. If Bigelow decides to attack them, then I don't see how they can hold out."

"Friend Dave, we will have to rescue our Hawk friends."

"But what happens if we are too late?" asked Arlana. "What can the four of us do against Bigelow's whole army?"

"I don't know Arlana. I know we have to try. I do have an idea. Right now, I need to talk to Hiszt."

Drinking the last of their tea, they packed up and resumed their journey with urgency. The large smooth-barked trees gave way to heavy turf covered with low flowering bushes about three meters high. They smelled like juniper, overlaid with a sweet floral scent. After two miles, Dave began to recognize some rock formations on the cliff wall, and the larger trees looked familiar. He found a trail he had used previously, and the walking became easier. Finally, they emerged into the broad area in front of the dragon caves. The meadow was much changed. Everywhere the once-green grass was charred. Even the trees at the edge of the meadow were smoldering stumps. A large green lizard sunned himself on one of the flat ledges before a dragon cave.

Dave walked boldly up to the meter-long head and said, "Ho, Hiszt my friend, I hope you are not on sentry duty."

A large eye opened and studied Dave. Slowly the dragon rose on his stubby legs and stretched his wings. "Dave Schuster, my human friend, I did not expect to see you for many days. What brings you back so soon?"

"There is trouble up top in the next terrace. A great battle is looming and my people are in danger of annihilation."

"We have also faced danger here, Dave, my first friend from the realm of men. Two days ago, spiders swarmed up from below. We burned many of them. We burned so many of them that our fires are nearly extinguished. Finally, we beat them back and we are resting and recuperating our strength in case they climb up again from the terrace below."

Hiszt paused for a moment and studied Dave. "You are troubled, my human friend. What can we do?"

"I am worried for my human kin on the fourth terrace. What could you do? You can't fly up there and your fires are depleted because of your great battle."

Hiszt closed his eyes for a moment. "First, I will send one of the young green dragons to see if any more spiders are coming up from below. We have had many green dragons join us and we have dragon eggs to protect. We also have some small hatchlings with wingspans of only about ten to twenty paces. They are light enough to fly up to the fourth terrace as scouts. They are very young, so I don't know if I can trust them to be cautious."

"Please send the scouts right away to follow the spiders to make sure they are not returning. When you are rested and your eggs are safe, will you help us?"

"Yes," said Hiszt, "we will help you. You are our friends and allies. We stand and fall together."

Dave could do nothing but wait for the scouts' return. He set up camp on a ledge, well up from the terrace by the mouth of a subterranean passage. He hoped the escarpment would slow the spiders, but realized the arachnids had no trouble walking up a vertical surface. When they had moved their previous camp closer to the dragon caves, he began pacing back and forth.

"Husband, you will wear a trench in the rock if you don't calm down. Your pacing will not hasten the return of the scouts."

"I know Arlana, but I can't just sit here. Our friends could be dying up there."

"Still, it's wise to proceed cautiously. If we blunder in, our help may be wasted. We could do more harm than good, since we might wind up needing to be rescued ourselves."

"I know. But pacing helps me release tension, and I do my best thinking when I am walking."

He continued pacing, until eventually, Dave realized that his wisest course of action would be to catch up on his sleep.

More than a day later, Dave heard Hiszt's bugle call and rushed down the cliff at a speed bordering on recklessness. Not for the first time did he wonder where his fear of heights had gone. Hiszt was speaking with a number of relatively small green dragons. He turned to Dave.

"The news is not good. The spider army is much larger than we thought. They have climbed past the fifth terrace well to the southeast of us. They are mostly up to the fourth terrace already. We don't know where they are going."

"Do you think they will come back here, Hiszt?"

"No Dave, the spiders are attacking someone else. I think we are safe for now."

"Friend-in-arms Hiszt, I am going to head up the Spiral Ramp and make sure the entrance is clear of enemies. Come as soon as you can with as many of your folk as you can. We have no time to lose."

Dave, Arlana and Hanomer walked rapidly up the spiral ramp that had been cut by the captive rock-borer. The ramp had only a ten percent grade so they made fast progress, and emerged from the camouflaged entrance at the side of a rocky hill. There were no enemies in sight. Indeed, there was no indication of a looming battle.

Just then a number of small green dragons, some with wingspans of only five or ten paces, flew up over the edge of the escarpment and alighted near Dave. The largest waddled close to him and extended his head. Dave touched the dragon's neck to communicate by contact telepathy.

Lord Dave, we have been sent by our elders to help you look around. We were told not to be silly and to listen to what you say.

This was a very young dragon. He was bubbling over with excitement. *I think Hiszt is showing me great trust by letting me use these hatchlings for reconnaissance.*

Young master, I want you and your friends to circle above me and look along the terrace. Go as high as you need to, but stay above me, do not fly southeast because of the danger. When you see many men, circle around and watch them. Then all of you come back to me to report. Do you understand? Say it back to me.

When the young hatchling had the orders clear in his mind and had communicated to the others, Dave waved them aloft. He saw them climb higher and higher in broad circles, but they did not stray from overhead. Finally, after fifteen minutes, the hatchlings landed and conferred with one another. After the conference, the same hatchling as before waddled over to Dave on his four short legs and extended his neck.

We did see something, Lord Dave, but I do not know how to describe it. Would you like to see a picture?

Please.

Dave touched the dragon's flank and his mind's eye saw a rapidly receding terrace below him, and himself standing on the top of a hill looking up. As the hatchling recalled his climb, Dave saw further and further with each turn of the spiral. Finally, about eight kilometers distant, he saw the familiar butte through the dragon's eyes.

Its eyes were sharp, and it saw the butte crowded with Bigelow's men. Then he saw something else. There were three armies outside the butte. Bigelow's men were themselves attacked from the north and the south by two much smaller forces. On top of the escarpment, Dave saw a strange set of poles with flags on them. He saw the flags change, and then heard the faint blast of a horn.

Other rebels are trying to break the siege of the butte. But there are too few. Where are the spiders? Have they passed them by? It's still early morning. When will the others arrive? There is no time to lose.

An hour later, Hiszt poked his snout out from the Spiral Ramp's exit. Dragon after dragon followed him. Within minutes Dave had explained the situation, and the whole band began to move south. The dragons could move at a fast walk comfortably with their wings folded in a compact mass on their back. They made an incredible noise as they broke small trees, widening the path through the woods.

Hiszt kept the young hatchlings aloft gathering more news. Two hours later they left the forest and saw the battle before them. Dave arrayed the dragons in a long line with the largest ones to the east near the drop to the fifth terrace. The smallest dragons were on the west at the wall rising to the third terrace.

Something had changed on the battlefield. A hatchling came down and played his visual feed back for Dave and Hiszt. The southwest force of rebels had retreated onto the butte and a massive line of arachnids had charged into Bigelow's men, inexorably pushing them back.

Under Hiszt's command, the dragon line advanced. The armies were so concerned with the arachnids that, at first, no one saw them. The bugle sounded again and Dave saw that the flags had changed once more.

The rebels in front of the dragons began to disengage smoothly from Bigelow's men and file onto the butte. Now Bigelow's men saw the dragons advancing from their rear and the remnants of that shattered army either surrendered to the rebels and were taken onto the butte or ran towards the dragons, throwing their weapons away with their hands in the air.

Hiszt let the disarmed men run though the dragon line into the woods beyond. Now the spiders were upon them. The dragons spouted a withering fire, incinerating the spiders as they advanced. The dragon line stopped and kept burning the spiders as they advanced. Finally, the spider advance stopped. The dragons hesitated a minute to let the flames die down. Then they began to advance, hurling fresh flames into the mass of spiders.

Now they were even with the butte. The smaller dragons had no spiders to burn and circled behind the large green dragons, leapfrogging them to give them a short break. The battlefield smelled of burned chitin and of the cocktail that made up the dragon's flame.

The dragons came upon a cluster of much larger insects surrounded by a dense cordon of spiders. Hiszt led a contingent of the largest green dragons directly at this group burning them in an inferno of dragon fire. Then remarkably, the spiders began to scatter, and lost all cohesion as a fighting force.

The dragons were spent. They rested where they were, some waddling over to a stream cascading down from the butte for a drink of water. Larsen and Chartrand came down from the butte, shook hands with Dave and Hanomer, and gave Arlana a hug.

"Did Al find Pam and Little Thomas?" asked Dave.

Chartrand looked crestfallen. "No. We were on the way to the Eagles when we came across survivors of the Eagle camp attack. Apparently, Bigelow surprised the Eagles at night and overran the whole camp, taking them all prisoner except for a small band of warriors that managed to break through. The prisoners were all taken to Seth. That's where we went, but even after a lot of searching, we found no trace of Pam and Little Thomas."

"So, where's Al?"

Larsen and Chartrand both pointed to the flags at the top of the escarpment. "In his zeal to find Pam, Al managed to stir up all the slaves in Seth to rebellion while Bigelow was hunting the rebels. Apparently, among the rebels that kind of rescue puts the rescued under obligation, and so Al was made battle chief of all the slaves in Seth. He would have been with us down here except he took a pretty serious wound. You probably need to call him Lord Gleeson or something like that, seeing that he's become a big cheese." Larsen smiled.

"More like I should box his ears instead," said Dave. "He can't help but get into trouble when I'm not there to look after him." He glanced at Arlana who was rolling her eyes and shaking her head.

Arlana had been listening. "If Bigelow has Pam and Little Thomas," she said, "should we not make haste to find him?"

"You're right," said Dave.

"Chartrand and I took a careful look at the soldiers who surrendered. Bigelow wasn't with them," said Larsen.

"A lot of soldiers slipped through the ranks of the dragons when their ranks broke. Bigelow could have slipped through," said Dave.

"Or he could be among the corpses," added Chartrand.

"Let's set up six search parties and chase the fleeing soldiers," said Dave.

"Chartrand and I will get the best trackers to go with us. The last thing we need is to get ambushed by Bigelow and his men.

A week later it was a morose group that met at Al's base camp on the first terrace. Dave looked around and saw concern on every face. They had found no trace of Bigelow even though they had chased his men for many miles. Every captured man had said Bigelow had stayed in the command tent opposite the butte near the drop to the fifth terrace. They found the command tent rent by the spiders, but so sign of Bigelow's body or his special bodyguard.

Pam and Little Thomas had not shown up. The message from everyone was the same: no one could have escaped Bigelow's overwhelming surprise attack on the Eagle camp. Only a determined war band of veteran warriors could break through the cordon. Had Pam been killed in the attack?

Dave could see that Al had long been without hope. Hopeful development after hopeful development had been dashed. He had run out of ideas. And he had no place left to look.

Chapter 51

The Trap Slams Shut

Linder, Tandor, Thomas, and Makalo had just arrived at the Eagle village on their way back to the swamp and home. Their joy, beyond hope, at finding Pam and Little Thomas safe in the Eagle village still filled Linder with an optimism about the future he hadn't felt since he had heard about the kidnapping. Tomorrow when they took them to see Al—Linder could imagine the look of surprise and delight on Al's face. Then they could head home.

Pam had a long line of villagers coming to see her. She was firmly established as the village healer. *I hope Loktor isn't going to make trouble when we take her back to Al tomorrow.*

Still, Linder's optimism was beginning to give way to a feeling of uneasiness. He had a growing sense of foreboding that told him trouble was brewing.

I'm supposed to be a man of logic, a believer in cause and effect. So why do I give so much credence to these feelings?

"Perhaps, because they always prove to be correct," he muttered to himself.

His misgivings made him restless, and he began to pace. Pam gave him a quizzical look as if to say: "Why are you disturbing my patients?"

She's going to be awhile. I've broken one of my rules and that's why I'm feeling this way. Whenever I make camp, I always plan an emergency escape route. I didn't this time.

Having realized the source of his unease, he left the large healing tent and began walking around the village. The guards seemed to be in place and alert. *Where would I go if we had to leave in a hurry?*

He wandered over to the escarpment that led to the fourth terrace. It was not well guarded and he began to search along the rim for both a path down, and a hiding place. He saw several possibilities, all of which he disregarded either because the descent was too treacherous or because they would be too visible from the rim. Finally, he found what he wanted, a crevice that sloped down about fifteen meters and then ended at a ledge. He tested the descent. It was easy enough that they could manage it even in the dark. There were several shallow caves and possible paths for exiting the ledge to even lower levels.

His conscience satisfied, Linder headed back to the healing tent. He had learned when he first came, that about once a week, Loktor, the chieftain of the Eagles, issued a new password that had to be used to re-enter the camp. Earlier this evening the new password, "dragon's beard," had been passed from mouth to mouth.

As twilight deepened, Linder saw an Eagle clan member in ordinary worker's garb, gathering firewood. Something about the gatherer alerted Linder's suspicions. The man was just too aware of his surroundings, constantly checking for others. In a zig zag route, the gatherer moved further and further from the camp and seemed to be searching for firewood in a place where there were few guards and little deadwood. The man waved to one guard as he approached, and the guard waved back.

The hair on the back of Linder's head stood up. He remained stock still in deep shadow. When the gatherer's back was turned, Linder advanced quietly to the next shadow, far enough away that he would not be heard.

When well past the camp, the gatherer looked around searchingly, then dropped his bundle of sticks and walking rapidly, went deeper into the forest. Linder crept after him, listening for the cracks of breaking deadwood, to keep on his trail.

Finally, he heard the hoot of a night bird, only to be answered by an answering hoot. *Maybe he's just meeting his lady love*, thought Linder. But he didn't believe it.

Coming to the edge of a clearing, Linder heard subdued voices ahead of him and made out the words, "dragon's beard." Now there was no doubt. Linder moved back to the camp as quickly as he could, without making a racket. When he reached the perimeter, he gave the new password to the guard and said, "There are men in the woods dressed like us. I heard one of our people giving them the new password. We're being attacked by Bigelow!"

"Stranger, how do I know it's not you who's part of the attack, even though you know the password?"

"You have to tell Loktor, the chief, before it's too late."

"I can't leave my post. You tell him."

As Linder left, he saw a couple of men approach the sentry, and give the password. One stayed to talk and the other ambled into camp.

It's too late. There's no time to try to find Loktor. I have to get my people out of here.

Linder ran back to the healing tent and said breathlessly, "We have to leave now! We're under attack."

Pam was just putting her supplies away. The others looked at Linder uncomprehendingly.

"Now!" Linder shouted. At his tone, everyone began to move. Linder gave them thirty seconds to gather their things and then led them off to the cliff edge. The camp was still quiet. *Bigelow is getting his infiltrators into position and will attack in a concerted manner when all of his soldiers are in position. We still have time to get to the cliff edge before the carnage begins.*

Reaching the cliff edge, Linder swore under his breath when he realized they were about forty meters from where he wanted to be. But he soon found the path down.

"I'll go first, then Pam, and Little Thomas." Linder was already three steps down the narrow trail, helping Pam find her way, when he saw Tandor hesitate and then dash back toward camp. Thomas and Makalo stayed with them. Thomas occasionally took Little Thomas's hand when Pam had to negotiate a difficult part of the descent. Makalo kept an eye on the top of the escarpment, in case an enemy appeared.

Pam had Little Thomas by the hand while Linder guided her steps. They made it to the first ledge. Linder could hear shouting and the clash of weapons coming from the camp—the assault had begun.

Tandor reappeared at the escarpment edge, breathless, and scrambled down the trail at a reckless pace. Linder had the party hide in a shallow cave. The shouting of battle, the screams of the dying, and the clash of weapons—like hundreds of hammers beating on anvils—filled the air.

The six huddled together in silence. Even Little Thomas seemed to recognize the danger and did not whimper or cry out. At long last, the sound of battle diminished. Only the occasional scream of a wounded man filled the night air.

Linder quietly told them of the events that led to their escape. He described his search for the path, the traitor, and how he had tried to warn Loktor. "I knew I had no time to find him. I chose to save us instead."

They stayed hidden for another two hours, and then Linder led them further down the cliff face. In the dark, it was hard going, and treacherous.

There was a slide of rock, and Pam cried out. "Are you okay?" whispered Linder.

"No, I stepped on a loose rock, and badly twisted my ankle."

"Is it broken?"

"I can't tell for sure. I know I can't put any weight on it."

"Okay," said Linder, "we have to go to ground."

Linder left Pam and Little Thomas with Thomas while he, Makalo, and Tandor searched for a place where they could hold out until Pam was well enough to travel. That meant water, shelter, and food.

Linder moved southeast along the narrow shelf until he found a small stream of water cascading down the cliff face, and a couple of shallow indentations, but nothing that would protect them for any length of time. Finally, he found a round hole, about two meters in diameter with a tell-tale trace of round, pebbly gravel cascading down. *Rock-borer*, he thought. *That means it goes in a long way, but what if the borer comes back?*

Rock-borers moved at a slow walk but were virtually unkillable and unstoppable.

I have to hook up some kind of warning system, for the borer would never follow us along the cliff face.

Linder rejoined the others to compare notes. Everyone had found something, but his entrance seemed the best. No one wanted to hang out with a rock-borer, but ultimately Linder convinced them, that with proper safeguards, the tunnel he had found could work.

After immobilizing Pam's ankle, they slowly made their way to the cave entrance, with Linder and Thomas half supporting and half carrying her. Pam and Little Thomas waited at the round entrance while the others explored the interior. About one hundred paces in, the round tunnel entered a rock chamber with a small trickle of water on the far wall. There were several side chambers and a pebbly floor left over by the borer. Lumi-lichen gave the space a pale green-yellow sheen that kept the chamber from being completely dark, even when they covered their light gourds.

"I think we have shelter and water. Now we only have to worry about food," said Linder.

"I think I smelled a rock pigeon rookery nearby. That should provide us with eggs. And the pigeons can be delicious," said Tandor.

"I think we have enough food for a few days, and I need to set up our watches in case that borer returns. If you like, why not have a look for your rock pigeons," said Linder.

There was only one borer tunnel into and out of the chambers they had chosen, so Linder arranged it so that someone was always two hundred paces further in on a small rise watching and listening for the return of the borer.

Pam pronounced her ankle severely sprained, but not broken. Everyone worked to make themselves at home. After they were settled, Tandor approached Linder. He clearly had something on his mind.

"Linder," said Tandor, "When Al hears Chartrand and Larsen's news, he will head straight for the Eagles and into Bigelow's clutches. I must let Al know that Pam is safe, and warn them not to journey to the Eagles."

"Shouldn't I be the one to go?" asked Linder.

"Al depends on you to keep Pam safe. Besides, I know my way around the terraces and have the trust of the rebel tribes."

"How are you going to do it?"

"The third terrace has too many enemies, but I think the fourth terrace will still be relatively free, except for small dragons. I will use that." Tandor packed up and was gone in fifteen minutes.

The days passed uneventfully. They filled their time with guard duty and foraging for food. A week later Tandor returned, emaciated, and his clothes in rags. Bigelow was already on the fourth terrace. His soldiers had hounded Tandor, and only now had he been able to return.

After three weeks, Pam insisted she was well enough to travel, but Linder wondered if she wasn't letting her concern for Al overshadow her judgment. As a consequence, he had been postponing their journey until he was sure. Today he was taking Pam on a small climbing test to see how her ankle performed.

She was better going down the cliff than climbing up. More than once, her saw her wince as she had to stress her ankle to reach for an awkwardly-situated rock projection. When they returned, he was still unsure.

"What's wrong with everybody?" asked Pam.

Linder looked at the cave mouth. Everyone except Makalo was sitting outside the tunnel entrance with their supplies piled around them.

Chapter 52

The Rock-Borer

Linder was about to ask about Makalo when the latter appeared, puffing. "The rock-borer is definitely coming—Oh, hi Linder. Am I glad you're back."

"Okay," said Linder, "Let's move away from the tunnel opening. Over there, the ledge broadens out."

"Do you think the borer will follow us?" asked Thomas.

"I don't think so," said Linder, but I don't know enough about them to be sure. He might view us as dessert."

The cliff side shook with a dull, low frequency throb, as if a train were passing through a tunnel just inside the rock. The noise gradually grew louder. Suddenly, large thick tentacles emerged from the tunnel mouth. The tentacles spread out like a giant sea anemone and a grey tube, two meter in diameter, emerged, projecting about five feet beyond the end of the tunnel.

The tube opened up and a cascade of small round pebbles the size of marbles spilled down the mountain side, adding to the scree already there. When the cascade stopped, the tentacles searched the area around the tunnel mouth, and pulled organic matter from the cliff surface into the maw of the monster. Finally, some of the tentacles lifted off the surface of the cliff as if sampling the air.

"You'd almost think," whispered Linder, "that the borer can sense that we're here." He felt the old chill he had first felt in the worm caves, when he had been pursued by a borer through the tunnels.

Suddenly, the tentacles retracted, the protruding end of the borer became bullet shaped, and the monster pulled itself back into the mountain.

The six friends breathed a collective sigh of relief. "I never stop being amazed at rock-borers," said Linder, "If you had told me I would meet a creature so completely symmetrical it wouldn't have to turn around in a tunnel, but simply open up a mouth at its other end, I would never have believed you."

"You know you sound exactly like my brother Al when you talk like that," said Thomas.

"Is that a bad thing?" asked Linder looking anxiously at Pam to see if the reference to Al had distressed her.

"No!" said Thomas.

"Yes," said Makalo, "it shows you have been spending altogether too much time with him." Makalo grinned broadly.

"I think," said Linder, also smiling, "that I have been spending far too much time with the lot of you. I need some new friends. You folks know me far too well. I have no secrets. I'm an open book."

"A book with mostly blank pages," added Makalo helpfully.

"Okay, enough of this. Let's get moving. Pam, you have your wish. Maybe this rock-borer was a sign from God that it's time to find Al."

"Maybe!" said Pam smiling, ignoring Linder's cynicism.

Linder led the way down. After lowering Little Thomas by rope, Pam and Thomas were next. Makalo came last. Following three hours of steady progress, they reached the fourth terrace then stopped for lunch. Pam put up her ankle.

"Let me have a look," said Linder. He could see that it was swollen. "On second thought, this looks like a nice spot. We'll make camp here."

"But we have lots of daylight left," protested Pam.

"We need to get some food, and game seems plentiful here. We have fresh water. A rest now will help us make good time tomorrow."

"This is really about my ankle, isn't it?"

"It's pretty swollen, so that's part of it, but my other comments are true and valid."

Pam harrumphed her displeasure at the delay, but bit back any further retort.

Two days later, they were continuing northwest on the fourth terrace with Linder in the lead, when he came back to the rest of the group at a lope, his index finger to his lips. "Trouble!" he whispered. Without another word he led them back to the cliff wall. They crouched in a hollow among the rocks.

"What spooked you?" asked Pam.

"Spiders," said Linder. "Big spiders, the size of a large dog."

"You don't mean," said Thomas, "those bugs we saw in the terrace below?"

"Yes, that's exactly what I mean."

Linder climbed out of their depression, which was shaped a bit like a sand bunker on a golf course, and peered back along the cliff. Then he came back down into the depression. "I don't believe it. They're climbing up the cliff the way spiders walk up walls. There are thousands of them. The whole escarpment wall from the fifth terrace is covered with them."

"Are they coming this way?" asked Pam, a tremor in her voice.

"I don't think so, but I can't be sure. I am sure the main body of them is heading away from us northwest."

Linder periodically peeked out to see if the spiders were gone. Finally, the terrace ahead of them looked empty, and the cliff wall was also bare.

He wanted to wait to be sure it was safe, but Pam insisted they make a dash for it right then. Ultimately, Linder agreed.

Retracing their steps to the edge of the woods, the group headed back the way they had come. With Linder in the lead, they stayed under cover as much as possible, glancing up at the cliff every few minutes, afraid they might see arachnids. But they made it to a rocky gully without incident. In the bottom of the gully a large, deep creek meandered. They found a natural rock dam, which allowed them to cross. At Pam's insistence, they pushed hard to put as much distance between themselves and the spiders as possible before nightfall.

Finally, Linder called a halt. "We need to decide where to go," he said.

"I want to find Al," said Pam.

"Of course, you do," said Linder, "but we don't know where he is. We need to get you and Little Thomas somewhere safe."

"We have to avoid the arachnids at all cost," said Makalo.

"But all our friends and allies are northwest, the direction the arachnids have gone," said Thomas.

"So, we also have to head northwest. But do we go up or down?" asked Linder.

"I don't want to go up and risk meeting Bigelow," said Pam with a shudder.

"So, we go down to the fifth terrace and try to meet the green dragons," said Linder.

"The green dragons," said Pam. "are you sure they're safe?"

"They've saved our lives several times," said Linder. "I have to go on what I know."

So, they climbed down to the fifth terrace. But their pace was slow. After several days of journeying, Pam's head was spinning. She had asked incessant questions about the green dragons. Having lived with the Eagles, she knew their fear of dragons, but what she was hearing from Linder made her realize the green dragons were different. Still, she knew the adults looked like a cross between a small *Tyrannosaurus Rex* and a huge bat. *I'm not going to let their appearance frighten me.*

When they finally came out of the woods to a broad, burn-scarred meadow, her fear intensified, but she would not allow herself to show fear in front of Little Thomas.

Then she saw a tunnel mouth on a broad ledge. From Linder's description, she knew it to be Hiszt's lair, but where were the dragons?

Just then a green dragon spiralled down, landed on the ledge, and waddled into the tunnel mouth.

She felt panic. *Dare I go in there? What if the dragon doesn't know me and fries me to a crisp?*

She steeled herself, reminding herself they hadn't walked this far only to sit at the edge of the meadow in indecision. Pam transferred Little Thomas' hand to his uncle Thomas and walked boldly into the meadow. Makalo and Tandor followed.

"Is this a good idea Pam?" asked Makalo.

"This has taken far too long already. Desperate times require desperate measures."

Pam stopped well below the ledge so that she could still see the tunnel mouth, and called in her no-nonsense voice in the Common Tongue, "Hiszt, are you in there Hiszt? It's Pamela, Al Gleeson's wife— I mean Al Gleeson's mate."

Pam was just about to call again when a green dragon waddled out of the tunnel and peered at her and the others, swiveling its eye stalks from one to another.

"Welcome Pamela, mate of Hiszt's human friend, Albert Gleeson. I am Hirsa, Hizst's mate. My Common Speech is still poor. Come up here so we can communicate mind-to-mind. I have much news."

Pam scaled the small wall to the ledge slowly. Her ankle still gave her a twinge from time to time, especially when she was climbing. She reached the ledge with a grunt of pain, having twisted her ankle with the final exertion.

Drawing a deep breath, Pam approached the green dragon. "Friend Hirsa, I cannot speak mind-to-mind like Dave Schuster, but maybe you can speak to me using mind-talk the way Hanomer, our *Hansa* friend talks to us.

She put her hand on Hirsa's neck, which was as thick as a small tree trunk. Suddenly pictures and information bubbled out of Hirsa. Pam heard of the battle and the victory in great detail.

Finally, Pam interrupted the dragon's flow of thought. "But where is my mate, Albert Gleeson?" Pam asked out loud.

Ah, of course, you have been separated from him for a long time. Albert Gleeson has been wounded. He has returned to the human town of Seth.

"Seth," said Pam in despair, "how am I ever going to get there with my child?"

I will take you, human friend Pam.

But Hirsa, the air is too thin for you to fly.

I am strong and I will take you by the great Spiral Tunnel.

After a hasty meal, Pam and Little Thomas settled onto Hirsa's back, as she walked rapidly up a tunnel. True to her word, even though she waddled, Hirsa moved as fast as a cantering horse.

"Are we going to see Daddy again?"

"Yes, soon my love. Are you afraid?"

"No, this is fun."

Chapter 53

The Grand Council of Seth

Al's wound still pained him as he sat in an ornate chair at a round table with his Grand Council—his chieftains and advisors. Both the Hawk and Eagle clans now owed him allegiance, or so he had been told, since he had rescued them. Still, that didn't stop them from bickering like fishmongers over the price of herring when he wasn't issuing edicts. Issuing edicts was just what he was trying to avoid.

Loktor had the floor. "We canna hold Seth if Meglir comes against us. We will be snared rabbits if we stay here."

Dave cleared his throat and quietly stood up as Loktor continued his lament, arguing that holding Seth was a foolish move.

Finally, Al said, "Thank you Loktor. Our colleague Rokodor has been waiting quietly for some time to speak. Please give him the floor for a few minutes."

Loktor sat down. Dave looked around. "Esteemed colleagues, our colleague Loktor is right. We are in a dangerous and precarious position. Bigelow has escaped and wants nothing more than to retake Seth and re-establish himself in the good grace of his master, Meglir. Then he will resume his hunt for all of us. Holding Seth is dangerous, but relinquishing Seth is more dangerous still.

"If Bigelow retakes Seth, he will extend the switchback road to the third terrace and harass us at every turn. We cannot go back to how it was before. We have become a force and a great danger to the Bent Ones."

"What do ye suggest, or are ye simply a crow bearing bad news?" muttered Loktor.

Dave's acute hearing as an Ancient had no trouble picking up Loktor's mutters. "No Loktor, I am not simply a crow bearing bad news. We need to strengthen and hold Seth for as long as we can, but we also need to plan for its loss.

"The terraces have always been the route of invasion and trouble for Bigelow and Seth, for us it is the way of escape. We should improve the road to the second terrace and build fortifications protecting the road entrance at the first and second terraces. We should consider whether we should finish and fortify the road to the third terrace as well. Finally, we should extend the north and south walls right to the edge of the escarpment since we must hold that road open to let our people escape. If the predictions of Loktor come true, and Meglir attacks us with overwhelming force, we must hold the way of escape open at all costs. That means holding the rim of the escarpment to keep the enemy from shooting us as we flee."

Chartrand stood up. Al acknowledged him. "Rokodor's plan is sound, but we also have reason to hope that the Bent Ones will not bend all of their might to destroy us. Meglir is new here, and he has already suffered a setback with the Dark Council because of his defeat at Halcyon. He cannot afford the loss of further prestige by asking for help in regaining Seth. He will come on his own with a much smaller force. To me that is all the more reason to hold Seth."

Loktor rose again and Al acknowledged him. Looking at Al he said, "Ye be my liege Lord, by rescuing me and me people, and I will honor the oath, but I still say ..." he stopped, his eyes going wide, looking beyond Al. A murmur went up in the room and everyone looked behind Al.

Al turned around. Standing in the door way was a woman in torn clothes with dirt on her face holding the hand of a boy. Recognition dawned. Al bolted from his chair feeling a stab of pain in his side. Grabbing his side, he lurched forward.

Pam ran to him and embraced him. Al felt himself grinning like a fool. He had given up in despair, yet here they were, whole. Al picked up Little Thomas who was getting too big to scoop up, and hugged the two of them together.

This display of affection will do nothing to enhance my stature as battle chief, but I don't really care. Not even a little bit.

Chapter 54

A New Beginning

After several weeks had passed, it was well before dawn and they were on their way back to the swamp in the country of the Necroans.

"So, you two—or should I say three—are not coming back home?" asked Thomas as he turned from his horse to look at his brother and friends.

"No Thomas, we care too much about the people here, and we can't leave Dave and Arlana to do the work alone. After all, I'm the big cheese around here now and everyone seems to owe me their allegiance."

"I feel badly about leaving you here."

"Don't! We need someone to look after our property, and since you're between jobs, you are just the person. Remember we need that property in order for Dave and Arlana to get back to Feiramar."

"He's right," said Dave. "Arlana and I want to convince the Gurundar Council that this is our chance to finally rescue and redeem Abaddon and put an end to the reoccurring scourge of their attacks. We are finally taking the war to the enemy and redeeming their land."

"I'm pretty sure, I'll be back," said Linder. "Pam is much too good for you Gleeson, and I have to check in to make sure you're treating her right.

"As for you, Arlana, why in the world you ever married a man-child like Schuster, I'll never know. I'll have to come back to check on you two as well."

"Well," said Arlana, "my husband does test my patience at times, but you have to admit Linder, that he has done well. None of my friends back home have husbands who have become dragon riders, descended to Sheol, and returned."

It was early in the morning and they were heading back toward the swamp using the mine road.

"I'm glad," said Makalo, "that your chieftains saw the wisdom of improving the switchback road and extending it to the third terrace."

"The walls around Seth have been extended right to the edge of the escarpment," said Al, "the strongholds on the first and second terraces are almost complete and the one on the third terrace will be finished in three months. If Meglir comes, he will be surprised how hard it will be to drive us out of our home."

By dawn, they had arrived at the now-abandoned mine from which Tandor had been rescued. Except for Pam and Little Thomas, who were heading back to Seth with a warrior escort, the other friends proceeded on foot all the way to the black swamp oaks to see Makalo, Chartrand and Larsen off. Tomorrow they would return, and Thomas and Linder would make the trip.

As usual, Hanomer led, making sure they were safe. They reached and crossed the swamp without incident.

Makalo, Chartrand, and Larsen settled into the black swamp oaks and the others stayed until late afternoon, when they left the swamp and sped back to the butte which had been their camping site when they had first come to Abaddon. They spent a watchful night, but the Necroans did not appear.

Early the next morning, they repeated the whole procedure with Linder and Thomas completing the trip through the swamp oaks. In the afternoon, Al, Hanomer, Dave, and Arlana met the returning-warriors escort and rode with them back to Seth.

"We've talked about Meglir," said Dave, "but what about Blackmore? Do you think he's here, Al? And will he give us trouble?"

Al thought for a moment. "Knowing Blackmore and his political acumen, I'm sure he's here, and will cause us trouble at some point."

Dave nodded. "I wish we had seen the back of him. Meglir is trouble enough."

The three made it back to Seth, which already looked to be a happier place than it had ever been under Bigelow. People laughed as they chatted in the streets, and children were playing outdoors.

Daily patrols went across the plain and up the road in order to be able to provide plenty of warning, in the event of Meglir's approach.

Each day, escaped slaves from the other cities added to their numbers. Light had begun to dawn in the dark of this long-troubled land.

The tiny spark that Al had ignited in Seth had become a flame that promised to burn a cleansing fire throughout all of Abaddon.

The End

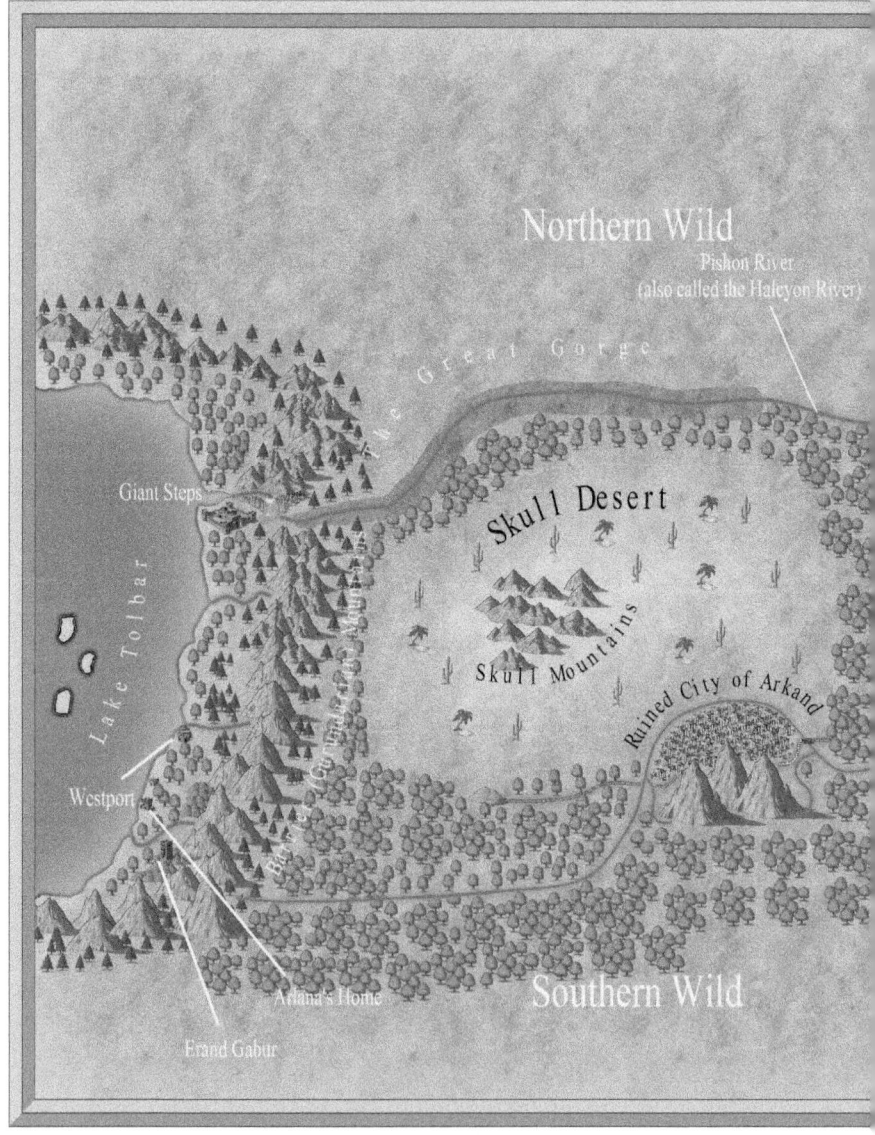

Wood Island

Deadman's Reef

New Jerusalem

The University of Halcyon

Botany Creek

Morfen (Part of The Great Southern Fen)

Culman Swamp

Kellbur

Goose's Neck

Great Southern Fen

0   50

Scale in Miles

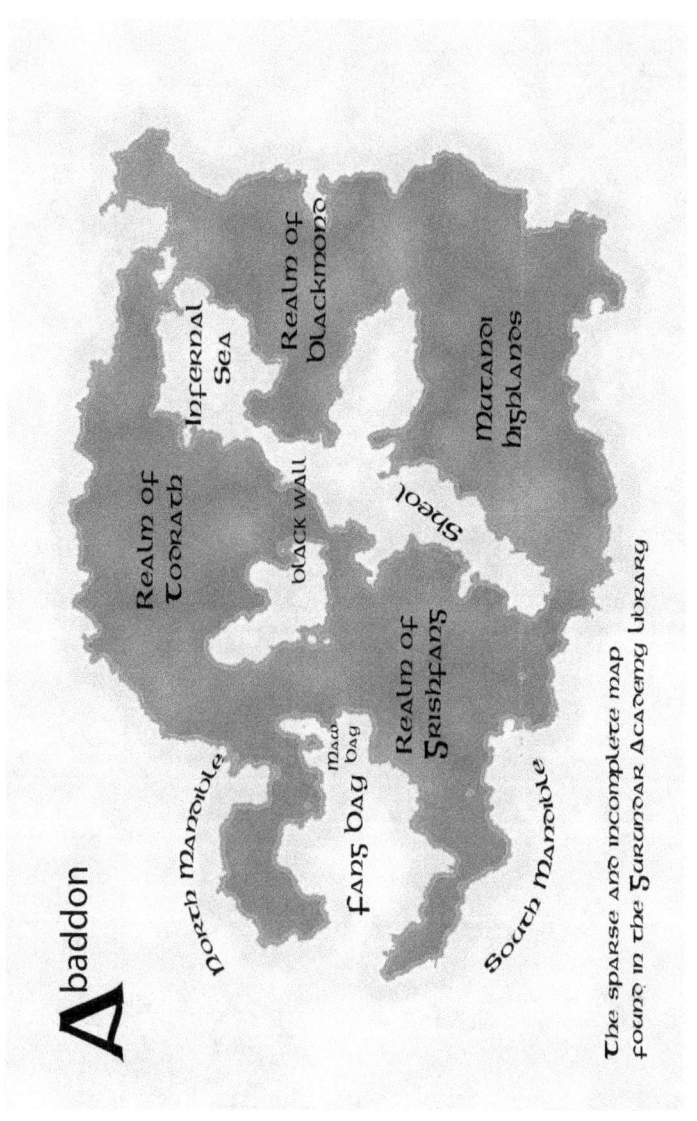

Abaddon

North Mandible

Realm of Toorath

Infernal Sea

Realm of Blackmoor

Black Wall

Mataroi Highlands

Sheol

Fang Bag Bag

Realm of Grishfang

South Mandible

The sparse and incomplete map found in the Surander Academy Library

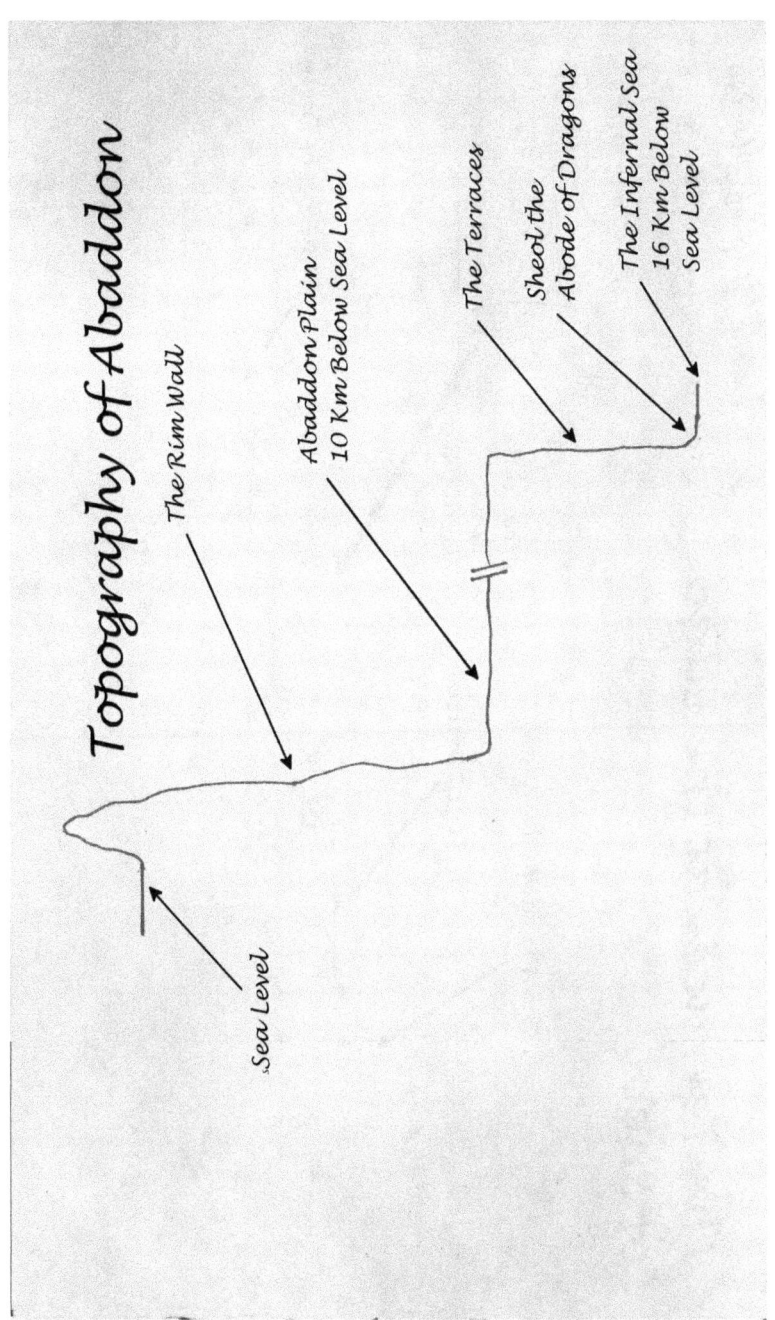

Topography of Abaddon

Sea Level

The Rim Wall

Abaddon Plain
10 Km Below Sea Level

The Terraces

Sheol the
Abode of Dragons

The Infernal Sea
16 Km Below
Sea Level

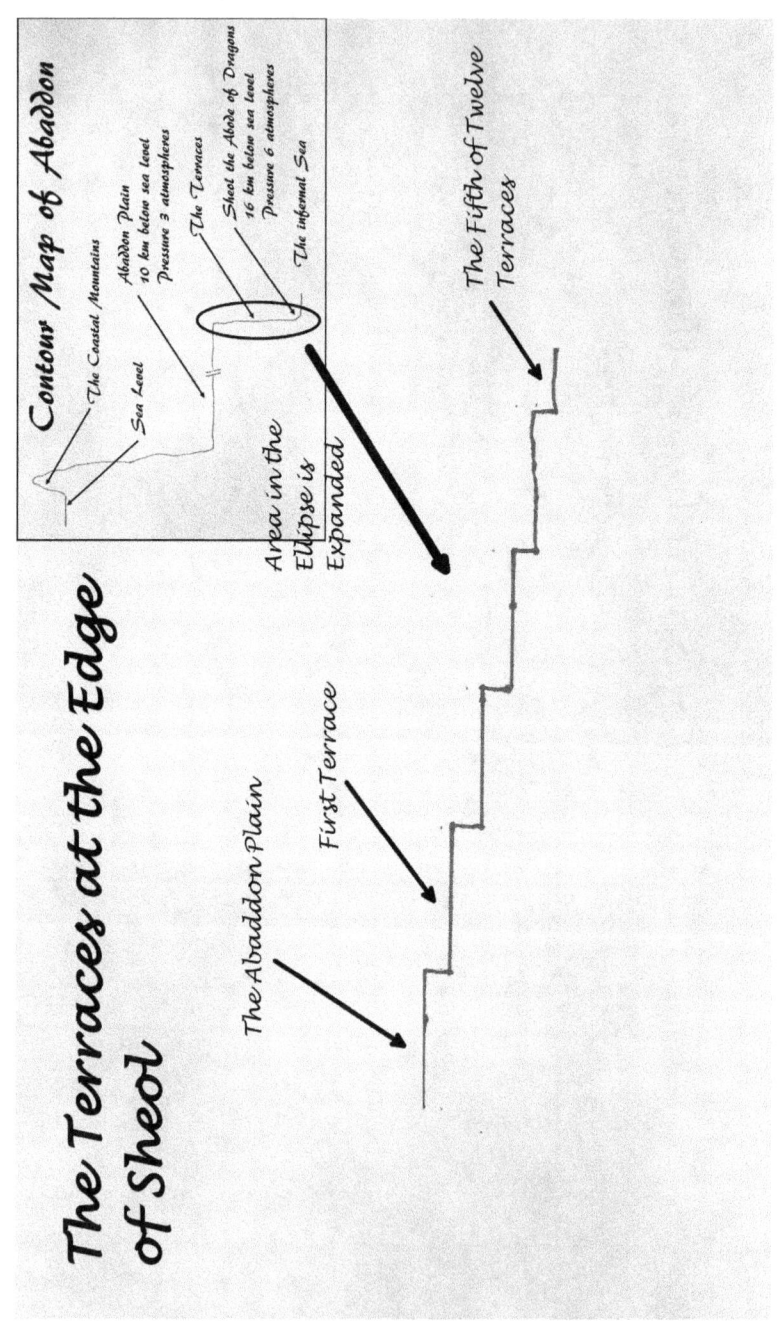

The Terraces at the Edge of Sheol

Contour Map of Abaddon

The Coastal Mountains

Sea Level

Abaddon Plain
10 km below sea level
Pressure 3 atmospheres

The Terraces

Sheol, the Abode of Dragons
16 km below sea level
Pressure 6 atmospheres

The Infernal Sea

Area in the Ellipse is Expanded

The Abaddon Plain

First Terrace

The Fifth of Twelve Terraces

The Southern Marches
Of Abaddon

Seth

Terraces to Sheol

Road to
Mutandi
Highlands

Pachydon Grasslands

Black Swamp Oaks
Necroan Fen

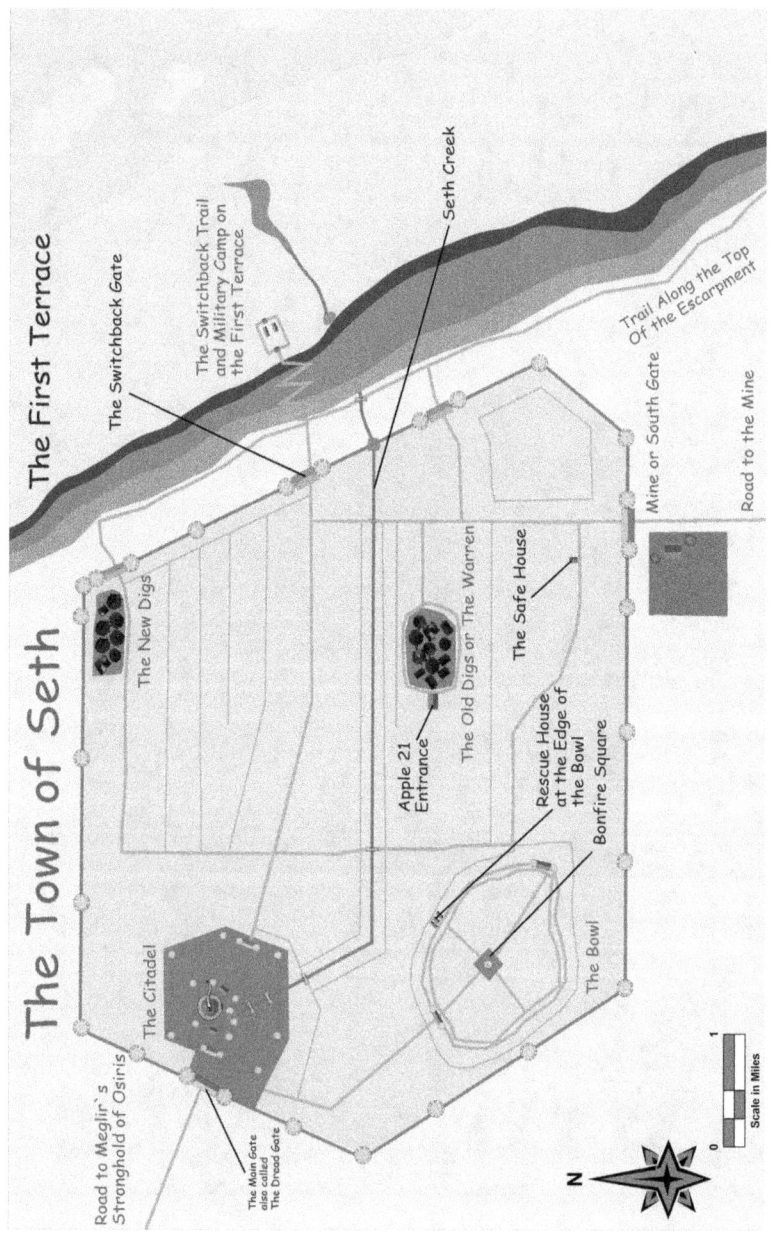

The Town of Seth

The First Terrace

The Switchback Gate

The Switchback Trail and Military Camp on the First Terrace

Seth Creek

Trail Along the Top Of the Escarpment

The New Digs

Mine or South Gate

Road to the Mine

Apple 21 Entrance

The Old Digs or The Warren

The Safe House

Rescue House at the Edge of the Bowl

Bonfire Square

The Bowl

The Citadel

Road to Meglin's Stronghold of Osiris

The Main Gate also called The Dread Gate

Scale in Miles

0 1

N

Glossary

Abaddon (A-bah-don): A continent to the east of Halcyon, which consists of a continent-wide crater surrounded by a ring of tall mountains. The Abaddon plain is about ten kilometers below sea level, while Sheol is about sixteen kilometers below sea level. The high air pressure at this depth and the warm temperatures sustain many large and unusual life forms that cannot survive at one atmosphere of pressure. Abaddon is the home continent of the Bent Ones.

Alandro: A 5th level thief in the Guild. His sister is Vixa.

Ancients: A race of beings that inhabit the continent of Feiramar. These people were separated by the Great Plague unleashed by Meglir. The Guardians or *Gurundar* (the contaminated ones) live east of Lake Tolbar and are not permitted to cross over to the western shores. West of Lake Tolbar live the *Naromundar* (the pure ones). The two sundered peoples only meet on the Callabar Islands in the middle of Lake Tolbar. After one of these infrequent meetings, those *Naromundarians* who met with the *Gurundarians* must stay in quarantine on the islands for three months before they can return home.

Ap: Hansean for "son of." This designation is used instead of a surname.

Arch Tree: A carnivorous tree found in the Mutandi Highlands. The tree consists of two trunks with vine-like appendages near the ground that act as trip wires. Breaking these vines causes a series of two-foot-long, serrated thorns to be plunged into the unsuspecting prey. The impaled victim is then slowly digested by the plant and the thorns are gradually returned to their "loaded" position. This plant was likely one of the experiments by the ancient wizards in the Mutandi Highlands, which work to develop lethal plants and animals.

Arachodor (err-RACK-oh-door**):** Kelldor's chief rival on the Council of Thirteen, the governing council of Gurundar. Arachodor believes Lesser Men are not much better than Halfmen and need to be exterminated for the safety of the Guardians.

Arkand (ARE-kand): A great city that was the capital of the Ancients before the capital was moved to Tar-en-Nar. It is guarded by the *Gurundar* for it contains many libraries and much knowledge.

Arlana (Are-LAHN-uh): Arlana is a *Gurundarian* who is the daughter of Kelldor, the chief of the *Gurundarians*.

Bandomer (BAND-oh-mer): One of the *Hansa* members of the Council at Eleytheria. He accompanied Al and Pam back to Halcyon to rescue Little Thomas.

Bent Ones: Bent Ones come from the continent of Abaddon off the east coast of Feiramar. The Bent Ones only come infrequently to Feiramar. They are Ancients who have given themselves over to evil. They bend and shape living things through their arts in support of evil.

Blackcloaks: Are of rank lower than Redcloaks. Blackcloaks may be Bent Ones (perverted Ancients of Abaddon) or humans who have long been in the service of evil.

Black Swamp Oak: (Also called swamp oak and black oak.) A kind of fast-growing travel oak that grows in swamp. This tree with black leaves forms a pear-shaped profile and can hold one person for transport to a twin black swamp oak elsewhere. This oak produces one large double acorn which gives rise to the two linked sister oaks when the halves are planted.

Blackthorn: The assistant steward of slaves in charge of construction projects at the Seth fortress.

Blade Trees: A species of tree in Feiramar with long blade-like leaves that has the extraordinary property of taking an iron or steel blade that is embedded into the living tree and transforming it into a molecularly engineered composite blade of extraordinary strength and sharpness. The process whereby the iron is slowly replaced by the composite, takes hundreds of years, so the Ancients established groves of these trees with embedded blades for future generations. These blades are so strong and sharp that they cut through ordinary steel as if it were light wood.

Boat Weed: A living plant used by the *Hansa* and the Ancients to build boats. A boat frame of cut reeds or wood is constructed and then planted with boat weed. The plant takes on the shape of the boat and makes it watertight while acting like camouflage.

Bossman: the title given by the Guild to a battalion leader who is in charge of a group of thieves and servant workers for hire.

Brotas (BRO-taz): A travel bread which does not go stale and is nourishing for long journeys.

Callabar Islands (CAL-eh-bar): Islands in the middle of Lake Tolbar used for negotiations between the Gurundarians and their sundered kin the Naromundarians. After the negotiations, the Naromundarian delegates must spend several weeks in quarantine to make sure they have not been infected with the Great Plague caused by Meglir.

Camgar: Second in command of the Eagle rebel band.

Celyddon (SELL-e-dawn): Best friend of Kelldor, and adopted father of Dave. He is also a member of the Council of Thirteen.

Cloaks: The generic name given to the highest level of society in Grishfang in Abaddon. There are Redcloaks, Blackcloaks, and Greycloaks. Cloaks can kill any soldier, steward, merchant, or slave on a whim without any questions being asked.

Da: Word in the Ancient Tongue meaning "daughter of."

Donovan Barclay: Dave's pseudonym while trying to locate Al on Halcyon.

Dorai (DOOR-eye): Aquatic mammals that the Ancients ride when they travel over the sea or up rivers.

Dwight Larsen: An old friend of Tom Chartrand and Al Gleeson.

Eagles: A rebel band that rescued Pam and Little Thomas from Bigelow. The Eagles chieftain's name is Loktor and his battlechief is Camgar.

Edward Makalo (Mah-KALL-oh): a physicist who helped discover many of the properties of black swamp oaks and of swords made inside a blade tree. His grandfather was an Igbo fighter in the Nigerian civil war.

Endowyn (ENN-do-win): Hanomer's wife.

Erand Gabur (ERAND ga-BUR): A fortress belonging to Kelldor's chief rival Arachodor. Arachodor believes Lesser Men are not much better than Halfmen and need to be exterminated for the safety of the Guardians.

Falcor: Captain of the brigantine, the Eagle and Ferris's friend.

Feiramar (FAIR-a-mar): The name of the continent that contains the *Hansa* and the Ancients. The island of Halcyon is off the east coast of this continent.

Gram: The name Dave gave to his sword from the blade tree in the Kellburg.

Granomer (GRAN-oh-mer): Chief Loremaster of the *Hansa*. Loremasters store up knowledge for the *Hansa* since they keep few written records.

Greycloaks: Are the lowest tier in the cloak hierarchy. Greycloaks may be Bent Ones (perverted Ancients of Abaddon) or humans who have long been in the service of evil.

Grimbor: The blade meister teaching at the Gurundar Academy for Guardians and Rangers.

Guardians: Also called *Gurundar*. They are the remnant of Ancients that guard the plague lands. They avoided Meglir's lair in the City of the Dead since only through them could Meglir capture a new body and be freed from his pillar prison under the mountain. For this reason, the *Hansa* thought the Guardians had all left and had abandoned the fight against Meglir.

Guild: Also called the servant Guild. A clandestine organization that rents out their services to the underlings of the Bent Ones to help them accomplish their tasks. Slaves are so persecuted and unreliable that these underlings look elsewhere to accomplish their assigned tasks. Periodically the Bent Ones clamp down on the Guild and enslave them.

Halfmen: Halfmen are short, powerful bipeds with long arms. They crudely speak the Common Tongue and use weapons including short bows. They have been created by the Bent Ones, from the captured Ancients by breeding them with apes so as to weaken them and make them susceptible to suggestion and control. Unlike the Apemen, who must be controlled directly, Halfmen act on their own, often fight among themselves, and have an abiding hatred for most living things.

Hansa (HAN-suh): *Hansa* are furry bipeds that have a prehensile tail that ends in a hand. Although not overly intelligent, they are given to music and poetry and have a highly developed sense of honor, justice, and are self-sacrificing in their service to others. There are left-handed and right-handed *Hansa* depending on the handedness of their prehensile tail.

Hanomer (HAN-oh-mur): Is a *Hansa* chief and friend of Dave Schuster.

Happenone (HAPP-en-own): The compound name given to the active ingredient in Happy Berries which led to Renegades.

Hawks: A rebel band contacted by Al when they climbed out of the depths. Later, they held Dave, Arlana, and Hanomer captive.

Hirsa (HERE-sah): A green dragon, Hiszt's mate.

Hiszt (HISST): The chief green dragon.

Hollidor (HAUL-i-door): Kelldor's brother, father of Ferris, and fellow member of the Council of Thirteen.

Horatio: The name of Dave's lup that he raised from a pup.

Hyperhap (HIGH-purr-happ): A derivative compound of Happenone that can be used to control Renegades, and to make them into fearless, strong soldiers called Bezerkers by giving them voice commands at the same time as a Hyperhap injection.

Kelldor (KELL-door): Kelldor is the leader of the Guardians and father of Arlana.

Kendor ap Karnellian: The author of the one history book of Abaddon called The *History of Abaddon*.

Kilk: The *Hansa* name for Apemen.

Klengar (KLENN-garh): The chief slave steward of Seth who aids Al.

Krachodon (CRACK-oh-dawn): A large crocodile-like creature with ten tentacles around the mouth to capture prey.

Kree ah na koo (CREE AH NAH COO): An exclamation in the Ancient Tongue which means "May the Creator help me."

Kyra: A young woman kidnapped (with her daughter Sophie) by Bigelow as he fled Halcyon. She and her daughter were rescued from Bigelow's fortress by Al and his friends.

Lake Tolbar: The long lake that separates the western lands from the eastern plague lands. In the middle of the lake are the Callabar Islands, the infrequent meeting place between East and West.

Le Blanc, Bernice: Blackmore's executive assistant.

Little Thomas: The son of Pam Lowental and Stan Bigelow. He is kept in the Staycare Centre, and in principle, Pam is able to visit him whenever she likes.

Loremasters: *Hansa* who specialize in remembering the past, and lessons from ancient times. They teach other *Hansa* to broaden their education.

Loktor (LOCK-tore): Chieftain of the Eagle rebel band.

Low Town: A neighborhood in Seth in a natural bowl bordered by cliffs and city walls. It was used by Bigelow as an internment camp.

Lumi-Lichen: Lichen that coats most caves in Feiramar. It gives off a pale green light.

Lupi (LOOP-eye): (Singular is lup.) Large, intelligent wolf-like creatures that can plan and coordinate attacks.

Matthews, Hugh: The lookout at New Jerusalem. He was a participant at the Battle of City Port, and decided to join his cousin at New Jerusalem.

Meglir (MEG-leer): Meglir, a great king of the Ancients who grew corrupt and became a tyrant, re-opening ties with the Bent Ones who live on another continent called Abaddon.

Morfang (MORE-fang): Morfang is a Bent One who travelled to the ruined city of Arkand to seek knowledge from the great libraries there. He was discovered there by Kelldor.

Mutandi Highlands (MOO-tan-dee Highlands): A region in southern Abaddon inhabited by wizards who use their arts with warped organisms to create new and bizarre lifeforms.

Myrodon (MY-roe-dawn): Celyddon's door warden at Giant Steps.

Naromundarians (Nar-roe-mun-DARR-ee-ans): "The pure ones." Ancients west of Lake Tolbar who are cut off from the Gurundarians. The Naromundarians still fear the ancient plague caused by Meglir and will not allow any Gurundarians to Naromundar.

Necroans (neck-CROW-ans): Huge, man-like creatures three to five meters tall that live at the foot of the precipice in south Abaddon. Although their bodies are huge, their heads are of average man size which gives them an odd appearance. They frequently raid areas to the north capturing men as slaves and as food. It is rumored they were created from ordinary men many years ago as an experiment by the wizards of the Mutandi Highlands.

Northborough: The village of the Gurundar near the Giant Steps and the nearest village to Celyddon's home.

Pachydons (PACK-i-dons): Huge elephant-like creatures that inhabit the southern plains of Abaddon and attack any interlopers that come near them.

Pishon (PEESH-hawn): The *Hansa* name for the Halcyon River.

Plague: About five hundred years ago, as he was being besieged, Meglir unleashed a plague that killed most of the Ancients and all of the Lesser Men besieging The City of the Dead. Meglir retreated into his obelisk as his host also died, while the Gurundar were sundered from their western brethren and The City of the Dead was declared off limits by the Gurundar in case the plague reoccurred.

Ragnor (RAG-nohr): A minor battle chief of the Eagles. He was captured and held in the Low Town. He organized a vigilante group to keep peace among the prisoners.

Rangers: Rangers are Guardians who travel alone to scout out and observe the vast territory under their guardianship from Lake Tolbar to the Eastern Sea. They are the elite of the Guardians.

Raynor (RAY-nohr): An assistant to Ragnor and Al's shadow in the prisoner camp.

Red: The new chief of the Guild after the Central Digs were raided. Red has bright red hair,

Rickets: A small lakeside village near Arlana's house.

Rokash (ROW-cash): A large bipedal reptilian carnivore about four meters tall.

Rokodor (ROW-ke-door): Ancient name that Arlana gave Dave as she came up with the idea to make him Celyddon's adopted son.

Rokomer (ROW-coe-mer): Dave Schuster's *Hansa* name bestowed on him after he killed the *Rokash*.

Rolomer (ROLL-oh-mer): One of the three *Hansa* that accompanied Pam and Al to rescue Little Thomas.

Sigor (SIG-ore): The name of Ferris' Dorai.

Siph (SIFF): A golden colored drink made by the *Hansa* that can be drunk cold or hot.

Skene Dhu (SKI-ann-doo): The name given by Dave to his blade tree knife. It is Gaelic for a small Scottish knife.

Sophie: The young daughter of Kyra who was also rescued from Bigelow by Al and his friends.

Sorgai (SORE-guy): Small floating rafts of seaweed that are used by the Gurundar for refuge and rest when on the ocean.

Spectres: Ancient evil beings who descended into Sheol to create great beings so large and powerful that could only live at high air pressure, including the dragons.

Staycare Center: A 24-hour nursery, and daycare center for mothers at Halcyon University. Women at Halcyon are encouraged to continue their studies and their work and leave the raising of their children to professionals. Mothers are permitted to visit their children whenever they like, and to stay overnight with them.

Sugar Gum Bush: A bush which grows two meters tall with variegated leaves. The root is used by the *Hansa* to make *siph*.

Tandor (TAN-door): A rebel, Guild member, and slave of Bigelow in Abaddon. His belief in a prophecy that the Bent Ones will be overthrown causes him to help Al and his friends in their quest.

Tar-en-Nar (TAR-en-nahr): City of Light. The Ancient name for the dead city before Meglir corrupted it.

Tar-en-Gorg: (TAR-en-ghorg): City of Death. The name for Meglir's city once the great plague was unleashed, killing most men east of Lake Tolbar. Meglir and his lieutenants ruled through the apemen.

Taromer (TAR-oh-mur): The third of three *Hansa* companions accompanying Al and Pam back to Halcyon to rescue Little Thomas.

Teledon (TELL-e-dawn): The son of Arachodor and suitor of Arlana.

Terraces: A series of wide shelves or ledges, about three kilometers wide that lead down to the Infernal Ocean and Sheol. Small dragons can only fly up as high as the fifth or fourth terrace because of the relatively thin air as compared to Sheol. The rebels live as nomads on the first to third terraces to avoid the Bent Ones and the dragons.

Thicket Islands: Small, low islands covered with brush at the mouth of the Tor River that obscure the Tor River from the Pishon (Halcyon) River.

Therien, Ed: Dave's pseudonym while in Halcyon looking for Al.

Trail Talk: A method of communication used by the *Hansa* in which directions and intentions are marked on a stick. Trail Talk sticks are usually left by an abandoned camp fire.

Tranomer (TRAN-oh-mer): The *Hansa* warrior who left in a coracle to report to the Elders about the siege of Torburg.

Tranquor (TRANK-quor): A custom of the *Hansa* that everyone should be allowed a time of quiet reflection in the morning before being interrupted by the day's tasks and worries.

Traveller: The name of Dave's bay (reddish-brown) stallion.

Travel Oaks: A single tree that grows in multiple stems that form a ring (or grove) of stems and allows travel to daughter groves that grow from cuttings from the original tree.

Vixa: A young woman in Seth that causes trouble with her flirting.

Vul: A large, carnivorous bat-like creature with a fifteen-meter wing span found in the Mutandi Highlands. The long, snake-like neck and sharp teeth make it deadly. The name comes from its vulture-like appearance. However, this creature kills as well as feeds on carrion.

Warren: An underground network of dwellings used by the Guild in Seth that is built under a rubble heap of levelled buildings. The Warren is about three square kilometers in size.

Wogogs (WOE-gogs): The name for lupi in the Ancient Tongue.

Zambor (ZAM-bore): A wizard with a fortress in the southern reaches of the Mutandi Highlands who was visited by Bigelow.

Acknowledgements

A multi-year project like *The Dragons of Sheol* confronts the author with many challenges: writing an exciting sequel, managing character development over several volumes, and maintaining consistency with the earlier works.

This process was helped immeasurably by a number of people who contributed their time, their skill, and their enthusiasm to make my work much better than I could have accomplished on my own.

First and foremost, I would like to thank my editor: Patricia Paddey. She untiringly worked to remove extraneous material, make sure the characters remained consistent and to correct obscure or wordy passages. Her emendations proved invaluable and measurably improved this book.

Kathy Kazmaier's careful reading of the final manuscript helped me see the work with "new eyes" and corrected numerous oversights and errors. Phil Kazmaier meticulously read early drafts of *The Dragons of Sheol* and constructed a much better map of the continent of Abaddon than I had achieved. For his diligence I am deeply grateful.

Special thanks are due Jacques Boudreau for his insights into the game of bridge and his instructive comments on the chapter entitled *Contract Bridge*.

I would like to thank the many readers of *The Halcyon Dislocation* and *The Battle for Halcyon* who encouraged me to complete *The Dragons of Sheol*. Your interest in finding out "What happened after the return?" kept me writing.

Finally, I would also like to thank the staff at Word Alive for helping with the details of the publication process. Wholehearted thanks to Jen Jandavs-Hedlin, and Tia Friesen.

As a Christ-Follower I claim no special aid or guidance in this work except in the humblest sense. I can see how following the Lord Christ has helped me grow as a person and without His grace and people He was able to use to encourage me, I don't think I would have had the courage to attempt an audacious feat such as writing a novel, much less a book series. Still I readily acknowledge that no work is ever perfect or complete and this story is no exception. The errors, shortcomings, and omissions in this book are all my own. Those who have worked with me, have helped to make my book better, and for that I am deeply grateful.

About the Author

The Dragons of Sheol is Peter Kazmaier's fourth book and the third in *The Halcyon Cycle*. In these works he has been able to pursue a life-long dream of writing fast-paced novels that explore the intersection between adventure, science, faith, and philosophy.

J. R. R. Tolkien's *Lord of the Rings*, C. S. Lewis' *The Chronicles of the Narnia*, Stephen R. Lawhead's trilogy, *Song of Albion*, and Robert Jordan's series *Wheel of Time*™ are among his favorite and best-loved books. He also enjoys science fiction classics such as Robert Heinlein's *Tunnel in the Sky*.

Dr. Kazmaier has spent most of his scientific career as a research scientist in industry. His strong background in science enables him to bring authentic scientific insight to *The Halcyon Cycle*.

He was married to Kathryn in 1976 and they live in Mississauga near Toronto. They enjoy spending time at their cottage near Seeley's Bay, Ontario on the Rideau Canal.

He blogs at www.peterkazmaier.com and delights in feedback from his readers.